To Travis, old friend
& good company

POSSESSED with Jared
& others, over the
years,

Good memories of
hikes & camps & canoes,
in the VP & Canada,

From
Arnold C. Naylor
April 2014

A NOVEL INSPIRED BY TRUE EVENTS

POSSESSED

Philip J. Crowley and **Kenneth C. Wylie**

SUNSTONE
PRESS

SANTA FE

Sunstone books may be purchased for educational, business, or sales promotional use.
For information please write: Special Markets Department, Sunstone Press,
P.O. Box 2321, Santa Fe, New Mexico 87504-2321.

Book and Cover design › Vicki Ahl
Body typeface › ITC Benguiat STd
Printed on acid-free paper
∞

Library of Congress Cataloging-in-Publication Data
Crowley, Philip J., 1949-
    Possessed : a novel inspired by true events / by Philip J. Crowley and
Kenneth C. Wylie.
       pages cm
    ISBN 978-0-86534-963-6 (softcover : alk. paper)
    1. Family violence--Fiction. I. Wylie, Kenneth C., 1938- II. Title.
    PS3603.R75P67 2013
    813'.6--dc23
                                          2013025980

WWW.SUNSTONEPRESS.COM
SUNSTONE PRESS / POST OFFICE BOX 2321 / SANTA FE, NM 87504-2321 /USA
(505) 988-4418 / ORDERS ONLY (800) 243-5644 / FAX (505) 988-1025

To my wife Ashley Ann Crowley

To my father Laurence V. Wylie

1

"**D**o you, Iris Crandal, take Rodney Harris for your lawfully wedded husband, for richer or poorer, in sickness and in health, until death do you part?"

With obvious rapture Iris looked at the older man whom she had known only three months, as if to seek reassurance. He smiled warmly, with a slight nod. Flooded with joy she replied, "I do."

"Do you, Rodney Harris, take Iris Crandal...?" The judge continued the familiar ceremony, and Iris thought back to her meeting with Rodney at the Michigan Training Unit, a medium security prison for young men, in Ionia. Iris was visiting a cousin who worked at the training unit as a counselor when she had been introduced to Rodney in the cafeteria. Charmed by the older man, Iris found herself involved in a conversation ranging widely across many topics, full of humor and common sense. Rodney invited her to dinner, and Iris accepted, only slightly concerned that he was obviously older. But she liked his viral good looks, his crinkly, weathered face, the way his eyes twinkled when he laughed, his air of confidence and experience. Always a good listener, Iris sat spellbound through dinner as Rodney roughly outlined his life from birth in Sandusky to fortunes made and lost in Baltimore, Miami, Phoenix, and most recently in the small mid-Michigan town of Ionia. At fifty-four Rodney wore success well. He dressed in accordance with his station as a prosperous real estate salesman, natty blazer and maroon tie, light blue shirt, his somewhat garish maroon trousers neatly pressed, swinging his crossed legs to an internal rhythm as he tapped the table for emphasis, the dim light of the restaurant gleaming on his polished oxfords. He flattered her with an obviously absurd guess at her age.

"You can't be more than thirty-one or thirty-two, Iris."

And when she giggled in disbelief he squeezed her arm warmly and chuckled, "Maybe thirty-three."

She confessed to thirty-eight, captivated by this attentive, mature man who took such an interest in her. She remembered that Rodney said little about his personal life, even as he touched on the highlights of his varied career, though he briefly mentioned his recent divorce. Apparently, the ex-wife now lived in a small house near Lansing.

Iris gazed lovingly into Rodney's eyes as he responded, "I do." This was the happiest moment of her life. She glowed with delight as they turned away from the judge. Rodney had arranged a small reception for close friends at a local restaurant, and she fairly skipped out the door. This she'd never expected. In fact, she'd almost given up hope of ever finding a suitable man.

Her first marriage had ended just after graduation from college in the late fifties. She and Jim hurried into marriage at eighteen, during their freshman year at Michigan State University, when almost no one "lived" with a lover outside of marriage. Despite the early passion, the marriage had slowly gone sour; Jim drifting further away each season, the things shared becoming rare, until, days after graduation he had joined the service. Iris then moved to Detroit to teach inner city children. Their divorce came just days before Jim received notice of deployment to Vietnam. One year later he became one of the first American soldiers to die in that country. Still hurt, perhaps still loving her first love, Iris had not sought another husband though she lived with a Wayne State University grad student during the sixties. Steve was verbal and volatile; and they often argued loudly, the neighbors complaining. Then Steve had gone west, and Iris last heard of him from Berkeley in 1970. He was a counselor at a free drug clinic near the University of California campus. Though unreliable, Steve was stimulating and often fun. After his departure, Iris gradually came to believe she would never find a suitable man. Her hopes of romance faded with the years. Now Rodney had changed everything.

From the very first he was attentive beyond anything in her experience. Jim and Steve had more or less taken her for granted. When, during their first formal date, Rodney asked permission to call in the future, she gladly agreed. The calls began almost from the day of her return home to Detroit. On the phone, he was endlessly flattering, his rugged voice forming loving and caring words. Within months he convinced Iris to move to Ionia at the end of the school year; and, over Memorial Day weekend, he asked her hand in marriage. Though Iris's friends and relatives were skeptical about such an early commitment, Iris consented to a June wedding. Though she knew little of Rodney's life and there was a difference of some fifteen years between them, Iris wondered if she had more time. The big "Four-O" was only two years away, and few women found decent men after that unwelcome watershed, not if they weren't rich or famous.

So she had agreed to a civil ceremony since each had been previously married.

The honeymoon was in Washington, DC. A perfect choice since Iris had visited the capital as a child, squired around the great monuments by her parents. She had good memories of the grand capital city; but Rodney insisted on driving rather than flying, revealing the first shortness of temper she'd seen, when she had briefly demurred.

"We'll get a better feel of the country if we drive. So let's not argue about it. Okay?" he stated emphatically, eyes narrowed slightly. She quickly agreed.

Now they had been at the restaurant for more than three hours. What was to have been a brief reception dragged on until it was almost five o'clock. Rodney, who had downed several drinks, showed no signs of wanting to leave. Though she had seen him take a few bourbons during their brief months of dating, she had never seen him consume so much. She was worried because of the long drive facing them. She supposed the drinking was merely his way of celebrating. Finally, at five-thirty she convinced him to leave. To her surprise, he seemed unaffected by all the alcohol, cheerful and energetic, as she had always known him.

"You're the eager beaver," he joshed, a wink to the few friends who remained at their table waving goodbye.

Then they were on the road, married. Happiness seemed to beckon. For several hours Rodney spoke with restless energy, as if the freedom of the road awakened him from a good night's sleep. He told stories of the strange characters he had known in his varied career, entertaining her as he had when they first met. Iris admired him up close, drinking in his strong, clean-shaven face. It was something she thought; that they hadn't slept together despite all their previous experience, and despite the fact that neither was young. She was relieved that Rodney hadn't pushed for sex as most young men did. Now she looked forward to it. Rodney, though thickened a little around the waist, was a powerful man, dark haired and well-muscled, and his sinewy wrists evidence of the strength in his long arms, thighs bulging on the car seat. She wondered if he sensed her eagerness for the intimacy to come. It had been a long time. How long had it been for him? She was wonderfully aroused by his closeness, a bit drowsy from the wine and the late hour, but alert and ready to stop. They passed motel after motel as night fell. Still Rodney drove on, silent now, as they passed the outskirts of metropolitan Detroit, heading towards Ohio, the myriad lights of the megapolis flashing past.

From time to time Iris studied the map, making suggestions.

"Sandusky seems about right, darling," she said softly at one point, placing her hand gently on his thigh. Despite tentative intimacies in previous meetings, she had never touched him there, so close. She could sense tension in him. "After all, weren't you born there? Do you still have family there?"

"I have no family," Rodney snapped, his normally deep voice seemed higher, hiding a note of anger. Then he touched her knee, his large hand strong and friendly, his tone jovial again. "Look, beautiful, the further we go the better. Let's go all the way to DC without stopping."

"But...but, Rodney. We just got married. I want..."

"Sure, sure. Look, I'm up to it. You can sleep if you want. I'm the one doin' all the driving. So you can't really complain." His chuckle seemed forced, but Iris succumbed. So the silver Thunderbird droned onward, along the Ohio turnpike into Pennsylvania. They stopped only briefly for gas and coffee. In one late night roadhouse Iris splashed cold water over her face and tidied her hair. In the mirror she thought her face seemed drawn, the wrinkles behind her eyes deeper than usual. She'd dozed on and off, but Rodney seemed unaffected by the lack of sleep. Was he always like this? She joined him in the car, dead tired, but still happy.

2

The sun was rising and glistening brightly on the waters of the Potomac when they finally reached the Holiday Inn in Alexandria. Exhausted, feeling dirty from the long drive, Iris wanted only to sleep, and she assumed Rodney was equally tired. But when he dragged the luggage onto the floor next to the bed, he took her in his strong arms, kissing her and caressing her body with knowing hands. Was it possible that this man, so considerate, humorous, charming, successful, was also a good lover despite his years, despite a recent divorce? Iris knew that many men had difficulty after a failed marriage. Her fatigue forgotten, she responded quickly to his touch, shedding her clothing and pulling down his pants. His hands felt incredibly good on her as he gently explored her inner thighs and moved his fingers over her breasts. She felt young again, lovely, beautiful, loved. And, though she had not made love for many years, entry was not painful. She was as ready for him as he was for her.

After their lovemaking Iris slept like a child until six that evening. She finally awoke to see Rodney, half dressed, long legs stretched out, sitting in a lounge chair reading the evening paper, a tall glass of bourbon in his big hands.

"How long did you sleep, dear?" she asked, half sitting against the pillow, feeling marvelous.

"Oh. A couple of hours maybe. Don't need much rest," said Rodney. Then he turned and smiled deeply, eyes gleaming, glass held high.

"Here's to us."

He drank the glass straight down.

The honeymoon was going beautifully. Rodney showered with Iris and slowly made love to her again. She was awakened as never before. Rodney knew things, ways to touch her; gentle kisses and caresses she had hardly imagined—save in an occasional fantasy when aroused by a spicy novel or hinted adventures in R-rated movies. He even persuaded her later that evening to watch an X-rated pay-video on the motel TV, making ribald comments at the often explicit scenes. She lay naked on the bed with him, unashamed and bold as he seemed to be. Truth was, though approaching forty, Iris had a secret pride in the body God gave her. She'd always liked her slender but voluptuous figure, the fullness of her breasts, now no longer pert and high, but not bad at all for her age, and her fine buttocks and slim thighs, with scarcely a trace of fat. She'd been previously shy, but Rodney now brought out a naughty impulse in her, and she smiled as she lay next to him, tracing a finger down his chest, twining it in his fine, graying hair, patting his beginning of a substantial paunch, caressing his penis and wondering at the almost forgotten magic that caused it to thicken and grow even as she watched. It was simply wonderful. They would explore new sexual frontiers together. Marriage would be a joy. Rodney loved her deeply. He was loving, mature, thoughtful, praising her appearance and ignoring the obvious signs of age, the wrinkles under the neck and chin, around the eyes, at the corners of her mouth. She was still young, pretty, wanted. A rush of good feeling came over her, and she bent to him with a moan, ready once more. It had never been like this.

They spent all of the first full day touring the historic sites and attractions, walking arm in arm like many other honeymooners. At the Jefferson Memorial Iris was infused with the power of the monument, the massive pillars circling the inner court, the latent but gentle strength of the bronze statue. Her heart raced as she read the eloquent, extraordinary words written by the man who had been her favorite hero in college history courses. The visit to John's and Robert's graves at Arlington National Cemetery brought tears; so much hope and promise crushed by the bullets of worthless assassins. Like many of her generation Iris believed that America's decline began on that awful November day in Dallas when Lee Harvey Oswald—acting alone or as part of a still mysterious conspiracy—took the life of the vibrant John Kennedy. She'd heard Kennedy in person when he stumped Michigan in the autumn of '60, and was captivated at once. She firmly believed that had Kennedy survived, there would have been no Vietnam, no second resurrection of Richard Nixon, and no Watergate.

Washington, as always, was alive with politics; and Iris tried to engage Rodney in some give and take, wondering if he had any politics, any strong and thought-out values, but he showed little interest beyond a quip, "It's all water under the bridge." They kept to themselves through the whole stay in the capital. Iris was not greatly disappointed; she had lost much of her early political passion after 1968. First King, then Bobby Kennedy, then Chicago—it had all been too much. She had only watched the Watergate hearings because all the revelations simply confirmed her youthful intuitions about Richard Nixon.

An evening was spent touring the magnificent Smithsonian. Iris accompanied by a patient, occasionally muttering Rodney, spent hours looking at the gowns worn by various First Ladies at Inaugural Balls. She examined the material and price of each gown before moving on to the next exhibit, and Rodney was politely attentive. What a patient, beautiful human being he was. She could not imagine why his previous wife had divorced him. You could never understand some women.

The third day was spent at Mount Vernon. Iris had been there with her parents as a child, but could scarcely remember the grounds and house, and the beauty of the whole estate was overwhelming. They saved the manse for last, walking first through the outbuildings and gardens. It was a perfect summer day and Iris luxuriated in the tour and in Rodney's presence. They took the path down to the wharf, walking past the many flowering shrubs and stately trees, the Potomac shimmering beyond. Even posted warnings not to touch the water because of pollution could not dampen her spirits. It was as if the great estate, a symbol of the nation's youth, had revived a time when she too was young and hopeful. Looking at Rodney, his head bare beneath the southern sun, she could almost believe they had known each other for decades, grown together into a perfect love. When they made their way eventually into the mansion and toured it, virtually alone, she literally glowed with happiness. Rodney was never more witty, joking about her in his best fashion.

"I can just see you, Iris, dressed up like ol' Martha. Bonnet and parasol, or whatever them ladies used back then." Chuckling, he squeezed her waist and moved her from display to display, joshing and kidding. "You'd a' been the belle of the ball, for sure. Every man jack of them, those ol' plantation boys, after you. Even ol' George." And he had leaned close and whispered to her, bringing the blood rushing to her face. Outside, they sat leaning against each other on the grassy hill overlooking the Potomac flowing through the valley below. From there no one could guess that the historic river was polluted.

A cool summer breeze drifted over their warm bodies as they lay beside each other talking of their future plans. Rodney was positive Iris could find a position in the Ionia school system. There was a demand for a speech therapist, and he knew Iris was qualified. He'd already talked to the Principal about the job. An appointment was set for their return from Washington. Iris was pleased, though mildly surprised that Rodney was so solicitous for her future employment. Certainly he made enough money for both of them, far more than she was accustomed to. In their brief acquaintance and marriage, he seemed to roll in cash, peeling away twenties and fifties, and writing checks without a second thought. Maybe it was the salesman in him that wanted control. He sure had a way with words, an inborn, natural eloquence and persuasive gift, a manner of projecting himself on others, of infusing the listener with a sense of importance—she'd rarely known anyone who gazed so intently when she spoke, as if no one else on earth existed. This she liked. All this was evident in spite of frequent grammatical lapses on Rodney's part, an indicator of his lack of formal education, proof of his unconventional youth and self-education. So she assumed. He was often rough-edged in the manner he used when ordering dinner at a restaurant, or in the way he spoke to gas-station attendants, but he seemed as smooth as silk in all that mattered, especially in his behavior with her.

Still, she wanted to know more about him.

"Why did your wife leave you, Rodney?" she blurted without thought.

He stared hard at her, eyes suddenly cold and dark as coal. She felt a brief chill, as if a dark cloud was passing beneath the sun. His face seemed suddenly older, the angles jagged, the beginning of jowls almost sinister, his skin nearly transparent. It was as if she could see through a door into Hell. But, when he did not answer, looking away to the river, the feeling quickly passed. She could ask again later, at a better time. In the sun everything glowed.

Later, in the Thunderbird, driving back to the motel, he reached out his big hand to her knee and began to speak, his voice quiet.

"Iris, I'm sorry if I offended you. Our past should remain just that. I don't wanna know about your previous marriage or any lovers, and I don't want to tell ya about mine. Okay? This is our honeymoon, so I'll make an exception this once. But never, I repeat, never ask me again." His voice seemed distant, but after a time he continued.

"We were married five years and, for some reason, she started drinking, tried to stop her, but it was no good. Finally, I couldn't take no more and threatened her with divorce. The next day I was served with divorce papers. She made allegations, never proven, that I beat her and held her prisoner. Just bull, all of it. The whole affair distressed me. You can understand why I don't want to talk about the matter. As far as I'm concerned the woman is dead. I never want to see her or hear her name mentioned again."

Iris, feeling sorry, leaned over and gave him a kiss on the cheek.

"I understand, dear," she said, vowing never to bring up the matter again. Soon they arrived at the motel and Iris took the initiative in sex. She kissed him immediately, deeply, as soon as they were inside the door, running her hands over him. Slowly, she unzipped his pants and removed his clothes. He seemed strangely passive through the initial stages, willing to let her see to his desires. They spent the rest of the day in bed, loving one another, and it was late when they went to dinner.

Now, Iris decided, curiosity roused in spite of her promise to herself, I won't ask about that wife. But there were other things. She gazed up at him. He seemed cheerful, loving, considerate, ready for anything.

"How come you never had any children?" she asked, as the waitress served a conventional motel dinner of steak, baked potato and salad. Rodney had already begun his second bourbon and was draining off a large swallow when his face began to change.

"I thought we agreed not to talk about the past," he boomed, his voice so loud the nearby patrons looked up in curiosity.

Taken aback by his anger, Iris sat frozen in her chair, fork suspended above the steak. It was the second time in the same day she had seen a different, a disturbing side of her new husband. Whenever she dared inquire about his past, he seemed to change.

Now, Iris was no ragmop of a woman. She had lived and worked and suffered loneliness and hardship. With Rodney, perhaps because of his greater age and experience, she often held back opinions, allowed him to lead and decide. She actually liked that part of him. Steve, in Detroit so long ago, had been fun and funny some of the time, but also weak and indecisive. In that relationship she had often made decisions, done the basic work of maintaining the apartment. When they had argued, it was usually because Steve had forgotten important tasks or missed appointments. Jim, her long dead ex-husband, had also willingly allowed her to make basic housekeeping decisions. But clearly Rodney was not that type. He was a man in charge, a man who controlled and planned things, or so he seemed. But she was not about to be shouted at in a public place, and he had got her dander up. She responded testily.

"All right, for Christ's sake," she said, stabbing the meat with her fork, "I'm sorry." But then she grinned, eager to show good will. This extreme sensitivity would pass she was sure, given time, given an opportunity to really get to know each other. Rodney would need to tell her more, and she'd be ready. She was an understanding, forgiving woman.

Rodney regained his composure at once, apologizing graciously to the people in the restaurant. Then he turned his attention to Iris. He signaled the waitress to bring him another drink.

"Iris, honey, I'm going to tell you everything about my past. I'm sorry I wasn't straight with you prior to the wedding. After you hear everything about me, all of it, if you want an annulment, I'll pay the legal fees. I don't want you to leave me and, to tell the truth, I was afraid my past might scare you off."

Iris, food suspended midway to her mouth, felt her pulse quicken. What could it be? A weight seemed to descend to her gullet, and she put the food back on the plate. Frightened, but nevertheless ready for compassion and understanding, she put her hand over his arm. The drink arrived and he took a long pull, downing half with one gulp.

"In the late forties," Rodney continued, "I married a woman in Baltimore. We were both just kids. But we had two children, a boy and a girl. The marriage wasn't happy. She was from a lower class background and had even less education than me. I guess I was impatient to make it, so I don't blame her for the failure of the marriage. It was a mistake on my part to try and change her. In the mid 'fifties, we moved to Lansing, and I went to work in a bank. I'd been in the loan business anyway." He paused, with a trace of a smile on his rugged face. "Now that was a racket, let me tell you." Now his face fell again. "Anyhow, I divorced her the next year. She got custody of the kids. The women always did back then."

"Where are the children now?" Iris asked, unable to restrain her curiosity. Watching Rodney's face, she thought for a moment he was going to cry. She could see tears forming in his eyes. His voice quavered as he went on.

"I don't know. That's the truth, honey. I don't even know where she is. We kept in touch for a year or so and then she just up and disappeared, like that." he said, snapping his fingers. "Without a trace. Even the friend of the court lost track of her and the kids. Rod and Marg would be in their twenties. Haven't seen either of 'em in years." His voice caught. "I miss the hell out of them."

At this, Rodney could no longer control his emotions. Tears glistened in his eyes, and Iris lovingly guided him outdoors, silently walking beside him, arm around his waist, looking into novelty shops. After an hour or so, they made their way back to the motel. Iris, holding Rodney's head on her lap as they lay on the bed, not making love, had never felt closer to Rodney. Even later they did not make love, though Rodney made a half-hearted desultory attempt, unable to rise to the occasion, and Iris felt deep affection and sorrow for him, for all the pain he had obviously suffered so long ago. She vowed then and there never to leave him.

3

They packed to leave the next morning, and soon the Thunderbird was purring along the open road, heading back to Ionia. Rodney seemed more relaxed, far more so than on the way down, and he offered to stop at Sandusky on the way home.

"Ever been to Cedar Point?" he asked in his old jovial tone. "If not, we can stop off and spend a day there and maybe even drive by the old neighborhood."

"Rodney. I'd love to," cried Iris, happy again. Surely things would remain open between them. Together they would free each other of the burden of the past. Rodney's willingness to confront the place of his birth and childhood seemed to her further evidence of his basic good nature, his healthy attitude. It confirmed what she had felt about him from the start.

Cedar Point proved to be the largest, most garish amusement park she had ever seen. They rode on all the main attractions, screaming like kids. Iris was amazed that a man his age would agree to ride the huge roller coasters, the Blue Streak and the Gemini; and, when it became time to leave the park he did not want to leave. He was like a child of ten again visiting Cedar Point for the first time. This boyish quality was endearing.

"You know," Rodney said as he looked around, obviously touched by these scenes, "my ma never took me to Cedar Point." His voice broke again. "She'd take my brother and sisters, but not me. Said I was too young and wouldn't mind. I remember one time she and her boyfriend took my brother and sisters to the Park and left me behind, locked in a fuckin' closet. Can you believe it?" his voice was rising. Iris had heard him swear only when telling a risqué joke. She wondered if he would break into a rage, or break down and cry. "Jesus, I was only six goddamned years old," said Rodney, his voice more controlled now. "They musta been gone hours, and I had nothin' to eat or drink. I messed my pants and had to sit there in my own shit till they got back." Iris held his arm, but Rodney was no longer talking to her. He was not talking to anyone in particular. It was a confession and a cry thrown out into the anonymous air. "Then, when they got home," Rodney said, "she beat me with a paddle 'cause I had soiled my clothes. Hell, I wasn't allowed out of my bedroom for a week, except to eat and go to the bathroom."

Though she continued to hold his arm and caress his back as he drove south towards their motel, Iris was shocked by these revelations. Rodney had seemed to be so straight, so well-adjusted, so mature, a man in complete control of himself. Now, watching him crying, even as he drove onward into the gathering night, she wondered. She hardly knew him...despite their closeness when making love, despite her previous sense of sharing all things. He had lived more than fifty years before she met him. Who was he...what was he? Her feelings of love, still powerful, were now tinged by the first shadow of doubt. She sighed, willing to put up with less than perfect. At least now she was beginning to understand why he had not wanted to stop in Sandusky on the way to Washington. Now she wished they had continued to drive straight home. Later, as she lay in bed next to him, his breathing quiet and regular, she pondered their future. What new revelation would tomorrow bring?

It was early when they woke to begin the final leg of the trip to Ionia.

"Is it okay with you if we drive back into town before we head on home?" Rodney asked suddenly as they finished loading the car. Iris nodded without comment. Rodney drove into Sandusky and then towards the lake front and then followed several jogs and turns into the west side of the city. Suddenly he pulled to a stop in front of an abandoned, burned-out, two-story home at the end of a street that led nowhere. The entire scene was ugly, sordid, a run-down dead-end street in a dead-end place.

"See that tree?" Rodney pointed to an old, almost leafless maple. "I was ten when I climbed to the top. When I tried to get down, I lost my balance and fell through the branches, all the way to the pavement. I hit my head and my arms and legs were all cut and bruised, and I had a big gash across my forehead. My ma came out; and, instead of taking me to the doctor, she took me into my bedroom and put me on the bed. Said she had a remedy that would stop the bleeding and take care of the pain. Then, next thing I knew, she was pouring salt into my wounds." Rodney paused to look at Iris as if to see if she believed this incredible story. "I begged and begged for her to stop, but she slapped me and told me to stop crying. My cuts were still bleeding, and she took this old, oily rag and put it over my open cuts. I don't know how long I was passed out after that, but she was gone when I came to. Next thing I remember was the sound of the squeaking bedsprings in the next room, and my ma making strange sounds. I guess her boyfriend was in there with her. I was glad when she burned up in that fire, even if it meant I had to live with foster parents. Anyone was better than my ma."

Iris listened, knowing the hard truth of his words. Rodney was not otherwise an inventive story-teller despite his gift for persuasion. She simply sat beside him on that dead-end street staring at the ancient maple, its barren branches reaching up to partly obscure barren buildings beyond, a litter of refuse at the base of its trunk. Bleak and alone it stood, and she too felt lonely, though her new husband sat beside her.

Presently, Rodney started the car and switched on the radio, dialing it to country music turned up loud. He rarely listened to music, but Iris assumed he wanted the diversion and made no small talk. For a time, as they drove into Michigan, past familiar scenes and into the central region of the state, Iris tried to comprehend what she'd heard. But Rodney seemed fine now, controlled, his old self. Near Ionia he began to joke with her. She wondered how he could have possibly adjusted so well and made a success of himself after that awful childhood. As they turned into Rodney's drive, the sun was shining and again Iris felt happier. He was obviously stronger for all his past.

Iris looked forward to seeing Rodney's farm for the first time. He had talked often about his acres and the old house and buildings located at Muir, a tiny settlement of some five hundred people, a few miles east of Ionia. Muir was half of the twin village of Muir-Lyons, which straddled the Grand River. A small Chrysler trim plant in Lyons was the only reason for the existence of the place. In the previous century when Michigan was being settled, Lyons had briefly been touted as the capital of the state, until Lansing had been chosen instead. Muir had languished, a somulent place, but it had charm nonetheless.

Mid-Michigan farms in the valley of the Grand were still mostly of the family type, vestiges of the norm that had once extended across America, from New England and the eastern seaboard to the great plains, symbols of an agricultural civilization that had created the most productive and hopeful rural society in history. In this segment of the state, the crops were potatoes, vegetables, rye and hay. There were a few scattered dairy farms, though far fewer than before World War II, and stock-raising was common. The pasture land was lush and extensive. The Harris farm, Rodney explained, was not a working farm despite several horses kept in the big barn. He used it during free time, on weekends and holidays, riding his horses and puttering around in a garden on the west side of the house. Smack in the middle of the ten acres was a small pond, a magnet for waterfowl and other birds. From one end the pond drained into a cattail marsh which fed a tiny brook. The house was large, square, two-stories high, with four bedrooms upstairs, a classic type for the region, built perhaps ninety years before, when rough-cut beams and hardwood sheathing were common. Its basement was dark and cool, supported by a fieldstone foundation nearly two feet thick. Rodney had purchased the place ten years before, remodeling and upgrading the plumbing, heating, and electrical system. He often worked inside during spare time, paneling and salvaging wherever door frames, window sashes, lintels and stairs could be stripped and varnished. Though the house looked typical of any old farm from outside, indoors it was modern and comfortable. The house had been added to in the past, since the cellar beneath, used for fruit and storage, could only be entered from an outside passage descending from slanting twin doors, exceptionally heavy. Rodney often used an upstairs bedroom as an extra office, and he had promised Iris that she could use the smallest bedroom as an office for her school work. The master bedroom above the kitchen, with a large window overlooking the rolling farm, was ready for the newlyweds; and they talked about turning the other room into a guest-room.

Standing beside Rodney and taking it all in for the first time, Iris was speechless. It was perfect. Clearly, her husband had planned for this. Such a place had been one of her girlish dreams. Now it existed in reality. It was hers as well. She explored the three barns, the largest sheltering the horses, its lofts full of timothy in neat bales for the big animals. It smelled like a barn should smell, earthy and fecund, and the buzz of summer flies brought back old memories. The medium-sized barn stored an old tractor, a snowplow and other equipment, and the smallest one, near the house, had been converted into a garage.

"Maybe I'll sell off the house in town," said Rodney as he guided her around the place, proudly pointing out each structure. "We could live here year around." Iris almost jumped for joy, laughing and hugging her husband.

"Oh, Rodney. I'd love it," she said, happy beyond words. She felt she might build real happiness on this rural place, near a small town, close to several larger cities, yet peaceful and isolated in a pocket of a bygone America. She had not lived in a small community since she had moved to Detroit in the early 'sixties. Frankly, she was pleased to move away from that city's Indian Village area. As a teacher, she'd never earned enough to buy one of the stately old homes lining Seminole and Iroquois Street, and had grown tired of apartment living, crowded into tiny rooms, yet always within sight of families who had spacious lawns and gardens and big room houses. Not one to resent the success of others, Iris nonetheless aspired to better things. She looked forward to breathing fresh air twelve months of the year, to watching the seasons pass over the woods and fields, and Rodney had promised to teach her how to ride and care for the horses and how to grow a garden.

At one point, as Rodney showed her the cool, dark cellar, playfully shutting the slanting doors on them, cutting off the light, she threw her arms around him and kissed him passionately.

"Can't we wait till we're upstairs in bed?" he joshed, returning her kiss.

"Sure, dear," she replied, shuddering slightly at the blackness and silence of the old cellar, liking its musty smell, but a little frightened by it. "This isn't the place to make love, is it?" But she kissed him hard again, probing his mouth with her tongue. When he broke away, laughing, and threw open the doors again, she noticed a stock of bottles, bourbon mostly, stacked with a few wine bottles on the old fruit shelves. Rodney planned for everything, she thought, even for parties.

4

The interview for the job at the school was a week away, so Iris spent the remaining time happily rearranging the house to suit her taste. Rodney protested little, though he would not have her touch the bedroom except to put up new curtains and a few pictures on the walls. For all his handiness and skill with tools, Rodney had no taste when it came to decoration; there was hardly a picture or hanging in the entire house. The neatly painted walls bare save for a calendar here and there. One, in the kitchen, had to go; it was a Penthouse calendar, not the kind of thing she wanted to gaze at every day. As she took it down to throw away, Rodney intervened, "Hey," he boomed in a tone of mock severity. "Let me have that. At least I can put the damn thing up in the barn and enjoy it there," he joked. She laughed with him, charmed as always.

Through those first golden days, neither of them mentioned Rodney's troubled childhood or his failed marriage. Iris preferred to approach the subject when the time seemed right, but things were going so well, she did not dare. Rodney acted as if nothing had happened, as if he had told her nothing, and every time their talk drifted towards the past, he quickly changed the subject. For some reason, he didn't seem interested in her past. Maybe, she thought, still euphoric and hopeful, Rodney was right; the past is past and should be left alone.

As for her own background, Iris was hard put to come up with interesting anecdotes. She'd been an ordinary child in a quite ordinary working-class home, well loved and cared for, actually hardly aware of the relatively modest means of her parents until well into high school, never wanting for the basics of life, even when, during the war, as a small child, she had fleeting memories of rationing and wooden toys. Even when, nearing her tenth birthday, her father had bitterly complained about having to give up a coveted new car, a hoped-for raise in his wages having been put off. At some point in the early 'fifties, her family had climbed with seeming ease into the ranks of the middle class. During a sociology class at MSU Iris had, for the first time, realized the parameters of her own upbringing, but she had never been particularly analytical about these matters, accepting her roles and opportunities. As a co-ed, likewise as a high school student, she had been conservative of dress, conforming to mid-American fashions of the time. She'd had her hair in a bob, a sweeping fall to the shoulders, a bouffant (shades of Jackie Kennedy's influence), even bangs and pigtails during a brief period when the "natural" look, coming indirectly from the pervasive influence of the rebellious youth of the 'sixties, had changed the look even of the most conservative folk.

Through her first marriage and the extended affair with Steve, through college and work in Detroit's inner city, through the civil rights movement, the anti-war movement, the riots, through all the turmoil of her young adulthood, Iris had never questioned the values that sustained her, never doubted the value of her work, and, even when most lonely, she had rarely descended into self-doubt. She was simply not a depressive person by nature, having inherited a cheery disposition from her hard-working mother, a child of an old farm family from Pennsylvania. Never beautiful, as she understood the word, her nose too sharp, her face too broad, her hair too fine and thin, she nevertheless had a good figure and knew it. She had been a cheerleader briefly as a senior in high school, dating infrequently until college, but none the less aware that boys liked her, admired her in a swimsuit. Not beautiful perhaps, she felt pretty enough, especially when loved. Jim, her first husband, had been her first lover; and, indeed, she had lost her virginity to him only weeks before their marriage at eighteen, both of them freshmen in college, both without experience or money or the slightest knowledge of the strains of matrimony, the tug and pull of two separate egos trying to accommodate to the demands of student life. The failure of their marriage had been devastating to Iris. She remained outwardly busy and cheerful, channeling disappointment into her work, her young pupils, her career, and her vacations, often taken with other women of similar situation. The only real depression she had known was when she got news of Jim's death, years after their divorce, in some strangely named province in far-away Southeast Asia. And even that had come before the awful absurdity of the Vietnam War. But that too had passed an episode of "blues" and nothing to worry about. She had grown accustomed to living alone, working as a single woman, sleeping when and where she wanted, at home or on holiday, season through season. Her taste in books was largely determined by best-seller lists and book club recommendations, so she was not ignorant of the world, but never, through the years, had she had a real adventure. Never had she risked her career, never had she traveled extensively away from tour groups and tourist routes, never had she tried anything like this.

So it was a thrill, standing on the little porch, watching a circling hawk, sweeping her eyes across the vista of his (no, their) land, the barns and fences, the gleam of the pond beyond, and the moving lumps of the horses in the pasture. She reached down deliberately and unbuttoned her light summer blouse, just enough to reveal some cleavage. She felt incredibly sexy and alive. She wanted to sing. A breeze ruffled her hair as she stepped inside the house. She had never before felt so good, so beautiful. Rodney grinned at her, his eyes going to her breasts, and he put his drink down on the window sill, holding out his big strong arms.

"Well...look at you. All fresh and pretty. All ready for me. Let's go upstairs. I think it's time to try that bed."

It was a sunny day, and Iris was confident as she dressed for her interview. Rodney left early for work, but not before he woke her and made slow love to her, the most enjoyable and fulfilling and romantic love she had ever known. In the morning, even after a previous evening of love making, he had exceptional staying power, bringing her to climax again before he shuddered against her. This, she thought, was best of all. A man of such virile strength, despite the time it took him to reach orgasm, combined with his apparent need for her, seemed too good to be true. She knew there was much of the little boy in him, wanting comfort and craving care, but this endeared her and appealed to her instincts, her mothering nature, and enhanced the emotional ties she felt. His past may have been awful, but he was a marvelous husband and lover for all of that.

Rodney had pinned a note to the mirror as he left, and now Iris read it, smiling.

"May you have the best good luck, Iris darling. Thanks for the best time ever in bed"

The formal note made her laugh, so like him to make it sound official. The interview was at ten at the high school in Ionia, and it would take between ten and twenty minutes to drive from the farm, so Iris hurried through breakfast, leaving the dishes for later. She should have gotten up before eight to leave more time, but there was still plenty of leeway.

As she entered the garage, Iris was taken aback. She circled her VW Beetle in disbelief. All four tires were slashed and the windshield was broken. Without the car there was no way she could make the interview, not with barely a half hour to spare. Of course Rodney had taken the Thunderbird so there was no other transportation available. She could call for help from a garage, but she did not even know which one was quickest, or closest. Rodney could help, she suddenly realized. After all, she was married now, no longer on her own. Running into the house, she called, getting his secretary immediately and filling her in. Rodney, she was informed, was showing a house and wouldn't be back for at least an hour. Having no alternative, Iris called the school Principal, postponing the interview. Disappointed, Mr. Hayward agreed to see her after July 4th; but, at that time, the interview would only be for a position as a substitute teacher.

"I'm really sorry, Mrs. Harris," he said. "Frankly, I'm impressed by your resume. Your experience could be of real value here. I'll look forward to seeing you later then, and let's hope things work out for that substitute slot."

Iris was disturbed by this turn of events, but what could she do? Immediately after her talk with Mr. Hayward, she called the Sheriff's Department, quickly reporting the crime over the phone. A deputy arrived within minutes, followed by a plain clothes detective attached to the Ionia County Sheriff's Department.

Such vandalism on an isolated farmstead was not common in the region, the officers explained, puzzled by the scene. There were no signs of forced entry, and the officers surmised, after talking to Rodney later that same day, that the vandal must have arrived between five and eight in the morning, since Rodney had seen nothing wrong in the garage, swearing he had locked the door.

"Probably some punk kid," said the deputy, studying Iris as he spoke, looking her over politely enough, but with obvious interest.

"But why would anyone do this?" Iris asked, frightened by the vandalism. "It doesn't make any sense. Why tamper with my car like this?"

The police had no answer.

Later that evening, when Rodney drove in from a long and busy office day, Duke, the big German Shepherd, ran to the car, barking in delight. Strange, Iris thought, the dog had not warned her of the intruder that morning. Maybe the prowler had fed the dog a biscuit or something. But Duke was inclined to bark at the slightest pretext, especially at strangers, or so Rodney had said that first day when they moved in, reassuring her that the country was safer by far than any city street.

Rodney consoled her that evening.

"It's just as well, Iris. A substitute position is fine, and maybe next year a full time position will open up. So you go on in for the interview. You need to work a few days a week, I suppose. Hey! I've got an idea. Let's drive into Lansing for dinner at a good restaurant."

5

For the following two weeks, Iris cared for the horses and cultivated the garden. Rodney had let go the man who came out three or four times a week to clean the stables and check the animals, now that Iris was there. She enjoyed the chores, the free time, and, for a while, wasn't even certain she really wanted to teach.

Rodney certainly made more than enough money. One night she explained her feelings to Rodney, and he was sympathetic.

"Sure. It's all right with me, but look, Iris, you might get bored out here in fall and winter. Maybe you'll want an outside project." Then he passed her a drink, downing his own.

Except for his drinking, which seemed to be steady through most evenings, and sometimes even in the mornings when he was at the farm, Rodney seemed to have few faults. He spoke easily with her, listening to her with apparent attention. He seemed to be loving and kind in and out of bed. He was a member of the local chapter of the Elks and the Chamber of Commerce, well thought of in the town. Every year, he played an active role in preparing the city for the onrush of people at the fair, one of Michigan's best. He seemed a good citizen, successful with his business, and an outstanding husband. Though she'd rarely prayed for years, Iris thanked God every night for sending her this wonderful man.

On July 11th, Iris drove into town for her interview, her VW repaired, new tires all around and a new windshield. Rodney had paid the deductible without comment. The drive along M-21 was lovely and comforting. Though this region of Michigan had no turquoise blue lakes, few majestic hills, no mountains, no vast forests like other parts of the big state, there was something very soothing about the rolling farmland. She and Rodney rarely went anywhere, but soon she realized what a nice region it was. It possessed a simple beauty unmarred by the spread of industrialization which, radiating from cities like Detroit and Flint had so altered the once charming countryside of southeastern Michigan where she'd grown up. Iris did not know the names of the budding wildflowers or the shrubs and trees that lined the roads and drives, encircling the modest houses with shade and color. The fields swept away on both sides, green and shining in the July sun, bursting with the promise of harvest, and here and there the shimmer of a pond, a creek, the bend of the Grand River glimpsed in the distance. Ionia loomed quickly, a town of some seven thousand, most of who worked in the various state institutions. If the town had any fame in the state, it was because of these large and often misrepresented institutions, a large state prison and a state training unit. The old and legendary asylum, the hospital for the criminally insane, had been closed then reopened as a prison.

The interview took barely an hour. Iris knew she had impressed Mr. Hayward when he mentioned that it was a shame she had missed the earlier interview for the full-time job.

"I'll probably call on you in the fall fairly regularly, maybe as much as twice a week. With your experience, Iris, you should be able to substitute for any class, except maybe boys' gym." Haywood spoke in a manner befitting his office, precise and measured words, like the man, his hair cropped short, tie in place even on this hot summer day. Iris liked him and looked forward to working with him. She also liked the sprawling but unexceptional school, similar to others she had known as a youth. Inwardly she was pleased at the interview, glad she still had the knack. So many years in one system in Detroit had not dulled her ability to impress.

On the way home, she stopped off to tell Rodney, inviting him to lunch. They took their time, more than an hour and a half. When he returned from paying the bill, Rodney had an announcement. He'd call the office and take the rest of the day off.

They left the VW in the parking lot and took the Thunderbird. Rodney drove silently for more than an hour, telling Iris to be patient when she asked twice where they were going. Soon they were droning through a strange desolate region, hardly a house in sight. The road was old and cracked, the few houses run-down and ramshackle, the roadside grass uncut. It had been many years since Iris had grappled in the seat of a parked car with one boyfriend or the other, at least twenty-two years since she had lost her virginity to Jim in the backseat of his '52 Chevy. That had been the first and last time she had ever made love in the backseat of a car. Was this to be a second time? With Rodney, who was fifteen years her senior? She was secretly excited by the idea, ready for him even as she dreamed. If there was one thing about Rodney she knew, in spite of his steady maturity, it was that he had the capacity to surprise her. The idea of sex in the back of the Thunderbird, perhaps under some spreading old tree on a back lane, brought back the feeling of youth she had felt with Rodney the first time they made love back in Washington, DC. And he did not disappoint her, pulling the car finally into the drive of an abandoned farm, no one in sight, only the droning of bees around a honeysuckle bush, the muted songs of birds in the oaks, the shadow of an occasional cloud falling over them as they moved from the car to the grass, moving with each other in naked passion under the summer sky.

By the end of July the summer had begun to drag. Rodney had been right. She would be bored if she stayed home all winter. Some relief came in the form of the Ionia Free Fair. Though she had gone four years to the university in nearby Lansing, Iris had never been the fourty-odd miles to Ionia. And she enjoyed it hugely. She had never lost the childish delight in the bright midway on a hot August night, the heady smell of popcorn and candy apples, peanuts and hotdogs, the sounds of the old machinery cranking and clanking as the rides spun and whirled. The cries of children running from one amusement ride to another. That first summer she and Rodney went to the fair every night. Rodney seemed captivated by it, just as he had been by the park at Cedar Point. Perhaps it was his terrible childhood, passed without such pleasures. Perhaps it was the both of them, thought Iris, so much in love and so good for each other. On the last night of the fair, Rodney took her to the grandstand to see Sonny and Cher. The Ionia Fair always managed to attract big-name entertainers. Iris was beside herself when the famous couple appeared to thunderous cheers from the mostly young crowd, and she swayed in Rodney's arms as they watched, singing to herself through the familiar lyrics that boomed forth from the loudspeaker.

Driving home that night, the stars spangling the sky—undimmed by the kind of obliterating light that dimmed the heavens in the vicinity of big cities—Iris cuddled against Rodney, grasping his arm to her breast, leaning against him, humming "I Got You Babe" as the Thunderbird roared down the empty road.

Towards the end of August, Rodney was away much of the time, attending seminars for Real Estate Brokers in Detroit and Traverse City, and his business took more and more of his time. Sometimes he was not home until midnight, coming in with the smell of bourbon on his breath, but outwardly sober, dutifully making love when Iris wanted him, but often with self-centered disregard. Could it be, Iris wondered, that he was taking her for granted? But she quickly stifled such thoughts. He was, after all, no young man.

Left to herself, with only Duke and the horses to keep her company, Iris grew lonely. Nevertheless, she managed to keep busy with housework, with chores around the farm, and preparation for the coming school year. Always methodical about her teaching, Iris soon had plans and outlines ready for almost every contingency. She would not, she vowed, be one of those subs who simply filled in time when a regular teacher was absent. She would keep those students on their toes, entertained even if they did not know her at first. Iris also found time to join a local civic group concerned with upgrading and renovating downtown Ionia, and, almost without thought, she began attending Mass. Iris had fallen away from the Church while still young, not going to services since her freshman year in college. Religion, with its rituals and disturbing requirements, had seemed less important than school, than parties, and the adventure of the college years. But now she was drawn back to the old patterns, taking comfort in the familiar ceremonies and the litanies, only vaguely missing the resonant Latin rites of her childhood. Rodney never attended church, though he did not comment on her renewed interest, nor criticize her. Of course, she was unable to receive the sacraments because she was both divorced and married outside the Church. Still, she took comfort in her attendance and offered her own prayers to God.

The end of August fell muggy and hot. Everything seemed heavy and thick, and daily the great thunderstorms advanced out of the west, rolling in across the vast farmlands. Iris enjoyed the spectacular show of nature, the black thunderheads forming and rolling forth as if going to war, the air reverberating. Often she sat alone on the porch as dusk fell, watching the sky, waiting for Rodney, lonesome but never low. Sooner or later she knew Rodney would be home, the lights of the Thunderbird sweeping into the drive. However late he came, she always waited.

The farm was not a frequented place. Desolate was the better word, since no one seemed to visit. For some reason Rodney's many acquaintances never stopped by. Why this was, Iris did not speculate. Perhaps folks sensed the need for the newlyweds to be alone, perhaps Rodney preferred his social life to be separate from his home life, and perhaps...she simply had no idea. There were times she desperately wanted visitors, especially at dinner time or in early evening, but, in spite of the loneliness, Iris was not frightened. She found the farm peaceful. She enjoyed the quiet days and marveled at the regular sound-and-light shows staged by God almost every night. Years of city living had dulled her natural senses, she thought, and now they were being renewed. So she said nothing by way of complaint, welcoming Rodney home with a hug and kiss, always solicitous, ever the helpmate. If he had grown more distant of late, surely it was because of his work, his preoccupations. She could be patient. They would find time together, like before.

The worst storm of the season struck less than a week before school was to begin. Weather reports gave some warning, but nothing to prepare for the severity of it, the ferocious wind and driving rain, the seemingly endless crash of lightning, thunderclaps rolling into one increasing roar. It seemed to Iris the worst storm she'd known. Maybe in the city, among other people, surrounded by houses and buildings, such a storm seemed less dangerous, but maybe not. Whatever...she was alone. Rodney was in Lansing for a business meeting and had called at five, saying he would spend the night at a Holiday Inn. Iris cooked a meager but tasty dinner of left-over chicken casserole and early corn, the ears cooked slowly in a saucepan. When the storm increased in fury around eight or so, Iris scurried about pulling drapes and closing windows. She pulled the plug on the TV, on her stereo set, on other appliances. When the lights went out she was prepared with candles set at strategic places. Frightened as the storm battered the house, the rain pounding the windows, the wind howling and shaking the structure to its old but solid fieldstone foundations, Iris took comfort in her preparations, lighting candles one by one. Without TV, she thought at one point, she would have no warning if a tornado was sighted. She could then run outside and enter the old cellar, a perfect shelter if it came to that. But the odds were against a direct hit, even if one came. For a while she looked for a battery-operated radio without success. For what seemed hours, Iris sat, candles burning down, watching the storm. Despite waves of fear that came and went she was in control, only wanting Rodney to be with her, to comfort her when the lightning seemed to endlessly light the sky and the thunder roared. As the storm grew in intensity Iris could hear trees falling near the house, toppled by gusts so powerful the window panes seemed bowed inward, rippling almost like sheets of water even as the rain coursed upon them. When the phone rang, Iris started, not expecting it. It must be Rodney, she thought, as she ran to pick it up, her heart pounding.

"Hello," Iris shouted over the storm. Now there was a brief lull in the thunder and she could hear breathing. "Hello?" she repeated, scared now. Who could it be?

"Get out! Go...leave that man while you still can," came a voice. "Leave tonight while he's gone."

Iris listened, holding her breath. The voice was flat, almost emotionless, not threatening or raspy like in some Hitchcock movie. It seemed to be a woman's voice, but, amid the storm and the hissing static, Iris could not be sure. She did not recognize the voice. Fearful, she spoke into the receiver.

"Who is this? What do you want?"

"Just get out. Please, for your own sake, get out," came the voice and then a click, followed by the dial tone.

For the first time since moving in Iris was really frightened. Still holding the receiver Iris felt a chill of terror literally raising the fine hair on her neck and back. Was it some kind of awful practical joke? Who could it be? She had no real enemies. She replaced the receiver, briefly considering then rejecting a call to the police. What could they do? The damage to her car a few weeks before still worried her. Could this be connected? Maybe the same person? The voice had not sounded male, but it might have been, distorted as it was by static and noise. Was someone watching her? If so, why? She had never hurt anyone. Terror almost overcame her as the candles fluttered at a blast of wind so fierce it penetrated the house. She would turn to Rodney, her husband. He would help. He would know what to do.

Rodney answered before the second ring. She had asked the desk for his room number, and was connected at once. He listened without comment as Iris, crying a little, told him about the phone call.

"Now calm down, Iris. Just take a deep breath...that a girl, now take it easy, okay?"

His soothing voice had an immediate effect, and Iris's near hysteria waned. In control now, she followed Rodney's instructions and locked the doors, running back to the phone when she was done. Then he told her not to leave the house. He would check out and leave at once, skipping a morning meeting. It would take him less than an hour to get there.

"Goodbye, Iris. You just wait. I'll be there in no time, beautiful."

"Oh, Rodney, darling. I do love you," Iris cried. She hung up the phone and returned to her chair, throwing a comforter over her shivering body, her terror gradually subsiding. Soon the storm ended. Presently, Iris began to feel foolish, and before Rodney arrived she opened the door to the porch and peeked out into a damp, cool night, the eaves dripping still, the sky clearing to brilliant stars. Maybe Rodney had not left yet. She went quickly to the phone, determined now to handle this silly thing. Some prankster, no doubt. Rodney could stay and finish his business in Lansing.

The phone rang just as she reached for it. It was the same voice.

"Get out! Now! He has just left the motel, and you have half an hour to escape. If you don't go now, you'll be trapped. Believe me. He'll try to possess you. I know. I was his possession once. Don't become his possession. Live your own life. Get out while you can."

"Who is this?" Iris cried into the phone, her voice cracking. "What do you want? Why are you telling me this?"

But the phone was dead. Iris held herself, trembling to her toes. None of it made any sense. This could be no simple practical joke, no prankster. Someone was watching Rodney. Was she being watched too? What could she do? What if someone had monitored her call to Rodney? Maybe the caller was outside now? Fear spurring her, Iris ran to the window overlooking the sweeping drive and stared into the night. The moon illuminated the rain-swept landscape so visibility was good. She could see nothing unusual, the loom of the outbuildings, the woodlots and the gleam of the pond. One of the horses had ventured into the barnyard, its hooves sloshing in the mud puddles. Iris looked out the other door, behind the kitchen. Nothing. She sat at the kitchen table, flooded with light, waiting for Rodney to come to her.

About three quarters of an hour later Iris heard the crunch of car wheels on the gravel drive. It had to be Rodney, she thought. But what if it isn't? Frozen in fear she willed herself to move. The door opened. It was Rodney. Flooded with relief Iris ran to him, throwing her arms around him and hugging him close. For a long time she would not let him go. Then laughing, gabbing, she began making coffee. Hurriedly she described the last phone call.

As she talked Rodney's face changed. He had been frowning when he entered, now his scowl had transformed his face into a mask of hatred.

"That bitch." he muttered. Iris could barely hear him.

"What?" asked Iris, confused. How could he know who it was?

"Nothing," said Rodney, looking away. "Just thinking out loud. Forgot to call my secretary about my appointments. She's okay, but she never takes initiative. I have to tell her every goddamn thing."

"Oh," said Iris. "I thought..."

"Look, beautiful. Don't you worry. It was probably a prank call. Someone who guessed you were here alone. Maybe someone who knew I was in Lansing."

"But, Rodney."

"Like I said, Iris. Don't worry. All that stuff about possession. Sounds like someone has seen too many old horror movies. Anyhow, I don't want to possess you...I just want to love you the rest of my life. I've never been as happy as these last couple months. Look, if it makes you feel better, I'll call the sheriff's department in the morning."

Relieved, Iris went to him again, nestling her head into the crook of his strong neck, kissing him on his unshaven cheek. Gently he patted her back, and then as she began to kiss him on his face and lips, his hands moved in familiar intimacy, down her back to the swell of her buttocks, under the elastic band of her pants and panties, against the smooth naked skin.

"You go on up," Rodney said, reaching across her to open a cupboard. "Just get in bed and wait for me."

"No," said Iris, playfully pulling at him. "Let's do it right here." And indeed that is what she wanted. She was ready now. But Rodney firmly pulled himself away, and avoiding her hands, quickly poured himself a tall drink, filling his favorite tumbler with the dark amber of straight Kentucky Bourbon.

Rodney looked at her, a long, slow look. He did not smile.

"I said go on up," his voice had an edge to it. But then came a slight grin. "I'll be right behind you."

He turned and drank deeply, draining half the glass at one pull. Iris began to mount the stairs, hands at her breasts, feeling the hard nipples, moving very slowly, waiting for the sound of his heavy tread to follow. If ever, she thought, she wanted to be possessed, it was now...

Rodney brought some boxes into the bedroom. "Look what I got for you," he said, holding up an expensive pants suit, one that Iris had admired in a Lansing store window a week ago. He must have gone to considerable trouble to get it, she realized, since the store had been sold out of that particular item, except for the display window. How thoughtful of him.

"Look what else I bought," Rodney added, smiling. "For us." It was a black negligee, lacy and transparent.

In front of the mirror, Iris felt proud. She knew with her fine figure, that the negligee would set it off to good advantage, accentuating the swell of her breasts, slimming her thighs. Rodney came to her at once. As he thrust into her deeply, again and again, she cried out in joy. It was so good with him.

But late that night something brought her awake. She looked around the dark room, its spare furniture just visible. Rodney still resisted any change in the arrangement of the room, any addition to the furnishings. Why, she had no idea. Looking at the bedside stand, on Rodney's side, she saw the gleam of the tall glass, now empty. Had he drained even that last drink? How, she wondered, could he hold so much and not show it? She rolled onto her side and watched him slumbering beside her, his mouth open to a soft snore. She could smell the bourbon, but also there was the rich odor of his male body and the healthy aroma of love. Her mind wandered, into sleep, then dreaming again. Then she came awake the second time, scared by a fearful dream. The dreadful image faded quickly. What was it, she wondered? Suddenly it came to her. Why...why had he said "That bitch," immediately, his first words that night, after she had explained the second anonymous warning? How did he know it was a woman? She was not yet sure of that. Even after the second call, not distorted by static or thunder, Iris was uncertain. Was it possible that he knew who it was? What did he know? Worried, wondering, Iris did not sleep until dawn.

6

It was now several days since the incident and Rodney was gone again, this time to Grand Rapids. Fall was on its way, the days were growing shorter. Even as Iris gazed out the kitchen window the sun was setting. The shadows lengthened on the road, and Iris saw a figure approaching, walking alone along the roadside. She moved to the larger dining room window and saw that it was a woman, walking slowly, limping, but with a steady gait. The strange woman turned into the drive, hobbling up to the house and then up the steps onto the front porch.

Who could it be, thought Iris, this stranger with a pronounced limp, middle-aged, exceedingly thin, dressed in a shabby old shift. She went tentatively to the door, looking the woman over carefully before opening the door.

"Can I help you," asked Iris, facing the woman now at close range, disconcerted by this apparition. The lady attempted a smile, revealing missing teeth. Her thin lips seemed to be cracked and old, though the eyes gleamed with hard intensity. There was something in that gaze...something both lost and determined, like the gaze of one who might have become resigned to tragedy, accepting it, yet not willing to ever again be hurt. The woman wore thick unfashionable glasses, scuffed walking shoes. Her sallow skin, though deeply creased, was stretched tight across a face that might once have been attractive.

"Are you Iris Harris," said the woman in a flat, almost mannish voice. At once Iris recognized the voice. This was the person who had called her twice that stormy night.

"Yes," Iris stammered. "Who are you?"

"I'm Julia Harris," said the woman, her crooked smile once more revealing gaps in a row of yellow, uneven teeth. Iris stared, reaching a hand back to the porch swing to steady herself, not knowing what to say. This was the caller. She felt a shiver run up her spine and yet it was obvious there was no danger from this emaciated woman who looked weak, lame, and old. Then the smile faded and the old woman began to cry, reaching a thin arm out for support against the house.

"Come in...come in," Iris led the lady into the living room, guiding her to a seat.

Blowing her nose into a handkerchief, the woman explained who she was, her words tumbling forth. In moments, her mind whirling, Iris began to understand. This was Rodney's ex-wife, the former Julia Elizabeth Logan. This was the ex-wife Julia, who according to Rodney, had turned to alcohol and falsely accused him of beating her. Finding her voice again, Iris tried to gain some control of the conversation. Her mind was full of questions.

"Would you like coffee, Julia?"

"Oh, sure, I'd like that, if you don't mind..."

"Well, let's go into the kitchen," and she led the way.

As the coffee brewed, Iris could see that Julia was thirsty. She asked, "Can I get you water or something?"

"Water's fine, till that coffee's ready," Julia attempted another smile. "That is, lest you got somethin' else."

"A drink maybe. I have cold beer."

"Beer's fine, till that coffee's perked," Julia said, with a sigh, obviously hoping for something stronger. So, thought Iris, it's true, the woman is an alcoholic. How else explain the ravaged face, the emaciated figure, the pronounced limp and trembling hands.

"How old you think I am?" Julia said rhetorically, quickly answering her own question. "I'm forty-two. Hell, I know I look older. Don't lie to me, Iris. I do look older."

Taken aback, Iris stared. Could it be so? The woman looked more like sixty, and Iris could not disguise her shock. But then, drink did awful things to people. She felt real sympathy, but what did this woman want of her? She was determined now to get to the bottom of this mystery, but, before she could speak, Julia continued, her flat voice almost toneless, as if reciting a litany.

"I married him five and a half years ago. I wasn't bad looking then. It started out just fine, and beautiful, and I never felt better about any man. He seemed to me the finest fella you ever saw. So loving and caring. It was just fine for a while...but then things changed. Oh, things changed. I don't know what started it, but I remember the night when things went bad like it was yesterday. He was out working one day and come home late for dinner, I waited on dinner till it was too late to cook somethin' decent. I was heating up hot dogs on the stove when he come in the door, just stormed right in took that pan off'n the stove and throwed boilin' water at my face. I was lucky, I tell you, 'cause he missed. But then he took that there pan and started beating on me, all about the head and shoulders, yellin' at me, calling me a goddamn fool cooking shit for him, callin' me a whore and all kinds of other names. I don't know how long he kept at me. I just remember how it hurt. I was black and blue all across my face and shoulders. I remember how he laughed, just laughed at me, called me a worthless bitch. Tellin' me how I didn't deserve to live with him. I was sure he was gonna kill me, but after he stopped he just up and left the house. He didn't come back for four or five hours, and when he did, y'know, it was like nothin' had happened."

Stunned, unbelieving, Iris hovered over the woman. The coffee was ready now, so she busied herself with it, trying to frame a question, confused and scared. Surely this lady was mad, or half mad, probably paranoid. She had read that such delusions were common to alcoholics in the later stages of that malady. She recalled Rodney telling her that his former wife had once accused him of beating her, but that the charges had been false, and even the woman's lawyer had doubted her. She was about to ask Julia to leave when she found herself, for some reason, asking more questions.

"But you were married to him so long, about five years wasn't it? If all this is true, why did you stay?"

"Because," Julia cackled, her voice heavy with sarcasm. "Cause I loved that bastard. No matter how bad he beat me or how often, and, believe me, there was plenty after that first time."

Iris wondered how this could be true. How could anyone, she thought, remain with someone who beat her regularly? Only a masochist maybe. She was torn between an impulse to see this crazy lady to the door and a desire to learn more. If even a small part of this were true she would have to confront Rodney.

"Why did you...finally...I mean, divorce him?" Iris asked, the question mumbled. She was confused.

"He let me go," said Julia calmly, "because he met you."

"No! It's not true. It can't be," cried Iris. She slammed her coffee cup down so hard the hot liquid spilled, burning her. Julia, on the other hand, now drank steadily from hers.

"He was already divorced," Iris went on, forcing self-control, "when he met me."

"No," said Julia quietly, her gaze level now. "I remember...that night he come home from work. He tol' me he met someone new, another woman. Said I was free to go." Julia looked intently at Iris, studying her face, the hard lines softer now. "You don't have to believe me. Check the divorce file at the courthouse and look at the date the complaint was filed."

Iris tried to drink the remainder of her coffee, mind whirling. All this was too much. She believed most of what Julia had told her was a pack of lies. But it was disturbing. Maybe it was true that Rodney had only divorced this singularly unattractive woman, obviously ill-educated, just after meeting her. It was possible. More probably the woman was demented. Crazy people, she surmised, could lie with a straight face. Julia, if she was lying, sure carried it off with an air of assurance. Her demeanor was radically changed, no longer the crying old woman, Julia now seemed in control. Nevertheless, Iris vowed, forcing herself to drink the rest of the coffee, she would get to the bottom of this one way or the other.

She looked up, about to ask another question. Julia's face, somehow much younger now, seemed to reflect a range of emotions; sympathy, concern, curiosity, it was hard to tell.

"Did you notice how I limp?" asked Julia, with a tiny smile.

Iris nodded. It was impossible not to notice.

Julia stretched out a bony leg and removed the shoe from her right foot. Even before the plain brown stocking was removed, Iris could see the stub, lacking toes. With horror Iris stared at the now naked foot, the stump where the toes had been was red and puckered, ugly.

"He done it with an ax one evening," Julia said, studying her own stump and moving it in a circular fashion, then pulling the stocking back on. "I was sittin' in the kitchen. He come in mad and drunk without warning tied me to a chair. Then he tied my leg to that chair." Julia was looking straight at Iris again. "It took three blows with that ax, but he finally chopped all the way through. I fainted, but my toes was gone when I come to."

Unbelieving, Iris stared, speechless.

"You wanna know what he told the doctor?" Julia laughed, a low sound that chilled Iris to the bone. "He tol' the doctor we'd been out choppin' wood and I cut my own toes off by mistake. Can you imagine that?" Again came the chilling laugh. "You'd think they wouldn't believe it. Well, they did, I tell you. That man can make practically anyone believe anything he says." Julia, having finished her coffee now, pushed the empty cup away, both hands palm down on the table, leaning towards Iris.

"I always liked a drink now and then, I admit. But it was after that I started really drinking. Hell," she laughed again, this time in what seemed to be real humor, "I tried, but I could never keep pace with him." Julia paused, as if to ponder her words.

"It was after that, after he cut off my toes, he kept me prisoner." This was uttered in a near whisper, with an undertone of urgency.

"That's why I called the other night, when I seen him at the motel. I work there as night maid and I seen him come in. I read about how you two was married, in the Ionia paper. I was gonna warn you before it was too late. Then when I seen him I just went to a pay phone and called. 'Course I knew the number out at the farm." Julia's voice trailed off a moment.

"So...you see. You gotta understand. He ain't what he seems. If you don't leave now, while you still got a chance, you'll never get free of him." Then came the terrible laugh again. "Leastways, until he finds someone else."

For a long time, both women sat silent. Iris, speechless with fear and wonder, did not want to openly accuse this sad woman of outright lies. She was obviously very sick, but it was hard not to believe some of it...perhaps in her sick mind the woman had distorted real events, making a mash of fact. Maybe some deep resentment towards Rodney had created a paranoid world of fantasy. When Julia rose and asked the way to the bathroom, Iris busied herself in the kitchen. From the bathroom came the sound of retching. When Julia returned, she was muttering incoherently, obviously deranged. "Got to get dinner for him. Gotta hurry. He'll get home any minute."

Iris took her hand gently and led her to the door, the way she had come, speaking gently to her as if to a child.

"D'you need a ride, Julia? It's almost dark."

"No. I'll walk. Gotta get some hot dogs, I'm always short on hot dogs. He don't like 'em, but he don't give me enough money for decent meat. The store ain't far. I'll be back in plenty of time if I hurry."

Firmly, Iris helped the incoherent woman down the front steps, speaking comforting words to her. "Okay. You go on home now, Julia."

For a long time Iris stood in the gathering darkness, the lights from the house spilling onto the lawn. A horse whinnied behind the barn. Cicadas buzzed in the shrubbery, their harsh song to the waning warmth of the dying summer. She wondered if the woman was safe. Maybe she should call the sheriff's office, but she felt they had been bothered enough. Truthfully, she was relieved when Julia had disappeared. Now she could think this through. She would not let it ride, no matter the extent of Julia's lies. She would look into it.

When she returned to the house and made ready for night, she made sure all the doors and windows were shut tight, locked. Then, worried, tears barely held back, she poured herself a shot of scotch drinking it down in small gulps, like fire in her throat. She knew sleep would not come easily.

7

Iris was up early the next morning, agitated and tired, but eager to complete all her errands before Rodney returned from Grand Rapids. He was expected around four o'clock. It took but twenty minutes to reach the Ionia County Courthouse, an old stately building of three massive stories, block-like and imposing. Without difficulty, Iris requested and received the file of Harris versus Harris from the County Clerk's Office on the first floor. For a time she hesitated, wondering if she really had the right to probe. But she repressed her fear and went ahead, driven by curiosity.

She could hardly believe her eyes. Here in black and white was the recorded date of the Judgment of Divorce. It was May 26th, only three days before Rodney had asked her to marry him, not long after they had first met. The date for the Complaint of Divorce was February 3rd. Julia had been telling the truth, at least on this point. Thinking back, Iris realized that this was the day after she had first met Rodney in Ionia. Suddenly her throat was dry, burning.

"Is there a place I can get a drink of water?" she asked the clerk.

Drinking from a fountain down the hall in the old building, Iris tried to control her thoughts and use reason. Could everything Julia said be true, then, if this part of her story checked out? She found a chair within sight of the clerk and read further in the file. The next document was titled: Petition for Injunctive Relief. The petition was even worse. Inside it was alleged that Rodney Harris had repeatedly beaten, threatened, abused, and committed various acts of violence against Mrs. Harris, including an attack on her person with an ax. Included was an Injunctive Order signed by the Circuit Judge, restraining Rodney Harris from harassing, molesting, abusing, annoying, or committing any acts of violence against Julia Harris. The Judgment for Divorce, also in the file, included a property settlement indicating that Rodney was to receive the farm property near Muir, the Thunderbird, and all the household items except those specifically belonging to Julia Harris, as personal items. Rodney was directed to pay Julia a cash settlement of $5,000.

Iris read each document over again, trying to control her feelings. She wanted to scream and cry, to throw the papers away, to burn them, to run into the street and show them to everyone, to take them home with her. She knew she had to control this flow of irrational anger. Calmly, forcing her mind to the task, she read through the stack of papers, this time looking for clues beyond the legal words. It might still be mere allegation, the basis for all this, she thought. Julia might have made it all up. After all, if it were true that Rodney had beaten and abused Julia, then why had the property settlement been so much in Rodney's favor? There was no mention of the house in Ionia. Maybe Rodney had only rented that. In any case a settlement of $5,000, plus personal items hardly seemed fair to the divorced wife. Why was this? Was it possible that an investigation had revealed the allegations to be untrue? Had Julia imagined everything? Hence the settlement in Rodney's favor? It had to be so.

Determined to learn the truth, Iris rose and asked the clerk for access to a copy machine. She would copy everything and confront Rodney with the evidence, to back up the visit by Julia the previous evening. She would learn the truth from him this very day or else leave forever.

Rodney was late, the car turned into the drive at five-thirty. Springing up the back steps and into the mud room, Rodney held out his big arms. Iris, for the first time in the marriage, did not respond. She stood frowning, arms crossed on her breasts. Turning her back to him, she advanced to the table and gestured to the pile of papers strewn across it, a cup of coffee steaming where she had been waiting. Hands shaking, she pointed, the words not coming at first.

"I've been to the courthouse, Rodney. Julia visited me last night. I had to find out." Now words failed her. Iris's determination wavered at the look of bewilderment and hurt on her husband's handsome face. "All the records of your divorce from Julia are there. And the...the...what do you call them? The petitions."

"The Petitions and Orders to keep me from beating Julia?" Rodney too had found his voice. It was deep and grave, controlled. He nodded, a look of pain crossing his face.

"So much went wrong with that woman, that marriage," said Rodney sadly, throwing up his hands. "I suppose I should've told you everything, but..." Then he interrupted himself.

"Did you say she came here? Did you say that? She came here?"

"She sure did. And...oh, Rodney, she said the most awful things." Iris had begun to cry. She stood forlorn beside the table, the papers strewn before her. She wanted him to deny it all, to assure her that poor Julia was mad, sick, insane, a pathological liar, anything. She wanted his big arms around her, firm and comforting. She wanted the nightmare to go away.

"She came here?" Rodney repeated his litany. Now he paced the kitchen. "That goddamn bitch, that little bitch, that mother fu..." he caught himself. Turning swiftly, he grabbed up the documents from the table, reading each quickly. Half way through, he threw the rumpled sheets down, turning to Iris; arms raised high, menace in his face, eyes blazing. Iris shrank back, instinctively raising her arms for protection. But Rodney fighting for control let his arms fall. He reached out gently to take her into his arms, but she resisted, pushing him away.

"No. Don't."

"I'm sorry, Iris. Jesus, I'm sorry. That woman...well...I'll tell all of it. Now, come on, sit down." He pulled up a chair to the table and pushed the papers to one side. "Now sit, and tell me everything she said. Everything."

So Iris did, crying a little as she spoke. Before she had finished, Rodney reached out gently to take one of her hands in his, just touching her softly. His touch was so comforting. Still suspicious, she nevertheless wanted his touch so. Then he began to speak in turn.

"I did tell you she made charges against me, of abuse. Didn't I? It ain't hard y'know, to get restraining orders in a divorce. But that don't mean the allegations are true." Rodney's words flowed rapidly, his voice flat and toneless. There was an undertone of sniveling in his words, but mostly he seemed hurt, indignant. "Julie has mental problems, serious problems. She seems to get better, then she gets worse. I don't know what caused it, but she changed not long after we got married. Maybe she always had the problem, I don't know. But I didn't see any...any symptoms, or whatever, when I first met her."

Rodney had been speaking with his head turned to the window. Now he turned to look at Iris. "She wasn't bad looking then, y'know."

"So she said," Iris responded, to her surprise. Withdrawing his hands, Rodney ran them through his thick hair.

"Anyhow," Rodney continued, "she started having them delusions, and before I knew it, she was accusing me of abuse. Look, I don't know quite how to say this. I never been the type to kiss and tell...but Julia, she was funny, in bed I mean. Sometimes...she kind of liked...y'know, me to be a little rough. I think maybe she actually wanted to be hurt. But I never hurt her."

"Believe me, Iris; I never laid a hand on that woman. Maybe a little... spanking...and that...in bed and all. But I never hurt her. You gotta believe me."

It all seemed so improbable. And there were the records, still on the table between them. Suddenly she wanted to destroy them all, to forget the last night and the morning, to obliterate every bad thing that might come between them.

"What about her foot?" Iris asked, surprising herself with her firm query.

"Oh, that. Jesus H. Christ. That ax incident. Okay, let me tell you the whole thing. It was when we went out together one time, to get wood for the fireplace. She was pretty clumsy, but I still don't know exactly how she did it, if it was really an accident or not. Y'know, she could be pretty crazy at times. Like when she was here last night." Rodney watched Iris closely, to see her reaction. "But, anyhow, I heard this scream, and I come running to her. All the toes were cut off, right through. She had on them thin sneakers, y'know. So I picked her up and rushed her to the Doc, blood all over the floor of my car, and he tried to rejoin the toes, but it was too late and the wound was too rough. I gotta tell you, it sure surprised me when she started to tell that doctor that I did it. Can you imagine? She told him I cut them off. It was unbelievable." Rodney looked at Iris, eyes darting away and then back. "Look. If you still don't believe me, after Labor Day, we are going in and we are gonna talk with my attorney and with that doctor. Okay? They'll tell you the truth."

"Then," said Iris, wanting to believe him now. "What about that property settlement? I guess she didn't deserve...?"

"About that," Rodney continued, "you're right. After she accused me of abuse, I talked to my lawyer about her behavior throughout the marriage. We discussed the possibility of maybe committing her to a hospital, but, when my attorney approached hers, well, they came up with this agreement as to the property. It was a bargain, sort of."

Rodney rose and made his way to the cupboard, fixing himself the familiar tall drink of bourbon. He drank more than half a glass in one gulp, sighing. "I don't know whether you believe all this, Iris, but you will when we talk to my doctor and my attorney. And, just to clear everything up, we'll go to the police too. They made a report on that ax injury."

He made his way next to Iris, finishing the drink and placing a heavy hand on her shoulder. She looked up at him, smiling now, nodding, and believing him.

"If you still want a divorce after that, it's yours, Iris. But I want you to stay." Pouring a second drink, Rodney set it on the table before her. "Go ahead, you sure as hell need it more than me." Iris drank, almost choking on the straight bourbon, but the warmth quickly spread through her. She did feel much better now. Rodney put his arms around her from behind and she now took his hands in hers where they rested near her breasts, pressing them to her, her head turned to receive his kiss on her neck. It was all fine now.

"Iris. I love you too much to live without you. But, if you have any doubts at all, I want you to feel free to go. I am not an animal. Have I ever hurt you?"

"No," she said softly, and it was true. Then she began to cry, and, from behind, she could feel Rodney sobbing too.

8

Labor Day weekend was hectic. Rodney had invited several people over for a cook out at the farm. They arrived in several groups, the cars quickly filling the drive and the yard and spilling down towards the barn. There were kegs of beer, lots of pretzels, potato chips, watermelon and new apples. The afternoon was spent with the fifty or so odd people taking turns riding horses, playing catch, pick-up softball on a makeshift diamond in the pasture, eating and drinking. It was a hot afternoon and growing more humid as evening approached. One younger couple ran hand in hand down to the pond, plunging in with clothes on, then stripping to undies, while everyone laughed and applauded. Iris stood watching, the late sun sparkling on the droplets of water as people waded in and splashed each other. Rodney had already consumed more than anyone. She was amazed at his capacity, but used to it by now. Looking around, Iris realized that her husband was easily the oldest person present. Nevertheless he seemed to be the driving force behind the various activities. He adjusted saddles and stirrups, and led the less confident guests around holding the reins in his own hands, expertly advising the bolder riders as to the points of balance and control over the big animals. At one point, to demonstrate, he had mounted the big mare, the fastest and most spunky of the horses, and rode her hard at a gallop down to the end of the pasture and back, clots of earth flying, folks shouting. Iris was proud of him, and a little scared at his physical presence. She knew his incredible capacity to drink impressed others; they too had come to expect it of him. Most of the people she did not know, though there were familiar faces present; Mr. James, president of the local Chamber of Commerce, and his large wife, several of Rodney's business associates, a banker, the owner of the old but still busy grain elevator, one of the Sheriff's deputies and his pretty young wife. When the barbecued beef was ready, everyone sat and ate huge helpings, dipping out scoops of salad that Iris had prepared, gabbing and singing as the sun began to set. Rodney had fixed up a borrowed stereo system in the barn. Iris, having finished her food, went into the kitchen. She was working there, washing and trying to get a little ahead of the incredible clutter already spilling over the countertop, when Rodney entered. It was now full dark and she could hear the boom of music from the barn.

"Ain't you coming," said Rodney, putting his arms around her. She could smell the heavy odor of booze on him. It permeated from him. "We're off down t'the pond, it's a custom of the Harris farm, a bunch of us go skinny dippin'. Do it every year at Labor Day. So, ya comin' or not?"

For a moment, Iris almost agreed. But, though not modest about her body when with Rodney, she was shy of others in that regard. Dark or no dark, she did not wish to swim in the nude, especially in that pond. It was none too clear or clean. So Iris busied herself and Rodney clumped out the door, mumbling. He was gone till nearly midnight, by which time Iris had the kitchen spic and span, the outdoor tables cleared. She drifted down to the barn looking for Rodney, but he had not come back. She watched for a time as half a dozen couples tried, with what seemed to her rather awkward lack of skill, to dance to the loud rock music. Laughter and shrieks drifted up from time to time from the pond, but she did not walk down, afraid she would be forced to strip and join the roistering gang. Then she looked up to see the young deputy standing next to her. He looked cool and handsome in his civilian clothes.

"My wife's inside. Looking for the john," he explained. "Where's Rodney, haven't seen him around?"

Iris studied the youthful figure. He was several years younger than her, maybe in his early thirties.

"Oh...Rodney," Iris laughed. "He's down there, with..." She gestured toward the pond. The young man nodded knowingly. "My wife wouldn't go either. Not that I made a big point about it." She could see his smile flash in the light from the overhead bulb that dimly illuminated a corner of the loft, leaving the dance space in shadow.

"You want to dance?" asked the deputy.

"Sure," Iris smiled, holding up her arms to be guided onto the planked floor where the others now swayed to the slow rhythms of a Barbra Streisand ballad.

"Are you doing okay?" asked the deputy after a time. Iris was embarrassed that she could not remember his name. He had been one of the cops who came when her VW had been vandalized. Now the question seemed out of place. She looked up sharply at the man, pulling away slightly. He was a good dancer and she had naturally drifted closer, enjoying herself.

"Of course. I'm fine," she said firmly. "Rodney is a wonderful husband," she added, realizing it must sound foolish to say it.

"He sure is something else," answered her partner.

Then Iris felt a heavy hand on her shoulder, spinning her away from the deputy.

"What the hell are you doing?" It was Rodney, standing over her, his hair wet, the reek of bourbon now overpowering. Iris allowed him to guide her away from the dance floor, into the outer darkness. Beyond she saw the form of a woman, apparently watching. Who was that, she thought? The figure seemed vaguely familiar. It was, she realized, Rodney's secretary, a flashy and outgoing woman slightly younger than Iris. As the woman turned and walked towards the house, Iris could see that her hair too was wet.

"Look," growled Rodney, his hand gripping her so hard on the upper arm that Iris almost cried out. "You wanna dance, dance with me. Okay? I'm your husband, so you dance with me."

With that he guided Iris back into the barn, a somewhat sheepish smile on his face as they passed the deputy, who watched now with his wife as Iris and Rodney joined the dwindling party on the dance floor. Rodney, she realized, was very drunk, unable to coordinate his steps and they reeled and clashed for some time, almost falling more than once. His iron control over himself, while drinking, Iris realized, was largely a show.

Nevertheless, Iris soon allowed him to guide her into an old stable, out of sight of the others, where he began pawing her in familiar anticipation. Slightly aroused herself, Iris held him off, whispering, "Not here, not here..." and then leading him into the house and towards the stairs. Pushing at him from behind as he reeled upwards, she returned to look out the door into the night. All but two couples had gone now, one of whom was the young deputy and his wife standing next to their car, waiting for the car ahead of them to pull out.

"Goodnight," Iris called, waving.

The deputy seemed to hesitate, staring at her, then he climbed into his car beside his wife and drove away into the darkness.

Upstairs, Rodney was having trouble getting one of his shoes off. Iris helped as Rodney ran his hands freely over her body. Quickly she undressed him, then herself, and stretched out beside him. The reek of booze was still so powerful she almost gagged, but she began to kiss him fondly, running her hands over his chest and down. But it was no use. He was not able. Again and again she tried, using every trick he had taught her, but to no avail. An hour at least passed before he gave up, cursing, turning his back to her angrily, snoring almost immediately. Iris did not sleep for a long time.

All of Labor Day was spent quietly. Iris cleaned up the yard and the barn while Rodney slept. She fixed him brunch just after mid-day, but he ate little, sipping instead from the ever-present glass of bourbon. Though he had looked awful when he came downstairs, within forty minutes, sipping at his drink, he looked almost normal.

"So? Didja have a good time last night then?" Rodney asked, grinning, his old self again.

"Yes, darling, it was fun."

"Sorry you missed the skinny dip down at the pond?" Rodney said, gazing at her out of the corner of his eye. "You gotta learn to loosen up, beautiful."

Iris, remembering the way he had pulled her away from the deputy, was about to retort, but she held back. Loosen up indeed, she thought. What went on down there, she wondered? Well, not much could happen with so many people sharing the pond, dark or no dark. But she did not like it.

"We go in tomorrow, remember?" said Rodney, changing the subject. "To see that doctor and my attorney."

"How could I forget, dear," said Iris, without a trace of irony in her voice.

9

However, their first stop next morning was the Ionia County Sheriff's Office. After a short wait, they were joined by a Sgt. Sanders who opened the police report filed by Julia. Sanders explained that, at the time, he had been a patrolman for the Sheriff's Department and had taken the original complaint himself.

"We had problems with Julia before this incident," said Sanders. "Truckers traveling on M-21 would report she was wandering down the road in her nightgown during the wee hours. This happened several times. M-21 is close to a mile from your house. I remember trying to talk to her, but she was completely withdrawn, shy, almost unable to respond. Like she was somewhere else." Rodney nodded at this, looked from the Sergeant to Iris. "In fact, Mrs. Harris, I remember once, after one of those incidents that I recommended to Mr. Harris that he should probably get help for Julia, at an outpatient clinic, or..."

"You even suggested I might have to get her committed, didn't you?" Rodney said, triumphantly.

"That's right," said Sanders. "In this business you get pretty good at telling...when..."

"Someone has gone looney," Rodney interrupted.

"Well...whatever," Sanders shrugged, continuing his narrative. "On this particular occasion, I got a call about five-thirty to get right over to Dr. Hargood's office. A woman was complaining of assault and injury, so the Doc's receptionist said, was screaming that her husband had attacked her with an ax. Well, I got to the Doc's after they had taken Mrs. Harris...uh... Julia, over to the hospital. When the Doc told me who was involved, I frankly had my doubts about any attack, but I followed up, of course. At the hospital Julia was...well, beside herself."

"Out of her mind," said Rodney, but the Sergeant looked up shortly, not appreciating the interruption.

"She told me Rodney here tied her to a chair and cut off her toes. It seemed incredible to me, and still does to tell the truth. Mr. Harris here has a good reputation in the community as a hard worker and good husband. He's active in lots of civic affairs. So Mr. Harris, who was very patient, I might add, while Julia screamed at him, managed to explain how they had left the house around one o'clock to cut wood. Sometime later, while Rodney was stacking cordwood in the wood lot, he heard her scream for help. When he got to her, the toes were gone, sliced right off. It's some distance to that wood lot. Mr. Harris carried her all of a quarter mile to his truck. By the time he got her to the hospital it was too late, I guess, to save the toes. Anyway, I checked with the nearest neighbors that same night and one of them saw the truck at the stop sign across from her house, with two people in it. Furthermore, no one heard any screams or the like coming from the house, though it is some distance to the nearest neighbor."

"Maybe you'll find this unpleasant, Mrs. Harris," continued Sanders, "but it wasn't really an ax. It was a hatchet she used. That wound was apparently self-inflicted. You see, the next day, after Mr. Harris told us where they had been cutting wood, one of our deputies went out to the woodlot and found the hatchet. The prints on the handle were Julia's. That's it, I guess." He stood and let his breath out. "Any questions? It's all in this report, including, of course, the alleged attack. I consider the case closed. As it says here our investigation determines the probable cause of the wound to be self-inflicted injury."

Iris was convinced despite the awkward language. The report supported everything Sgt. Sanders said. She read through it quickly.

"About the lie-detector...?" said Rodney.

"Oh yeh. Almost forgot. We were planning to put both subjects through a polygraph test, not binding of course, and Mr. Harris readily agreed, though because he was taking Valium, our expert wasn't ready to test him while he was on that substance."

Iris turned to look at Rodney in surprise. This was news to her. Valium? Well, it was hardly a rare thing these days.

"Further," said the Sergeant, "it is our examiner's policy not to test an alleged defendant unless the alleged victim is tested first. And Julia... well, her state was...she was barely coherent. We just dropped it. We closed the case, but not before we recommended to Mr. Harris that he think about committing Julia. It was obvious to everyone that she needed help. I firmly believe she was, and still is, dangerous to herself, if not to others."

As Iris waited in the hall, Rodney and the Sergeant talked quickly, heads together, then shaking hands. Iris was now certain that Julia was very ill, filled with delusions. Then they drove to Dr. Hargood's office.

The doctor was a smallish man, sallow and pinched about the mouth, revealing yellow teeth as he showed them into his private office, ushering them past the several waiting patients.

"I've been expecting you. A most unfortunate affair..." he said clucking his tongue, producing a vivid "tut-tut." Iris almost laughed; the whole thing was becoming ludicrous. She had had enough convincing. Nevertheless, she sat dutifully, hands folded on her lap, nodding.

"I must," said the doctor, "be careful, of course, doctor-patient privilege and all. So I will answer only such questions as I deem appropriate." He cleared his throat of what seemed to be a large amount of phlegm, fiddling with his shirt pocket. Iris realized he had only recently quit smoking. The fingers were still nicotine stained, like the teeth. "First," said the doctor, "let me outline the case as I understand it. I treated Mrs. Julia Harris for an injury purportedly inflicted on her foot with an ax. To be specific, the toes were completely, if rather clumsily, severed from the foot, leaving a bleeding stump. In my opinion, the wound, which I treated only in first-aid manner before sending the patient directly to the hospital, was of such a nature that it might have been either administered accidentally, it might have been self-inflicted, or possibly inflicted by someone else. However," again he cleared his throat, coughing with the smoker's characteristic cough, "I did state that, in my opinion, the latter possibility seemed remote. This, of course, I stated to the police. This was so because the angle of the cut which severed the toes, seemed to indicate that the blow came from behind and probably a bit above. Rather like this!" The little man made a savage slashing gesture as if at his own extended foot, holding an imaginary hatchet.

"Any person other than Julia Harris herself, who might have administered such a blow, would have had to stand rather awkwardly behind her, or off to the side at least. Which idea, of course, stretches one's imagination, I should think." The doctor seemed self-satisfied, crossing his small arms. "It seemed likely...as I still believe...that the wound was self-inflicted."

"What did Julia say?" Iris blurted, surprised at her own voice.

"She gave two versions as I recall," said Dr. Hargood. "As I bandaged the foot and instructed my receptionist to call the ambulance and hospital, Mrs. Harris kept repeating, 'It's my fault...it's my fault.' But then, as I rode with her in the ambulance to the hospital, she told her frankly incredible story about her husband chopping off her toes." The doctor screwed up his small face, now suddenly wrinkled, and waved a hand as if to dismiss such rubbish.

"I am a physician, not a detective. But, of course, it is rather absurd. I mean, let alone the difficulty of any other person inflicting the wound, there is the matter of her husband, a businessman of reputation as you know, having no conceivable motive."

Julia wanted to ask more questions, but the doctor was finished. He rose and offered his hand to Iris, then to Rodney, who had uttered not a word. "Is there anything else?" asked the doctor.

Only later, as they drove off in the car, did Iris realize that she had planned to ask the doctor about Rodney's valium. Why did he take it, and when, and how often? Wasn't it merely a tranquilizer of some kind? That would have to wait. Maybe the prescription was from a different doctor. But it couldn't be very serious. Julia was apparently quite sick, and nothing the woman said could be believed.

Suddenly she was sick of the whole affair. She merely wanted it to pass. Now, she could see why Rodney wanted the past to remain past.

"Do we really have to see that lawyer?" she asked. Rodney was, however, determined.

"Julia," he said, "filed for that injunctive relief, or whatever, where she accused me of abuse. My lawyer will explain all of it. I want you to hear all of it."

Indeed, Rodney's attorney, one Howard Jackson, had much to say. In contrast to Dr. Hargood, Mr. Jackson was large, almost as tall as Rodney, though much thicker in the middle, with a rather high rapid voice that seemed to well up from the ample depths of flesh.

"Ah yesss. I remember vividly how Rodney came to me disturbed when he was served with a Petition for Injunctive Relief alleging physical abuse." Jackson waved the papers from his file, leaning back in his large chair as if to display the abundance of his vast stomach. "I began investigating her behavior. Rodney filled in the details on the ax incident, and by then I already guessed that she was in need of therapy. So, I approached her attorney on the matter."

Now he let the chair come back, its springs and swivel squeaking under its burden of weight. He looked intently at Iris. "In the course of my investigation, I discovered that she had been committed to a psychiatric hospital ten years before her marriage to Rodney. I so informed her attorney, also advising him that I would begin the same process again, that is, to have her re-committed, unless these charges of abuse were dropped. Furthermore, as part of the agreement, that she consent to the property settlement, as stipulated." Jackson tapped the document with satisfaction. A good lawyer who had done his job well. "Naturally, Julia agreed, not wishing to risk the chance that she might end up in the hospital again."

Jackson shifted his weight and looked at Rodney, who nodded.

"I must tell you, Iris, that Rodney called me recently. We have discussed the wisdom of committing Julia now. I'll review the situation. You see, I am convinced that Julia badly needs professional treatment. She is dangerous, at the least, to herself. Unpredictable at best. I am sure you won't want her showing up unannounced at your house again."

Iris nodded. That she did not want.

"The procedure is as follows. First we must establish that she is mentally ill, and that, as a result of this illness, might reasonably be expected in the near future to seriously injure herself or others, and that, in the past, she has engaged in acts supportive of this belief, and, because of the mental illness, is unable to attend to her basic physical needs. Things like food, shelter, and the like. Or that, because of the illness, she is unable to understand her need for treatment. The burden of the case is that she is unsafe to herself and others. According to the statute, mental illness means a substantial disorder of thought or mood which significantly impairs judgment, behavior, and capacity to recognize reality or ability to cope with the ordinary demands of life."

For several minutes, Mr. Jackson outlined further details. Iris, glancing at Rodney, could see the bland expression of satisfaction on his face. For a moment, watching, half listening to the drone of the lawyer's voice, she felt a deep flash of concern, of worry, of doubt.

"So, if you leave it to me," Jackson was saying, "I'll proceed as planned, and prepare the affidavit for your signatures."

Iris tried to listen with an attentive ear to the legal language, watching Rodney closely. With every tick of legalese Rodney pursed his lips, mouthing the words that he apparently knew well, turning one finger in after the other in a count. He was clearly satisfied. So too, Iris thought, should she be. But she was not. Something nagged beneath all the words, something incomplete. Turning her attention again to the lawyer, she listened to the final details, and there was mild comfort in the language of law.

"Naturally," Mr. Jackson said, winding up his speech, "if we are to make this work, both of you will have to testify. You are the only witnesses who can support the circumstances with facts."

"I'll have to testify?" Iris said, dismayed. "I really don't know her, I mean..."

"I'm afraid so," said Jackson. "Your testimony will be required by the prosecutor. Perhaps you should discuss this between yourselves." His eyebrows went up, looking from Rodney to Iris and back.

"We'll let you know the first of the week," said Rodney, his voice resonant with confidence and decision. They thanked the lawyer and left, hand in hand. In the car Rodney gathered her into his arms. "Now do you really believe, really believe me?"

She murmured into his shoulder. "Yes, I do, oh yes, Rodney. It must have been awful for you." And, filled with compassion for his past sufferings, she held him tight, asking his forgiveness.

"You'll never leave me?" he asked. "Never?"

"Oh, Rodney, never," she cried.

10

A week later the decision was made. Rodney expressed doubts but Iris pushed, convinced now that Julia needed help. In the meantime, Mr. Jackson's investigation had continued, revealing that Julia's work habits of late had changed. Until June, she had been prompt, though her work was often slow. Then she had become withdrawn and depressed, often coming to work late. Only a week before, the manager of the motel had found her on the floor of the women's restroom unable or unwilling to speak. Quickly the paperwork was prepared.

Events moved as predicted. Julia protested an examination. The probate judge ordered her hospitalized for the purpose of such an examination. Julia was duly examined and certified by a psychiatrist. All the proceedings were followed in order, and, following a Preliminary Hearing, probable cause was found to certify Julia as in need of hospitalization for psychiatric treatment.

The hearing was in early October. At the beginning two psychiatrists testified that Julia was suffering a serious mental disorder. Specifically, they translated the medical terms for the court; she suffered from substantial disorders of thought and mood. This was based on their interviews with her, during which she had stated that God took care of her, protecting her during her marriage to Mr. Harris. She had spoken of Mr. Harris as a devil. Furthermore, she had stated that God spoke to her, and told her it was her duty to protect Iris Harris from the devil who would possess her. It was at God's request, so Julia had said, that she went out to the Harris house to warn Iris. And then, when Iris refused to listen to God speaking through her, she became depressed and could not work. Furthermore, Julia had informed both doctors that she would refuse medication since God would not allow her to cloud her mind with drugs. The gist of the case was that both doctors agreed; as a result of her mental illness, Julia was dangerous to herself, could no longer attend to her basic needs, and did not understand her need for treatment. Therefore, she should be committed for treatment.

Over the objection of Julia's attorney, Rodney was called to the witness stand. He spoke clearly, with confidence, a note of sadness in his voice, as Julia wept, looking away from him throughout the questioning. The Prosecutor, despite objections, managed to get in the fact that Julia had apparently cut off her toes with an ax. Despite the fact that the incident was no longer relevant to the case at hand, having occurred three years previously. Julia had not a chance.

Iris did not testify until later. Then, and only then, did Julia come out of her sullen and increasing inattention to the proceedings. Iris had watched her grow more and more distant, sitting slight and bent next to her attorney, wearing the same faded blue dress, scuffed old pumps, nervously scratching at her scalp, eyes empty or turned inward as if to see no one, to acknowledge no one. But when Iris began to speak, she came alert with sudden energy, crying out loudly.

"All I wanted to do was help you. Why don't you believe me? You must get out! You must run! God will protect you if you listen."

Iris watched as everyone sadly turned away, embarrassed by this confirmation of the diagnosis. The lady was crazy, the eyes seemed to say. It was all to the good, this awkward proceeding. Looking at the poor woman Iris teared up, but she finished her testimony. More than ever she was sure of the rightness of it.

At the conclusion, the judge ordered Julia Harris committed to the regional hospital for sixty days for the purpose of treatment. As Iris knew, this period might be extended indefinitely, depending on Julia's progress. Julia seemed to pay no attention to the judgment, but then, as Iris walked to join Rodney, Julia lurched forward, her hands extended.

"Ask him...ask him about the others! I'm not the only one..."

Iris turned away in embarrassment. It was grotesque.

"Why did you conspire against me?" Julia ranted, "Remember, remember that I warned you." Then she was taken gently away.

Rodney took Iris north the next weekend. As he predicted, the color was magnificent. As the hills and glacial ridges of northwestern Michigan rose around them, flaming maples and sumac, yellow poplars and birch, russet and scarlet oaks, the leaves blowing along the rolling highway behind the rushing cars, Iris relaxed, letting Rodney tool the powerful car over dales and rises, flashing past rushing trout streams and blue lakes. It was lovely almost beyond words, she thought, feeling at peace for the first time in weeks.

"I have a surprise for you, honey," said Rodney, as they wound their way through the grand sweeps of US 131, north of Cadillac, the October colors so brilliant against the blue sky they seemed to be painted there. "I have property in Kalkaska County, a house and some acreage. I bought it for fishing. That's where we're headed. I can make the place livable with a bit of work. We can come up any time we want."

Iris was pleased. Rodney was full of surprises.

11

Iris had been "north" before but never so keen to the subtle beauties of the region. It was as if Michigan, despite its apparent clean geographic division into Upper and Lower peninsulas—together making it the most varied state east of the Mississippi—had conspired with nature to create another less obvious division, the one between its northern counties (all within the lower peninsula) and the southern counties, mostly industrialized, mostly flat, quite different. For a while, as Rodney drove, she toyed with this distinction, as millions have done, captivated by the ever-more-evident changes as they pushed north. The trees grew bigger, the hills and ridges higher, the rivers faster (she had twice seen canoes as they flashed past high bridges), the valleys deeper. Oak and hickory wood lots gave way to endless forests of maple and beech, and great swaths of deep green pine and cedar. The contrast of autumn's color and clear sky, of cobalt lakes framed in shimmering stands of birch, of tamarack and spruce-studded swamps filling old lake beds, and the blazing hills beyond seemed to match the change in the very air; now it blew fresh, pine-scented, invigorating, into the car and across her face and hair. Near Manton they had almost hit a large doe, her startled leap carrying her from roadside almost over the car, then with a second great bound, as if in super-slow-motion, back again into the shelter of a shaded poplar grove. Iris saw her young, two of them, quite large now in

October, standing alert in the trees, ears straight up. Heart still fluttering, she had put her hand on Rodney's big arm, thankful. Chuckling, he accelerated the powerful car up to speed.

"Use' ta hunt 'em," he said.

"Why did you stop?" To Iris, the idea of shooting such graceful animals, putting out the amber light in those great doe eyes, seemed intolerable, but she did not say so.

"I like fishing better" said Rodney.

This was typical of him, Iris thought. She looked at him closely, wondering. This, she knew, was hardly unusual. This sense, common to newly married people of any age, that their mate was a stranger at times, unknown and unknowable. But there was so much of Rodney's past...that she did not know.

Her father had hunted back in the 'fifties when his rising wages and relative affluence made the purchase of expensive rifles and hunting gear possible, when virtually all of his male friends made the annual fall migration in search of the elusive but abundant white-tail. She remembered the catch phrase, "Did you get your deer?" that men asked each other in those crisp November weeks. Her father had been a kindly man, speaking rarely and in short sentences, sometimes drinking too much after work or on long weekend nights with his friends at the local bar, but she had never been able to picture him actually shooting and killing anything. Trying to remember her long dead father, she wondered if he had ever got his deer. Tearing her mind away, not wanting to think of him, she vividly recalled her mother instead. A long and terrible illness, a prolonged death-watch. She pulled her mind to the present.

"Did you ever get your deer?" she asked, knowing somehow that Rodney, good at almost anything involving coordination of hand and eye, had probably done so.

"Sure did," Rodney flashed a grin. "I shot my limit five years running, back in the early 'fifties. I've hunted in Pennsylvania, Colorado, upstate New York, Michigan, even Canada. Got deer, moose, antelope, y'know, and bear too." And for the next ten miles he told Iris the story of one of his hunts and of the rip-roaring celebration that followed from tavern to tavern in some north-country burg.

It was a familiar story. She'd heard tall tales before from young men in college, from older men too. Even the cadences were familiar. What was it about hunting stories, about men in groups who hunt, that urged these tales? She did not openly doubt the truth of them, or the obvious pleasure in them that she sensed, even now as Rodney spoke, remembering events so long ago. But why, she wondered, did they usually involve hints of sexual conquest, of boozy nights and less than proper women—and where did all those willing women come from to populate all those back-country bars where the hunters flocked for two riotous weeks?

Iris was not much bothered by this, however. She often found herself questioning things but rarely pursuing the logic of her questions. Mostly satisfied with the outward shape of events, with simple rationalizations, she did not delve deeply. Her father's drinking, for example, following a pattern so familiar and widespread among the fathers of so many of her peers in school, had never been questioned. Her mother had accepted his "binges" with resignation, and Iris, an only child, had loved him as only a girl-child loves the man who bounced her on his knee and played with her for hours. When he grew distant as Iris entered puberty, either ignoring her or snapping at her, she continued to love him, even when late one night he had smacked her hard across her mouth for "giving him lip" about staying out too late. Like her mother, she had forgiven him that, attributing it to the booze and the late hour and to male temper. She took it for granted, like her mother, that grown men lost their temper when a woman, particularly a wife or daughter, "talked back." She had learned not to do so, repressing her naturally sharp mind, her quick but undeveloped sense of logic, her questioning nature. Women, she felt—virtually all of her women friends over the years—seemed tuned to the inner life, to family relations and how people treated each other, and how people acted. They talked about it, yes, they gossiped freely about it. They pushed for intimate detail and yet, in her experience, only rarely did they question the accepted patterns of male-female relations. Iris herself had rarely done so, though she read enough to know that others were doing so. She was vaguely aware, mildly disturbed at this, but not really bothered.

"When did you buy the place, at Kalkaska?" she said, breaking into Rodney's story.

"Oh...a while back," said Rodney. "Like I said, I got the place for fishing."

"What kind?" Iris did know a little about fishing. Jim, before his death in Vietnam, before their divorce, had been an avid fisherman. She had gone with him several times and remembered the strange thrill of seeing a trout rise to the bait, the secret sudden tug on the thin filament, the sudden explosion of action and the test of fish against rod and hand.

"Oh...all kinds, y'know."

"Good." Iris was thrilled. "Would you take me fishing, Rodney?" she piped, happy. "My first husband, Jim, he used to..."

"I don't give a fuck what he used to do," Rodney hurled the words at her, his face changed instantly. She felt his anger like a cloud. "I don't want to hear about him. He's dead ain't he, so let the dead alone."

"Sure, honey," Iris reached out to touch his face to calm him, but he threw her hand off and the car lurched sideways, almost into the ditch. He fought it back to the road. "I'm sorry, Rodney," Iris continued, "I won't mention Jim. But I would like to fish, and if you..."

"I said, forget it." Rodney pushed the car up to eighty and Iris turned away, frightened.

"Would you please slow down a bit, honey?"

"Okay. Just don't bring him up again, okay?"

"I won't, darling. I'm sorry."

They did not speak again until the Village of Kalkaska was announced, the roadside sign printed big in white letters on green. Like so many northern Michigan towns, the old Indian word carried with it an aura of remote forests and wild swamps, rapid rivers and logging camps, and prehistoric mystery. Not that the town itself was old, quite the contrary. It was hardly older than certain old codgers who sat in the sun, remembering the days when the loggers had cut everything down for as far as the eye could see, when the railroad carried off huge loads of timber and when the sluggish river was full of pine logs awaiting the sawmill. The logging days had been Kalkaska's only real boom time, a short-lived and wasteful time, at least until the 'seventies when large oil reserves had been discovered in the ancient reef far below the deceptive surface of woodlands and lakes. A town almost forgotten for long decades, Kalkaska had grown slightly in the prosperous 'fifties and 'sixties, serving a few outdoorsmen, mostly hunters and fisherman, who came to roam the wild lands on all sides. Indeed the entire county, of the same name and one of Michigan's least populous, had barely five thousand souls in it by the 1970 census. Then the oil boom had transformed everything. The once slightly seedy main street (for long years, the town's only real street), quaint and unplanned with a certain rural charm, now sprouted everything from the familiar golden arches of McDonald's to Big Boy, from chain motels to trailer parks. By the mid 'seventies, the main strip was hardly distinguishable from scores of other similar "strips" in other towns, extending outward from a once distinctive core where false-fronted stores had faced a sprawling railroad yard. All character and idiosyncrasy (perhaps still present beneath the neon glare) was overwhelmed by the kind of "progress" that delights the heart of real estate salesmen.

"It's still booming," said Rodney as he slowed for the village limit. "The place is three times as big since I bought my land up here. Hell...it's them oil wells did all this, brought all this."

Iris, looking around curiously, saw nothing especially prepossessing about the town. True, the name was arresting, and indeed the approach from the south through endless miles of forest did herald the town's essential isolation. She had hardly seen a farm worth mentioning since Lake City, and Kalkaska did seem to spring like some gaudy bauble of late twentieth century technology from a vast primeval landscape. But the big main drag, four lanes wide and thrusting north, seemed to her rather featureless, an unplanned sprawl without particular grace or charm.

"I can see that," she said, laughing to cover the note of irony that had crept in.

"Place was the fastest growing town in the state a while back, maybe still is," said Rodney. "I sold real estate up here, lots of it. Had a partner in it, fella from over in Traverse City. Easy to sell land here...y'know, to developers and the like, and especially to people who want a little cottage in the woods. We got the National Trout Festival here every year." Rodney stopped the car, pointing to an incredibly large statue of a trout, mouth open ravenously to the sky, perhaps twenty feet high, garishly painted. "Not bad, eh?" he said. Iris stared. Vaguely remembering the trout, she realized she had passed through this town on the way to Traverse City during her college years, riding with college friends up to Grand Traverse Bay. Traverse was one of Michigan's most lovely resort regions, where one of Lake Michigan's spectacular bays made a deep forty mile dip into the hilly moraines formed by the last great glaciers, a place of almost indescribable beauty. Kalkaska, she now recalled, was a place to get through, at that time not even a convenient place to stop for food. It had changed greatly, which was why she had not recognized it at first.

"Thing looks almost alive, doesn't it?" said Rodney, driving away from the gigantic fish.

To Iris, looking back, it seemed unrealistic, devoid of the grace and power she had herself witnessed when fishing for trout with Jim so long ago, perhaps in streams that flowed not far from this very town.

"You can have a lotta fun here," Rodney continued, talkative again. "They got snowmobiling and skiing in winter, both kinds, and ice-fishing, and hunting and fishing and camping. The law is tough up here too, y'know. They don't take no duff from anybody. Pretty much all white too, no niggers to speak of."

Iris reacted nervously to her husband's choice of words. She had barely mentioned her years of work In Detroit, her close acquaintance with black children, her often noisy and unruly, but always affectionate and vigorous remedial classes, her meetings with parents whose deep concern for their children sprang as much from their own lack of education as from an un-extinguished faith in the American dream. She really did not know this man. She would have to sound him out more, and carefully reveal more about her own past as well.

"I sound," Rodney laughed, sensing her nervousness, "like I'm selling real estate to you. You'll see. You'll love this place. Wait till you see the cabin."

They were there in a few minutes, turning down Valley Road and then another tiny dirt track and then into a long almost invisible drive through jack-pines and scrubby young maples. The cabin sat like a child's Lincoln Logs structure, square at its base, a simple gabled roof shingled in cedar. Behind it ran a small brook.

"It's only a summer cabin," explained Rodney leading her to the door. "We can fix it up anytime and make it livable. Some insulation, y'know, and a good wood-stove. Could be cozy from April to November, if you don't mind roughing it a bit."

"Oh no, Rodney. I'd love that. We could come up on weekends whenever you have time."

"Sure, and whenever you have time, beautiful," then he scooped her up and lifted her through the door, pausing inside to kiss her long, taking her tongue with rising passion.

"Are we still on our honeymoon, darling?" Iris breathed against his neck.

"You're damned tootin' we are," then he gently placed her on her back across the single, low bed, beneath a small four-paned window that looked out towards the brook and the scarlet sumac that grew there in profusion.

When he entered her she gasped and moved as if all control had gone, crying out against his rough cheek, secure that out here in this wilderness there was no one to hear except the birds and animals, no one to bother. They were truly alone.

12

The color tour was marvelous. The next day, rising early and eating breakfast in Kalkaska, they tooled west on M-72, then through crowded Traverse City, catching glimpses of the twin bays East and West, that pointed like cerulean fingers at the famous resort town. Then they turned to the north, up along the shore of the western arm of the bay some fifteen miles to Sutton's Bay, a tiny village backed by steep drumlins covered in brilliant maples, nestled around the deep bay of the same name. It was breathtaking. Iris had somehow missed this corner of her native state, this winding two-lane road where every turn revealed another view of the bay, so blue now in October it surpassed language. There was no adjective to match its force, she thought. On this day a wind from the west had blown up whitecaps and the effect was to deepen the color of the water, setting off water from sky, contrasting the colored hills and their fall finery. Though it was October and she knew the water out there would be cold, this bay was after all but an inlet of Lake Michigan, there were two or three sails in sight. Weekend sailors out for the last time, probably, braving the chill. She felt a twinge of envy, quickly repressed. Things were going well for her too.

In Sutton's Bay they found a busy restaurant and bar in the Country Inn and Rodney ordered a hearty meal for both of them; the food ample, a little overcooked, but basic. She felt almost as if they were in New England. White clapboard buildings, restored Victorian structures, piney new tourist traps side-by-side with slightly tacky older stores, and over it all the aura of the successful resort village, most of the people casually but expensively dressed, a mite gaudy sometimes in their autumn clothes. After eating, Rodney led her into the adjacent bar. Iris, sipping a glass of wine, Rodney tossing down one, then two, straight bourbons, they scanned the array of faces. Locals, she guessed. Tanned cherry farmers, long-haired carpenters, one or two Indians, a gaggle of young men just old enough to drink boisterously shouting at each other. A white-haired drunk with an exceptionally handsome face moved over next to her, squeezing in on the side away from Rodney. Friendly, eloquent in the fashion of the intelligent dipsomaniac, he engaged her in conversation.

"Haven't seen you before...just visiting? On our color tour?"

"Yes," Iris answered, smiling. He was nice enough.

"Where from?" said the man, modulating his voice, speaking clearly, controlling every consonant, as if teaching elocution. She recognized the pattern.

"From Ionia," Iris said. "I'm really from Detroit though, I lived there for years, and..."

"So did I," said the man. "Back in the good ol' days. Taught school there, for about twenty years, a hopeless task, I might add."

"Me too," Iris laughed, enjoying this guy.

"Well, put 'er there," he shook her hand warmly. "Where did you teach?"

"Several places," Iris said, happy to chat. In all her time with Rodney, he had never asked her about her previous career, only from time to time questioning her about her first marriage and then cutting her off just as she began to explain the details.

"Well, shoot, just tell me. I know 'em all in that town. All the schools. I was quite a city boy. Got around a lot, all the jazz places, too, the night spots."

Iris felt pressure on her hand. Rodney's grip was tight and growing tighter on her. Nervously she sipped her wine, turning away from the man, embarrassed. Rodney's iron grip relaxed and he took his hand away and ordered another drink. But the white-haired man intervened.

"It's on me, fella, and for the lady too. Set us all up, Johnny," he called to the bartender.

"Well thanks," said Iris, speaking for herself and Rodney. "We just stopped in for a moment. My husband and I..."

"Husband, eh," said the man, leaning in closer. Despite his inebriated condition, the man was still attractive. "You could be his daughter."

"Well she's not!" Rodney's voice came from behind her. His hand now gripped her shoulder hard, cutting deeply, hurting her.

"No offense," said the man, throwing up his hands in mock fear. "I'm just being friendly."

"Are you coming?" Rodney said, his voice ringing out as he pulled Iris from her stool.

"Rodney," Iris whispered, mortified. "Calm down, he didn't mean any harm." But still he pulled her. "Rodney, my jacket."

"Well, get the goddamned thing then." He slammed out the door, Iris running to catch up.

"Hey," shouted the friendly drunk. "Aren't you going to finish your drinks?"

All the way back to the cabin, Rodney drove very fast despite the bourbon in him. Neither spoke. Iris framed questions but she repressed them. What could she say? The man was just a happy drunk, being friendly, harmless, obviously liked by the other patrons in the place. She had sensed this at once. A local character. Talking with him had been fun, might have been more fun. What was wrong with Rodney, what terrible jealousy did he harbor? It might be different if he had reason to worry, but she was in love with him, she would never let things get out of hand. The man had given every sign of being friendly to them both. He had merely been teasing.

"Rodney...Rodney, I simply don't understand."

"What are you talking about?"

"That bar back there. That man meant no harm."

"Naw...he was just trying to get his slimy paws on you, that's all."

"Rodney, he was not. He..."

"Can it! Can it, will ya." Rodney's voice became shrill. His foot heavy on the pedal, he turned the car too fast as they entered the dirt road that led to the cabin, and swept into the bushes, knocking leaves and twigs into the air, the wheels digging to regain the road. She did not bring up the subject again.

They returned to Ionia the next morning, barely speaking.

October passed in a blur. Iris was called on to substitute almost every school day. The Principal used her at every opportunity; the students grew accustomed to her, bantering with her in the halls, visibly brightening when she entered a class unannounced. Once she heard a girl, one of the better students, whispering clearly, "Mrs. Harris is here. Terrific." These rural kids were infinitely more obedient, accepting, and yes, respectful, she thought, than her former charges in Detroit, though sometimes she missed the challenge of smart, street-wise kids who could discern a phony in moments.

The school began to occupy her thoughts even on weekends. Rodney was off much of the time closing business deals in Lansing, Grand Rapids, and Detroit. It was the last weekend in October before they could get away again. Most of the leaves had gone, the trees stark and bare against a gray sky. The air held a promise of chill in it. The evening before they left, talking with Rodney in the kitchen, she saw flurries outside the window.

"Rodney, darling, remember that teacher's conference I told you about? The one up at Gaylord?"

"Yeah, what about it?" Rodney sipped a coffee-mug half filled with rum. He did not look at her. In fact, he had hardly looked at her or spoken to her for several days.

"Why don't we go up in separate cars to the cabin in Kalkaska and meet there? Then I could stay on to attend the conference. It only lasts two days."

"Is that right?"

"We could have the weekend together, and then I could..." She stopped, aware of Rodney's hard glare, his eyes unblinking, the angry set of his face. It was that awful stranger's face again. Why should anybody be angry at such an idea? Gaylord was not far from Kalkaska, she could use the cabin if he didn't want her to stay in some motel.

"Rodney," she rose and went to him, playfully twisting his hair in her fingers, stroking his head. "Why not? You're a big boy. You can get along without me for two or three days can't you?" It was, she realized, more than a joke, more a real question than a statement. She moved her hand playfully down over his chest, down his stomach. She began to move her tongue in his ear. He would agree...she would seduce him to it. Everything would be all right.

Sure enough, an hour or so later up in the bedroom, Rodney agreed. He lay naked on his back, hands crossed under his head, his powerful chest still heaving from his exertions. She lay next to him, fingers running through the graying hair on his chest.

"I suppose it's a good idea," he murmured. "For you to get away by yourself for a few days. I mean, we'll be together on the weekend, and then..." he raised himself onto an elbow, "you can come back. Will you be driving alone, I mean, or will someone be with you?" His voice rose on the last words.

Iris gazed at him in disbelief. "I'll be alone of course, honey." She wondered, why did he worry so? It was true that her newfound friend Betty

Jean, a teacher at the school, was going to attend the conference. They had hoped to drive up together in the VW, but Betty Jean's retired parents had a place near Grayling and one car simply would not do.

"That gal, that Betty Jean," said Rodney, as if reading her thoughts, "she won't be going with you then?" His voice was petulant, unconvinced.

"No. I told you, Rodney. She has to visit her parents. She can't drive all the way up there and not see them. So she needs her own car. She's staying with them all three nights of the conference."

"I thought you said two days."

"I did. But she has to stay three nights. The conference is only two days." Iris, exasperated, felt as if she were explaining herself to a child. Why did he act like this, this loving man of hers?

13

The morning was crisp and clear. Frost lay everywhere, like a thin dusting of snow. Winter loomed close. Iris listened to the radio as she ate a light breakfast of orange juice and toast, waiting for the state-wide weather report. Rodney was already gone, driving off in the Thunderbird. He said he wanted to get in some early fishing before she got to the cabin. She had seen no sign of fishing gear, not a rod or reel, but maybe he planned to use the single old spinning rod in the cabin. Anyway, she did not want to drive through an early snow storm, so she waited. She had had the car checked the day before, filling the tank. Her suitcases were ready in the mud room. She looked forward to the weekend, to joining Rodney at the cabin, and especially to the following three days on her own to the conference in Gaylord, to talks with Betty Jean and other teachers, maybe to an evening at some good local restaurant. She had seen so little of others since her marriage. She had greatly enjoyed her marriage so far. She basked in the glow of Rodney's obvious passion for her, but he did not give her half enough time for her own interests. Years of living alone had accustomed Iris to self-sufficiency and she had experienced none with him. He simply had to cut her some slack, to ease up, to let her explore and meet others. To get out on her own. This weekend would be marvelous, a perfect combination of time with her husband and then several days on her own, going to the conference and meeting others, followed by a loving return to her husband. After the separation they would make love with more passion than ever before.

It took her only moments to load the VW. Duke, roaming without a leash, trained to remain on the farm but free to guard it, ran into the garage and put his head to her groin. Stroking the big dog, she said, "Goodbye, boy. Rod will be back soon. Me too." Duke would be fed by one of the men who usually cared for the horses in winter. Duke lay on the drying grass wagging his tail. She was fond of Duke. He came with Rodney, with the farm, he was part of all this. Rodney was good with him, like with the horses, firm but gentle. She was glad the big dog was there to watch the place.

Turning the key in the ignition, Iris felt her heart sink. Nothing happened. She tried again and again. Nothing. Goddamn it! I hope this is not an omen. She turned the key and looked at the fuel gauge. Empty! It registered empty. How could that be? She had filled up the day before, had the car checked out. She felt her heart beat faster as she circled the car, looking for any signs of vandalism, like the previous time. Nothing. Then she remembered the pump near the smaller barn, attached to a huge fuel drum, for the tractors and other equipment. Quickly she ran to the pump, cursing again when she saw the lock. Of course, Rodney kept it locked and kept the key on his key ring.

She sat down in the crisp air, hardly noticing the still wet seat of the lounge chair where the frost was melting. Who can I call for help? Rodney is on his way to the cabin. He'll expect me in about four hours at least. There's no phone up there. Besides, he won't want to drive all the way back down. Who could help? There was really no one. Nothing could be done. Finally she decided to call the Sheriff's office in Kalkaska and ask the deputies if they could get the time to drive out to the cabin and leave a sign on the door for Rodney to call her. She knew no one else in that town, that county, and, she realized, hardly anyone here, in or around Muir or Ionia. She got the Kalkaska Sheriff's office quickly and left the message. The polite and helpful dispatcher promised that an officer would leave a message on the cabin door. Then, though Rodney had discouraged personal calls to his office, Iris decided to make a call there. It would be open until noon on Saturday. Sally, Rodney's secretary, answered immediately. Quickly Iris explained, eager to get Sally's advice. Maybe Rodney would call the office en route, to check on business. Saturday was a busy time for realtors and, despite a competent staff, he liked to keep tabs on everything.

"I...I see," said Sally, her voice querulous over the phone. Iris remembered the sight of Sally, hair wet from the pond, standing in the shadows that night of the big party on the farm. Standing behind Rodney, watching. "You say, he's on his way...up there now?" The pause was long, the voice surprised. Sally's image flashed into Iris's mind. Blondish, not naturally for sure, about thirty, buxom, abundant curves, a provocative walk. Also single, she recalled. For a moment, curious jealousy clouded her thoughts. She'd heard talk, not much, but enough. Sally was something of a swinger. Rodney often worked late at the office, and Iris, not by nature possessive or jealous, had felt minor twinges of concern. That night when Rodney had gone skinny dipping down at the pond, obviously Sally had been there too. She remembered Sally's figure in the darkness just visible in the light from the barn. Sally had been clad only in wet panties and bra. Iris repressed these thoughts. She simply had to figure out how to get up to Kalkaska, and then to Gaylord for the conference, and how to let Rodney know there would be a delay. She'd have to arrange for someone to drive out with gas. It might take an hour or two, maybe more.

"I really don't understand, Mrs. Harris," Sally continued. "Mr. Harris left no word here that he was leaving town. I thought he was coming in today."

"That can't be!" Iris shouted into the receiver. Controlling herself, she lowered her tone. "I mean, he must have forgotten. We planned this. I'm supposed to meet him at the cabin."

"Well..." Sally responded, the word drawn out in disbelief. "I have no way to reach him up there unless he calls. I certainly will pass your message on if he does. I'm sorry I can't help much."

Hanging up, Iris immediately called Betty Jean, who had planned to leave this morning, to stay a few extra days with her folks. No answer. She sat at the phone, racking her brain, when it rang. It was Sally.

"Mrs. Harris? I don't know if I should say this. But it just popped into my mind. I forgot about it when you called a minute ago. You see Mr. Harris was scheduled to attend a seminar in Grand Haven, y'know, one of those meetings where they hash over the new laws about mortgages and so on. Maybe he forgot about it, but I made reservations for him in a motel there, and..."

"You what?" Iris shouted, furious now.

"I just told you," Sally's voice was cold.

Bothered by the tone, worried and hurt, Iris was speechless. Sally continued, "Didn't he mention the seminar to you?"

"I guess...I mean I think he did," Iris stammered. "I'm sure he did. I guess I got mixed up. I'm sorry to bother you, Sally. Oh, Sally, do you remember the name of that motel, the number maybe?" Iris wrote the number down, furious at having to lie, furious with Rodney for this inexcusable screw up. He had apparently forgotten the seminar and forgotten to tell her. Surely he wouldn't be at that motel. She would give it an hour or so and then call, just to be sure.

Later, full of coffee, she went into the bathroom, the small one near the kitchen. Earlier she had used the upstairs bath. That's why she missed the note, taped to the vanity, not in the most conspicuous place available, in Rodney's somewhat crabbed hand.

"Iris sweety I forgot. I got to attend a realtor's seminar in Grand Haven. Got no choice but to attend. So I have to go there instead. I'm really sorry. Have a good time at the cabin and the conference. I love you, Rodney."

Though disgusted by his forgetfulness, Iris regained her composure. She had only the problem of getting gas for the car. She would miss him, of course, but her trip was only delayed. After all, the conference didn't start until Monday. She looked forward to cleaning up the cabin and stocking it with food, stoking up the new cast-iron stove, maybe getting to know some of the storekeepers in Kalkaska. It would be fun to be alone.

She tried Betty Jean once more. No answer. Obviously she was on her way north. It was noon when the truck from the Shell Station in Lyons pulled into the drive. The man poured three or four gallons in, then signaled for her to crank it up. Nothing. He raised the rear hood of the little beetle and gazed inside the engine compartment. Then he came around to the window, a quizzical expression on his face.

"Mrs. Harris. You should have checked back there. No wonder it won't turn over."

"What do you mean," said Iris, following the man around to the back to see.

"There ain't no distributor. It's ripped out. That's why it won't even turn over." He pointed to the tangle of wires, hanging empty. In spite of herself, Iris cried out "No." Hands over her face, she began to sob.

"Maybe you oughta call the cops?" said the man as he walked to his truck, shaking his head, "that there ain't no accident, that's for sure."

For the first time in years Iris poured herself a glass of bourbon and began to drink it, sitting alone at the kitchen table.

14

Twice more she called Rodney's office but got no answer. It was closed at noon of course. Dismayed at being stranded, perhaps for three days, Rodney at the seminar, Betty Jean on her way to Gaylord and not available by phone for hours, Rodney obviously not yet checked into his motel, perhaps not till evening; there was no one to turn to. By the time she finally got up enough gumption to call the Sheriff's office it was late afternoon, and she'd drunk too much. Mortified at having to explain the situation, embarrassed at what must seem to others as complete idiocy, frightened by this second act of vandalism, she waited for the promised patrol car, trying to counter the effect of the booze with coffee. Twice more she tried the motel. Rodney had not checked in yet.

Iris stood up unsteadily when she heard the tires on the gravel. It was a patrol car, and she recognized the youthful deputy from the party last summer.

"I...I've forgotten your name," Iris said, shaking his hand as he stepped onto the back porch.

"Deputy Barnett," he said, following her to the garage, explaining why he had come alone. A detective would be along soon to inspect the evidence.

"Strange," said Barnett, shaking his head, gazing with Iris at the tangle of wires. "Do you have any idea why anyone would do this?"

"It's terrifying...Mr. Barnett," Iris said, so frightened by the implications that she allowed herself to grasp his arm. "I mean, both times, my car, leaving me stranded..." She could not finish.

"You have no idea who...who might be doing this?" Barnett peered closely at Iris.

His eyes were clear and kind, interested. "Well, whoever he is, he wants to keep you here." Suddenly he stopped himself, aware of the effect of his words on Iris, who gasped. She had not allowed herself to think the same thought. It was obvious though. "Maybe not," said Barnett quickly, "Maybe it's just another prank. Maybe someone who wants to get back at Mr. Harris?"

"Why would anyone want to do that?" Iris was suddenly interested

"He's a businessman. He sells real estate. Some people...they get..." Barnett searched for more careful words. "They get angry if they lose out on deals. Maybe the vandal goes for any car he finds."

"You say 'he', like you know," Iris said, "like you know it's a man."

"Just a manner of speaking," Barnett muttered, glancing quickly at her. "Most crimes are committed by men, you know."

Iris led the deputy inside where he searched the house with her. They found nothing unusual. He was still there making notes on a pad, when she got word that her husband had checked into the motel. The operator put Rodney on at once from his room.

"Oh, darling!" Iris cried in relief, the words tumbling forth. She was almost unaware of Deputy Barnett, still in the room, shifting uncomfortably from one foot to the other, until he cleared his throat. She stopped, interrupting her explanation to Rodney, to thank the deputy.

"I guess I don't need you now," Iris waved to the deputy as he left the house "Thanks." He was gone.

"Who's that? Who are you talking to?" Rodney shouted, his voice shrill.

"Just a deputy, Rodney," Iris explained. "When I couldn't get you, or anybody, I called the police, and..."

"Well, Iris, you just sit tight. I'll be there in a flash."

Iris knew Grand Haven was a good drive. She would be alone well after dark. She held back, but a slight headache throbbed, probably brought on by the bourbon. Remembering how Rodney handled such things she poured herself another drink, determined only to sip until Rodney got home.

Somehow the drink disappeared, and Iris poured another. Underneath the knowledge that Rodney would be with her soon was fear, inchoate, inarticulate fear. The drink helped. She poured a third. And then...

Rodney stood above her. She lay on her back on the couch, his face was blurred a little, his voice seemed distant.

"If I knew you were gonna have a party, I would'a stayed. How long did that deputy hang around here anyway?"

"Oh," Iris held out her arms to bring him down to her. Her head swam.

"Hell, you're drunk woman," said Rodney, laughing. "I might as well join you." He sat beside her on the couch, propping her up with a big hand, offering her another sip from the glass of bourbon. Then he took the remainder down in one huge gulp. She hardly remembered him carrying her up the stairs.

Later, she remembered him rubbing her back and the sound of her own somewhat slurred voice explaining, describing. He listened and then he had turned her over and caressed her over her breasts, down her belly and into the soft vee of her. She was only vaguely aware of him entering her until besotted but aroused she climaxed against him.

The next morning, hung-over but mind clear, Iris had questions that needed answers, and she hurled them at Rodney when he joined her for breakfast.

"Why didn't Duke bark? He always barks, like when the deputy drove in."

Rodney threw up his shoulders, shrugging.

"Maybe he was out chasing rabbits. He does that y'know. That would explain it."

"Yes," Iris agreed, "but twice in a row? It worries me." She didn't argue but Rodney's explanation seemed weak. Duke could hear a strange car half a mile away and usually ran barking to the head of the drive minutes before Rodney drove in from work. In any case, Rodney got on the phone and arranged to have the car towed in and fixed. Iris went back to bed before noon to sleep off her hang-over while Rodney did odd jobs around the place. She drifted off, vaguely remembering that the promised detective had not shown up. Well, what could he do anyway? Whoever vandalized her car was very clever. She knew there would be no prints, except hers and Rodney's, even if they got around to checking.

When she woke, feeling decent, she brought up the question of the conference, explaining to Rodney that, if they fixed the car on time, she could still drive on up alone and use the cabin and attend the important teacher's meetings in nearby Gaylord.

Rodney would have none of it.

"No! That's it! I won't listen to this. You went through too much, Iris.

You're staying here, with me. That's all there is to it." Then he promised her a fancy dinner. They would drive into Lansing again, to a good restaurant, that very evening. And they did.

Less than a week later, Iris was bitterly disappointed again. A cousin who lived in Flint had called, planning to visit friends in Lansing, wondering if Iris might want to get together. Iris excited at seeing Mable again had invited her to stay at the farm after the visit to Lansing. She hadn't seen Mable, a mother of four grown children though only one or two years older than herself, in two or three years and had always liked the big hearty woman, her mother's brother's daughter. They had been fairly close during college years. They had married about the same time, though Mable's marriage had worked. She was still married to the same guy after all these years, a college teacher at the University of Michigan in Flint. All of her kids, it seemed, were doing well.

But Rodney did not like it. At first he had listened calmly enough as Iris explained.

"You'll love her, Rodney. She's great fun. Full of stories and funny," Iris explained, "sort of like you, Rodney. You two would really get along."

"I'm sure," said Rodney, nodding, but he seemed unconvinced. "Let me think about it. We're awful busy around here, y'know, and the guest bedroom ain't ready yet. Where'd we put her? I don't know."

Later, she tried again, trying to argue without anger, just explaining how nice it would be to have Mable for a day or two. Mable had the time and wanted to come. So why not? Rodney, this time, listened with less patience.

"I said we don't have room. No place for anyone to stay."

"No room?" Iris exclaimed, voice rising. Now she was getting mad. It was silly. Rodney's excuses made no sense. "We have this whole goddamned house. We have room for a regiment of friends."

"Now, don't overdo it," said Rodney. "It's true we only have one bedroom ready, and that's our own. I mean, do you want her to sleep on the couch?"

Iris got nowhere. She was prepared to argue her case again, to make it an ultimatum the next morning, convinced that it was time to have people stay over. She had seen none of her relatives since the wedding—and even then Mable had been unable to attend—and already her few good friends in Detroit had drifted away. Out of sight, out of mind. One or two had called, but Iris had not invited them up, when so early in the marriage she had not wanted to disturb the intimacy of their relationship. But now it was time. Winter was coming. She needed others in her life.

Two days later Rodney settled the whole thing by announcing that they were going up to the cabin near Kalkaska on the very weekend that Mable had hoped to visit.

"But it's not insulated for real winter, is it?" Iris protested.

"No," Rodney agreed, "but that's why we're going up. I already called the lumber yard up there and the insulation will be delivered when we get there."

Iris agreed but at dinner that night she blurted out her feelings, "Rodney honey, why don't you want anyone to visit? Not even my relatives." She watched his face change as if a mask was being drawn across his normally benign and handsome features. "Why don't you like me to leave the farm unless I am with you?" she asked. Iris paused, holding her breath, surprised, wondering at her words.

"What are you talking about?" Rodney exploded, rising from his chair and knocking it back to the floor, arms spread in fury. He did not wait for her answer, raving on. "Are there bars on the windows? Do you see locks on the doors to keep you in?" His voice raging, he grabbed her purse and took out her keys, dangling them before her. "Here, take the fucking things and get your car and go. Go! You're free to go any time. Any time. Any fucking time you want. What in the hell is wrong with you? Just because I want to spend Thanksgiving alone with you up at our cabin, you make a big deal of it. You accuse me of not wanting you to see relatives."

Iris waited until his rage subsided. Presently, he picked up the chair and sat down again at the table, pushing his food away. Iris had cooked one of her best dinners, pork tenderloin with julienne of celery and potato, and strawberry shortcake. She knew the signs. He would not eat another bite. Now he apologized, reaching out for her hands, his voice low.

"C'mon, honey. Please understand me." He pulled her closer to him and then his hands moved up her legs, already they were under her skirt, moving with knowing, practiced assurance. She moved her legs apart a little to make it easier, swaying a little to the thrill of his hands, thrusting her pelvis against his shoulder, her breasts into his face.

"I'm sorry, Iris. Really. I know you want other things. Just bear with me. I love you so much. I want you for myself so much." As he spoke, his hands continued to move, up into her cleft, and then sliding her panties down. She willingly stepped out of them, leaving them on the kitchen floor. Now she was helping him, guiding his hands, moving her other hand over his body. Even as she bent over him, he spoke softly.

"If you want to see your cousin, you go over there after Thanksgiving. Or, if you want, have her visit us. We could spend the last part of the holiday together."

Iris melted entirely now, murmuring in his ear. Then she pulled him down over her onto the floor, allowing him to take her right there.

15

Unfortunately, after they returned from the long weekend at the cabin, Iris's plans to visit Mable in Flint were ruined by a sudden change in the weather. The southern half of the state was hit by a huge storm that moved in on Sunday and stayed for four days. Iris and Rodney had barely made it home, arriving at the farmhouse only hours before it hit. Within an hour six inches of new snow carpeted the earth, and by midnight it was two feet deep. Travel was not only dangerous; it was out of the question. All the roads were blocked next morning, and it was Tuesday before they could get into Ionia. By then it was too late. Iris called Mable and put off her plans until Christmas. Then she would go to Flint, or Mable would come and visit. Rodney had informed her that it was one of his "Rodney Harris traditions" to throw a big bash two days before Christmas, so that was taken, but after that, well, he had said, it was up to her.

Iris threw herself into preparation for Rodney's Christmas bash with all her energy. The substitute teaching had tapered off for some reason, and for two weeks she was called to come in only three times. Apparently the teachers were enjoying extraordinary health for the time being. She did not mind, keeping herself busy with orders, lists, decorations, plans for surprise gifts for Rodney, special cakes and baked surprises.

The party date came quickly. Rodney invited a score of couples. Iris knew only a half dozen people she had met at the school, none close friends except for Betty Jean who came early with her husband Hank.

In the kitchen Betty Jean bustled about helping. Iris, pleased at her early arrival listened to Betty Jean talk about her English classes, asking pertinent questions about certain students she had come to know. Then suddenly Betty Jean stopped behind Iris, taking her by the shoulders and turning her. Hank was in the living room with Rodney fixing the punch. When Iris faced her, Betty Jean spoke in a muted tone, directly.

"Has he been beating you, honey?"

"No! Of course not." Iris was shocked, "What makes you think that?"

Betty Jean dropped her arms, turning to pick up a salad bowl. "I just thought. I mean, the way he's jealous of you. I just wondered?" She threw a fearful glance at the living room door.

Angry, Iris rounded on her friend, "Look, Betty Jean. Rodney would never do that to me."

"Well, I've heard a few things, and I just had to ask."

"What things? What have you heard?"

"About Rodney and that previous wife. It's common knowledge in town that she accused him of abuse. You can't keep secrets in a place like this."

"That's obvious as hell," said Iris with asperity. "But Julia is sick, crazy as a hoot owl. She's certified. She imagines things, makes them up. She hallucinates. Don't tell me you believe that shit."

"I never said that, Iris. I just wanted to be sure."

"Well, now you know."

After that encounter the party seemed loud and intrusive. Betty Jean acted as if nothing had happened, apparently submitting to Iris's explanation. Iris tried to enjoy the growing crowd as the house filled with guests. Before nine, seventy or more people showed up.

It was a come-as-you-are affair since remnants of the big snowstorm still covered the countryside, and several guests who brought snowmobiles came inside after stacking snowmobile suits on the porch chairs, a few came in cross-country outfits, skis fastened to the tops of their cars. Every couple brought a dish, so the food was heaped on the big table in the dining room, and Rodney placed himself near the huge punch bowl, periodically refilling it with fruit juice, pre-mixed in the kitchen, and spiking it with vodka. Twice Iris brought him another fifth to pour into the big bowl. A fire crackled in the living room fireplace, the first time in weeks that Rodney had burned anything in it, and people surrounded it chattering. A previous Christmas party, Rodney told her, had continued through the night and into the next day. Looking at all the food and drink Iris could believe it might happen again. She had spent three hundred dollars just for the liquor, decorations, baked cakes and cookies, and other tidbits. They had enough sweets and desserts for a hundred, and probably enough booze for twice that. Rodney spared no expense. From ceiling to floor in every downstairs room and even in the barn gaudy decorations were hung, lighted with oval Japanese lanterns, the front porch covered in colored blinking lights, the big spruces in front festooned with white lights, the big Christmas tree inside likewise.

Now she stood next to Betty Jean. Hank, a recovering alcoholic, looked forlorn as he sipped a coke, walking frequently to the sideboard to grab cookies. He was on the wagon, so Betty Jean said. But apparently no one else was. Certainly not Rodney. He had begun to drink at noon, and Iris wondered how much he had consumed. She knew it was a staggering quantity. She was hardly sober now. In fact since Thanksgiving Iris had fallen into the habit of drinking with Rodney after dinner. Though he started earlier, he urged her to join him and she had begun to relax with a mixed drink, usually bourbon and soda, letting her worries flow away.

They made love less, but seemed to get along well enough. Often she had found herself reeling up the stairs and falling into bed. Sometimes she turned to him, only to find herself alone. Once she went downstairs and found him on the couch, comforter thrown over himself, a drink in hand, eyes open, watching TV. At first she had thought it a mere late-movie, then she watched, eyes wide. It was an x-rated video. Only a few days before, Rodney had purchased a VCR claiming he needed the new technology to tape football games he missed while out selling property. So, this was what it was for. Following his directions, his hand patting the couch, she had joined him and together they had watched the pornographic flick all the way through. Before it was over, she was naked, cuddled under the comforter with him, playing, watching, titillated by the otherwise ludicrous images on the TV screen. They had ended making love with furious energy.

Now, watching him, at the center of a circle of laughing people, he seemed to radiate health and power and pleasure. His large head, hair showing a touch of gray in just the perfect places, turned and moved, his teeth flashing in a great smile. Among the other men he seemed clearly the most handsome, taller than most, broad and powerful, his deep voice echoing in the room over the noise. What a man, she thought. My husband. Mine.

But now Iris wanted to stay sober for several reasons. She did not want to nurse another hangover. She put her drink down and busied herself with her guests. She tried to count the people she knew. There was the school Principal, and their lawyer Howard Jackson with his wife, and Sgt. Saunders. In front of the fireplace, with several men leaning close and laughing, was Sally, Rodney's secretary, in a slinky dark dress showing too much cleavage. As Iris watched, chatting politely with one of Rodney's business associates, she saw Sally move close to Rodney and put her hand on his shoulder, saying something which made him throw back his head and laugh. There was something in that gesture, something of a knowing intimacy that hurt her to her quick. Could it be that...? No. She dismissed the jealous surge. Rodney was into his 'fifties. He was no superhuman. She gave him all the sex he could handle, she felt sure of that, all and more. Certainly she gave him all the love any man could want. Nevertheless, turning away to busy herself again, hurrying over to join Betty Jean, she vowed to cut back on her own drinking. She knew she had gone to the school once or twice looking less than well. Rodney could apparently handle it easily. She could not.

It was midnight or later when she realized that Hank was drunk. She had no idea when he had started drinking. He was not tipsy, but seriously sloshed. She saw him literally stagger to the bar for another straight shot of booze. Rodney clapped him on the shoulder and poured, seemingly unaffected himself. Iris looked for Betty Jean again, finding her with several other women squeezed into a corner of the kitchen, talking about the town's latest sex scandal; one of the older male teachers had been accused of the homosexual seduction of several schoolboys.

"Well, what I think is that you don't seduce any kid that doesn't want that, if you know what I mean," one of the women was saying. Iris reached in and grabbed Betty Jean by the hand, pulling her out into the less crowded mud room. "Hank's drunk," she said. "C'mon, I'll show you." Betty Jean followed.

"Oh, Iris. When he gets like this he doesn't really know what he's doing. He can get mean."

"You can stay here tonight. We'll get you home tomorrow."

"Oh thanks, honey," said Betty Jean.

Rodney did not like it. Iris felt no need to tell him that Hank was being driven home separately. Instead she made a point that Betty Jean needed to stay over for the night.

"What in hell is wrong with her place? Where's Hank anyway? I was just talking to him." Rodney looked around at the thinning celebrants, clustered now in little groups through the big house. "Why does she have to stay here?"

"Do we have to have every little reason, honey? She needs help tonight. Isn't it enough that she asked? She's my friend after all."

"Well, hell. Where you gonna put her?" Rodney spat the words out even as he waved goodbye to a departing couple, his face wreathed with a smile. Then he turned to Iris again, his face a mask of suspicion. How could he change so suddenly, she wondered.

"On the rollaway in my office, the one stashed behind the old bureau by the chimney wall."

"Well, shit. You want to get it ready, then go ahead. Why does she want to stay anyway?" Suddenly he grinned, his face alight again. "You sent him off home didn't you? You two. Cause he's drunk. You two put your little heads together and..."

"Christ, Rodney, that's enough." Iris turned on her heel, looking for Betty Jean.

His hand stopped her. They were alone in a corner of the room, people instinctively given them space. He pulled her in as if to hug her, waving goodbye to another couple. "You don't talk to me like that, Iris. Never. You hear me," he hissed, his voice low, menacing. "Never!" Then he let her go.

She almost bumped into Sally who stood in the middle of the floor, drink in hand, another hand saucily on her hip. She realized Sally was the only woman who came in a party dress. Somehow this had eluded her. If you could call it a dress, Iris thought. It was slit half way up both thighs and backless. The sound of roaring snowmobiles came from the back of the house.

"Hey," Sally shouted, "who's for a snowmobile ride? Hey, Rodney, how about you?"

"Sure. Good idea," Rodney said. "But what are you gonna wear, Sally? Where's your suit? Did you bring a suit?"

"I guess you'll have to find something for me, Rod, something suitable."

Everyone laughed and groaned and Iris watched as Rodney led Sally out to the mud room where he kept the winter gear. Then she went in search of Betty Jean.

Much later she and Betty Jean sat on the couch, close to the dying fire. Rodney and the others had just returned, the rumble of the snow machines up the drive alerting the few remaining guests. It was nearly four in the morning. They had talked quietly, ignoring the others, for two hours. The party was noisy enough to drown their conversation, but Iris was drained by what she had heard. Her heart went out to Betty Jean, yet still she was puzzled.

"But why didn't you leave him?" Iris said for the tenth time.

"Because I love him."

"I know. But how long can you...I mean, put up with it?"

"Believe me, Iris, it isn't like you think," said Betty Jean, rising now as Rodney and the others breezed in, bringing with them a gust of cold air and the overwhelming smell of booze. Iris got up too, and when Rodney held out his hand, she took it, surprised at herself. She was still simmering with anger at him for running off with Sally and the others and not asking her. But she would have declined in any case and stayed with Betty Jean. So, she allowed herself to be pulled in close to her husband, who announced that it was time for a visit to the barn. And out they all trooped into the cold night, the dozen or so who remained. Even Betty Jean ran along with them to see the horses and to enjoy the surprise Rodney had prepared. It was a surprise even to Iris.

"This," said Rodney proudly, opening a gate in the barn to reveal a bell-studded sleigh, "is for our special guests only. Those who earn the right to it by staying until the stars go out." Everyone cheered and applauded.

And, indeed, the party ended perfectly, the final half-dozen couples riding out into the silvery night in a sleigh, behind a jingling trotting horse, until the December sun rose pale in the east.

16

It was cold. As Iris made her way from barn to house the snow crunched underfoot. Every breath turned into frigid vapor, drifting upwards into the night. Even Duke, who normally enjoyed being outdoors, barked at the back door, begging to be let inside. The thermometer nailed to an oak beside the back steps registered a Siberian ten below Fahrenheit. With the wind chill factor, Iris had heard on the radio, it was negative thirty.

As she opened the door Duke rushed past shaking himself as Iris stomped the snow off her boots. A native of Michigan, Iris knew cold, but this was exceptional, ten days of extreme cold. The evidence was everywhere.

Stalled cars in driveways, icicles lengthening from eaves, animals huddled together in barns, the etchings of Jack Frost even on modern thermopanes. For days Iris had been alone at the farm. The Principal had not called her to substitute since before Christmas and her only contacts with others had been a brief shopping trip to Ionia and a lunch with Betty Jean. Rodney, of course, had been home most nights, but he came home invariably late. His tardiness had become a pattern. Every time she asked, he seemed to have a business excuse, working late at the office, late dinner meetings to sell property. Despite herself, she was beginning to doubt him. He's probably fucking Sally, Iris thought with rising anger. He sure isn't fucking me. The thought as she tried to pour coffee caused her to miss the mug and, even more angry, she cleaned up the spill, cursing. Rodney had been distant ever since the big party. He had not made love to her since. She was aching to talk with him about it, but every attempt was met by sullen dismissal. She knew his behavior might stem from several causes, perhaps his business was not going well, maybe it was the cold, or post-holiday depression. Several times she had considered asking Betty Jean to do a bit of spying for her, but Betty Jean was having enough trouble with Hank who was still off the wagon.

Now, upset at her doubts, Iris busied herself to make things especially good for Rodney. He had promised to be home in time for dinner, and she would make him more than welcome. For hours she worked, preparing a special salad, choosing the best steaks in the freezer, baking fresh bread and making her best onion soup. The wind rose, and the sturdy old house creaked and moved, but she felt secure. A fire crackled in the big iron stove and before six she built up another fire in the fireplace. By seven the steaks were thawed, the soup simmering on the wood-stove, the kitchen table laid neatly, candles lit, a bottle of Cabernet chilled. Just before he was due in the drive Iris ran upstairs and slipped into the black negligee Rodney had purchased for her in Lansing last summer. He would be unable to resist. Walking into the kitchen's glowing warmth she had never felt sexier. It had been too long. She wanted him badly. Ears perked for the sound of the car, she poured herself a glass of sherry and stood before the window. Cold though it was, the night was beautiful. Stars seemed to hang from the black arch of heaven, the snow glistened and even the wind seemed to sing. It would be good now, she had made everything perfect. Maybe he would take her immediately and they could eat later, putting the steaks on afterwards. The soup could simmer indefinitely.

She heard the car before she saw it and moving deftly she placed the steaks on the grill. She could pull them off if Rodney went for her first, and, in hopeful preparation, she slid one strap down over a shoulder, revealing part of a breast. Then he was at the door turning the knob. Excited she ran to him, kissing him full on his cold lips, waiting for him to warm to her loving. But his lips did not open. Instead he pushed her away from his rigid body, throwing his coat over the kitchen chair. She could smell bourbon on him.

"What the fuck is going on here?" Rodney shouted, looking around in obvious anger. "Can't a man have a simple meal after a hard day? What the hell is all this?" He swept his arm around, turning to stare at Iris, frozen in fear and surprise, standing there in the black negligee. For a long moment he looked her up and down and Iris hoped, trembling now, that he would calm himself and take her in his arms. She could feel her heart thumping, a vein in her neck throbbing. Then he pushed past her, grabbing the costly bottle of wine and stomped into the living room, where he threw it into the fire. The flames roared and sputtered and he turned on her.

"Where's my goddamned drink? My fucking bourbon? Can't you do anything right? At least Julia knew what I like to drink when I get home." Advancing into the kitchen, he hurled the steaks from the grill. Then, with a sweep of a massive arm he smashed everything from the table. Glass, candles, and plates crashed onto the floor. Iris stood terrified, holding both arms across her breasts, unable to think or move. She watched Rodney as if his action played before her in slow motion.

"And what the hell are you wearing that for?" Rodney sneered, approaching her, head thrust forward, arms hanging loose. "I suppose you think it makes you look sexy, eh? Hell, you're thirty-eight years old, you goddamned bitch." He thrust his big arm out and grabbed the negligee at the top, tearing it savagely from her body, ripping it from top to bottom. Iris was pulled almost off her feet since the fabric was strong. Staggering, she regained her feet, the bodice of the negligee hanging down, her breasts bared. Rodney was on her again, pulling and ripping until she stood naked before him. He thrust the destroyed fabric before her.

"You think this looks good on you?" he taunted her. "You bitch. You're almost forty and you know what," he leaned in closer, "you look it." His eyes gleamed and now he smiled. Iris held her breath, hurt, amazed, frozen in fear and terror. She did not know this man.

"Now, Sally," Rodney held up the tattered negligee, "she'd look good in something like this. She's young enough. Fact is, she does." He hurled it in her face, and she clutched it to her naked body, backing away. So it's true, she thought. He has been with Sally. Suddenly her pent up anger welled up, overcoming her fear.

"You son-of-a-bitch," Iris shrieked. "You aren't worth it. I work my ass off fixing a nice romantic meal for you and you dare to treat me like this. I don't have to take this from you." Suddenly, her voice broke and she began to sob.

"You're right," said Rodney, his voice rising, his eyes fixed and glaring, his face a mask of hate. Suddenly he grabbed her and forced her back, his hands in a grip of iron on her arms. He propelled her through the kitchen, into the mud room and out the door into the night. The door slammed and she heard the click of the lock.

Iris felt the cold immediately. It was almost comical, but she could not laugh. The porch was covered by a low slanting roof with hooks along one wall, so, shivering uncontrollably she looked for something to throw over her naked body. On a hook was an old snowmobile suit, ripped and worn, that Rodney had used working with the horses when it was cold. She slipped into it and though it was much too large it quickly warmed her enough to restore rational thought. She still had slippers on and she leaned to look through the back window into the bright kitchen. The lights went out one by one. Then silence.

Thinking carefully, Iris weighed her options. One by one she eliminated the obvious. The cars were no help since all the keys were inside. She had some idea how to start or drive the snowmobile that sat near the garage but the keys would not be in that either. The barn was close and the horses might provide some warmth, but the stalls were unheated and she had nothing to cover her head and hands, and the slippers were inadequate. Already numbing cold spread across her toes. She began to shiver. There was hay and if it came to survival she might burrow down in a pile near the horses, but they might also trample her. No, that was silly. And, there was no point trying to walk to a neighbor. The obvious thing to do was to confront Rodney, no matter how irrational he seemed. He was her husband. He loved her, or at least he had. What I'll do, she thought, is talk to him, loud enough for him to hear. He'll have to let me in. Then, I'll find some way to get to my keys and get away and go straight to the police. Whatever, I'm finished with this madman, she thought. I'll leave tonight and never return.

Looking inside again, she saw that a candle burned in the kitchen. What was he doing? The flame projected eerie shadows across the walls. Tentatively she knocked on the door, the sound seeming to echo. No noise came from within. Where was Rodney? Would he leap out at her? Would he hurt her? She knocked louder and still there was no response. When she tried the door knob, it turned. He must have unlocked it while she was scrambling into the old snowmobile suit. Gently she pushed the door in and entered the mud room, passing quickly into the kitchen. She looked around, alert as a cat.

In the corner lay Duke, raising his head and wagging his tail, his big eyes expectant. Ignoring the dog, Iris padded through the kitchen and into the dining room where by the flicker from the fireplace she saw a form stretched out near the door. She held her breath and heard deep breathing. Was Rodney unconscious? She bent over him, suddenly wondering if he might be too drunk to stand. Would this explain his behavior? She touched his shoulder, prepared to help him.

His big hand caught her unaware, full across the lower jaw. She fell sideways, recoiling, arms up trying to protect her body. Now he was on her, overpowering her. Twisting, she caught another blow on her breast and then across her back. Momentarily free, she scrambled towards the kitchen but he caught her, his face inches away now. She could see his face; it seemed to be wholly changed. There was something more than anger there. Was he smiling? It couldn't be. No, his expression was blank, like a man methodically performing some routine task. He hit her full in the face with the back of his hand and then with the palm, snapping her head back. His breathing was labored, heavy. Every word he uttered, punctuated by blows, was obscene. "Bitch," he said in a low tone, "cunt," then his voice rising, "fucking good-for-nothing bitch," and he hit her again and again.

Iris could not remember when he stopped. She had fallen to the floor, curled into a fetal position. The old snowmobile suit had provided some protection, but pain beyond measure seemed to fill her head, pulsing beneath every inch of her skin. The blows had apparently stopped and Iris opened her swollen eyes and realized she was on the kitchen floor. The candle still guttered on the table. She remembered Rodney's words as he kicked her prone body the last time, "I'm too good for you, you bitch."

Iris felt a chill. She rose slowly, fearful that he might be waiting to pummel her again. The outside door was open wide and then came the whine of the snowmobile engine. Then the machine roared away. Moving inch by inch, seared with pain, Iris managed to shut the door and stumbled into the living room where the fire still burned. She pulled herself onto the couch and managed to get the comforter over her. She heard Duke whine and then felt his cold nose. Vaguely she recalled his loud barking as Rodney beat her. The last thing she remembered before falling into oblivion was Duke's warm breath on her bruised face and his wet tongue, gently licking.

17

Darkness seemed to envelop her. Iris regained consciousness slowly, as if aware of life only through pain. Duke's wet nose sought her face again, and she could feel his body moving as his tail wagged. Heavy breathing filled the room and she realized it was her own. Moving inch by inch, almost afraid to contract a muscle she managed to reach a light near the couch. Rodney was apparently gone. Laboriously she got to her feet and made her way to the bathroom, a journey of moments, cursing the day she had met Rodney Harris. Seeing her grotesque visage in the mirror, Iris flinched. Red eyes peered back through swollen lids, and brown dried blood caked her nostrils. Her lips were puffed and red. Stripping off the ragged snowmobile suit, she inspected her body, wincing at the pain in her back and abdomen. There were no huge bruises, yet, but red zones were painful to the touch. Groaning she leaned on the sink and studied her face. "Can this be me? This is not me. This is not happening to me." Iris realized she was testing her voice, speaking to the mirror as her face wavered. A movement behind her, and she imagined Rodney was there beside her in the mirror, his face anguished. Starting, she turned and it was Rodney. He had entered the bathroom behind her, and now he stood over her, looking down at her. Instinctively she recoiled. Oh no, she thought, I am finished. Now he'll kill me.

But Rodney was trembling, tears coursing down his unshaven cheeks. He groaned and fell to his knees, reaching for her. But Iris backed away, hands out to stave him off, shaking her head.

"I'm sorry," said Rodney, "I'm sorry." He spoke between sobs. He was crying like a child. "I don't expect you to forgive me, but I'm begging you. Please, Iris. Please. You're the best thing that's ever happened to me. I don't want to lose you. I'll do anything you want. I'll even take you to the hospital, or the doctor, if you want. If you think I need help you can call and make an appointment for counseling. Just don't leave me, Iris, please."

Iris backed to the corner of the bathroom. Moving more quickly, as muscle memory returned, she grabbed her bathrobe from a hook on the door. She had no intention of listening to this. "No!" she shouted. "No." But he rose from his knees and sat on the edge of the tub. It was a high old tub and Rodney was so large that his face was almost level with hers. He hung his head, tears dropping to the floor. He sobbed with heaving gulps. He lifted his face and gazed at her. His eyes streamed and his mouth worked. Like a child she thought, just like a child.

"Oh...Iris, please listen. Please. I know you don't have to forgive me, but...I had an awful day. I lost...two big sales. I...drank too much. I know that's no excuse. But I lost control. I didn't know what I was doing. I mean it. Something came over me. It wasn't really me. You've got to listen. I love you."

Iris glared at him, but he kept on. He couldn't be acting. Not now. He needed a shave and his eyes were red. His big head hung again and every once in a while he glanced up at her like a child who had been caught lying or misbehaving. Without willing it, Iris touched his face. Then as she pulled her hand back, he took her hand in both of his. Tenderly he held it and she allowed her fingers to move over his face, giving comfort. She had gone through an enormous change of mood in minutes. Hate and fear now gave way to pity, and yes, to love. He had loved her and maybe he still did. She still loved him. He needed help. She suddenly wanted to help him.

"I'm cold," he said. "C...cold." Moving deftly despite the pain, Iris liberated a blanket from the linen closet in the hall and threw it to him. She realized that the house had become frigid. The fires in the woodstove and the fireplace had burned down. The thermostat was set low. Briskly she turned it up and began stacking kindling into the woodstove, shoving paper in and lighting it. Soon the roar filled the kitchen, even as the first rush of air came from the furnace below, up the old registers. The living room clock chimed. It was one in the morning.

Without a word, as Rodney sat in the blanket and watched, she made coffee and poured two cups. Iris was determined to think clearly. She had experienced an unspeakable assault, a criminal assault, at the hands of her husband, a man who professed undying love for her. Why, if he could beat her once, wouldn't he do it again, if provoked, or drunk enough? That he needed help was plain. But should she help? She remembered Julia's words. Now was the time to get out. It made sense. As she handed the cup to Rodney and sipped her own, keeping a distance from him, she decided to pack and leave as soon as possible. But outside the wind brought dark clouds and snow. No stars gleamed and the trees bent under the north wind. Where would she go? She had no steady job, no money? No place for immediate shelter. Betty Jean was having enough trouble with Hank. Mable might help, but Flint was a good distance off, and how long could she stay anyway? Iris looked closely at Rodney. He seemed genuinely contrite. He had stopped pleading, but his eyes radiated hurt and hope. The hot coffee gave her courage. Security was not the half of it, she reasoned. The truth was that she still loved this big confused guy, this man who had truthfully given her love beyond any expectation, who had wooed and won her and who, with a mere touch could turn her to jelly. He had beaten her, but maybe he could be helped, cured. After all he had not laid a hand on her previously. He could be helped. Her new friend Betty Jean was making progress with her alcoholic husband Hank, with outside help.

She could resurrect what they'd had, rebuild the foundation of their affection, rebuild it, and help him become whole. It was her duty. Filled with sudden resolve, Iris made her decision. She would stay and help him. She would try, but, if ever, Iris thought, he does this again, I leave. That will do it. I'll go.

"We have to talk," she said, sitting down across the table.

Rodney sighed, his face a study in relief. "I'm tired," he said. "But whatever you want, Iris. I'll do it. You name it. You just name it." He half rose in the chair, the blanket like a cape over his big shoulders. "Does this mean... that you're gonna stay?" his voice breaking on the last word.

"It depends," Iris said, "on what you do, Rodney." She held back the urge to touch him. "I want you to know...if you ever beat me again, if you ever lay a hand on me again, I'll go. I'll call the police and I'll press charges and I'll never come back."

He nodded vigorously. "I know...I know. You're right. Will you stay...will you stay then?"

"For the moment," Iris rose to her feet. "But I'm going up to bed alone.

You can sleep on the couch. We know you need help. You've got a problem and tomorrow we'll start on it."

"Oh...Iris," Rodney's voice returned to its normal basso profundo, resonant and manly. "I'm gonna do everything to make this work. It will never happen again. I promise. We'll talk about it then, tomorrow."

Iris, her entire body hurting, the coffee still having its effect, hardly slept. Every waking moment she wondered if she was making a mistake. Yet, despite the pain, she felt a surge of love for the man now sleeping alone on the couch downstairs. Near morning, waking for the third or fourth time, she even felt a rush of desire. She still wanted him, needed him. He had given her such pleasure, such love, had brought out such powerful affection in her. She owed it to him to try. She was his wife. Many women had far less. Rodney was successful after all. He possessed energy and resources. He was handsome, strong and full of vitality. Everyone knew Rodney was charming, with a kind of animal force about him, and possessed a gift of gab. When they went out, Iris was invariably aware of the glances other women shot in his direction, and she knew that men too sensed his magnetism. He was, as a friend had whispered at the wedding, "a catch." She would not easily give up on him.

She rose at dawn, wincing in pain, and padded down to look at him. He seemed to be sleeping easily. She took two aspirins and returned to her bed upstairs and fell deeply into slumber, finally free of pain.

When she made breakfast later, Rodney was gone. He called briefly from his office with a promise to return home early. Later in the afternoon she answered a call from the school. Mr. Hayward explained that a High School teacher had been hit by a car and would be laid-up for several weeks; could she substitute for five weeks or more? Eagerly Iris consented and scribbled a note for Rodney. She drove into town to buy materials for the English class. When she returned, Rodney was napping on the living room couch, where he stayed through the night. Wanting to talk with him and plan for his therapy, Iris knew it might have to wait until their respective schedules eased a bit. At the school, she hid her bruises with make-up, sunglasses and long-sleeved blouses with high collars. The English class went well, the students quickly warming to her. Only Betty Jean knew the truth.

The weeks flew. Within a few days Rodney returned to their bed, wooing her as before. They made love again. Even Iris found herself falling into the routine. But she had not forgotten. The tension remained. Rodney, though solicitous, managed to guide all conversation and activity away from the issue. Since that terrible night they had not discussed his problem.

This, Iris knew, could not work. Trust, once lost, had to be carefully rebuilt, so the tension remained. She was hesitant and fearful, sometimes breaking down and crying without warning. Often she found herself staring for long moments across the snowy landscape, now so bleak and stark it was hard to believe this was the same place where she had found such happiness last summer.

Once she watched a high circling hawk, thinking as she watched that she was circling, circling, and no closer to Rodney than that night after he had begged forgiveness and understanding. Somehow she had to hold him to his promise. Making love to him, submitting to him on little things, made it easier, but it was not a solution. The problem loomed beneath. As time passed she found it easier to forget, to push her worry out of mind.

It was early March when Betty Jean, sitting with Iris in the teachers' lounge, brought the subject to the fore.

"Was that the first time then?" asked Betty Jean. Iris needed no prompting.

"Yes," Iris said, speaking fast, letting it spill out. "I never expected it. I still can't imagine what I did wrong. I fixed a fine romantic dinner for him and he just exploded." She wanted to explain that he had acted strangely possessive during the trip to Washington, DC, at parties, in the bar at Suttons Bay, and on other occasions, but she repressed this. "It's been four or five weeks and he's been fine since. I don't think he'll ever do it again," she said hopefully, allowing the words to flow as a kind of comfort, half-believing. "He's been a marvelous lover, you know." This she blurted out and then blushed, laughing.

Betty Jean's eyebrows went up. "Oh? Is that so? Tell me about it." Then she asked more questions. Questions about when Rodney wanted her, whether it was at certain times, after so many drinks, and so on. Iris bristled and changed the subject, returning to her speculations. "I don't think he knew why. He was under strain y'know. That cold spell affected all of us, and he had too much to drink that night. I don't suppose I was much help, always nit-picking and bothering him about being isolated and so on."

"Quit making excuses," snapped Betty Jean. Iris looked up in surprise.
"Excuses?"

"Yes. Can't you see you're trying to take all the blame on yourself?"

"I am thinking. I'm doing the best I can," Iris murmured, knowing it was not so.

Betty Jean stared hard into Iris's eyes, patting her hand. "Have you two talked about that night? I mean since he and you made up?" Iris could not pull her eyes away. She felt her cigarette burn down to her fingers, shaking it and stubbing it out. She had taken up smoking again almost without thought, a reflex action.

"I...well, not really. No. I think what happened was some kind of fluke, y'know. Just the right combination of all the elements caused him to blow up that evening."

"And you believe that?"

Iris nodded, aware of her lame response. Betty Jean had put her on the defensive. It was true. Rodney had not seen anyone, or spoken with her once about the beating, nor sought mutual support or aid. Now the bell rang for the second time and Betty Jean rose.

Moments later, back with her students, Iris could not concentrate on the subject. She was half way through a sentence on the origins of Elizabethan drama when she broke down, sobbing, and had to run from the room.

18

A few days later, Ionia was bursting with excitement. The local basketball team had reached the State quarter-finals. "March madness" seemed to affect everyone. This was combined with another affliction that seems to hit with greater force the further north one lives. Iris knew the symptoms, increased tension and restlessness, shorter fuses, disgust with the smallest routines, the inability to concentrate. Known as "cabin fever", this malady had but one remedy, melting snow and sunshine. It had been a hard long winter.

At the school Iris caught the fever of the team's success. Her embarrassing breakdown had not been repeated (though it had occasioned a brief query from the Principal, who asked kindly if there was anything the matter), and now she had been asked to teach full time until the end of the school year. The hard work of teaching had forced her worries about Rodney almost completely out of mind. Rodney was working hard too, coming home late. Several times he had complained about his dinner not being ready on time, about his shirts not being washed, or about clutter in the house. Once Iris dared to hint, softly, that he might combine efforts with her to clean up and catch up. "That's women's work," Rodney had gruffly rejoined, pouring himself a tumbler of bourbon. He greeted the news of Iris's full-time employment with petulance.

"Oh fuck. Now nothing will get done around here till summer," and he had stomped out the door. Iris saw no sign of him until he stumbled in late that night. For the first time since the summer party he was visibly intoxicated as he swayed his way upstairs to bed. When the basketball tourney is over, Iris thought, we better talk. It can wait till then.

On the evening before the quarter-final game was to be played, Iris made ready. She had volunteered to drive some varsity cheerleaders to Jackson since the buses were filled. Rodney had grudgingly agreed that she could use the Thunderbird since the VW was so small. But now Iris was worried. Michigan was being hit by an ice storm. A cold rain which had started early in the day was slowly turning to wet sticky snow and predictions were for freezing rain later on. Driving would be dangerous. Outside the tree limbs groaned and creaked with every gust. As the day waned, telephone wires were coated with a fine thin ice, threatening to break the lines.

Rodney built up a fire in the wood stove and it roared as he fixed another drink. Iris had lost count already. On edge, Iris decided to make a drink for herself.

"Let's hope the roads are clear in the morning," said Iris, raising her voice above the stereo. It was Jackson Browne but Rodney was oblivious to the music, as usual. Rodney did not respond. He nursed his drink silently, eyes vacant.

"I hope the roads are safe tomorrow," Iris repeated, almost shouting now. "I have the responsibility for five other girls. I sure feel safer driving your car."

"What do you mean, my car?" Rodney asked, looking up suddenly, his tone sinister. Iris continued, fighting to moderate her voice.

"Don't you remember, honey? You agreed last week that I could drive the Thunderbird to take some of the girls to the big game in Jackson. It's still okay isn't it?"

"No! It's not okay." Rodney turned to face Iris, frowning. "I need the car to close a deal in Lansing. Before you ever ask me for my car again, remember, I have an image to maintain and driving some fucking VW bug don't fit that image."

"But you know the VW isn't roomy enough, darling. I'm taking five girls and myself. You promised I could drive your car," Iris felt a flush rising to her face. Angry and frustrated she tried not to raise her voice, speaking slowly, "I'm holding you to that promise, Rodney. I'm taking the car. You said I could, so I am."

Rodney sprang to his feet. Immediately Iris knew she'd gone too far. He advanced on her, face expressionless, eyes glaring and unblinking. For an instant he paused before her, a tiny twitch moving his cheek, then he grabbed her by the collar of her sweater, pulling her close. She could feel his hot angry breath and the smell of bourbon.

"Look, bitch. Where the fuck d'you get off telling me what to drive and what not to drive? I'm the master of this house, or did you forget your lesson, back in January?" Rodney's voice was rising, and it was full of menace. "Maybe you need another lesson."

Then he hurled her against the wall, charging in to pin her before she could move. As he began to slap her across the face, snapping her head back and forth, Iris tried to fight him off. But Rodney overpowered her. He seemed to have superhuman strength. Keeping his hand open he hit her again and again, the blows stinging, until Iris could no longer see him. She heard his voice, grunting, like a metronome, "no bruises...no bruises." Then, finished, he fell back, breathing hard, head lowered. Iris opened her eyes through a red haze and began to breathe again. Her face was on fire. Rodney, she realized, looked as if he were in some kind of ecstasy. He had a strange grin on his face, his eyes brilliant. Sobbing now as air rushed into her lungs, Iris slid to the floor. She felt her face, knowing he had deliberately hit her only hard enough to hurt, not enough to leave noticeable bruises.

"You bastard!" she hissed, unable to stay her words. "You miserable bastard. This time I'm calling the cops. I should have called the first time."

Moving carefully, she made her way to the phone, fearful of turning her back on Rodney, who sat at the table, holding a drink. Apparently the connection was bad, static hissed and cracked on the line. Iris returned the receiver to its cradle, dismayed. Rodney was up, moving to the sink where he filled the tea kettle with water, then carrying it to the stove. Iris tried again, getting through this time. The dispatcher at the Sheriff's office was terse, saying she would notify the nearest patrol car and send it over. Iris did not explain why, just saying she needed the police, and quickly. Fifteen minutes or so said the dispatcher.

"It's over." Iris said, pacing now. "That did it." Beyond courage, somehow, and filled with rage, she spoke in brief phrases. She was no longer afraid. The cops were on their way. Rodney could beat her again, but now he would have to kill her. Help was on the way. "You better believe it, it's over!" Suddenly she stopped before him, furious that he did not answer. "What's the matter, Rodney? Are you afraid now? You didn't think I'd call, did you? Not really. Well? Did you? Answer me, you son-of-a-bitch!"

But Rodney remained silent, finishing his drink. Rising, he washed the glass out in the sink and put it carefully away, looking around the kitchen.

"Iris," he said quietly, his voice low and controlled. "What's wrong with you? You better settle down before the police arrive." He picked up the teapot, now whistling, and poured two large cups of tea, the strong aroma filling the room. "I find tea relaxes me...want a cup?" He took a sip. Then he held out the other cup. "Here...maybe this will calm you down. The cops don't listen well to a hysterical woman. Here...honey."

Iris broke. Whirling around she spotted the ash tray and grabbed it. Rodney backed away, smiling, making a come hither gesture with both hands. She hurled it with all her strength at his smiling face. Easily he ducked the missile and it smashed into the wall, fragments scattered through the kitchen.

Inside the patrol car the two cops were tense. The road was slick with several new inches of wet snow layered on top of treacherous ice. Furthermore, domestic calls were often unpredictable and always unpleasant.

"D'you know these people?" Fitzgerald asked as he drove with all the care and experience he could muster, the car barely exceeding 25 mph. He'd picked up Deputy Barnett at the station as a back-up.

"Yes," said Barnett, "I met them before. Went to a party once, last summer at their farm. Can't say I'm a good friend of either of them, though."

"Party, eh? Oh yeah. I heard about Harris and his bashes. So you went to one of them didja?" Fitzgerald's tone was bantering. He changed his tone, deadly serious, all business now "There was a charge; wasn't it some time back? The previous wife?"

"Yes. Didn't hold up though. They put the other wife away. Seems she made it all up." Barnett remembered the new wife, Iris. He'd danced with her briefly, and he recalled how Rodney had come up from the pond to the barn, and how he had hauled Iris away. It had seemed a little strange. And Harris sure could put the booze away. The Sheriff seemed to like Harris, who had a reputation in the county as a successful businessman. Barnett was curious. Iris, he remembered, was...or seemed to be...a fine decent woman. Bright and graceful.

The two men had difficulty making it to the door, slipping several times on the dangerous ground. Barnett went ahead as Fitzgerald waited outside, standard procedure. Iris met him at once and he moved inside to a position where he could see everything. No weapons or anything dangerous in view. Already Iris was talking, then shouting, "All right. I want him out of here right now. Arrest him! Take him away from me!" Barnett could see that she was near tears, her face red with anger. He could see no signs of a beating.

"Now settle down, Mrs. Harris," said Barnett, using his most soothing tone. He saw Rodney off to one side, looking a little pained as if to say, 'It's beyond me.' To confirm this, Harris shrugged, a tight smile on his face. Barnett took Iris by the arm, firmly, and, exerting his considerable strength, moved her into the living room. "C'mon, let's go in here, where we can talk." Fitzgerald stayed behind in the kitchen with Rodney.

"He beat me!" Iris said, fighting for control, holding back her tears. 'He hit me across the face, he slapped me, over and over. Look! If you don't believe me, look!" Barnett could see that her face was brick red, but it was almost impossible to be certain. It might be anger.

"Here, sit down," said Barnett, taking a seat beside her. Then he began to question her.

"You say he beat you once before," Barnett said, a few moments later, after listening to a long rambling account, almost incoherent. "I think you said it was in January. Did you call the police at that time, or seek treatment?"

"It was January...yes...I mean. No. No...I mean I didn't call. I didn't think. What difference does that make anyhow? He beat me. Why are you questioning me? Why don't you arrest him?"

"It isn't so simple, Mrs. Harris. If he actually committed a crime. Now don't get upset. I wasn't here you know. I mean...you are the only witness. Do you have any other witness?" Barnett knew it sounded ludicrous, but so it was. He felt his patience straining. His hands were tied in this matter. He had a pretty good idea why Iris's face was red. She'd been beaten, of that he was certain. But his hands were tied by the law. He could not simply arrest the man on the basis of one person's accusation, without evidence. He tried to explain this patiently to Iris, controlling his own rising anger. "The law," he said, "states that for a misdemeanor a police officer may only arrest, without a warrant, for a crime committed in his presence. If such a crime was committed, in...a case like this, it would be assault and battery. That crime is a misdemeanor in this state. I didn't witness any crime, my partner did not, therefore, even if your husband did assault you, we cannot arrest him tonight." Barnett braced himself, knowing Iris would explode.

"So what the hell do I do?" she cried. "I don't believe this shit. I call the police to assist me when my husband beats me and I get this Catch-22 bullshit. Dammit! I want him out of here! I want to be safe from him. Are you telling me he can hit me anytime he wants and get away with it? What in hell good is the law? What good are you?" Iris spat the words at him. Barnett wondered, incongruously, if she remembered the time they had briefly danced in the barn. A devoted husband, entirely loyal to his wife, he nevertheless wanted to take this distraught woman into his arms. He dared not.

"I never said there was nothing you could do," Barnett continued, speaking carefully, trying to mask his frustration. "We'll prepare a police report on this and submit it tomorrow to the prosecutor. If he thinks there's sufficient cause, he'll authorize a warrant for Mr. Harris's arrest. And, if that happens, you'll have to appear before a magistrate and sign the warrant, under oath. Then we'll be able to arrest him."

"Oh. That's just fine!" Iris exploded again. "And just what am I supposed to do till then?"

"I'd suggest," said Deputy Barnett, "that you stay with a friend."

Iris flung herself at him. Vaguely she remembered him from the summer party and his quiet manner. She was not really aware. The emotions were so mixed in her; fear, hurt, rage, anxiety. "You...you stupid son-of-a-bitch." Barnett held her back, her arms missing him in aimless sweeps. Then she began to cry. "I didn't hit him. I didn't do anything. He beat me. Why should I have to leave?"

Soon she subsided, apologizing quietly. Barnett cursed inwardly. He hated these domestic calls. In these situations people always seemed exposed, somehow at their worst. All their frustrations seemed to spill over, all the hate and anger. He believed Iris, but he could not do more than he had explained.

His voice grew testy, "Look, Mrs. Harris. I don't make the laws. I just enforce them. You married the man, I didn't." He instantly regretted it, but it was out before he could stop the words. He had sensed the previous summer that this woman was too good for Harris. He had been dubious about Harris from the start. The man was strange in some indefinable way. He wondered if Sheriff Saunders had not been too long behind a desk. One got a sixth sense about these things out on the job. Harris was perfectly capable of this, he knew. But the law made no provision for a hunch, or an opinion. Now he cursed himself anew. Damn. I always lose my cool on these jobs, but why do these women expect miracles from us? He applied himself to calming her down again. It took some time.

In the kitchen, Rodney was speaking coolly to Fitzgerald. He had been cool from the start. "So you see, Bill, I'm still not sure what caused her to act that way...one minute yelling and screaming at me and the next throwing ash trays at me." His arm swept around. The shattered glass on the floor spoke the rest. Fitzgerald nodded his head in rueful agreement. "Y'know, Bill. I think she needs help. First thing in the morning I'm gonna call a doc and set up an appointment. First thing."

Rodney answered every question with aplomb and decisive certainty. He was the aggrieved one, the long-suffering husband. When Iris and Barnett re-entered the kitchen, they all talked for a while. Barnett and Fitzgerald got a promise from both that there would be no further incident, that there would be a consultation in the morning with an appropriate professional. Through it all Iris sat passive, not speaking. When she heard Rodney tell the deputies that he was not, after all, going to press charges against her, she almost screamed. But she repressed her anger. So long as she was in the same house with Rodney, she vowed, it was best to remain silent. As soon as she could, without Rodney knowing, she vowed to call Betty Jean. She would get out soon enough. Nothing would stop her now.

"Sorry for the inconvenience, fellas," she heard Rodney's voice at the door. Then the car was gone. For a moment she held her breath. Would he come after her? Probably not, she realized. After all, the police had just gone. Then he was in the kitchen, laughing.

"Well, baby...now you see? The cops can't help you. All you have, baby, is me. You might as well get used to it." Still chuckling he reached for the bottle in the cupboard. "Here, baby, want to join me, here, have a little snort."

And Iris, for the life of her, still unable to look at him, not wanting to see him, not talking, did not refuse the drink he placed before her. Nor the second, nor later in the night, a third.

Iris was first up next morning. Her face still hurt, but she could see no visible evidence of the beating in the mirror. That bastard. He did it this way on purpose. And her head hurt. From the beating or from too much drink? She was uncertain. Guilt and confusion muddled her thinking. Descending to the kitchen, a little clumsy as she fixed coffee and toast, she heard him clumping down the stairs into the kitchen. His cocky demeanor was too much. She knew then that she would follow through, she would press charges.

Rodney, fortunately, did not linger. As soon as he was gone Iris found the prosecutor's number and called at once, unloading her story to a secretary, outlining the events of the previous night, and the first awful beating. The prosecutor was in court, but he had already seen the police report and had left a note about it. The policy of the office, said the woman, was to take no action for five days on such complaints. Then, at the end of this waiting period, the prosecutor's office would contact the complainant who could then sign a warrant. At that time, a bond of $25 had to be posted. If, said the secretary, the case was prosecuted, the money would be refunded, but on the other hand, if the charges were dropped, the bond would be forfeited.

"I think you should understand, Mrs. Harris," added the secretary, clearly familiar with such cases, "that we have many of these complaints that seem to fall apart prior to trial. We have found this policy to be quite effective in reducing the groundless complaints."

"Mine is not groundless, believe me," Iris shot back in some anger.

"Yes...well, Mrs. Harris, someone will call you next Monday concerning this matter. Do you wish to take the call at your home, or at the school?"

"At school," said Iris immediately. She placed the receiver softly into the cradle. What do I do now? Where do I go for help?

By evening, when Rodney returned, she had numbed herself with drink. Vaguely she heard on the radio that Ionia had been beaten in double overtime. She stumbled to bed early, alone, in a mild boozy haze. And so the weekend passed.

On Monday, Iris got herself together and showed up for her English class. The students were unusually quiet, perhaps down because of the defeat in the playoffs, perhaps reticent because Iris had not helped with the rides. She could not explain what happened. Her face was unmarked. Who would sympathize, who would believe? Besides, she was only a substitute at the school. When, during third hour, the Principal stuck his head into her room—between classes—to inform her that a call was waiting in his office, she walked the hall with head down, arms slack, answering the call with a dead voice.

"No. That's right. I don't want to prosecute."

And in the office of the county prosecutor, the call was received with ironic comment. "I'm hardly surprised," said the prosecutor to his assistant who nodded knowingly. "They never do."

19

Spring came late to the vast peninsula, but it came with fooling play, with high temperatures into the fifties or sixties only to plunge the next day to below freezing. The snow melted steadily, but unseasonable storms brewed over the big lake to the west, bringing more snow and freezing winds. By April, however, the signs were unmistakable. Muddy patches of low ground, where the horses stomped in the barnyard, trapped massive puddles. Redwing blackbirds appeared in numbers, and robins hopped on brown exposed grasses, where the hint of green was a promise. The stark line of woods beyond the fields grew softer with new buds and a tinge of magenta brushed the sky at sunset. Flowers and leaves thrust forth in early May, and everyone celebrated, but with that hesitant air that people sensed, of change, of unpredictable setbacks, all part of the spring. Of course, April is not always the cruelest month and the second weekend in May brought freezing winds again, and, with the hard northwest wind, unwelcome snow.

Iris, buffeted within, seemed especially affected by this storm from without. On certain lovely days of sun and balmy southern breezes, she felt buoyant, able to tackle even her terrible troubles. At the school on such days people noticed and made polite comment. "Iris, you look fine," or "My, Iris, you look much better," as if she had been sick. And, of course, in a way, she had. For a while, when spring seemed irretrievably in, Iris cut back on her evening drinking, turning to her schoolwork, working in the flower gardens with trowel and fork, reading novels with renewed interest. But there were many days when it took all her will to go through the motions. She'd stood one day before the east window, overlooking a huge lilac bush now bursting with leaves, staring for long moments at the cold rain that fell from each tiny sprig, dripping, dripping. She had stood for an hour, and then longer, unmoving. As if hypnotized. She had not known for long moments that she was crying, her tears streaming down her cheeks. She had not known until Rodney, coming in from the barn, had come up behind her and taken her drink, refilled it, put it back in her hand, and then led her into the living room, to sit beside her. His old self, all charm and loving solicitude. He had made love to her that day, but she had simply allowed it, taking him but not climaxing herself.

At the school, Betty Jean had seen and understood, trying to help in the midst of her own struggle, but unable to do much. Once, in the women's bathroom, she had confronted Iris, trying to be at once kind and yet demanding honesty.

"How many times now, honey?"

"I'd rather not talk about it, Betty Jean."

"Twice? Three times? Believe me, unless you two get help, it'll happen again. It won't get better."

"I won't let it happen again," Iris had said, angrily turning on her heel. That she was certain of. Or so she told herself.

But, of course, Rodney was his old self again. He never mentioned the beatings or the aftermath. He pretended things were unchanged. He acted as if they had an unspoken pact that never would the incidents be broached, that the humiliation of the police visit, the dropping of all charges, all of it, had never happened. Rodney had gained power from the incident in March. But she dared not argue. She told herself she was biding her time. He'd maneuvered her into a situation of impotence regarding the law, or so she felt. He had made it impossible for her to act outwardly. So, she would bide her time. This she said every time she sat down to drink with him, especially when he made moves on her. Amazingly, his old potency was restored. He seemed, at times, insatiable. He wanted her often, sometimes every night. Almost always she allowed him to possess her, both fearful of upsetting his renewed sense of power and not wanting to terminate the rituals of the marriage bed, the conjugal show of love that she no longer felt inwardly, however much Rodney expressed it outwardly. She even went so far as to pretend she wanted him, again, faking her climax.

Not that she wanted him content. It seemed to Iris that she was never more acutely tuned to his every movement and action. She knew this did not stem from regard for him, but rather from fear. Yet, Rodney, though he avoided any reference to the beatings, did seem to want to put it all behind him. He worked hard at wooing her back. He brought gifts, flowers, he shopped for special foods, and he went out of his way to please her. For a time, Iris simply did not believe, and so long as the memory of pain kept her skeptical, she felt only disgust at his actions. Though pain is as immediate and intense as anything in life, human memory of pain—even as one recalls how awful it was—tends to fade with time. Perhaps mercifully, memory cannot resurrect that immediacy, or else, a famous physician once said, half of womankind would never have more than one child. And Iris though not forgetting, began to wonder. Then she almost began to believe again. Rodney spoke often of the good times (and those being undeniably good, he had a strong point to make), and always, whenever he drank, he plied her with drinks, and using them as he used gifts and flowers, he wooed her gradually back.

He even surprised her by announcing one spring morning that he had made an appointment with a psychiatrist in Lansing. And he kept the first two appointments. By the middle of May, he had convinced Iris that the beatings were an aberration, the consequence of the pressures of business, bad weather, too much booze, and his own love for her, a love so intense that he had become suspicious and jealous. He told her this was the burden of his meetings with the psychiatrist. Half believing, actually beginning to respond to him again in bed—surprised at this—Iris began to hope once more.

By summertime, Rodney dropped out of the treatment, claiming he was cured. Iris wanted to believe. Rodney appeared to be the considerate man she'd married over a year ago. To celebrate their anniversary Rodney took her back to Washington, DC to the same motel room they had used for their honeymoon. This time they flew direct from Lansing.

"To happiness. To love. To us!" toasted Rodney, sitting next to her on the bed. He tossed down more than half a tall drink. Iris sipped from her own glass. Rodney insisted. It was their second honeymoon, and time to celebrate. She agreed, though roughly aware that with the first drink she had a very human tendency to take another, never able to match Rodney, but going beyond reason, frequently losing control. Soon they were in bed, and Iris found herself once more taking the initiative, tearing his pants off and lusting after him. Fueled by hope and the romance of memory, by alcohol and need, she responded to him and their love-making was tender and romantic. She cuddled up to him, happy again, she held him close, feeling that they had weathered a terrible storm and they would grow closer and more loving.

Summer passed without incident. It was quiet in mid-Michigan, peaceful and lazy and serene. Iris stayed at the farm most of the time, content to care for the horses, puttering in the garden, planting and reorganizing the lawns and shrubs. She had long since read Rodney's books on horses and knew enough to handle basic care. She took pleasure in the sight of a clean stall, the pungent manure hauled away to the growing heap beside the barn, the fresh woody smell when she scattered the fresh sawdust bedding from wall to wall, and the glow of well done work, when the horses entered to drink and—like greedy children—when they rushed to their mixed grain at the end of each day in pasture. She soaped the saddles and adjusted the tack, swept away cobwebs, and groomed the big animals exactly as the books suggested. Sometimes he joined her at the end of his day, the two of them working side-by-side into the late evening, the sun still high until nine o'clock or later. She learned to ride moderately well, no longer hanging on to pommel with one hand, or bouncing uncontrollably, though she doubted that she could ever match Rodney's easy grace on horseback. Rarely did she go into town and then only for groceries or to join Rodney for lunch. Always he drank, but always he seemed to be in control, the golden liquid seemed to increase his wit and pleasure in people, to enhance his personal magnetism. Through most of the summer, Iris reveled in his attention. Only late in the summer did she begin to feel stifled, craving contact with others. Finally on a magnificent August evening, Iris decided to bring up the subject in a roundabout way. They sat together on the porch, gazing west across the pasture, watching a flock of starlings wheel in the lowering sun, the horses casting long shadows on the grass. Insects buzzed."I think," said Iris, "I'll go into Lansing this weekend and shop for a fall wardrobe for school. Maybe I'll stay over at The Kellogg Center, if you don't mind."

"Sounds like fun, Iris. I'll knock off work early Friday, and we'll drive over and have dinner. We can spend the whole weekend there."

"No, Rodney. I want to go alone. I appreciate all the time you gave me this summer, and everything, but you are not my father." She inserted a teasing note, trying to mollify him, "I'm a big girl. I'm sure you can get through one weekend without me."

Rodney put down the spiked coffee, leaned and gazed hard into Iris's eyes. She saw the cold anger, the deep rage, absent for many months. Recoiling, she waited, afraid.

"Out of the question," said Rodney in the flat toneless voice she had grown to fear. "If you go, I go with you. That's final. You're my wife, and you do not go about alone. The discussion is over. If you decide on the trip, let me know. Otherwise, I don't want to hear another word about it." He paused to see whether Iris would challenge him. She sat, eyes averted, tingling with rage but impotent to act. Fear held her back. She sensed what he would do if she disagreed. After a few moments, the silence enormous between them, Rodney rose and went inside, leaving her alone in the falling light.

The tears came but she held herself together and soon she controlled herself, unwilling to allow him to flaunt his little victory. She realized she was little more than a prisoner all summer, despite their rejoining, the love-making, the evenings together, the dinners and luncheons. She had no money to finance a divorce or keep herself thereafter. She had pooled her salary from the substitute teaching to make repairs on the house and outbuildings. Rodney had insisted that she bear some of the burden. He claimed his business was not doing so well.

But, she thought, there is a chance. Mr. Hayward was to call within a week or so about a possible full-time position at the school. Her teaching had been highly regarded. The students liked her. She reasoned that if she could land that job, nothing would stop her. She would quietly leave once employed, file for a divorce, and say goodbye to Rodney Harris forever. If she were careful now and bided her time, it would all be possible. She knew the school board was to make the decision before the new semester started. A regular job would set her free.

Several days later, Rodney was helping Iris prepare for his Labor Day party, planned this year to be even bigger than the year before. Iris was not in the house when the phone rang, and Rodney picked it up at once.

"Sorry, Mr. Hayward, Iris isn't here at the moment," said Rodney in his most businesslike voice. "Is this about the full-time position? I thought so. Well, Mr. Hayward, I can save you another call later. You see, Iris told me just the other day that she was not interested in a full-time position. She thoroughly enjoyed the substitution last year and I know she would like to continue that...No. No. I don't think you can change her mind on that. She was pretty firm about it when she told me. Well. Good luck then, and thanks for considering her. Bye."

As he replaced the phone, a smile flashed across Rodney's face. Just then Iris entered from the kitchen door.

"Did I hear the phone?"

"Yes. It was for me," said Rodney. "Business."

"Oh." Iris could not conceal her disappointment. She had been expecting Hayward to call. Maybe the full-time position was not going to materialize. She returned to the barn, her head down.

20

On the day of the big party the first guests began to arrive around six. Everyone was there from the previous time, and more. Iris kept an eye out and ran to greet Betty Jean and Hank when they drove in around seven. Rodney's secretary, the voluptuous Sally, was right behind them. Iris embraced Betty Jean, having seen nothing of her for many weeks. Hank was subdued but sober, his eyes clear, his face relaxed. Apparently he was still on the wagon. Warmly he shook her hand, his eyes taking in the impressive array of lights and tables, the several large outdoor barbeque grills, the signs of a big bash.

Rodney joined them, drink in hand, offering Hank food and drink.

"I'll eat," said Hank, "to my heart's content, but no drinks, thank you."

"That we'll have to see," Rodney rejoined, with a wink. Then the two men walked away to join another boisterous group, all talking about the Tiger's season and whether they might make the playoffs this year.

"When did he start up again, on the drinking?" Betty Jean asked.

"He never stopped."

"But I thought...with his therapy and all..."

"Well. You were wrong," Iris snapped. "He stopped the meetings with that shrink long ago. But at least he seems to monitor his drinking. He's never drunk as far as I can tell." She found herself talking in spite of her resolve. The fact that the teaching job had not come through was a setback, and she had drawn inward again. But Betty Jean was so friendly, so easy to talk to. They found a corner in the crowded kitchen, talking quickly and with growing frankness. Iris needed this, wanted this desperately, this communion with another woman, this communication, this give and take. Rodney had kept her so alone. Then Betty Jean dropped a bombshell.

"I still don't understand why you turned Mr. Hayward down. That job was too good to be true. I know you haven't taught much speech or history, but you'd be good at any subject."

"What?" Iris dropped her glass and the spill spread across the floor. She did not move.

"Iris," Betty Jean took her by the arm and led her into the bathroom. "Iris, honey, do you mean to tell me you didn't know about the job offer? The Board voted in late August and you were the unanimous choice for first offer. How the hell did Rodney keep that from you?"

"That dirty...bastard!" Iris burst into tears. Then she slammed her hands against the wall. "That lying son-of-a-bitch."

"Iris, listen to me," Betty Jean stood with her back blocking the bathroom door. "If this is true...If he kept it from you, think about why. Why? It's all about control. He simply doesn't want you to teach, to have your own life." From outside came laughter and shouts. People were gathering behind the house. The shouts came through the bathroom window. The revelers were heading towards the pond to skinny dip. Someone knocked on the bathroom door.

"Listen, Iris," Betty Jean said. "We'll talk more. Just keep this to yourself. Don't confront him. Be smart. Humor him. Play along. We both know from experience what will happen if you challenge him." Then they left the bathroom and walked out through the kitchen into the balmy evening air.

Outside, Rodney had gathered the adventurous into a cluster, and now he led them away across the pasture and towards the pond glistening in the distance. Iris tagged along with Betty Jean, more objective this time, and curious. She would not go in without clothing, but she intended to watch. Rodney was in his element for sure. At the pond he plunged in first, clothing and all. As he emerged like a massive humanoid beast from the far side, he ran dripping after several squealing women, throwing them in with the help of several men. Beer cans had been hidden on the bottom, anchored to cement blocks, and at once one young fellow found them, hoisting the cold cans up to the approving cheers of the swimmers. Others had brought large wine bottles and everyone drank freely. Rodney stripped to the waist, revealing his powerful torso, and then half submerged, peeling away his pants and shorts and swimming from side to side urging the others on. Two or three women joined him, then a couple of men, and soon the pond was full of people yelling and splashing, clothing flung onto the grassy banks. Iris and Betty Jean sat some distance away, silently observing. Normally they might have laughed, but the knowledge of what Rodney's abuse had done hung heavily over them, and soon, as darkness fell, they wandered back towards the house, following the sodden path trod by others. Iris had watched Sally in the pond, fully nude, large breasts bouncing as she splashed and played, often moving close to Rodney. But it all seemed innocent enough with so many people so close. It was, she knew, merely another way Rodney, by rousing mild shock and interest, attracted people to him, and played out his "life of the party" role. Later, when Rodney joined her in the house where a smaller group had gathered for shelter from the late summer dew forming on the cool night lawns, she pretended interest in his words. Pretended wifely approval. Rodney was effusive.

"Hey, Iris. How's it goin', honey?" he shouted to her, dressed in fresh clothes, the ever-present drink in his hand, face flushed with pleasure and booze. Had she not discovered his deceit, she might have been drawn to him, somewhat boozy, but handsome, the center of attention.

"Hey, folks. I got some wife here, y'know. Nothin' wrong with this woman, I tell ya. Got a mind of her own too. Right, honey?" He put his big arm around her and squeezed her affectionately. "I mean. She won't go skinny-dipping no matter what. Now that I like. Y'know, I like that. Lotta women, they'd give in...but Iris here, no. And I respect that. Yeah. But she's a damned good wife too, I tell ya. A real woman, none of the unisex bullshit with her. This woman knows how to treat a man." He bussed her for all to see, to some muted laughter. Iris noticed that Betty Jean, watching from across the room, managed an ironic smile. She knew, oh yes, she knows better. And, thought Iris, so do I. And you, she thought, looking up with pretended happiness at her husband. You will get yours. You'll find out soon enough.

But then Sally, clad in wet clothes that clung to her abundance, revealing everything, came inside giggling and flouncing, and took Rodney away, dragging him with a wake of laughing quests through the kitchen and out into the night where someone was playing a guitar. A bonfire was roaring. Reluctantly she followed, Betty Jean falling in beside her, a reassuring hand on her arm.

Later, towards morning, Iris was barely awake, waiting for him. She knew he would come. When he did, the smell of bourbon preceded him. It was truly amazing how much alcohol he could consume. She'd imbibed too much herself, and for a time her head swam, but soon she felt better. He almost tripped as he removed his pants, and fell muttering onto the bed.

"Goddamn woman...could'a waited f-me, could'a waited. Jesus...hadda say goodbye t'all them guests m'self. Goddamn it." As he lurched towards her, Iris almost laughed and indeed would have had she not known that he had cost her the teaching job, had lied to her, had lied to the Principal. He surprised her by pulling the covers back. She'd expected him, really drunk this time, to fall into a sodden coma, but he managed to raise his naked body over her. His hands were on her, his mouth at hers. His power over her despite the drink was both familiar and frightening, so she forced herself to submit, hoping it would be over quickly. Then he was astride her neck, wagging his half erect penis in her face. He was laughing, and Iris, without thinking, pushed him off with all her strength, jumping out of bed.

"Why you dirty son-of-a-bitch," she breathed in a low voice. "What makes you think you can do anything you want with me anytime you please? You didn't even bother to find out if I was awake." She stood beside the bed and looked down at his naked body. He did not look so good now, his ample belly hung, his penis had retreated into itself, his hair was mussed, his face sweaty. Discretion told her to stop, to get into bed with him and submit. There had been times, when impelled by love, she had gladly gone further than he expected in experimenting in the sexual intimacy of bed, but not now. Though she knew she should be careful, as Betty Jean had advised, Iris felt rage boil up inside her, and the words tumbled out before she could stop them.

"If you need a piece of ass so bad, why not call Sally? She'll suck you off good I'll bet. She'll spread her legs for you." Iris shouted, total out of control.

"What's the matter with you?" Rodney muttered, surprised by this outburst. He pulled himself up onto an elbow.

"You! You're what's the matter," Iris screamed. "You bastard! You lied to me. You intercepted a call from Hayward and told him I didn't want the job. I know all about it. Betty Jean told me he offered the job, with the Board behind him 100%. Why did you do that? I don't understand it. Why? What have I done to you?" She was near tears, ready to break down. "You bastard," she cried again. "You're fucking with my career. You have no right to interfere."

Rodney stared hard at her. He rose with the bed-clothes around him, draped almost like a monk. He seemed thoughtful for a time, but then he came around the bed, throwing off the bed clothing, standing naked. She recognized the transformation. He did not shout or raise his voice at all. But, she thought, with fear paralyzing her, here was Jekyll turning into Hyde. His voice when he spoke was high, almost like that of a child, and she shivered in terror, unable to move.

"When," said Rodney, standing over her, his head thrust out and down, "will you learn?" He stood with hands hanging loose. "How many times do I have to teach you? You are mine, you are my wIfe. You belong to me." His voice was higher now. He was not screaming, but his voice was piercing. "I told Hayward what I did because you are my wife and I decide how and when you work. You work here, not there. You belong in my house, not that fuckin' school. Do you understand me? I don't need you to work. I don't want you to work. I will not let you teach full time. The decision wasn't yours to make, it was mine. It always will be."

Iris got out one word,

"But..."

Then he hit her. He slugged her full in the face with his clenched right fist. The blow snapped her head back and she felt the warm blood gushing from her nose, over her lips, the pain blinding. Rodney pushed her away, cursing, and stomped down the stairs. Iris, holding her bleeding nose, followed without a word, passing by the bathroom and moving directly to the phone. Without a moment's hesitation, she called the police. By this time she had memorized the number.

21

Fitzgerald took the call, turning to Barnett who stood nearby. The dispatcher simply held the receiver up to him. "They're at it again," he said to Barnett.

En route to the Harris place, Barnett spoke cryptically. "Maybe it would be better..."

"What are you talking about?" asked Fitz.

"I was just thinking. What if they tried to kill each other? I mean," said Barnett, hating himself as soon as he said it. "I mean, it takes about twenty minutes to get out there. A lot could happen in that time."

"Forget it," Fitz laughed ironically. "We'd get there too late and one or both would be dead. But I get your point. I mean, in the long run, it might be a blessing for the both of them."

"I don't believe that," Barnett almost snapped at his partner.

"I didn't think you did."

The house was ablaze with light as they drove into the drive. It was nearly dawn, but Iris had switched on all the lights. Fitz entered first, and Iris met him at the door. The smell of alcohol was overpowering. Rodney Harris sat at the kitchen table, a coffee mug before him, looking bemused. Barnett followed Fitz inside, taking in the scene, swept by a sickening sense of deja vu.

Barnett escorted Iris into the living room, While Fitz stayed with Rodney in the kitchen. He listened dispassionately, knowing there was little he could do. As a cop, he wanted to close the files with a guilty verdict when a crime was obvious, but, though he believed Iris (since blood was caked under her nose and there were dried blood spots on her nightgown), he was forced to explain once more his limited powers. He told Iris that a police report would be forwarded to the Prosecutor's office, and that she would have to follow up herself. She only glared at him, grimly shaking her head.

"D'you want us to stay a while?" said Barnett, aware of the fear in her gaze.

Iris shook her head, rage bursting forth. "No. Just forget it. Just fucking forget it."

In the kitchen, Fitzgerald was finished with Rodney, having taken an oral and written statement telling his side of the story. As the deputies left Rodney watched them from the back porch. When the car was out of sight he turned back inside to find Iris just inside the kitchen door, her hands clasped around herself, furious. He looked at her a moment, smiled his cold smile, and advanced. Iris put up her hands.

"Okay, bitch," he said, a fist catching her full in the mouth. Iris collapsed like a rag doll. Her head cracked on the floor. Half conscious, she heard his voice, "That's for calling the cops." He stepped over her body and left the kitchen.

Near Ionia the officers talked sadly about the case. "Y'know what he said?" Fitz asked with scorn. "He said she ran into the bathroom door because she was drunk, and then blamed him. Can you believe it?"

"Yes," said Barnett. "I mean, he'll make up any story. But what can we do? She won't press charges." He cursed with disgust. "She'll probably stay with that dirty bastard no matter how much he beats on her." Fitz sadly agreed.

Iris, fearful of any challenge to Rodney, slept that night and the next several nights on the couch. He left generally before she was up and returned late each night, scarcely talking to her, treating her more like some dumb animal than another human. Outwardly submissive, Iris plotted. There will be a divorce, she vowed, as soon as I can save enough to hire a lawyer. She also made another decision, and at the end of five days she called the Ionia County Prosecutor's Office and asked for Mr. Johnson. The prosecutor was out, but Iris explained that since the five-day period had expired, she was now ready to post a $25 security bond in order to sign the warrant. Iris was instructed to appear in the Magistrate's office late that afternoon to sign the warrant. She got there at the appointed time and the District Court Magistrate issued a warrant for the arrest of Rodney Harris on the charge of battery, a charge that carried a maximum penalty of ninety days in the county jail. She left the office with a sense of pride and accomplishment. Now just you wait, Rodney Harris, you'll get yours.

That evening, Iris cooked Rodney a prepared dinner for the first time since the assault. Knowing that his tastes ran to the simple and bulky, she cooked steak, baked potato, green beans and a salad. She'd told the police to arrive at about eight since Rodney was expected around seven-thirty. The condemned man, she thought, deserved his last meal at her hands.

"So, what's the occasion?" Rodney asked in a jocular tone as he slid behind his plate. "Does this mean all is forgiven? Are you ready to be a good wife?" He smiled with obvious pleasure at her. Iris grinned back at him. Let him think I'll put up with this. He'll learn soon enough. Rodney was finishing his coffee when the patrol car swung into the drive.

"Were you expecting someone?" Rodney asked, staring at her.

"No. Were you?" Iris went to the door, pretending surprise, and watching Rodney's reaction when she ushered the two deputies into the house. Barnett shot Iris a quick glance full of appraisal.

"Mr. Harris," he said, glad to pronounce the formal words, "we have a warrant for your arrest. Will you come with us?"

Rodney was half way to his feet, stammering,

"What the fu... what's the charge? What the hell is goin' on?"

"Assault and battery," Fitz replied, "upon your wife. Please get your coat and come with us." Neither deputy expected trouble. That would come later when Harris was released on bond. Barnett, watched the big man reaching for his coat, shooting side glances at Iris, hoping she knew that it was a given that Rodney would be home before the evening was over. Iris seemed to glow.

As Fitz escorted Rodney out to the patrol car, Barnett stayed a moment, wanting to warn her. "Mrs. Harris. I just think you should know. He's likely to be released on bond in no time at all. He'll probably come right back."

"Can he do that?" Iris cried.

"How can we stop him?" said the deputy. "I'd suggest you visit a friend."

"But...but, I have no place to go."

"I'm very sorry," Barnett muttered in disgust. There ought to be some place...he thought...some place. But there was not, not in these years of the 'seventies.

Iris did drive out shortly after the police car was gone, aimlessly wandering into Muir and then into Ionia and back, turning down back roads she barely knew. She drove past Betty Jean's house, but there were no lights on and she did not stop and knock. It was late when she finally turned back to the farm, and seeing that Rodney's car was not there, she parked the VW in the garage and entered the house. For long moments she wandered upstairs and down, fiddling with her bags, searching to see how much cash she had. It was past midnight when she heard his car, and ran to the window to look. He was back. I should have packed and gone, she said to herself. Anything but this. Nevertheless she waited for him in the kitchen, almost expectant. What would he do now? Whatever he did, please God, she prayed inwardly, let him do it now, and get it over.

"Surprised?" Rodney's grin was almost radiant. "Did you really think they'd keep me at the jail? Listen, Iris. Maybe you should study the law a bit before you go off half-baked, signing complaints and all. I've been the route, baby, and I am a businessman of standing in the community. I don't have to post no cash bond, y'know. All I gotta do is promise to show up in court." He paused and came nearer, not threatening, speaking in his assured resonant voice. At least, thought Iris, his voice wasn't half an octave higher.

"Course, I won't have to appear if you drop the charges." Now he took her arm, almost gently, pulling her close. Iris did not resist, could not resist. "And that, baby, is what we gotta talk about. Don't worry. I'm not gonna hit you. Just think about it."

Finding courage, Iris pulled back. Trembling she walked from the kitchen, through the dining room into the living room. Rodney followed and took a seat in the easy chair near the couch. Iris sat on the couch, fully aware that his attention was focused on her. What kind of justice system, Iris wondered, required a victim to post a cash bond to sign a warrant, but allowed the culprit to go free on nothing but his promise to appear in court? She was disgusted and nauseated. Apparently Rodney was waiting for her to give in. He held a drink in his hand.

"Well," Iris finally spoke. "I have no intention of dropping any charges. You might as well forget it." Uneasily she rose and headed upstairs, determined not to sleep another night on the couch. Let him do that. Half way up she heard his voice, low, with laughter in it. "Hey, baby. We'll see, we'll see." And then, after a moment of silence, "Sleep well, Iris." The tone was so sinister that Iris hardly slept at all. Late in the night, she mixed another drink, and then another, before sleep finally came.

22

For the remaining days before the court appearance, Rodney did nothing. Nor did Iris speak with him, except when necessary, in short terse words. But on the day Iris was due in court, he woke her early, shaking her gently.

"Iris. Iris, I got to talk to you."

She awoke frightened. He stood over her, looking down. Oh God she thought, here it comes. But Rodney sat on the bed, head in his hands.

"I need help. Oh...Iris, please. I know it. Maybe this is what I need." He did not touch her or move closer, though his shoulders were heaving. She was not sure he was faking it. "I love you, Iris. More than anything on earth. I will do anything you want. I'm sorry, believe me. Please forgive me."

Through breakfast Rodney vowed that he wanted the marriage to work. Iris, sure that he had some trick up his sleeve, listened with reluctance, but he was hitting home, and she knew it. Except for the lapses, the beatings, their marriage had provided hope, excitement, and fulfillment such as she had never expected. If something could be done to end the threat of his lapses, then maybe it was worth trying. Despite herself, fearing the loneliness that faced her, she agreed to give it a try. "But I'm not going to drop the charges. You need to know I'm serious about this. You need help, and this is the only way I know of to make sure you get it." To her surprise Rodney nodded agreement.

They drove in separately, despite Rodney's insistence that they go in his car. Iris did not want to feel beholden at this point. Rodney was there just ahead of her, reading the heavy docket, obviously disappointed by the many cases on the schedule. At least theirs was first, the big black letters spelling out the name Rodney Harris, scheduled for arraignment.

Moments later, the bailiff asked all to rise. Rodney knew the judge, named Butts. They had played some golf and occasionally socialized through town connections. The Prosecutor, Johnson, was also a familiar face. He had bought his home through Rodney's real estate firm. Rodney flashed them both a grin, with a slight wave. Iris, watching, wondered again at the wisdom of this. He had so many acquaintances.

Butts, surveying the courtroom, glanced at the papers before him. Ten or more years presiding over such arraignments had familiarized him with the rights of defendants and he could recite the litany from memory. When he had informed the defendants of these rights, he read aloud from the top folder. "People of the State of Michigan vs. Rodney Harris," he intoned, his voice echoing. Rodney, hearing his name and knowing all eyes were on him, shifted his weight slightly. Judge Butts gave no sign that he knew Rodney as he read the charge. "How do you plead to the charge?" he asked officiously.

"I plead guilty," Rodney said, in such a low voice that Judge Butts had to ask him to repeat the plea.

"Well, Mr. Harris," said the judge after a short pause. "Instead of sentencing you immediately, I'm going to refer you to the probation department for a pre-sentence investigation. Please see to it that you meet Mr. Ruft, the probation officer for this court, before you leave the courthouse. Sentencing will be in two weeks." With a rap from his gavel the judge proceeded to the next case.

Rodney, having briefly chatted with Ruft in the probation office, left the courthouse head down. Iris, stunned, ran down the step to catch up. She had seen the look on her husband's face as he stepped from Ruft's office, and his posture of resignation. She fell into stride beside him; waiting for the words she knew would come, hoping for them.

"Iris, I can't go through this again. Please, Iris, don't make me come in here again, like this. Mr. Ruft told me you can still drop the charges even though I pleaded guilty. If I get sentenced I'm ruined in this town, maybe in this business. I'm damned good at it. You know that. And we've been good together. Except for...y'know, those times, when I lost...control."

"I know," Iris said. "But, Rodney, I can't risk it again. Maybe you don't know what you're doing, when you beat me half to death, maybe that isn't really you. But I won't live with you if you don't do something about it. I mean that. I've got to go through with this. I don't know any other way." The car was parked a block away and, as they walked, Iris saw Betty Jean's large figure near the supermarket, watching. She would have to talk to Betty Jean, she needed to. She nodded to Betty Jean, acknowledging her. She would call later. For the moment, Rodney required her attention. It was vital.

"Iris. You've gotta believe, I've learned my lesson. It's up to you now. Please, agree to drop the charges. I'll get help, and we'll handle this together." Rodney stood next to his car, Iris intently studying his face. His eyes were clear and his face had sincerity written on every handsome feature. She wanted this. If only she could be sure.

"I'll do it, Rodney," she found herself saying. "But only under certain conditions. Only if you..."

"Don't you worry none," Rodney said, a huge smile lighting his face. "You tell me the conditions, I'll abide by 'em. Anything, Iris. Anything."

At the farm, Iris heard the phone as she left the garage, running to answer it. It was Mr. Hayward, offering a substitute teaching job for two weeks. Rodney came in as Iris was agreeing to take it on. He waited until she hung up, and then spoke softly, "That's good, Iris. It'll be good for you, for both of us."

Then he went out to the barn, saddled up the big chestnut mare and rode off across the fields. From the house, Iris saw him from time to time, making a circuit of every section of the land, wherever the horse could go, sometimes walking, often trotting, cantering across the level expanses. It had begun overcast, now the day was clear. A high cool autumn day. Already the grasses were tawny, the goldenrod past its peak, the ragweed and chicory, fleabane and aster in profuse bloom. Muted colors, almost pastel in this pause before the full burst of leaf-color, seemed to blend across the scape of gentle rolling land. Iris had opened the window to let in the cooling air, not bothered by the spores and pollens that filled the air—her particular and mild hay fever came in the spring. Crows called from the woods, and a flock of blackbirds descended to the changing maples and oaks. Rust-tinged leaves on lower branches bordered the still green lawn which they watered on these drier autumn days, and Iris's plantings of flowers, roses, mums, marigolds, geraniums, and sunflowers seemed somehow to catch the sky, brushing it with swaying tips. There would be deer in the pastures at dawn, and honking geese on high. Soon frost would rime the withering vegetable garden, ruining late tomatoes but perfecting the squash and pumpkins. Listening, as she watched, she also smelled the land. The air bore that fall aroma so indefinably and unmistakably of autumn. It tugged at her heart, and she stood at the window and cried. She had truly come to love this land, this place. Never in her youth had she taken time to properly see and hear and sense the natural world, and then there had been the busy years of city life, and its endless but sometimes bogus excitements. The time with Rodney—before he went off center—had been good. This land, this place, this life—if only she could be sure he would never again hurt her—had much to offer, and Iris, watching from the window, cooking a large dinner for both of them, knew that she did not want to lose it. She had to fight to keep it, keep him—that man now riding in distant fields, in and out of view—and somehow preserve the marriage that made it possible. When she saw him ride into the barnyard in the gloaming, leaning expertly to undo the big gate, walking the horse into the barn, she sighed. She would fight...she would live up to her vow, for better, for worse.

Rodney seemed genuinely changed. There seemed to be no anger in him, but not fire either. He sat for hours at the kitchen table drinking alone. Often he was there when Iris went to bed and there when she awoke. Three days running he was there when she returned from the school. Always he recited the same litany.

"Iris. I've learned my lesson. I know you mean business...you're correct. I had no right to cancel your chance to teach full-time, or...to hit you. But I can't go to jail. Please don't go through with this. My business is suffering enough. If I go to jail I'll be ruined. D'you really want that?"

And it was true. Sally called from his office regularly and wondered if

Rodney was coming in. From his answers on the phone Iris knew that Sally was trying to get him back to what he did best. Iris knew he'd missed three closings within two weeks. Clients were growing restless.

But Iris, tormented by her own confusion, did not know what to do next. She was determined not to let him escape without paying a price for his cruelty. Only then, she felt, would he know that he could never beat her again, never hurt and humiliate her and destroy that smidgen of love she felt for him. He deserves some jail time, she thought, not that she was vindictive, only fair. Yes, she still wanted him and needed him. She wanted him cured; she wanted him as he was early in their marriage, but without the uncertainty that loomed constantly. Try as she might Iris could not erase the memories of their first happy months. Also, try as she might she could not forgive him the terror and pain. If he sought help, if he had to suffer even half as much as she had, as proof of willingness to change, then...maybe. Iris was determined to make the marriage work with equal resolve to protect herself. She'd started to save money for a divorce if that was the final option. It angered her that any counsel, any judge, even Rodney, thought her weak. She was determined to give him one last chance to seek help.

Thus, on the scheduled day when the Judge was to pronounce sentence Iris agreed to drop the charges. Rodney had agreed to attend counseling sessions with her, and vowed to resume individual treatments. This convinced her that he was sincere. But, she had held firm. "It's not," she said, as they drove into town, "because you don't deserve legal punishment. It's because I think you've really learned a lesson, Rodney; I mean, you must know, now, that if you ever touch me again in anger I'll call the cops and never again will I drop the charges."

She remembered his relief when she first announced her decision. How he grasped her arm fondly, "You won't regret this Iris. We're gonna start over from here." Then Iris entered the prosecutor's office, alone.

Mr. Johnson, whom she had not met before, was lean and tall, with a loose-jointed angularity to every motion. He could scarcely disguise his disappointment at Iris's request.

"It is difficult," he explained, "to withdraw a plea of guilty prior to sentencing. It can be done of course, but...well, if the judge allows your husband to withdraw his guilty plea, then you could notify the Court of your decision to drop the charges. At that point, the Court would dismiss the case. Are you aware that by dropping the charges you forfeit the bond posted?"

Iris nodded and Mr. Johnson continued, "More important, Mrs. Harris, is that by dropping the charges you allow Mr. Harris to get away with committing a crime. If this case follows the usual pattern, he will almost surely beat you again, and there's nothing we can do about it." Iris could sense his growing disgust and wondered if he was right. "I've seen many cases like this," Johnson went on, "when domestic violence complaints are dismissed by the victim, only to have the same situation come up again and again. Maybe I shouldn't be concerned. You're the one he is beating. If you are willing to accept beatings, that's up to you."

Iris recoiled at the sudden harsh words. "How can you say that? I don't want..."

"As I said, Mrs. Harris," Mr. Johnson spoke with hard deliberation, "It is up to you not to me." He threw up his hands. "You might as well have a seat in the courtroom till your case is called."

Iris tried to more fully explain her plans, how she knew Rodney would now keep his promises, how they agreed to work together to cure him of any future violence, how he had promised to stop drinking, how she had every intention of divorcing him if he ever again beat her but Johnson cut her off with a gesture with his long hands, showing her out his door, and gesturing towards the courtroom. She had so wanted to explain how she still loved her husband, needed him, wanted him, how he had promised and how he had worked hard in recent days to make their marriage work, and how full of remorse he had been, how he had revealed his even greater need for her to help him. She also wanted to tell him that as soon as she had the means she would be free to file for divorce, at any time. That would be her ace in the hole.

While waiting for Iris, Rodney had reviewed the docket of cases for the morning, and when she appeared in the hallway he fell into step beside her, all ears as she explained what was happening. The previous case was handled quickly as Judge Butts accepted a young man's not guilty plea of possession of PCP, set a preliminary examination and appointed counsel. Then the Judge called, "People of the State of Michigan vs. Rodney Harris." Pausing to glance at Rodney and nodding to Iris, he continued. "Do you have anything to say, Mr. Harris, prior to sentencing?"

"Your Honor, if I may," Johnson interrupted, "This morning I was approached by the victim and complainant in this matter, Mrs. Rodney Harris. She indicated to me that it was her desire to drop the charges pending before this Court." To Iris it seemed that the legal jargon rang hollow from the walls. Would the Judge want to make trouble about this? Surely he would agree.

"Is that correct?" Butts asked, gazing quizzically at Iris.

"Yes," said Iris in a small voice, barely audible.

"Well, I have a few comments. It is not the custom of this Court to readily grant motions to withdraw guilty pleas. In this case, however, since the victim-complainant desires to drop the charges," and here Judge Butts paused and looked hard at Iris as if to give her a last chance to reconsider, "the Court sees no reason why the motion to withdraw the guilty plea should not be granted. If the injured party does not wish to pursue the legal remedy available for this crime, and this is the type of crime in which the victim is the one who suffers, not society, the Court is not going to interfere in the domestic relations between the parties. It is my understanding, Mrs. Harris, that you posted bond to cover court costs in this matter. Is that correct?"

"Yes."

"The Court is going to forfeit the bond. Mrs. Harris, you cannot file these charges and get Mr. Harris into court and then just drop your complaint. The Court is going to advise the examining Magistrate to scrutinize very closely any further complaints by you. The system, Mrs. Harris, is here for your protection and assistance, but this Court is not going to act as a referee for arguments within your house. Keep that in mind in the future."

"I will, Your Honor," said Iris, sheepishly.

"Thank you, Your Honor," said Rodney, smiling broadly, his confidence restored.

"I hope you two live happily ever after," said the Judge, with a faint note of irony.

Or, thought Iris, did she just imagine it?

"We will, Your Honor," Rodney intoned in his normal deep voice. "Thank you, Your Honor."

23

To Iris the week seemed endless. Even after Rodney dutifully scheduled appointments with a marriage counselor in Grand Rapids, she dared to ask the obvious question.

"Why not in Ionia, there are two good ones right here?"

Rodney replied dully, "I don't want to get counseling in Ionia because it will affect my business image." Iris thought that was idiotic, given the rumors that already floated. "Hell Iris, you stick to that part time teaching. It will keep you busy, and I'll bring in the real money." She could not express her deeper worries. Knowing that the law recognized nothing of what she had suffered; the gap between dreaming of what should be and what could be was huge. She remembered her mother saying 'the thought is mother to the deed'. But that was not for her. So far the resort to the law had failed her.

Though she dutifully had sex with him, falling back on plays of affection that still brought an illusion of closeness, they seldom spoke. Even Duke felt the tension, curling up in corners to avoid the negative vibes. Iris knew that she had to confront Rodney and somehow get him to talk about their problems before another escalation, so she decided to cook a fine dinner. That might break the impasse. She started fixing a steak, with baked potatoes and green beans, moving to the cavernous oven where she liked to bake bread.

The odor of alcohol preceded him. Though he had apparently abstained for several days, Iris was not surprised when he grabbed another fifth from the cupboard, turning his bloodshot eyes on her.

"What the fuck is that you're wearing?" Iris backed up near the stove, but he hit her before she could answer, knocking her against the hot stove, then kicking her repeatedly as she fell to the floor, Duke scrambling to get out of the way. "Fuck you bitch. This will learn you not to wear Levis around me. Don't you ever learn?"

Then he lit into her with the riding crop. When he was finished, he straddled her, checking to see if she was conscious. "You goddamn whore. After all I done for you," Through her pain Iris understood enough not to move. She kept her eyes shut, feigning unconsciousness, but the words hurt almost as much. "You are gettin' what you deserve. Never, never, ever call the law again. You won't live through it the next time."

Rodney turned to the stove, flapped the sizzling steak onto a plate, and with the fresh bottle of bourbon in hand, stalked into the living room.

Pain ruled, pain was proof that she still breathed. Every pulse brought sharp but conscious agony. The noises seemed to make no sense at first, but soon she recognized the high yipping of a dog in pain. He was beating Duke. She struggled into a chair, the pain radiating from her back to her arms and legs. She knew where she was and who she was, and sensed what was happening. The bastard was taking out his hate on Duke. Damn him forever to hell! Iris hardly moved for hours, worried sick about Duke and terrified that if he heard her moving about he would go after her again. Eventually she pulled herself to her feet and, staggering towards the living room, hanging onto both sides of the door frame, she saw that Rodney was passed out on the couch, oblivious to Johnny Carson's familiar image and wit.

Iris pulled herself upstairs, and, afraid to look at herself in the bathroom mirror, gingerly sat on the bowl, surprised to find that everything worked. She removed the two hundred dollars from her lingerie drawer, and, finding strength returning to her limbs, softly descended and tip toed past her husband, his hateful face looking childish in soporific slumber, and made her way to the VW. When it started she sighed with relief. At least this time he had not disabled the car.

The night was clear as Iris drove along M-21 into Ionia. She found it difficult to shift the normally easy gears because of stabbing pain in her shoulders. It was nearly one in the morning. when she pulled into Betty Jean's drive. Her friend came sleepy to the door, eyes widening in shock at the apparition before her, Iris's face greenish blue-black and swollen. Crying softly, she instantly pulled Iris inside.

"Hank is gone off fishing with a buddy up north," Betty Jean explained. "so we have the place to ourselves. I hope you don't mind, with what you been through, but I could use a drink." She grabbed a bottle of wine, and they sat and talked, often crying, until dawn, half expecting Rodney to come barreling through the door at any moment. Betty without a moment of doubt agreed to loan Iris enough money to find a small apartment and to retain a lawyer. Two days later she rented a flat on Union Street near the High School. To her amazement she had not seen or heard from Rodney. Betty, with good local connections, scheduled an appointment with a well-regarded attorney, Harry Pool, for Friday.

24

Iris instantly liked Harry Pool whose name was stenciled on the outer glass door of his woodsy office. Gently he led her to a soft chair, then he sat behind his desk, peering out from behind thick, gold rimmed glasses. His bright blue eyes moved constantly, and his smile seemed to break his narrow face into parts. Pool directed Iris to start from the beginning, making notes as she told her tale. He questioned her closely several times, but Iris held nothing back, pouring out her soul, thinking that this kindly man might help her. Presently Pool came to the front side of the desk, resting his rump on its edge so that he stood directly before Iris. She felt his presence as a comfort.

"You did right, Mrs. Harris, to come to me. Our first order of business is to get the judge to sign a temporary restraining order, enjoining Mr. Harris from beating, wounding, injuring, or harassing you in any fashion." Pool paused, thinking of the cases he'd covered since his graduation from the University of Michigan Law School, class of 1965. He had emerged as a skillful and resourceful attorney, specializing in domestic relations law, and his reputation now extended far beyond the small town where he'd been raised, and to which he had returned after a successful start in Lansing. He was busy and expensive but he had already told Iris that he would charge her his rock bottom fee.

"I want you to file a complaint with the police. That comes first Iris, even if you have done so before." Pool tentatively touched her hand, where the bruises were less visible, though he could see that Iris had tried to cover her wrists and arms. He guessed he'd seen worse, far worse, but from what Iris had told him so far, she was almost certainly at risk.

"Michigan has adopted a no fault divorce law," Pool continued, "so we no longer need to allege any reason for the divorce aside from the fact that the marital relationship has been destroyed. Your complaint on file with the police would be a strong tool in reaching a property settlement, and in obtaining a temporary restraining order." Pool waited, watching Iris's reaction. He would get some satisfaction in helping this battered woman (showing all the familiar symptoms) in sticking it to the brutal s.o.b. who got away with so much only because the law on such matters was absurdly weak. Furthermore, every successful case on the record would help build data in support of stiffer penalties for abuse, and in support of better means for protection and redress on the part of the victim. He felt no need to say all this to Iris, but he continued with hardly a breath, "I know that at this moment you are only interested in getting your freedom. But I happen to believe, Iris, that you are also entitled to monetary compensation, and I believe we can act together to obtain such compensation. If you are adamant about refusing to press charges, at the least you must let my secretary take a few photos, as evidence." When that business was taken care of, as he scanned the photos, Pool picked up his chain of thought.

"Mrs. Harris I believe your life is threatened." He held up his hand at her protest, "I've represented many women in divorces who've been victims of domestic violence. Some—I dare say too many—come in here to retain my services, and they sign the complaint for divorce, and then almost immediately claim they are reconciled with the husband. Many return to the husband and face continued abuse. This could happen to you, Mrs. Harris, if you don't follow through with the proceedings. I'm not saying so because I want your fee, but because of my experience in such cases." Pool's manner was reassuring, confident, and intimate. "Let me warn you again, that once he knows what you have put into place, he is likely to lash out in anger. This might not come at once, but according to your own account, the pattern is there. It's vital," Pool stood up to emphasis his words, "that on the first occasion he violates the restraining order, that you contact me. At once. Do you fully understand? We cannot allow him to violate a court order. If he gets away with it again, well, it might only reinforce his brutal behavior."

As Iris signed the complaint Pool truly hoped she had the will and support to follow it up. He'd seen it often, a woman abused but deeply dependent, and still claiming to be "in love" and emotionally linked, needful of the very man who repeatedly abused her. Iris seemed rational and self-aware, well educated, a teacher, and mature in years. Maybe this one would work. What Pool knew from experience was that these things did not follow predictable patterns of income or social class. He recalled one affluent woman from a city half way across the state who had come to him bruised and defeated; recommended by a colleague who knew his reputation, and this rather stuffy woman had demanded confidentiality (hardly necessary), had demanded that the divorce be arranged quietly, secretly, backed up by the appropriate restraining order to protect her, and then, characteristically, she had dropped everything. The husband, Pool had discovered, was a prominent physician.

"This is my home phone number; you can call it if the office is closed." Pool shook Iris's hand gently, something she noticed with a soft smile.

Outside, Iris looked at the sky with wonder. For the first time in days she allowed herself to drink in the sensations of a lovely fall day. The smell of burning leaves, the darkening sky already sparkling with stars, the orange glow of a full harvest moon rising above the trees. Life held hope again. Though it hurt to walk, she set off to her apartment at a steady pace. She had taken positive steps to change her life.

25

By mid-November Iris had been in the flat for more than a week without a word from Rodney. She knew his business was picking up, and somehow this both relieved and bothered her.

On Sunday she rose early to attend the 7:00 o'clock Mass. Of course she knew, having married outside the Church to a man twice divorced, that she could not receive communion, or any of the sacraments, but attendance provided solace. As she turned her little beetle into the avenue leading to the Church, she spotted the Thunderbird parked down the street. It was still dark and the car's lights were on. She drove on, but as she turned into the parking lot, Rodney slowly cruised on past. Iris stayed alone in her pew, far off to one side, long after the Mass was over. "Please God, let him be gone. Holy Mother of God please protect me." She was aware of the Priest, since she stayed on well after the pews emptied, and the Priest had returned through the central aisle nodding to her, a kindly face. There were no secrets in a small town, but she wondered how much the Priest knew. She was wondering if she should beg his support, if not a real confession, but as she walked through the portals, there Rodney was, parked in full view of the Church. Iris paced to her car and drove towards her flat, the Thunderbird tooling along behind. She checked from the window once inside, and there it was, parked not two hundred feet away, his large frame visible. This had to be illegal.

Of course it being Sunday Pool was not in his office, though she tried, and the more she thought about it, she did not want to call the Sheriff's office. She felt that both deputies who had answered her calls were, well, if not hostile, far too friendly with Rodney.

When she saw the Thunderbird parked only a few feet further away the next morning, Iris called Pool, disappointed to find that he was in Flint for a trial and would not be back for several days. When Pool's secretary suggested another of Pool's partners, Iris left a furious message, "You tell Mr. Pool that Rodney Harris is stalking me. You promise to tell him?"

She knew this was not helpful, to get distraught and angry so that others might wonder if she was at fault. For three days the pattern continued, and Iris cursed herself for not calling the police. She found herself wondering; how did he eat, or go to the bathroom, and she recalled his uncanny ability to go without sleep, or to sleep lightly even when drinking, to somehow ignore the normal urgencies of the body. But three days? It was ridiculous. Impossible. But there he was day after day, night after night.

Then on the fourth night the phone rang and she answered, nothing but silence on the other end. How could he have obtained an unlisted number so fast? Now sleep came hard, with what her long dead first husband had called waking dreams. Rodney kept calling and not speaking, until she grew so exasperated that she broke down and shouted into the phone, "I know it's you, you bastard Rodney. What do you want? Answer me!" She began to sob, gradually realizing that she was the one speaking, as he sat silent, and heard her angry voice.

Teaching was difficult. Iris could hardly do the homework, far more than students imagined, as if she could just stand up there and teach vital lessons. On Friday, knowing his car would be there and that the silent phone calls would come, she decided to confront him directly. Sure, she knew that if she made deliberate contact with him, that if he avoided doing so in public with her, that her case would be weak. Nonetheless, she waited until most of the students and staff had gone home, preferring that no one she knew would witness what she planned. She walked directly past her VW, up to the Thunderbird parked behind it. Rodney waved with a huge smile and pulled his car out and pulled away.

"You son-of-a-bitch," she screamed. "Come back here." A few lingering students and the janitor paused to stare. Iris realized as she stood in the parking lot screaming at her husband, that she, not he, appeared to be crazy. Head down, humiliated and in tears, she ran to her car and followed him very close until he turned into the drive leading to his office. She knew how he would make it look but she could not stop herself, charging directly into his office behind him.

"Where'd the bastard go?" Iris screamed, heading towards the door to Rodney's private cubicle. Sally stepped out and tried to block her, but she pushed by with a curse, into his inner sanctum, filled with animal taxidermy, and began with words she had rehearsed for days.

"I need to talk with you," she shouted, even more furious as he produced a huge grin, "Why can't you leave me alone? Why are you harassing me, day and night? You know I have the law on my side. Pool drew up the papers. If you even call me once on the phone you break the rules." She realized that Sally hovering at the door behind her would not be a sympathetic witness, but Iris could not help herself, her voice rising to a pitch of hysteria. "I am going straight to the police. They will arrest you immediately."

"Sit down Iris," Rodney gestured to a chair, taking his own seat behind the desk, reaching for the inevitable bottle, pouring a drink, then pouring another for her, he held it out.

"Here," he said without a sign of strain, his voice mellow. "Let's discuss this rationally, like adults."

"Adults?" Iris screamed, infuriated all the more by the insult, her face contorted, "You don't know what an adult is, you fucking liar!" She yanked the glass from his hand and threw it at him. Quick as a cat Rodney moved sideways, but some of the bourbon splashed across his pants. He advanced careful on her, the stains visible on his crotch, but Iris shrank away as he reached the door.

"Sally, come in here," Sally, already at the door, stepped in and turned with outstretched arms towards Iris. "Go ahead Sally," Rodney ordered, "we have to remove her, she's totally lost it. She's out of control drunk." Sally, tentatively taking Iris by one arm, began to pull her gently out of the cubicle, but Iris pulled back, "Get your dirty hands off me you whore!"

"Iris," Rodney said in the maddeningly precise tone he used when the cops were around, "I'm only asking you to leave my place of business. By coming in here you are in jeopardy. This is unacceptable invasion of privacy, and you are doing this with a witness who will back me up. If you don't leave quietly, now, I'll have Sally call the police."

"No. Not till you answer me, you bastard." Iris backed away, trying to put the desk between her and them. "I'm the one who should be calling the cops." Knowing she was losing it, making things far worse, Iris had the uncanny sensation of watching herself from afar, but she got her hands on a stack of papers on the desk, scattering them. Rodney watched with a sardonic grin, shaking his head. Sally ran into the front office, returning in a moment, "They're on the way, promised to come straight here."

She swept everything on the desk onto the floor, including his drink, the rich smell of bourbon filled the room. Rodney merely watched with an ironic grin, shaking his head, almost laughing. Sally looked dismayed at the mess, stooped to begin cleaning it up, but Rodney gestured, "Go to the front door, and just bring them back here. Let them see for themselves."

In the patrol car Fitzgerald spoke first, "I hate this shit...you never know with these domestic brawls. One of these days, with these two, anything could happen," he tapped his sidearm pointedly. Barnett nodded, feeling hollow in the pit of his stomach. Not that the two of them were in mortal danger, but simply that he hated every minute of it.

At Harris's office the deputies noted two cars, the wife's VW and the husband's flashy big Thunderbird. Fitzgerald led the way inside where Rodney waited, opening the door and waving them inside as if they were guest to a dinner party. "I don't know what the hell is eating her, ah Deputy Fitzgerald, if I got your name right." He escorted both officers through the larger front office to the more private inner one where Iris stood quivering with outrage, as if at bay. "I asked her to leave, officers, but she refuses. I don't want to touch her, since they have injunctions out against any contact. But Sally here can't remove her, so we had to call you. I want to be clear that I am not asking you to arrest her. But she has to go. Apparently she needs help."

Barnett noticed how smooth Harris spoke, how cool he seemed. He came around to the fore while Fitz moved to the side, and spoke firmly but quietly in the assured tone of a veteran cop, "Good afternoon Mrs. Harris," he caught her eye, though she looked away, her expression of outrage matching her high color. The room reeked of alcohol and soaked papers were scattered everywhere. "Mr. Harris has asked you to leave, so you'd better do so." Unspoken was the threat to remove her by force. Iris moved back until she stood directly under the head of a bull elk. Her eyes were wild, "If you don't come quietly Mrs. Harris," Fitz spoke firmly, "we'll be forced to arrest you for trespassing." Barnett continued with a softer tone, in the way a team of two cops learn from long experience, "Look, Mrs. Harris, if you're having difficulties with your divorce, surely that can be settled by your attorney," he gestured her towards him, "C'mon now."

Iris laughed, "Sure. You come running the instant he calls, but you ignore all my pleas for help. How much is this bastard paying you? Why are you on his side all the time? It's just like a man to side with a man."

"Please Mrs. Harris, come with me," Barnett said, moving to usher her out, but Iris grabbed a brass paperweight in the shape of an eagle and held it cocked in her hand. Fitz circled to the other side. Furious but not wanting to be manhandled, Iris lay the paperweight down. She held her head down as she shuffled out the door. Behind her Barnett slipped on the mess, almost falling.

"Don't worry officer. I'll clean this up," said Rodney. "Thanks for your quick response. There's no telling what she'd have done next if you hadn't got here right quick. She gets like this every once in a while. I love the lady, but believe me, she needs help."

Barnett, as they escorted Iris to her car, resisted the impulse to cuss Rodney out, or to turn back and smack him in the middle of his liar's face.

In the patrol car Fitz was less sure who was at fault. "Y'know...it isn't cut and dried. I don't know which is worse. I mean she seems pretty goddamn bitchy. Every time we get a call she's hysterical, swearing like a drill sergeant, full of bile. If my wife acted like that...whoo-eee. Y'know what I mean?" He shook his hands as if freeing them of something. "Those two deserve each other, if you ask me."

Barnett kept his own counsel.

26

Well into the evening in her lonely flat Iris turned to drink. First she poured a glass of Sherry, the remainder of the Amontillado she had planned to share with Betty Jean. When that disappeared she turned to a bottle of cheap California Chablis. She tried the TV and flicked it off in disgust, hating the fake laugh-tracks of a sitcom. She dug out a liter of Canadian, almost full, and put it within reach. Iris never believed that she had a high tolerance for alcohol, though with Rodney always happy to encourage her, she had turned to the solace of that elusive high of just one more. She was aware, especially after long talks with Betty Jean, that her intake when in Rodney's presence far exceeded the normal range of social drinking. Since the first beating, however, she more often welcomed the mellow release of a second or third wine, or a sip of bourbon, always in abundant supply with Rodney around. Several drinks, carefully spaced through an evening brought a kind of numbing comfort. A few times she had drunk herself into bed with the room wheeling about her, only to regret it the next morning, especially if it was a school day.

It was late when the phone rang. It stopped before she could reach it. A few minutes later it rang again and she let it ring, certain that it was him but holding to her vow. Time passed and she was pouring a glass full of Canadian when without thought she dialed the farm.

He answered at once. "Well, it's you Iris. I knew you would call back. I'm listening Iris."

His voice was comforting, its deep timbre resonating in her ear like the bass of a church organ. She needed this, wanted this, craved his arms, his company. She was lonely, hurt, angry, needful. He was her husband still. "I...I'm not sure I believe you can change," she said, "How can you make me believe that you're serious, that all you want is to discuss the settlement?"

"Iris, all I am asking is to see you on equal terms. I could come there, if you would let me in, but it's better if you come here, where you belong." He allowed himself a deep chuckle, "You know, I was getting ready for bed, and I was sitting here in my skivvies thinking of you."

He'd have her back in his bed in no time. His pretty Iris, his wife, and he would have all the control he ever wanted, all he ever needed. His voice thickened, "Iris, if you feel better I'll come right there. You don't have to make a move. Is that okay with you?"

"I don't know. I guess so."

"You just sit tight. I'll be there in a jiffy."

Iris hustled to tidy herself and clean up the little flat. She ran a comb through her hair, brushed and gargled, shaking her head to clear the cobwebs.

When he came in the door she stood silent, trying to control a smile. He looked around quickly taking in what there was to see in the tiny apartment, and, characteristically asserting himself he took a seat at the formica table.

"Now that's better. I brought us a drink, in case you want one," he pulled a bottle of Jim Beam from his jacket and plopped it down, stretching his arms out. "Ya know Iris, it's fun to see where you live, nice place you got here."

"I'm not sure..." Iris murmured, still slightly woozy and not ready for a drink. She put up a hand to deny the bottle, but she seemed to have no control over her movements and found herself sitting across from him. Rodney looked wonderful, freshly shaven, his face shining in the stark light of the single overhead bulb.

"You've done a fine job decorating this," he said, sweeping his big arms around, indicating the cheap prints on the walls; a Van Gogh sunflower, a larger Constable landscape, both free from the bank when she opened her new account, and a circus poster on the door to the bathroom. He was lying, but it was typical of him, the same old charm.

She did not correct him, since she liked the cozy atmosphere of her tiny flat. "Well, thank you Rodney, I guess," she said.

"The ol' house sure misses your woman's touch," he continued, "have you got a glass for this?" She fetched a plastic tumbler, and he held up two fingers, so she put down another one.

"Now Rodney," she replied, not lurching to her feet when he put his hand over hers.

"I sure as hell know I ain't the only lonely one, Iris. I want you back almost as bad as you want me back. I think about you day and night," he chuckled, since it was hardly a stretch. He had followed her day and night. Iris could hardly believe his brass.

"I think about the way you kiss when we go to bed," he said, "and how you make love to me, and how you..."

"No. Stop. Rodney, I'm sorry. We agreed to meet only to talk about the divorce, and the settlement. That's all." Her hand found the tumbler and she tipped it up, and instantly felt the effect.

"Right, which is why I'm here. This, just between us, that's the way to handle these things. To hell with them lawyers."

Iris shook her head, but in spite of herself she was pulled towards him. He was friendly and fun, and she did miss him and his large knowing hands.

She moved to the counter top where she had prepared cold cuts for them, trying to avoid looking at him, but he moved easily up behind her and stood close. "Rodney! No..." she protested meekly.

He laughed, reaching around her with both arms. "D'you miss this even half as much?" he whispered, his breath on her neck. Iris was afraid to answer. The truth was, despite her anger, hurt, and fear, she did miss his homey presence, his strong body, his knowing hands, and the familiar sensation of his body close against her from behind. She dared not think. He was too close. Then, as if he knew her mind, he allowed his body to move closer, and she felt him pressing into her soft behind, his member rising. Oh...yes, she wanted that, she wanted him.

With a shake of her head, slightly reeling, Iris pulled away and turned to face him. Still silent, only able to mouth a "No", she shook her head, her hair sweeping from side to side. Her mouth came open to tell him off, to deny what he wanted, and what she wanted. His lips came firm and open to hers, and forced her mouth further open, and his tongue went to work, and she could not stop hers from probing too. Her breath came faster, and without willing it she allowed her arms to slide away from where she had been pressing against his chest. Her pelvis was moving now in synch with him. His voice in her ear whispered, and she groaned, and when he slid down onto his knees, slipping her pants down and knowing where and what to touch she came almost instantly and began to cry.

When he picked her up from the kitchen floor and carried her to her bed, with barely enough room on it for both, she was his.

27

Less than a week later Iris considered her options. They were few and she knew it. True she had gone back to work, and had only communicated with him by phone after he had left her apartment the morning after their stolen tryst. Despite the warm kitchen and a free Saturday ahead, her prospects seemed bad. She could continue to pursue the divorce; that seemed the obvious course. But the courts, given the police record Rodney had manipulated to his advantage and to make her look unstable, would most likely not be able or willing to help her.

Rodney had staged enough acts in the presence of witnesses, including two police deputies and several officers of the court, to make Iris appear as the culprit in any court where testimony is required by oath. She had been foolish. Betty Jean was right; Iris had behaved like the boy who cried wolf once too often. The wolf was devouring her. She could not remember all the times she had called the cops for help and found that they could not follow through. Was that her fault? Bitterly, she recalled a talk with Betty Jean, arguing that the whole law enforcement system was stacked against her. Rodney would win as usual.

Iris considered calling Harry Pool, probably the only man who could help. Even though she included allegations of abuse against Rodney, her divorce case would probably leave her destitute. Pool was a tough pro and would do what she asked, though she still owed him about half his already low fee. He might already be back in town, so she quickly found his card, the office number stenciled on it and his home phone scribbled on the back, and stepped to the phone to call him when it rang.

"Hi honey, it's me," Rodney boomed, his voice full of robust cheer. "Fine morning, ain't it. I don't know if you knew I was out of town, up north checking out deals in Kalkaska. I just called to tell you that I got to be at my office for a few hours, so if you want to reach me...you can call me there. Hey, maybe it's better if I just drop by. Just to see you would make my day."

Iris was tongue tied, "I...I have thought about this. I can't see you here, not now, not in broad daylight. Rodney, wait. Listen." She spoke deliberately, having rehearsed what she wanted to say, "I thought we agreed, I mean I thought you knew that I will proceed..."

"Proceed, you mean with the divorce?"

"Yes. I am calling Pool about that."

"What? Iris, wait a minute. You gotta understand. I am setting things up to prove to you that I love you, and to make sure you are taken care of. I have a lawyer working on a property settlement. All we need to do is talk about it."

"Well, I guess we could meet at Pools office. If you want to talk about a divorce settlement, that is the place to do it." Iris could hardly believe her brass, expecting an explosion.

"That's fine with me," he actually chuckled. "I will have my guy contact

Pool. But hang on there a minute Iris, would you consent to me taking you out to dinner tonight? No harm in that."

"I guess so," she said, not thinking there was danger in it.

Iris pondered all this with mixed emotions. Rodney was assuming she would eventually return to him. That was a scary prospect, since she of all people understood the risk. Then again there was the loneliness of her despair, the lack of money, partnership, affection, and comfort. The latter had hit her with terrible force; living in the tiny apartment with no one to talk to for days on end brought home with terrible clarity the fear of being alone. Her time with Rodney (she shuddered, repressing the bad parts) had made the previous years alone seem empty. She let her mind range back, forcing herself to think with honesty and logic. Long ago she had dreamed of children. She and Jim talked about it, and for a time he was eager too, but with months of trying without success, and without telling Jim, she arranged a complete physical. The news was bad. She would never conceive. She had been young, so she considered adoption, but by this time the marriage with Jim was on the ropes. After the divorce, and his untimely death in Vietnam, she felt some relief. At least she did not have a fatherless child. But, she remembered how she had longed for that un-conceived baby who might have been created by that clear adolescent love, a child who might now be in college, or perhaps a mother or father.

She caught herself. That could never be. It was far too late. Children would never be part of her life. Rodney had grown children by at least one previous marriage, though he apparently never saw them or voiced the slightest interest. He'd asked her why she had none, and had seemed relieved by her cryptic reply, "I can't and never will be able to have any." She recalled a comment Rodney made in his cocky manner in the early weeks of their marriage, "It's just us two, Iris, and nobody else," as if that confirmed something. And, it was true. Friendly enough with many, happy to entertain large groups, he had never invited a single couple to dinner, or even a small party of six or so. He had no close friends in the normal sense, and had done all he could to keep Iris from having any. In effect they had remained a couple, that and nothing more.

In her confusion Iris did not push her thoughts with vigor. Like her mother she tended to drift on emotion, falling back on Old Testament admonitions about the proper duties of a wife to a husband. She remembered her mother quoting one of St. Paul's epistles that required of women a dutiful submission.

She gazed outside as the snow vanished in the warming sun, thinking it was warm enough for shirt sleeves. However, standing in the doorway, she put her arms around herself and shivered. The pale northern light was low and slanted, and though the sky was clear, the sun did not bring warmth, though the temperature was in the high fifties. A young couple walked by, the father carrying a child in one of those new back pack contraptions, the two youngsters leaning their heads together, whispering and laughing. The young mother looked back at Iris. She had not seen them before, but the girl's glance, though not hostile, carried recognition. Obviously they knew of her, or had heard. Flooded with gloom she stepped back inside.

Tears came easily, but brought no relief. What have I done to my life? Why has this happened to me? Iris looked at the cupboard where she kept her liquor. She moved a step forward and then back, holding her head. There was no physical pain now, but pain of another sort. Something in the chill beneath the unseasonable warmth, the small distant sun, repelled her. She had been to the tropics only a couple of times, on brief vacations, to sun in the Caribbean. She actually knew little of those climes, except for that sensation the amazing heat of the sun provided. Now she craved the sultry comfort of a tropical beach, the lukewarm sea, a wade in tepid waters where waves gently broke on white sand beaches under an equatorial moon. She stemmed her tears, sniffling and putting the kitchen in order. The day loomed empty. She could hardly wait to see him.

28

They met for dinner in a busy bar restaurant in Ionia where a waiter, who obviously knew Rodney, showed them to a booth in a more elaborate ante-room. She did most of the talking as the dinner arrived, baked ham with greens for him and chicken with dumplings for her, and for an hour or so Iris thought it was the best and most candid talk they had had since the marriage. Eventually he made the concession she expected, since she knew he would do all he could to keep her in his orbit. She figured—though Betty

Jean was scornful when she broached the idea—that she could go ahead with the divorce, while at the same time, in order to get even half of what she deserved of his considerable assets in some kind of payment plan, she might be forced to see him from time to time.

"Rodney, aside from the settlement which I'm sure Pool will agree with, I need more than your word, I want it in writing, somehow, that you'll be decent with me, I mean even if we have a drink or two, that you won't go off into another rage and beat me up again?" There, she'd said it.

Rodney leaned across the booth and took her hands in his own big paws. "I love you Iris, That won't change. You trust me enough to go through all this stuff about a settlement, and I am cooperating all the way. But I sure don't plan on saying goodbye."

"I still love you Rodney," she said, too late to stop. "But let's face it, love isn't enough. You must give me time enough so that I know you will let me live my own life, too. I know how you value your independence, well it's the same for me. I will live my life from now on without anyone telling me what to wear, where to travel, which friends to have, all of that. I mean it. I admit I want your friendship, but it's like my teaching, I know full well what you have to offer, but, well, at the school I have a life and a career and nothing you can do will change that."

"Sure. Jeezus Iris, did I ever say anything different," he lied.

"I am not some possession of yours, like your horses or your dog, that you can do with as you like," she sniffled, taking out a hanky.

He nodded, his hand on hers, "Will you come to visit, if only to see Duke and the animals?"

She knew he was dangling the bait. She'd worried about Duke, only learning later that Rodney had not mistreated him. Or so he said. "Duke is always finding new animal paths, and leads me to the deer scat and such," Rodney added. "I don't know if you heard about it, but them deer come around more now into this area than I ever saw. Used to be mostly up north past Clare, now they got more browsing down our way, so I see them out there, and figure the state will allow us a hunting season on them. And you should see the geese hanging around the pond."

"I'd like that, if...if you agree that I only stay for dinner. I'd be glad to cook one on the big range."

"Now you're talking." Rodney grinned happily. "Iris, while I got you with me let me show you something..." He reached in and pulled legal papers from his inside breast pocket. "I am jumping the gun to show these, but Pool and my lawyer won't care, since what's in here is my doing."

Iris looked through the papers quickly. She knew he planned to be generous in the settlement, but she could hardly believe what she read. The sum and substance seemed to be that once proceedings were over, she was entitled to half of Rodney's property, both personal and business. There were no figures listed, just the percent. She would demand that Pool read every paragraph. She tried not to reveal it, but she was delighted. She simply could not believe that Rodney was so devious that he would agree to all this, and then proceed to abuse and beat her. That would totally undermine every word, every sentiment, every promise, every written word on the subject, and he might easily lose it all.

Iris wanted a life with someone, and there was no one else but Rodney out there, to share those simple and obvious things, like the wildlife, the woodlots and fields, the pond and the geese now sheltering on it.

"I'll need time to think this over." She handed the papers back.

"You got all the time you need. All the time in the world," said Rodney. "Now seriously Iris, can't you just drive out tomorrow? It's a Sunday after all, and I will not go in for work, so we can stroll the acres, and I can crank the old range up and I'll find a good steak and you can cook whatever goes best with it, for both of us."

It was on.

Church the next morning was busy, its isles full for early Mass, and Iris found the far corner of a rear pew. She prayed earnestly, hoping for guidance. No answer came, at least not via the homily, or the familiar verses that the Priest favored from the Old Testament. Was she being punished? No. Iris could not believe that her sins were all that awful. She was fallen from the Church, and without access to the Sacraments, but she was vaguely optimistic about the kindly Priest, Father Kowalski. Perhaps he could help. If not, what was a Priest for? After the Mass she thought of speaking with him about her dilemma, not asking for a confession but merely to tell her side of the story (about which he surely had heard mostly lies). But she did not.

She had Pool on her side, and Rodney's signature was on the forms of the property settlement. She had leverage. Feeling far better after the rituals of the Church, and her own determination to clear herself and keep Rodney content with the hope that she might return, Iris went home to the empty flat.

Two days later she got a message of a call from Pool via the school intercom. "Call for Mrs. Harris." She escaped a clatch of teachers in the lounge and picked up on the open phone in the central office.

"Iris, Harry Pool here. Sorry I missed you, but business is business. For starters I am not displeased about this document you signed in the presence of my secretary yesterday. D'you realize Iris that according to the terms of this agreement, we've got far more than we requested in the complaint for divorce? Normally, had I known you were going to sign anything without consulting me first, I would have objected. I don't know exactly how you managed to get Mr. Harris on board, but you, well, you've achieved more than I thought possible, with your husband. Congratulations. How on earth did you manage to convince him to sign?"

Iris hesitated, knowing Pool would not like what she had to say. Pool would not approve of the fact that she had spent the previous evening with Rodney at the farm. She remembered how Duke greeted her happily, and how welcome were the warm confines of the farm house, made more appealing by the large fire Rodney had built in the dining room hearth, and the comfort of his familiar embrace. She was alone in the school office, so she spoke freely.

"I've decided to return to my husband, Mr. Pool."

A long silence on the other end was broken by a single word, "Why?"

"Look, Mr. Pool I've spent some time with him, and I truly think he has changed. He is reasonable about us working together to make it work, and I believe him. If I am not happy with our reconciliation, and if he has not continued the counseling, well I still have you and other friends to help us make it through this. And, Mr. Pool, we both wondered if it might be possible to adjourn the hearing on the divorce until after the first of the year."

Pool broke another long silence, "Mrs. Harris. You'll recall that at our first conference I warned you that you would be exposed to extreme pressure by Mr. Harris to get you to return. I anticipated that, and frankly given what has happened before, I am hardly shocked. My experience in these matters is considerable, but I admit that this ploy of his takes all. It is a clever, cunning, and unforeseen maneuver. He has managed to undermine both your good will and, frankly, to virtually place you under his control via your need for financial security." Iris, hearing the repressed anger in Pool's voice, waited, not wanting to argue. "If you persist in this nonsense, I will ask the court to adjourn the matter. This goes against all my training and against what I know of the parties involved."

"I want you to proceed with the...the adjournment," her voice small but firm.

"Okay. I see no difficulty in that since obviously Mr. Harris will consent to the adjournment, you two being...ah...reconciled." Pool sighed loudly, and continued, "Mrs. Harris, I feel it is my obligation to note that what I am saying now is being recorded on a Dictaphone. Once again I advise you that I continue to believe that you are in serious danger. Despite any verbal agreement you may have made with Mr. Harris, any promises about filing this agreement and so on, well if things go bad again you will face a situation far worse. From your own testimony, which I have on record, you already know that Rodney Harris is a dangerous and unstable man. You know this as well as I do. Mrs. Harris, I will take no further action on this matter until you contact me again. Have a pleasant day."

Pool hung up before Iris could say goodbye.

As Christmas drew near Iris and Rodney grew closer. Iris felt her initial wariness falling away. She still did not completely trust him—memories of the things he had done were too painful to ever forget or completely forgive—but she sensed that he had changed. His behavior was more open, more respectful of her person, and he seemed more loving than ever, in bed and out. He also seemed to listen more, to attend to her feelings and anticipate her wishes. On December 22nd Iris called Pool to inform him that she wished to drop all divorce proceedings. Pool advised her that it would first be necessary to sign a reconciliation form to be filed with the Court. Iris drove in and signed it the next day. Rodney and Iris settled in to spend Christmas together, the two of them at the farm. Iris felt quite happy once more, once more her life was in order, her loving husband with her.

29

"Rodney," Iris said hesitantly. She sat across from him at the spanking new bar that spanned half the kitchen. He'd added it during her absence, and they sat opposite, sipping drinks. Dinner time was approaching, and she blurted her concern, "I don't want to complain, but I saw your car parked near the school today. I mean..."

"What of it?" Rodney snapped, gazing benignly outside at the snowy expanse.

"Well...there's been comment on it." She did not add that Mr. Hayward had mentioned it, even going so far as to suggest she speak to Rodney about it so as to avoid a complaint to the police. Iris felt awful not standing up to him more firmly, so she blurted her thoughts, "It's not just me, Rodney. You know you can trust me, but the talk around the teachers' lounge is that you have been parked near the school several times." She paused, wondering if he was up to his old tricks.

"Just forget it!" he snapped, slamming his bourbon down. He wiped the slight spill with his shirt sleeve and took another swig, "I like to check up once in a while. What the hell do any of them know? It's for your own good Iris. All them boys...especially at that age. Hell, didn't I read about a teacher being raped last week?"

"But that was in Lansing, not Ionia," Iris replied. It was absurd, her Principal practically ready to call the cops, and Rodney was pretending to protect her from school boys, parking nearby and watching her every move.

"I said forget it!" he shouted, his mood turning ugly.

Iris dropped the subject, moving to the stove to stir the chili. Rodney downed what was left of his second drink, walking into the mud room where he donned coat and boots and disappeared towards the barn. Watching him go, Iris turned the burner to simmer. He might be gone minutes or hours...his behavior becoming increasingly erratic. She considered calling Harry Pool, but it would be humiliating to admit how wrong she was to return. Worse yet, Hayward had told her she could not be employed full time until the following autumn, though she would remain on the top of the list of substitutes. The thought that Rodney would find out sooner or later was scary enough. What would she do with the rest of winter in the confines of the house with just her and Rodney? She shuddered, a wave of fear sweeping her, when she heard a noise from outside. At first she could not identify it, a high wavering yowl like a frightened child. Then she realized, it was Duke. What was going on out there? She wrapped herself in coat and scarf, slipped on her boots and ran outside. As she drew near the barn Duke's piercing yowl seemed to pierce her head, but she pushed on, moving slowly into the circle of light from the small side door, the big barn doors being closed in winter. She heard a whistling sound, and peeking carefully in, she froze in horror. His back to her, facing the wall, Rodney thrashed the dog, arms rising and falling. She could hear his grunts of effort as Rodney, feet planted wide, brought the riding-crop down on the helpless dog time and time again. Duke's whines reverberated, and the horses in the stalls shied and whinnied with almost every blow. Duke cowered, his paws and body trembling. The big dog attempted to rise but Rodney kicked him down. Then Duke growled.

"You goddamned stupid fucking mutt!" Rodney shouted, kicking the dog again. "Don't you dare growl at me. I'll teach ya not to growl..." He turned and reaching around feeling for something more sturdy, eyes wide with rage. He spotted Iris, watching tearfully, her hands at her mouth. He glowered at her, stood for a long moment his long arms hanging loose like some great ape.

"What're you lookin'at?" he asked, moving towards Iris. Duke, his tail between his legs, whimpering softly, moved to the far corner. Iris could see open wounds where the riding crop had cut through hair and skin, and she stooped down to embrace him with arms outstretched, a thoughtless but natural reaction. She knelt and touched Duke's muzzle, and when he growled again she murmured, petting his head. Behind her Iris could hear Rodney's heavy breath, feel his looming presence. She looked over her shoulder at him, "How could you?" She held the dog close. "What did he ever do to you?"

"None of your fucking business," he said, voice rasping. "Since when is he your dog? He's mine. I trained him up, and I discipline my own damn dog. So get your ass back in the house." Rodney moved in, as Iris continued to comfort Duke, checking out the bleeding slashes visible through his heavy winter pelt. She saw blood on her hand, and turned towards Rodney to show him what he had done. Duke, calm now, wagged his tail tentatively.

"I said, get your goddamn ass inside!" Rodney's voice rose sharply. Iris knew the signals well, and she stood up, a bit shaky, still holding Duke by his collar.

"Okay, I'll go in, but I am taking him in there with me. He needs to have these wounds treated."

As she turned to lead the dog away Iris felt herself propelled violently from behind. Though she felt no pain through the thick coat, she tumbled onto her hands, scattering straw, sawdust and old manure. The barn was not clean. She realized that Rodney had let things go.

She glanced around and saw that he had Duke by the collar, screaming obscenities at the dog, who had come up to protect her. Gaining her feet she followed the snow path to the house, planning to call Pool at once. Having memorized his numbers, she got to the phone in the kitchen, dialing without removing her coat or scarf. The phone rang once, then twice before it was ripped from her hand.

"Who the fuck do you think you are? What in goddamn hell makes you think you got a right to call anyone without my permission?" Rodney ripped the phone from the wall socket, and approached her, moving to block her exit from the room.

"I'm leaving. You can't keep me here. I'm going through with the divorce."

"There will be no divorce," Rodney spoke each word separately, in the high pitch almost childish tone she had learned to fear. "No divorce! Not now or ever." He pulled back his arm and she cringed, expecting heavy blows, but he did not hit her. Instead he grasped her by the arm and, with the enormous force that anger gave him, propelled her through the mud room and out into the cold night. Oh no, she thought, he's going to lock me out. Maybe this time he won't let me in. Iris resisted only for a second, realizing she was warmly dressed; boots, coat, and a scarf on her head. She could simply walk to the nearest farm for help. But once in the yard, Rodney moved quickly to reach her at her pace, looking around at the barn and other outbuildings. What was he thinking?

"You can't keep me here, you sick Bastard." She resisted his grasp, hardly aware of her challenge. As she pulled, he gripped harder. "You settle down, woman," he ordered, holding her with both hands, his grip hurting through the thick coat. "Goddamn it! You're mine. When will you get it through your thick skull? You belong to me." Then, despite her frantic struggle, he dragged her around to the side of the house, flinging open the big slanting doors that led down to the cellar, making the snow fly. As he did so he needed both arms, and Iris, standing free for an instant, began to run. He had her in two or three strides, turning her body and smashing her in the face. She went down, but so did Rodney, slipping on the snow. Again she scrambled away, propelled by panic, and again he caught her. He hit her again and she felt the gush of warm blood from her nose. Face down in the snow, she lay unmoving. He turned her with frenetic range and struck her again several times. Face up to the moon, she lost consciousness.

A musty odor stirred in her nostrils. Where was she? Feeling around in total darkness, she sensed earth and stone. The cellar, of course. He had thrown her into the old cellar, the foundation of the original house. She felt encrusted blood on her face and pulled herself up. Crawling, she found the old fieldstone wall, moving along it until she found her bearings and stood. Along two walls were shelves, laden with stored goods, even some canned goods. She remembered that some were emergency stores, including one or two crates of potatoes. Despite her bloody nose she could smell the tubers. Another wall of shelves contained several bottles of wine, and even more bourbon. At least, she thought bitterly, I won't need to worry about what to drink. She had no can-opener, no knife, no way to access the canned food, but the raw potatoes might sustain her. She could unscrew the bottles not stopped with corks. Somewhat reassured, she found the nearest crate and sat on it. It was reasonably warm, heat radiated from the house above and from the adjacent crawl-space which led to the newer "basement" where the water heater and furnace were located.

Rodney had put that in, but it was impossible to reach directly from the old fieldstone cellar. He had boasted that the fruit cellar had almost perfect year-around temperature, ideal for storing winter foods like squash, and with its earth floor, perfect for wine. But there was nowhere to dig. The fieldstone had to extend far below and the earth outside lay within inches of the frame structure of the house. Iris felt some warmth through a small opening that led to the crawl space, enough to prevent freezing. But it would not be comfortable. She still had her coat, boots, and scarf. She reached up and touched the rafters, maybe seven feet above. There was space to move, perhaps four paces from side to side. Slowly, easing herself to lessen the pain, she paced back and forth. She did not cry. Presently she rested. When she woke a second time she could sense dim shapes. Dirt clung to her face and she brushed it away, wincing. Her face was swollen, and her hair hurt at its roots where he had jerked it around during the beating. Some light leaked in, from where she could not tell, but enough to discern the walls, the old shelves, and the door of solid oak built when the house was erected, situated at the bottom of the steps leading to the outside slanting doors. She got to it, but it was locked, so there was no escape that way. Despite a headache, Iris began to search, mostly by feel, but in time she found an old grub hoe on a lower shelf. Then she remembered…at one corner of the kitchen, under the area behind the new bar, was a trap-door leading to the cellar. Once, he had told her, there had been a ladder leading down from there, long since gone.

She moved a potato crate, and standing on it, found the trap-door. Above, she knew, a rug covered it, and probably at least one stool. It had a rotary latch fixing it from above. She took the grub-hoe and standing on the potato crate began hammering at the trap door. It was excruciating, forcing the heavy tool upwards, above her head, the accumulated dirt and dust of decades falling onto her face and into her hair, her arms aching. Her headache grew worse. But for long moments she kept it up, silent when she rested, listening, then going at it again. If Rodney was in the house he would hear her hammering from below and react. She wanted that. She wanted him to communicate, to acknowledge her. Otherwise she was even more alone. Obviously he was not home, since no sound of life came from above. For perhaps an hour she beat away at the trap door with no noticeable results. When she finally fell, exhausted, pain racking her back, her upper shoulders and arms, her head reeling, she could smell and feel splinters on the earth floor. Later, she felt along the bottom of the trap door where the grub-hoe had made slight grooves in the old pine boards. It might take days, but sooner or later she might break through. For hours she sat huddled in what seemed to be the warmest corner. Sleep came in phases and then awakening to realization of where she was, she ran back through her mind the days and weeks since she had returned to Rodney. What a fool thing to do...what a mistake. Almost from the first, despite outward protests of affection, despite increasingly ritualistic sex between them, he had inexorably returned to his previous patterns. For hours he had sat in front of the TV, silent, watching and drinking. When he wanted her he'd ply her with drink and force himself upon her, cursing her if his performance was less than complete, almost never caring to see if she was responsive. She remembered an awful tirade when, unable to sustain an erection, he shouted obscene insults.

"You're a lousy fuck. You know that? Maybe I ought to fuck you in the ass. You're gettin' old too. You know that?" He'd dragged her naked to the mirror, swaying drunk, leering over her, pulling at her breasts without erotic joy, "Look...See how ya sag...you ain't young anymore. Ya don't know how to make love anymore." If Iris dared try to actually make love, to somehow touch his remembered tenderness, by forcing herself past the humiliation and the insults, until she somehow found a way to arouse him, enough to join him, he would cease any closeness, leaving her hurt and depleted and unsatisfied, until she found a restless sleep.

Even then Iris had pitied him. She understood that it was not the form of sex that did not work when his brutality came to the fore, but the unloving nature of it...she supposed it was the same baggage of his brutal childhood that made him so uncaring, capable of hurting her with bitter words that seemed almost worse than his fists. Yet, she remembered loving moments when both had indulged in the full pleasure of things she had been forbidden as a young girl, the sort of give and take they both enjoyed, in the discovery of each other, things that came from mutual need, quite natural and right. Now in his transformation some of the intimate acts had morphed into ritualistic abuse. No matter what he promised in the daily routines of life, or in the marriage bed, always he needed more control, more power over her. She sensed with sickening clarity that this need extended beyond the house, to the school, the town, to the world outside.

Lying in the dark cellar, she remembered a bizarre incident when her cousin Mable had written her a letter just as Iris had moved back to the farm. Rodney found it in the mailbox and when she got home triumphantly waved it at her face, holding the opened letter before her, "This is the crap you get from some bitch cousin?"

Iris scanned the handwritten letter. In it were several wise and thoughtful questions. Was Rodney off the bottle? Had he abused her physically in any way? Was he still in therapy? Was their reconciliation based on real progress or mere hope? Further in the letter Mable also noted that Iris had apparently been cut off from regular communication with others, and in view of her isolation, maybe Iris should drive over to visit her in Flint. Or, if she could not get away, Mable promised to visit Iris. They could talk.

Iris folded the letter, looking up at Rodney, knowing she was trapped, not by the simple truths in the letter, but by the terrible fact that invading her privacy in this manner made his hold on her more frightful. She was hardly surprised when he ripped the letter out of her hand and lit it on fire, until the ashes scattered onto the floor.

"That Mable," he laughed mirthlessly, "Shit. I know she means well, baby, but she's probably some frigid bitch with some milquetoast of a husband, just jealous of what we got."

As he raved, Iris remembered how he poured more drinks for both of them, until he took her upstairs, compliant as a slave.

In the cellar's blackness she saw her mother's face, frowning with distaste at some minor verbal cruelty from her father. The images out of black darkness came in full color; vivid also was the smell of oatmeal boiling on the stove, of eggs frying in the pan, and four quarts of fresh milk in bottles delivered before dawn, which she was given to shake so that the cream mixed with the skim. Her mother's face was pink, her hair blond but shading to gray, though she had only a few years to live, eventually dying of ovarian cancer at age forty-seven, and her father passed soon after, downed by a stroke at only fifty-five. Both gone before Iris was twenty-five; an only child left alone. In her dream Iris's father's face was colorless, as pale as a ghost; then it morphed into Rodney's.

"Iris, dear, you deserve this," said her mother.

"Sure do, you dumb broad," put in her father, in his own voice but with Rodney's face, adding for emphasis, "and don't tell me you repent your divorce from that fine fellow who died fighting for his country in Vietnam. Don't you get it Iris? This so called marriage is doomed. If I had lived you would never have married him."

"But you did," her mother added, "and now look what you've got."

It was then she woke, remembering where she was.

She did not know day from night when she began beating away at the trap-door with the grub-hoe, until finally she realized her terrible thirst, finding a bottle of cheap wine with a screw cap she chugged until the wine dripped from her chin. Then came stuporous sleep, but without the nightmare of her parents visit. Time passed without a sense of measure, hours or days, it seemed to make no difference. Chafing her hands and feet until they tingled, aware of the effect of the cold on her, filthy and itchy, she found a corner to defecate. She must not soil herself...and once more she explored her prison, mounting the crate for another assault on the trap-door, when she heard him moving above. She banged on the joists, screaming. His footsteps went away and she waited. Much later, she began to beat on the trap-door with the old tool, and then came his voice, muted from above, but clear.

"Are you comfy, Iris? Maybe a couple of days down there will teach you. You've got to learn your lesson. Never again mention divorce. Don't even think about it. Have pleasant dreams."

"Rodney," Iris shrieked, "I'm sorry. I've learned my lesson, please let me out." She began to sob, totally out of control, but his footsteps retreated. Trying to regain a smidgen of sanity, she began reciting trivia, naming the fifty states in the sequence of their joining the Union, something she had mastered in high school. She managed it the second time, and then began a geographical listing of all the nations in the U.N. continent by continent. She had gone through South, and then Central America, and starting with Africa (not remembering half, since the names had changed so much) when his voice came again.

"Are you still there Iris darling?" His voice was jocular. "I'm sorry but I have to leave. Lots of work at the office to close four new deals..." and his footsteps faded.

"Please Rodney, I can be trusted," she screamed. "Oh, please God, make him answer!"

Silence, then after some minutes came the muted sound of a gunshot. More silence. Iris lay huddled. What was he up to? Was he going to kill her? Then she heard the outer doors being thrown open, light came through the latch of the inner door, then she heard the turning of the lock. The bolt slammed open and then the door. Blinded by light, Iris recoiled. Gradually she regained vision, it was apparently late in the day, the waning light still seemed too bright as she squinted. He stood in the doorway grinning, holding something in his big hand. Peering out Iris saw a collar. Duke's collar, she realized as she backed into the cover of the open inner door.

"Hello Iris," Rodney boomed, "I hope you enjoyed your stay down here. Cozy ain't it? Here. Look what I brought. Your very own memorial."

Pulling a hammer from his belt he tacked the collar to the inner door.

"Nothing or nobody turns on me. Just remember that, Iris." She saw the clots of blood on the black leather.

"What have you done? Where's Duke?" she dared not ask more, understanding the awful truth.

"This is a reminder," he said with a mirthless grin. He stood back to admire his handiwork. "You just promised me you can be trusted. Iris, this is to jog your memory in case you ever forget." He turned to face her, one foot blocking her on the inner threshold.

She sank to the dirty floor, sobbing, "Duke. Duke." Then he turned to climb the steps, and moments later she heard the back door slam shut. It was growing dark now and the cold wind blew fine snow down the steps, through the open oak door, into her face. She realized dimly that he was leaving her exit from the prison cellar. She made her way painfully into the yard. Not a hundred feet away was the garage, with her car. She could reach it in seconds. But the keys would not be in it. Maybe the phone, but it was inside where he lurked. He had killed Duke. He is capable of killing me. If I provoke him I am dead. Is this just another trap? Iris considered the road, but she was weak from hunger and thirst. She moved to the back steps, and shuffled wearily into the warm, bright kitchen.

"I see you learned your lesson," Rodney grinned, raising his glass in a mock toast. He sat at the new bar, clean and neat, hair combed, in freshly pressed clothes.

"Iris, I'm no fool. I know you're thinking of the car. I know exactly how you think, my sweet. It would do you no good to try. I not only have the keys, I've fixed the VW so it won't run. The phone is disconnected, and there is an alarm on the garage door." He paused to look her up and down, not a glimmer of sympathy in his face.

"You should see yourself."

Standing in the kitchen, Iris was aware that the cellar dirt covered her face and hands, clung to her clothing. Her hair was grimy and filthy. She reeked. She could smell herself in the warm kitchen, and he chuckled, apparently enjoying her degradation.

"Sit down darling. Why don't you have a drink? Don't tell me you don't want one."

"No. Not till I take a bath. If you'll let me." Iris climbed the stairs. She had nothing else to do.

30

Through the long winter and into a delayed spring Iris endured long hopeless days, waiting on him, daydreaming about the past, fantasizing a future without him. Nightmares, often similar to those she endured in the cellar, tortured her and she slept badly even when she had too much to drink. If she woke in terror, she found herself fearful of sleep, since more dreams might come. Sometimes it was her mother or father casting blame and sometimes even friends like Mr. Hayward, or Betty Jean, or her cousin, but usually it was Rodney spewing accusations as he often did in waking life, though in some of the dreams he was a giant, his features altered like a Hollywood ogre changed from husband to werewolf. He would catch her, throwing her to the ground, and then take her, shouting, "You are mine. When will you learn? Mine!"

Some dreams were pleasant. She was free of him, teaching in Detroit or in a Flint suburb with Mable nearby. Rodney was dead in these dreams. But she would wake up to hear his stentorian snores beside her. His being in the same bed was another burden. He assumed her compliance, and fearing any reaction if she refused, she allowed him to use her. What did surprise her was when he began rewarding her with cash for sex. He seemed so uncaring that when she play-acted the ritual, pretending no affection or tenderness, it hardly bothered him. He even joked about it, saying it was her "part time business" to serve him. Having access to no money Iris complied in the loveless charade, hiding the money. By May she had stashed several hundred for the day of escape. That she would do so, she had no doubt.

Most of the time a cloistering depression mastered her days. Watching TV (almost never a program she liked when Rodney was in the house) eating bags of potato chips, enduring his endless stories of triumphant real estate deals, hunting trips in the Rockies and Canada, she even listened quietly to his angry perorations about any and every politician. If an elected official revealed the slightest humanitarianism, the more Rodney despised him, his cynical curses about do-gooders echoing in the void. Iris, though sick of his bigotry, did not argue. She sat long hours staring out at the landscape she had once loved, hating the monochrome of white on gray. She read escapist fiction which Rodney bought in bunches, paying little attention to title or author so long as they were in the "romance' section. She watched daytime TV until she began to put on weight, and came to welcome the second glass of wine after dinner, and sometimes the third, while Rodney as usual, could hold half a fifth of bourbon without apparent effect.

It was a perfect day in May when Rodney took her on a drive into town. Everywhere spring was greening and birds singing, but Iris was oblivious, having but one thought, how, how could she escape. Once parked in Ionia he was all business, rapping orders.

"I'm gonna let you come in," he said. "You just sit quiet in the front office till I'm done with some phone calls, then we'll go shopping. Maybe after, if you're obedient and don't try anything, I'll take you out to dinner. After that I might even buy you a present."

She noticed that Sally was not in, wondering why, since, she thought vaguely, it was a Friday. Later cruising down Main Street through busy traffic,

Rodney, always in a hurry, fell in behind a slow moving Olds. Rodney honked in annoyance, but the driver was oblivious. The Olds swung without warning around an old Dodge, which braked hard, and Rodney barely managed to stop in time. Cursing loudly, he shouted, impatient with others as always. No sooner had he put the T-Bird into gear when they were smacked hard from the rear, and pushed into the car in front with a crunch of metal. In a flash three angry drivers were in the street, Rodney by far the loudest.

Iris immediately realized that the accident was hardly fifty feet from Pool's law office. Her heart pounding, she saw that Rodney and the other drivers were pointing out the damage, searching their wallets for insurance cards. She was so scared that her sweaty hand slipped on the door handle, but she was out quickly, almost breaking into a run but moving at a fast walk, then she was at Pool's door.

Rodney spotted her. "Iris, you come back here," he yelled, pocketing his wallet and moving quickly up the sidewalk, a grim smile on his face. She pushed the door open, breathing a sigh of relief when she saw Pool standing right there.

"Harry. Gosh am I glad to see you." She could hardly believe he was there, looking out the door at the minor crash, which had created more noise than damage.

"Hi Iris, what brings you here?" said Pool, sticking his head out to study the accident. "Is that Rodney, your husband? Well, it sure is. I guess that's a silly question."

It took Iris only a few minutes to explain. She saw Pool's friendly face change as she described the cellar and the killing of Duke. Before she finished her story Pool began taking notes on a legal pad. He called in his secretary, who listened as Harry asked questions. Shaking his head, not so much in disbelief as in visible disgust, Pool dictated a complaint for divorce, particular to the new information from Iris, plus an affidavit for a temporary restraining order.

Iris kept looking at the door wondering if Rodney would simply force his way in and take her away. Pool was rangy, neither small nor weak, but few were a match for Rodney Harris. Pool sensed her fear, and looked out the door again. "Well, he's parked in his Thunderbird not far down the street," said Pool. Then he ordered his secretary to call the cops if Harris even poked his head into the office. Pool always worked quickly so Iris was gratified when he got the office of the Circuit Judge to arrange for an immediate signing of a restraining order. Iris called the school, hoping to get Betty Jean, but she was crushed to discover that her friend had moved to Ann Arbor not long after the New Year. The school had a forwarding address and a phone number, and Iris managed to luck out, Betty Jean answering at once. Iris began to cry as she explained her situation, but within a few minutes Betty Jean interrupted, "Iris, I can help. I mean it. This time it will be different. Hank is actively into A.A. and I have a teaching job here. All you have to do is get here."

Meanwhile Pool worked the legal routine with the familiarity of easy professionalism. Before the end of business at the Courthouse he had the restraining order in hand. Now he only had to serve the papers on Rodney. Normally Pool would have waited for the Sheriff's office to serve them, but this time he wanted it to happen now. Before he left the Courthouse he called his secretary, confirming that Rodney was still parked on the street near his office. At once Harry Pool loped with the strides of the halfback he had once been, directly to the silver Thunderbird. He came up from behind, rapping on the window on the driver's side. Rodney turned in surprise.

"Mr. Harris," Pool extended the sheaf of papers through the open window, thrusting them into Rodney's hands.

"I'm serving you, Rodney Harris, with a new complaint for divorce, and a restraining order enjoining you from any contact whatsoever with your wife." Pool almost hoped Harris would make a fuss. Pool was rangy and fit; he worked out on a home-gym and jogged fifteen miles a week.

"So the goddamned bitch did it again," Harris muttered, making as if to open the door, but Pool held hard against it.

"She's gone, Harris. And you better move your ass out of here," Pool put all his angry force behind his words, smiling at Rodney with genuine malice. "Let me tell you Harris, and you listen good. If you violate one jot of this restraining order this time I'll personally call the police. And, before they get to you, I guarantee that I will beat your ass." With that he wheeled and walked to his office, feeling much better.

Iris had been busy too, from the office she arranged to catch a bus to Ann Arbor. Pool saw Iris off on the five o'clock bus scheduled to arrive in Ann Arbor around eight that evening.

Despite several bus stops at small towns along the way Iris was elated. She managed to slide open the window beside her, letting in the soft spring air, which began to mix with light fragrant rain as the bus rumbled and she dozed.

Ann Arbor was the beginning of hectic but not unpleasant weeks. The Benchley's rented three bedroom house, located about two miles from the University of Michigan campus, was convenient, if cramped, and Iris had access to the phone so long as she repaid the long distance calls. Within days through contacts Betty Jean and Hank had made there, they met with a domestic assault team. For the first time Iris felt that the professionals were on her side, and through their legal support she moved so quickly that even Harry Pool was impressed. By the end of June, they were divorced. Since there were no children, Pool had petitioned the court for an early resolution of the matter.

Nevertheless she felt stuck, her hopes for a decent life dashed. Her spirits lifted in midsummer when at a Tiger's game she ran into an old college girlfriend, Jill Dunn, who taught at a high school in Boulder, Colorado. Jill was visiting her parents in Detroit, and within moments they caught up on the missing years. Jill had once lived with her first husband in married housing at MSU, right next to Iris, and though they had exchanged Christmas cards for a time, had lost all contact. Jill had eventually divorced her physician husband, and with one child grown and another in high school, found a teaching job in Boulder, a mountain community. At forty, Jill was coltish at about 5' 11" and smart, athletic and single. They immediately agreed that Iris should join her for a serious job search. Iris could live with Jill until she found a teaching job, and move on from there.

31

Was it possible? Was she actually on her way to Colorado and safety? The VW contained all her earthly possessions, most of them stuffed into a carry-on travel bag in the small trunk up front. On the back seat a large trash bag bulged with the rest of her stuff. She'd had to leave all her books, except a couple of novels, one of which lay beside her on the seat. It was a book of high adventure and humor across the plains and into the mountains where she was headed, about a captive white boy brought up as a Cheyenne.

Just before the ramp to the expressway that was to be her escape Iris turned into a gas station to fill up. She fought an impulse to turn the car around, aware of the tug of him, of images that came in flashes of almost sinful pleasure. During negotiations—carried out by Pool with protective gusto—to retrieve and fix her VW she was glad the legal system kept them apart, since she missed not only his physical presence but craved the sounds he made just being there, the feel of his breath when he whispered in her ear, his lips upon her, the touch of him.

Driving across the Illinois prairies she remembered the litany, almost laughing at the memory. She recited it out loud, grinning at a passing driver who stared, thinking she was singing a song.

"Obedience first."

"He requires this in small things at first, beginning with petty things. Like the order in which I must serve dinner. Like how to place the toilet paper. Like the way I tuck in the bed sheets (his have to be the army way). Then comes control of my every movement, to and from work, even shopping or visiting a friend. Then come restrictions as to my behavior, even my movements about the house or barn. These come in gradual portions, hardly noticed at first, but relentlessly and inexorably they build. Soon I am in a prison, the barriers are sex, food, and company. They continue to build. Eventually I am a mere possession, a sexual play thing, a submissive listener unable to disagree or counter his mindless rants on all subjects, from his scorn for blacks to his disdain for protesting youth, his murderous attitude toward "queers." Then come further restrictions as to when and where I can shop, even to stop off for half an hour on an unscheduled errand. Then comes his manipulative intervention in my career. I am not allowed to work, not even as a teacher in a school only a few miles away. He deliberately sabotaged two good offers for full-time teaching. Finally, after repeated attempts to patch things up and make it work, comes the successful attempt to cut me off from friendship, from any contact with anyone he does not invite. Then comes the deadly mutual isolation. I am alone with him and he with me. That is the way he wants it."

Trying to commit to her move she recited a stanza from Elizabeth Barrett Browning of poetry memorized in school:

"If thou must love me, let it be for naught
Except for love's sake only. Do not say,

'I love her for her smile—her look—her way
Of speaking gently,—for a trick of thought."

What an odd thing, to remember a love poem at such a time without love. It was so awful in its implications that she cried as she recited it out loud.

Into Nebraska on the evening of the second day, the memory of the cellar kept her moving west. Lightning played across the sky before her, dark looming thunderheads obscuring the stars from horizon to horizon, a wind rising and bending the lingering stunted trees that grew back behind the endless ditch behind the expressway fence. Checking her money, she found a motel outside Grand Island about a hundred miles west of Omaha. One night for twelve bucks. She paid and entered the musty room while the great storm raged across the plains outside. Frightened at the howl of wind and crash of thunder and endless brilliant lightning, she laid wide-eyed and alone until the storm waned hours later. Once, just into sleep, she woke with a start, convinced that he was banging on the door, that he had followed her, had come in the silver Thunderbird across the land to possess her. But it was just a loose screen door on the next unit banging in the wind. She slept fitfully since it was not a fantasy that he could follow her. He would find out where she had gone. He had done worse before now.

Finally about twenty miles east of Denver she saw the mountains. She pulled over and stared, breathing deep of cool air blown down from the vast massif. The storm had brought high clear air and blue sky, the peaks rose distant and majestic. The desolate land behind her, mountains blue and green ahead, she almost hoped to hope, almost dared to dream. Then she entered the Denver megapolis and wound her way through streams of cars out towards Boulder. As they drew closer, the mountains dominated her attention, drawing her west into their shadow through the glorious foothills right up onto the slopes of the folded range itself. As she followed Jill's directions, seeking the new apartment building, she felt as if God was guiding her up into the rare and brilliant air. Jill's directions were easy to follow, and there she was at the cantilevered deck, waving. As she carried her meager belongings up to the chalet-like flat, into a warm hug, Iris felt things would work.

Perhaps disappointment was inevitable. The high heat seemed more bearable, dry and thin, so the heat of summer did not hurt so much, but time pressed on and the first easy days vanished. For a week or so Jill took time to guide her, and they rode horseback down near Nederland. They drove to Vail where Iris felt hopelessly out-of-place amid the crowds of stylish jet-setters. Returning by a different route, through a high pass where the storm of the previous week had left summer snow melting amid large puddles, they stepped from the car. Hiking with Jill into an alpine col so high that no trees grew, gazing to the east from whence she'd come, Iris felt liberated, almost believing that God might listen now. In that high place, she believed, at least for a time.

But reality intruded when she began the search for work. Her Garden of Eden, so lovely to look at, was stark and empty down in the streets where people worked and lived. For years the region had attracted people of all backgrounds, especially young professionals. Every position in every school was filled. Waiting lists greeted her even at day care centers. By August Iris was desperate. The money she received in the divorce was almost gone. She knew Jill could not put her up indefinitely. Finally she looked into every advertised job no matter how poorly paid.

In the midst of this Jill lost her job, receiving notice that her employer was letting go dozens of employees who had short term contracts. Iris found a job that same week at a nearby restaurant, at the insulting wage of $3.50 an hour. A few days later, Jill found a job as an executive secretary in an architect's firm in Colorado Springs, at least a hundred miles away.

"Naturally," said Jill, elated at her new job, "you can stay on here if you can foot the bill. I talked to the Aspers, my landlords. They know you might have some trouble paying and will give you some slack. Don't be downcast, Iris. I'll be only a couple of hours away. I've got to take it. I'm too old to turn this down. It may be my last chance to really make it."

So Jill was gone within a week and Iris was left to herself, friendless in a strange city. She realized that Jill's promise to help Iris look for a decent job was well-intentioned, but Iris's qualifications would limit her there as well. Teachers were over supplied especially around Colorado Springs, and she had never upgraded her skills outside of education.

Depression was unavoidable. Her work began at seven-thirty in the morning and ended each day at five when she returned to the apartment to a pre-cooked heated dinner, to TV, and then bed at ten-thirty or so, only to rise at six and start it all over again. She had no friends or acquaintances except for her landlords, the Aspers, who invited her to dinner once each week. They were understanding and supportive. Nancy Asper especially would inquire kindly about her doings, trying to help. But Iris had nothing to say, her life so mundane day in and day out that she could not remember from week to week anything worth speaking of. At work, Iris tried to banter with the other overworked waitresses, her dour and humorless boss, the occasionally witty or friendly customer; but the place was one of those fast-food establishments where the turn-over was fast, even among the help. The job wore her down. When she realized that she could not pay the steep rent and keep her car, Iris sold the VW. Now her world was limited to the five square blocks from her apartment to the restaurant. No local bus service existed there. Even the mountains on whose very slopes she lived were out of reach. She could only stare out from her balcony across the town to the Flat Irons in the West. Sometimes, just to be with people, she'd eat at the restaurant where she worked, sometimes at other places within her tiny budget. Most often, however, she went home alone, lived alone, slept alone, cried alone. She felt she was growing old alone and there would never be another chance.

As depression won over will Iris found it harder to rise each morning and face her work. In early November, she called Jill and asked if she might take a bus down for the weekend (for weekends were worst of all), but Jill was busy and only promised Iris an invite over Christmas. Iris managed one interview that same week with a local school, but nothing came of it. Her appearance was ghastly. She'd lost weight, but not in the healthy glow of activity. Rather she was worn and thin, the lines of her forehead and mouth deeper, her neck stretched and her face haggard, black circles around her eyes. The job rejection hit her especially hard since it seemed to confirm her fear that she was no longer competitive, that in early middle age she was on a downward slide to oblivion. No matter where she looked, she could see no evidence to the contrary. Despair seemed to grow in proportion to her isolation.

One desperate evening she went to the mirror and gazed at her face. For a long time she studied the image, trying to see beneath the expression. Try as she might, she couldn't summon the will to produce anything but a grimace, the grin of a skull. Inadvertently she cupped her breasts and cried, sobbing until the tears would not come. At least she could cry. But she knew she now cried too much, beyond the healing process. Tears now became a proof of feeling, evidence of life, and that too seemed to be dying. When she had control of herself again, Iris tried to remember how it was.

She had been alone for many years in Detroit, before Rodney. Alone, she had managed better than many. She cultivated friends and sought diversions. She'd loved her work with the inner-city kids, the routines of classes and school affairs, the night work and preparation, the parties and outings with other teachers and friends, the occasional thrill that a date might bring titillating yearnings and, if not, at least another funny story to tell her friends the next day in the teachers' lounge. She'd used her savings to travel a little, and had been to Europe once on a group tour that included London and the southeast of England, and a jaunt to Paris. She knew much of the U.S. and had—just about the time she met Rodney—even planned a trip to China and Japan. She had made elaborate careful plans for the future and had even anticipated retirement as a single woman. She had more or less given up, before Rodney, on finding a man, a lover, a husband.

Was that it then? Had that sudden chance, the deep need for that part of life prompted by Rodney's attention, destroyed all of that? Had she been so weak, so vulnerable? Now she could not even listen to a popular love song without bursting into self-pitying tears, could not watch a TV show that showed a love relation without resentment, so filled with anger and hurt that she would sometimes scream at the inanimate glimmering screen, "No! No! You lie. It isn't like that!" Sexual feeling, once so powerful in her, especially in the early times with Rodney, was now so suppressed that she found it hard to believe that she had bought into the idea that true love existed. She no longer felt what others felt, revealed daily in the media everywhere she turned. And she would curse, using the foul language Rodney had used, dulling what feeling she had left.

Looking at herself in the mirror, Iris tried to make the Iris she had once been rise to the image and come forth. Where was that woman? Could she be there, somewhere, beneath that drawn and sorrowful face? She shuddered. She had seen that drawn hopeless look before. Oh no! Was it the same drawn expression of pain held in that made Julia look twice her age, the worry and sorrow in the mouth, the despair in the eyes?

She did the same the next night and the next. Fully aware that she had coped, had actually enjoyed life, had made her way in the world, had built friendships and activities and anticipation and hope, she now began to doubt that she could do so again. It was Rodney who had made that impossible. It was not herself. He had destroyed something...something inside, something vital. In that despair, hoping only for a friendly voice, she thought a terrible thought.

"He still cares. Rodney cares. He may have beat me and imprisoned me, humiliated me, but he cares. I know he cares. He cares about me. He wants me still."

A few days later a letter came. He had found her address. Fearful at first, Iris tore it open, heart racing. The words brought tears, mingled tears of fear and hope.

> Dear Iris,
>
> It took some doing but I found you. Up in them mountains eh. I wonder how you manage though. You could never handle details, like me. Am I right or not? I mean things like keeping the place going, getting the car fixed. I bet you miss that.
>
> God, Iris, I miss you. I am nothing without you. Since you left things have gone to pot. I am planning to move to Kalkaska, soon, to take up with my real estate company (the one I joined when you came back to me last time). This damn farm is too big and empty now. I plan to live in the cabin and fix it up even better. I am not drinking much, believe it or not.
>
> But I don't know if I can make it without you. Do you feel the same? I know you do. I know you, Iris. You and me were made for each other. It was destined. I think about you all the time, every day and every night. I remember how we were together, all the dinners and the fun times and how we loved in bed, and all those things. But I am nothing without you.
>
> I need you Iris. Please write, or call. If you can't call, just write. A word from you will make my day. Please, please, Iris, just write me or call me. I love you,
> Rodney.

She read it over several times. Every word imprinted in her mind, she sat to write him back, and then on impulse decided to call. Hesitating several times, she rationalized, "He knows where I live so he can find me. So what harm is there in calling? He cannot hurt me over the phone." And so she called.

She recognized his voice immediately, responding without thought to his hello.

"I need you, Rodney," said Iris and she began to cry. Then fear swept over her and she hung up before he could respond, his voice ringing in her ears, that one word—"Iris?" resounding. For hours she sat alone on the couch until the sun hit her face, barely affecting her. Desperate to call him again but knowing what it would mean, she finally rose numbly, decision forming. The phone did not ring. She half expected it, remembering the energy he could bring to bear. If he had found her address, he would find her telephone number. Twice she opened the medicine cabinet to stare at the pills and twice she sat in despair, finally she poured her hand full of every pill she could find, swallowing them fast followed by a glass of water. She remembered making it to the bed.

"C'mon, Iris, help yourself. You must walk..." the voice came more clearly. It was Mr. Asper and he was holding her on one side with his wife on the other, forcing her to walk back and forth. "It's lucky we expected you for breakfast. When you didn't show up..." his voice trailed off, and Iris was aware of being led outside to an emergency vehicle.

32

Two days later, she was pronounced fit and released, a card in her purse with the address of a counselor who had looked in on her in the hospital. But Iris, thinking she didn't need a psychiatrist, had lied, only promising to follow through so she could leave the hospital. What could a shrink do? Nothing in the situation she faced each day could be changed. She was sure a search through her past would not help. Resigned to despair, she returned home, mutely accepting the kind words of the Aspers. Her employer, duly notified about her problem, gave her two weeks extended leave, and she accepted the time without question. She remained alone.

Then Thanksgiving loomed. A hint to the Aspers brought an explanation that they were committed to visit relatives in Denver. Jill had other plans. Then her employer, expecting her back immediately after the holidays, suggested that Iris take up his standing offer for a free meal on

Thanksgiving Day, something he had done for employees for several years. Hating the idea at first, Iris finally agreed. Anything was better than being alone in her apartment on that day of celebration and family. She entered a bit early, hesitantly. Shown by her boss to a table in the corner facing the wall, Iris smiled and nodded, accepting his kindness. The noise and clatter of the customers subsided as they hurriedly finished snacks or coffee. Was there going to be no one else in the restaurant for a meal this day? An older couple came in and read the menu, nodding at the special prices and the heaps of food promised. They were shown to a table on the far side. Iris sank into herself, not watching, not listening, alone. When the food arrived, she thanked the waitress, a casual friend, chatting briefly, not able to feel a smidgen of light behind her forced smile. Then, could it be so? It was...it was his voice, Rodney's voice, "Iris. Iris. Thank God, Iris. I found you."

Could it be a dream? She looked up. It was real, it was him. She felt his hand on her shoulder.

"Iris, for God's sake, it's me. I've searched all over. May I sit down?" She nodded, unbelieving. It simply could not be true. But it was.

"I haven't slept a wink since you called, and then when I couldn't find the number at your apartment, I decided to come on out. I drove straight through..."

She allowed him to reach out to touch her hand, but pulled back when he tried to grasp it. She was aware of a curious glance from her boss, but then all her attention was focused on her former husband. Unable to tear her eyes away, she studied him, noting every detail as he talked.

"Iris I'm here. Everything will be okay now. Just let me join you. Here, let's get me an order, if that's okay." His voice was throaty with emotion, a basso sound that resonated to her feet and caused mixed sensations. His familiar face was lined and thin, but handsome as ever. The fringes of hair that curled back over his ears were gray now, though the thicket on top was dark still. In his bright and twinkling eyes she saw that dampened fire, the interest that had drawn her from the first. Somehow, though clearly tired, he looked clean and fresh. He had found her. She looked again into his eyes. Behind that gleam of interest, of true concern, burned something dangerous and awful, that she knew; but she suppressed her fear. She turned her attention to his words, words she had heard so often before, "It was all my fault, of course. I'm sorry, Iris. I heard what you tried to do. I blame myself for it. Now, once we get you well...I'll leave, you can count on that. But, in the meantime, it's best if I stay close by. No matter what you think. No matter what I did, you've gotta believe me. I do love you. You can reject me, but you can't change that. I love you. I love you."

His voice was low, and Iris felt tears coming. Embarrassed by her lack of control, she turned away, wiping her eyes on a napkin, shaking her head slightly.

"I don't know, Rodney," she managed, looking away again out into blue sky and a view of mountains. The restaurant was popular for that, despite its so-so fare. The view was spectacular.

"Y'know how I found you," Rodney was saying, "I called every school I could find to see if you applied." He smiled and tapped his temple. "To get your address after that was easy. I knew better than to knock at your apartment, so I asked a neighbor and got directions to this restaurant. I figured you'd be here. How do you like my timing?"

Iris stared. Unwilling to voice feeling, even to ask questions of him, she kept her silence. She let him talk. Deep inside was fear of him, knowledge, and an insistent voice. "Stay away. Give him nothing. Allow him nothing. It is because of him that you are in this mess. It isn't your fault. You must be firm. Keep him off and force him to leave. You can make it on your own. You must, Iris, you must. Don't give him an inch. You know what he will do with it. Don't be a fool."

Still he jabbered, full of apologies and explanation. Still she was torn and drawn. Attracted in spite of everything, she thought, "I know his moods. I can be careful and watch. I can predict the dark moods. He needs me. He loves me."

"Iris. Iris. Is something wrong?" He touched her hand again, breaking through her thoughts. For the first time, she laughed. What an absurd question. Everything was wrong. Nothing was right between them. Didn't he know that? She laughed again and with the bark of intended scorn she felt fear of him flee, as if a dark shape was emptied and her mind was clear. She wondered if it was real, this feeling. She focused her attention to him, to his words. Her laughter had brought a thin smile to his lips, his even teeth revealed in a brief flash. Her heart gave way.

"Iris...you look like you're a thousand miles away." Then he really laughed, too. His words had caught her, and their absurdity made him laugh at himself. It was his old charm. Like taut strings on a harp, she felt plucked and swayed, vibrating to his rhythm, to his bass voice. It was his magic. She tried to resist, pushing her food away. Then she spoke, the words so soft he had to lean in to hear, "Rodney. Rodney." She felt tears and the harp vibrated in her.

"If you're not hungry, Iris..." his hand was on hers, his voice as low as hers had been, his body leaning to her, "we can leave. Can we go to your apartment? We can eat later if you want."

"I don't know. I don't know." Iris looked at the uneaten food, which only moments ago she had faced alone. Now she had no appetite. He was right about that. What could she do? What could she say? She looked at his eyes, bluer than usual as they caught the Colorado sky. His face was open, his expression concerned. He cared. She knew that. The words came without thought.

"Sure. Why not. Let's go."

Rodney moved in and they shared the place until Christmas. As before Rodney was careful of her at first, often expressing sorrow at what had happened, even seeming to tear up at times. For most of two weeks he did not press her, allowing her to live by her routines, supporting her rather than challenging her. But he drank. Cheap bottles of bourbon appeared and disappeared in succession. In her own place, aware of where things belonged, Iris was amazed at the quantity he put away. It seemed that Rodney functioned more effectively the more he drank. Of course his smug manner soon wore thin and he began to harry her. She'd made the mistake that first afternoon, on Thanksgiving Day, of accepting his advances, and she'd slept with him. This kept him subdued, if not grateful, toned down, apparently controlled. He made love to her with less passion than before, almost as if resigned to the obvious degeneration of his powers, the lessened capacity and the more frequent failure that even her best efforts could not alleviate. Then for several nights he did not try and she did not initiate. One night he sat with her drinking, talking, holding a glass out to her. His talk was turning raunchy, always a prelude to sex.

"You look pretty good, Iris. This work is good for you. C'mon over here." He patted his knee, one leg moving slightly in and out, the ankle planted on the floor. "I got some more work for you. You were always good at this..." He unzipped his pants and grinned. "C'mere," he gestured.

Somehow warned by his mood, Iris hesitated. She shook her head.

"I said, get over here!" his voice stentorian, higher. She recognized the timbre of threat, the tone of danger. Iris approached slowly, murmuring now, afraid, wanting only to mollify him and satisfy him, to do anything to avoid the change she could sense in him.

"Sure, honey. Sure. Just relax. I'll do you fine. Here." As she leaned in closer, reaching her hands to take him out, his still soft member in her hand, still murmuring to him, he gripped her suddenly by both hands, then he smacked her smartly across one cheek, then across the other. Her head snapped and tears came. Sobbing, she did not struggle. "I deserve this. I deserve this. I am a fool. I deserve this. I knew he would do it. I deserve this." She accepted the pain, barely aware of his words coming more rapidly now from his grinning mouth, "You knew it, didn't you, baby? You knew it. I knew you would come back to me." Then sensing her submission, he shoved her head down to his rising member "You knew it, Iris. This is what you want. This is what you need. I know you. You are mine."

Within a week, he beat her twice more, harder each time. Less than a week before Christmas, Iris was reduced to mute and fearful quiescence, in terror of provoking him, submissive yet alert to his moods, knowing he was capable of far worse. Fear held her. Fear and her own almost total lack of self-respect, the disgust she felt for having allowed this again, the need and weakness that provoked it, the loneliness and despair that allowed it. I am nothing, thought Iris, not even to myself. I exist only for him to use and abuse. I am that and nothing more. If she needed proof, Rodney provided it with every passing day.

A few days before Christmas, Iris hid a black eye behind dark glasses. One of the waitresses noticed. In the women's room, trying to explain, Iris broke down. The concern, even of a casual friend, was enough to summon up what remained of will. She allowed the woman to drive her to the police station, but at once she recognized the familiar pattern of weary disbelief, of an incapacity to help, of an unwillingness to understand. When two officers took her home to confront Rodney, she wanted to laugh. He was as clever and charming as ever, confusing the issue, offering rapid-fire explanations and contradictions that had the cops shaking their heads, grinning behind their helmets. When they left, he simply laughed in her face.

"I'll get you for this," said Rodney, turning away to watch the flickering TV, "later. Right now I have better things to do."

And he did get her that evening, beating her about the head with his open hand and later with his fists, concentrating on her torso, breasts and stomach and smashing her hard against the bedroom wall until the neighbor next door complained. Not satisfied, he raped her.

As Christmas approached, Iris was overcome with gloom. The Aspers invited her and Rodney to a Christmas party, but Rodney had refused.

"Why should we spend Christmas Eve with them goddamn people? I'd rather spend it alone."

"Then spend it alone," Iris shot back in anger, "I'll go to the party by myself. If you want to be alone, be alone!" She regretted the words at once.

"Shit," Rodney sneered, "you know what I mean. Just the two of us, like in the old days."

Sure, thought Iris, like the old days. When Christmas came, it was as disappointing as she expected. No spirit of the holiday was evident, not an ounce of cheer in the apartment. Rodney, watching pennies—living largely off Iris's meager paychecks despite his having sold the Muir farm—did not even allow a tree or simple decorations. Dinner was cheeseburgers, potato chips, and, his only concession to the season, a bottle of egg-nog for Iris with a pint of rum to spike it. Rodney preferred his bourbon.

As Iris cleaned up that evening, Rodney spoke the words she had been fearing all along.

"It's time for us to go to Kalkaska."

Iris did not reply.

"Didn't I tell you I moved up there? Sold most of the stuff with the farm last summer. Tell you the truth, Iris, you were lucky to reach me at the farm when you called. I was only there to close the deal."

Iris knew he was planning to sell the farm and move to Kalkaska. Just my luck, she thought, remembering the cabin and the things he had done to her there.

"I modernized the cabin," Rodney continued. "You'll find it quite comfortable. Small and easy to clean. I work part-time in the town for a real estate firm. In three or four days, I can still sell more than any of them younger guys can move in two weeks."

"I don't want to go back there," Iris said, turning away. "I've got this job, I want to stay here." She could feel his eyes boring into her. Afraid but angry, she tried to confront him. "I don't want to go anywhere with you, Rodney. I called because I was afraid and alone, but you are up to your old tricks. We're no good for each other. I want to live by myself..."

He moved in closer, eyes fixed, his mouth a slash across his face, teeth visible, bared as he spoke. She knew the signs.

"You forget, bitch. You belong to me. You'll never be free of me. Why don't you accept that?" He held her by both arms as if to shake her, then he stepped back a pace and held his arms wide, letting them fall slowly to his side, "Or do I have to teach you another lesson?"

"What about the apartment? And this stuff I bought?" Iris indicated the cheap furniture and decorations, aware that she was pleading.

"I've taken care of that already. I called your boss and told him you are quitting. He promised to send the last check to Kalkaska. I've told the Aspers, too. They agreed to buy the furniture. So all we need to do is pack and go. I've taken care of everything."

"You have no right. You can't do this. I'm not going!" Iris cried, backing away, surprised by the strength of her objection. She could not do this. To stay with him now would break what was left of her will, the last thread of independence. But Rodney only smiled, asking her to repeat the words. She watched his eyes, his face, and saw the tale-tell glitter in his eyes, the tight forward thrust of his jaw. She knew his voice would rise now, his expression yet more fixed. By now she knew the signs as well as she knew the outlines of her own face in the mirror. Still, she objected, "I'm not going. You can't make me."

For a moment, he advanced on her, then suddenly he turned and walked into the bedroom. At once he emerged holding the riding crop in his hand, striking it across his thigh. This proof of his deliberation, his intent to beat her and hold her, broke Iris's resolve and she sank back, hands covering her face. He had brought that awful thing all the way from Michigan...now everything was clear. There could be no doubt.

"I'm not asking you, I'm telling you. You are going back to Michigan with me, and you damn well better not make a fuss about it. D'you understand Iris? Or do I have to use this?" He flicked the crop at her, catching her shoulder, then he let fly with a hard lash across her torso.

"I'll go, I'll go," Iris cried, but once he had begun she knew he could not stop. Before he was satisfied, he hit her more times than she could count, lashing her prone body where she fell.

When he finally spoke, he was breathing hard, his voice unnaturally high, "Now get your ass in gear. Start packing, now! We leave in the morning. If you ever cross me, you know what to expect. This is only a sample."

Iris, crying in pain, rolled to the wall and half rose, holding her head. She realized he had not struck her face. All the blows had fallen on her body, all the welts concealed beneath her clothes. Then she saw the rictus of his face up close as he stooped down over her, "Oh, I almost forgot, Iris. Merry Christmas."

33

The trip to Michigan took barely a day and a half. Rodney pushed the Thunderbird straight through, making pit stops only for food and drink. Iris huddled next to him, unable to enjoy the landscape rushing past, though she remembered happy trips across the plains. He seemed driven. The fuel on which he thrived, pint after pint of bourbon drunk straight from the bottle, was evidenced by the litter in back where he threw the empties.

Finally, on a cold clear afternoon, they turned down Valley Road, the car skidding on the icy surface. A light snow had coated the road so driving was dangerous. Passing through Kalkaska, Iris wondered where the people were. A few cars moved down the main street but the sidewalks were empty. Now the road wound through dense forest, a thin mantle of snow on the evergreens and the unplowed road. Maybe that explained the lack of people. Iris had never felt so alone in her life. Then they were in the drive, the cabin looming before them. Throughout the trip, neither had spoken more than a dozen words to each other. Now Rodney, haggard and drawn, his eyes sunken and hollow, was suddenly talkative.

"Well, here we are. The place has an oil heater, but I put in a wood stove to save money. I just hope no pipes have frozen. Now, Iris, you carry the stuff in. I'm gonna light that stove and warm the place up. I hope the guy I pay to plow the drive looked in like he promised."

Iris, lugging heavy suitcases from the trunk, looked down the drive through the lonely woods. She remembered that no other house was close by; the nearest cabin was about a half mile away. A chill gust caught her hair and wet snowflakes brushed her cheeks. It was snowing harder. Shivering, she went inside, dropping the luggage in a corner. The interior was greatly improved. At least he had not lied about that. She hugged herself, shivering as he busied himself with the fire. The wood crackled and smoke rose up the stove pipe, the metal ticking as the heat increased. Rodney grabbed an ax propped near the stove. Turning, he offered it to her, handle first, the sharp blade in his big hand.

"Here, you might as well warm yourself twice. We need more wood in here, split to this size," he indicated the small pile next to the stove. "So go out there and get to work."

Mutely, Iris went into the cold yard. She'd noticed an extra room added on to the back, forming a new wing. There were now two separate bedrooms plus the combination living room-kitchen. I'll sleep in the new bedroom, separate from him, that much I will demand.

A few miles away, but a universe apart in nearby Kalkaska, County Prosecutor John Stone contemplated the snow outside his office window, cursing under his breath. Twelve inches had fallen in a couple of days on top of nearly two feet in the past three weeks. At mid January, the average depth must be nearly three feet. Already the snow removers were creating mountainous piles at the corners of intersections. In many places the sidewalks, few enough in Kalkaska, were lost under heaps of snow. Stone sipped at his third coffee of the day, and it was not yet ten, making a face as he tapped his pen against the desk. The goddamn north Michigan winter blues already. The temperature was close to zero and the weatherman said even colder air was pushing down from Alberta. From goddamn Canada, as if it weren't bad enough already at this latitude, half way between the equator and the north pole. Might as well be the north pole...

Detective Frank Shaw interrupted Stone's reverie, sidling into the office like a cat, incredibly agile and graceful for a big man.

Shaw, never one to make light talk, began to speak, but Stone interrupted, "Hi, Frank. I hope to hell you've got something for me today. If it's more teenage B and E's and DUI's or speeding violations, I'm going into the library and start throwing law books through the fucking $900 per pane plate glass insuseal windows and let in some of that fresh clean goddamn north country air."

Shaw raised bushy eyebrows as if to accentuate the heavy eyelids that half covered his large wide-spaced eyes. He lifted a mighty paw and let it fall, as if to agree, shaking his huge head. Christ, he is big, thought Stone. At least he's on my side up here. An ally in my lonely struggle to bring enlightened law enforcement to this lovely part of Michigan. Lovely maybe in the summer…

"No, John. Sorry," said Shaw, literal-minded as always. "In fact, I almost hate to bring you this case, especially in your mood. One of our deputies responded to a domestic violence complaint last night, off Valley Road. Mostly basic stuff. The missus claims her hubby beat on her, and he denies he laid a hand on her. He says she went crazy and threw stuff around the cabin out there."

Shaw tapped a police report, "It says here there was shattered glass all over the floor, so I guess that sort of confirms the fella's story. But, I don't know. Let's see…the man's name is Rodney Harris, the lady is Iris, either his ex or current wife, I'm not sure. They moved out there 'bout a month ago. Actually, he's been around before, selling real estate. He's had that cabin for some years. Now he works part-time selling realty, but I gather he spends a hell of a lot of his time in the bars. We haven't got much on her. Anyhow, they had a talk after the complaint and surprise, surprise, the lady told the deputy she didn't want to press charges."

"Typical," said Stone. And it was. All too often the abused spouse failed to follow up. He knew that from experience. "Stupid broads. You tell them time and again what's going to happen if they don't act and sign the complaint, and then they just go back for more."

Shaw nodded in sympathy. "I know. I used to hate covering those complaints. Still do. There's not a man in the department that doesn't. You try to help some poor abused lady, marks all over her, half scared to death, her old man liquored up, and nine times out of ten she won't go past the initial call. This one looks typical, but who knows. Here's the report." Shaw slapped the file down on Stone's desk. "Maybe you can do something. The lady says she has prosecuted Harris before, in Ionia, I think. She gave an attorney's number down there. It's on the report. The deputy said he didn't like the way Harris acted. Something's very wrong out there."

Then Shaw was gone as quickly as he had come.

Stone scanned the report, pouring another cup of weak coffee. It was hardly exciting reading. Both parties had made written statements, neither especially instructive, but he could read quite a bit between the lines. This one had the earmarks of a longstanding problem. The language reeked of it. During his term as County Prosecutor, John Stone had handled perhaps two dozen such complaints, of which only five had gone past stage one to the signing of a warrant. Of those five, none had gone to trial. Invariably, within a few days if not hours, the abused woman would beg that charges be dropped. The language was always similar, "We had a long talk and he promises not to hit me anymore. It was just a misunderstanding. So I'm going to give him one more chance, and if he hits me again I sure will press charges. It was the alcohol that made him do it. He's stopped drinking now, so it won't happen again. Besides, God will protect me. And I love him. He loves me, too." He knew the language by heart. Stone, at first appalled by the complaints, hardly aware at the beginning of his term that such things were fairly commonplace in any environment, now had little sympathy remaining. Like the old saw, "you can take a horse to water, but you can't make him drink", you could only do so much, go so far. You could prepare an arrest warrant for an abused woman, but you sure as hell couldn't force her to sign on the dotted line. He read Iris Harris's statement through the second time. It was pointed and brief:

> "Rodney came home late. He'd been drinking. After about an hour, he started talking about Sally. She is a woman we knew downstate. I told him to shut-up, but he wouldn't. He taunted me about her. Finally I lost my temper and threw an ash tray at him. He immediately began to hit me. I ran into the kitchen and grabbed a broom. I don't know if I hit him or not. If I did, he deserved it. All I want is him out of the place. I will not press charges."

Here we go again, thought Stone. How stupid can you be. He read Harris's statement:

> "I was sitting in the living room minding my own business, having a drink when she started accusing me of carrying on with Sally. Now, we both of us know I did once have an affair with the woman but that was months ago before we got back together. I never kept that a secret. She was accusing me of a recent affair. Sally lives downstate and I haven't seen her in months. Anyhow, she keeps at me and I tell her to lay off and then she starts throwing stuff at me, screaming at me. Let me tell you this. This is not new with her. Such behavior was common in Ionia, and there are police records to prove it. You can check with the Sheriff's Department if you don't believe me. Anyway, so I get up from the couch to calm her down and she runs into the kitchen for this broom and starts swinging

the thing at me, hitting me on the shoulders. You can see the marks.
Well, finally I take the broom from her and she calls the police.

When she lived in Boulder, she tried to kill herself. You can check
with the hospital out there. She's unstable. I love my wife, but she
is disturbed and needs counseling. I plan to set up an appointment
with a psychiatrist next week. I don't plan to press charges, I just
want to have her get help."

Stone swore. Damned bastard...probably telling just enough half truths
to make it look good. He had seen this plenty. He wrote across the front of
the warrant request, "No action—since neither party desires to press criminal
charges. File with miscellaneous police reports." Then he threw the file in the
proper bin for his secretary to handle. There were other things to attend to.

At that moment, Iris sat on the couch. Rodney was in the kitchen fixing
a drink; she had no idea how many he had consumed since his return at four
in the morning. They hadn't spoken since his return.

"Iris," Rodney's voice boomed as he advanced, drinks in hand,
smirking, holding out a full glass for her in one hand and tossing down a huge
gulp from his own, "you gotta relax. You know that? When are you gonna
learn? The cops can't help you. No one can help you. You belong to me. You
are mine alone, and you'll never be able to leave me again. Sometimes I
wonder, Iris, if you understand this. When are you gonna learn to accept the
inevitable?"

Iris kept her thoughts to herself. Talking did no good. Nothing helped.
She had not pressed charges knowing that nothing would come of it. Now
he had her again, the local cops alienated already. She wondered, almost
beyond caring, if this tirade was the prelude to more beatings, or would he
try to force himself on her? She took a sip of the drink, its warm-spreading
effect working on her at once. At least she got some comfort from the booze.
If he took her, she would feel that much less, and care less. If he beat her,
she would hurt less. Even if all he did was talk at her, she would hear less.
The less the better. She withdrew into herself.

"Julia tried," said Rodney, launching his peroration, "and I don't mind
telling you that other women have tried. To no avail, Iris, to no avail! Julia
forced me to tie her to that chair and use an ax on her." He paused and
leaned closer, studying Iris for reaction. "You wondered about that, I'll bet.
Sure I did that to her. She told the truth about that. It sure made it harder for

her to walk after that. And she deserved it. And you know, it didn't surprise me how easy she came back after you left me that time. She wanted to, y'know, she had to."

It came as a surprise to Iris that the two of them had gotten together. Iris listened intently, but she kept her eyes shut as he continued his amazing confession. He leaned in yet closer, his mouth near her ear, making sure she heard every evil word. "Yeah, we lived together for a couple of weeks until she started acting crazy again. I had her recommitted. No one was surprised she hung herself."

What he said next was an even bigger surprise.

"Joan was the one that got away. She was damn lucky, and I was young then. She took the kids and split. I searched for her all over, but she somehow stayed one jump ahead of me. But my mother, y'know, and that fucking boyfriend of hers, they weren't so lucky. I knew they was sleeping upstairs in that dingy dump in Sandusky. They didn't smell the smoke till it was too late. The cops and the school guidance counselor all agreed it was an accident. I was too young, they said, to know what I was doing. I could've stopped my brothers and sisters, too, and maybe got them outa there, but the fire got out of control, and they deserved it too. They was always my mother's favorites, y'know. So they deserved to die too. They, all of 'em, treated me like dirt, and they got what they deserved."

Suddenly he poked Iris. She had put her drink down and now held both hands over her ears, trying to shut him out. He pulled her hands away easily. As if willed to it, she opened her eyes and saw his up close, bright, that unnatural brilliance in them. She was overcome with fear.

"You hear, Iris? I want you to hear it all. I want you to know, Iris, that you will never leave me. You are mine to the end. So don't ever think of leaving, just don't even dream about it. Unless you don't value your life. I've killed before and I'll do it again."

Each word seemed to reverberate inside her skull, each separate word as clear as if printed on her brain. She was aware of the high-pitched tone that seemed to dominate him, taking over his voice, the voice of Mr. Hyde, the monster.

To punctuate his message, he shook her, cursing in foul obscenity and hate. When she tried to pull away, he hit her with his open hand, again and again, snapping her head back, until bright flashes like crimson explosions in her skull brought an end to pain, brought darkness.

34

White on white. Everywhere white. For three days endlessly falling, through dark and light and without letup, the snow fell into the woods, layering white until the white of the sky and land were one. When the sun showed at all through the snowfall, it merely glowed like a bright circle, and the light was diffused as if it came from everywhere. From the cabin windows, the white seemed to come in closer. Iris felt enveloped, closer and closer. A chill mantle of shroud-like white fell and Iris despaired. Motion and sound no longer seemed to help, not even the cry of the jays helped. She neglected the feeder and the birds no longer came. Inside it was warm, but Iris never felt warm, huddling and holding herself. Sometimes, when he was gone, she cried; always, however, the tears came without relief. There was no expiation.

For several days, now mounting to over two weeks, there had been a kind of truce in the isolated cabin. Rodney went about his business almost as if nothing had happened. As he began to drink even more, she too sipped her way into hazy oblivion. It was the only way she could sleep. She thought about escape, but now she did not mention a word to him. Perhaps confident of her fear and obedience, he left her alone much of the time. The phone was available. True, he might later see any long distant calls she made when the phone bill came, but there was the leeway of several days, weeks, before he would know. So twice, emboldened by brief periods of sun brilliant on the snow, by a touch of humanity felt through the TV tube, she had called, speaking fast, desperation in her words. She called the Aspers in Boulder, learning that the apartment was available if she returned. Mr. Asper even offered to buy a plane ticket for her—she could repay it later he said—if she would agree to fly out soon. Her ex-boss in the restaurant was willing to give her another chance. Another call confirmed the reservation.

But how could she make it to the airport in Traverse City, almost an hour away? The cabin was isolated and it was dangerous to walk any distance in this stuff. Along the road, drifts were piled high. Rodney had now been gone for hours, the snow falling and falling. From the cabin, she could no longer see Valley Road. But she had devised a scheme. She would seduce him into taking her into town, to one of the bars he hung out in, to eat and pass the evening.

Once in Kalkaska she would escape him. It might be possible to hitch a ride into Traverse City. The ticket awaited her at the airport, paid in advance. She had time, more than fourty hours to make it. Maybe she could get help from the cops...no that was not a good idea at all. But if she could get into town, then, then...

She had no idea how long she watched the snow piling up, before she saw the headlights through the swirling white. It was the hired snowplow, working quickly, backing and roaring ahead until the drive was reasonably clear. She waited. It was hours, nearly eight o'clock when the Thunderbird finally appeared. He was in the door quickly, exuding energy and decision. Almost bounding across the floor, he went to the bourbon and poured two drinks, his arms waving. What was happening?

"I...I'm glad to see you, Rodney," she said, smiling, trying to sound cheerful, frightened by this mood of his. "Out here alone all day in all this snow, I thought maybe we could drive into that bar, y'know, the one where they make those great three-quarter pound burgers that you like. Make an evening of it there. Maybe even dance a bit. I heard on the radio, they have a band in there, starting tonight at ten. It would do us good, don't you think?"

"What in the hell," Rodney halted the glass halfway to his lips. "You're all turned on, ain't you? But I got plans too. Big plans. We are leaving here, you and me, soon. I have a big deal cooking up at the Soo. There's money in the land up there, and I been looking into it."

So that was it. He was planning to take her even farther away, across the Straits to the Upper Peninsula; that explained his energy.

Careful of her words, Iris pretended interest, determined that somehow she would use his euphoria and get into town this night. Somehow she must.

"I think that's a good idea, Rodney. But why don't we talk about it over a good dinner in the tavern. I haven't got it in me to cook tonight, and nothing's ready here. D'you think we could drive in, sit in the warm bar and talk? It does sound good, Rodney."

He stood in the kitchen, not moving, gazing at her. He tossed down a swig and moved to the stove and shoved more wood in. The chimney roared and he raised his voice, "No. We're not going to town. It's hell out there and comin' down harder. Why drive anywhere? It's cozy here and you can whip something up. Hell, you haven't cooked a decent supper in weeks anyway, so what difference does it make to you? Just get to work and cook something. We're staying in tonight."

"But, Rodney..."

"You heard me, dammit. The subject is closed."

Something gave way then in Iris and with the loss of control came a lessening of fear. This time, instead of throwing something or grabbing a broom, she spoke with icy hate, the words spewing out.

"You goddamn son-of-a-bitch. You bastard. You can't do this. I am leaving, and you are going to take me into Traverse City tonight. Now! You are going to drive me there and I am leaving for Boulder. It's all arranged. Do you hear me, you bastard? Nothing will stop me. You'll have to kill me to stop me."

Rodney's eyes glittered, the pitch of his voice rising, "You just forget it. You will never leave. Unless you go with me, you go nowhere. I told you once and I'll tell you one more time. You belong to me!"

Iris stood firm, facing him, unwavering. "I'm packed, and the only way you'll stop me is to kill me." She flung the challenge at him and turned to enter the small bedroom.

"Bitch! Look at me." He grabbed her at the door and threw her against the bed. "You never learn do you?" He hit her hard on the face with the back of his hand, then again and again. Resisting, Iris tried to protect her face and kick out. He easily avoided her feeble resistance and hit her harder.

"Do I have to keep this up all day," he panted, shouting, finally backing away to catch his breath.

Rolling away, Iris grabbed the lamp from the nightstand and threw it hard, grazing him on the shoulder, "I'm calling the police. They will get me out, and I will never come back." Sobbing, she rose, moving towards the door, throwing the clock-radio.

"Like hell, bitch. You watch this," and he dialed the Sheriff's Office.

"Hello? Is this the Sheriff? Yes. Well, this is Rodney Harris out on Valley Road. My woman is acting up again, throwing things, out-of-control. I think she might hurt herself. Could you please send a car before something happens?"

As he spoke, Iris came screaming through the door after him, "You won't stop me, bastard, I'll kill you, you fucking bastard..." her voice loud enough to be heard at the other end of the line.

"Can you hear that?" Rodney asked. "Get a car out here, she's half crazy..."

He turned to her, arms held out, speaking in a low voice so it could not be heard on the phone, taunting her, "C'mon, Iris...that's it, keep it up, bitch, keep it up, you stupid cunt. Keep screaming and goin' nuts and I've got you right where I want you...c'mon, bitch." He backed away, grinning, the light in his eyes brilliant, his anger seemingly gone now.

Detective Frank Shaw picked up the phone, listened for a moment as the dispatcher described the Harris complaint, and then slammed it down hard. He hated calls like this. All the patrol cars were miles away. He would have to go. Rising, he moved quickly to his coat, patting his shoulder harness automatically, as he had done a thousand times, striding through the dispatcher's office with a wave and a curse, "Shit, the paperwork can wait," he spoke to the dispatcher, "Where did you say, out on Valley Road somewhere?" He listened to the directions, "Okay, I'll go alone. But these things can get ugly. Be sure to have all other units alerted in case I call in for help. It's probably routine though."

Pushing the big Plymouth slowly through swirling snow, unable to see more than fifteen or twenty feet ahead, Shaw cursed. Just getting there might take twenty or thirty minutes. No one should be out on such a night, though he felt mild guilt knowing all the patrol cars were busy with minor accidents, helping motorists who had gone into ditches and drifts, trying to get from one place to another on nearly impassible roads. His thoughts drifted as he controlled the car, knowing the way as he did on all the backcountry roads in the county.

Frank Shaw was a lonely man...that was for sure. Sometimes depressed, he hated being alone like this. His wife of nineteen years was downstate for two weeks with their teenage boy, visiting her parents in Pontiac. But, even when she was home, he felt a growing sense of isolation. It was hard to put it in words, even to think it through. This looming sense of distance between himself and his family, between Ellen, whom he had married at thirty (she being twenty-seven then, a secretary in a small business in Traverse City), and his uncommunicative son. It confused him and angered him. He'd hoped he might enjoy having the house to himself, being free to eat out, to drive down into Traverse City for a good movie, or to go out with some of the deputies on the snowmobiles on a clear night. But he had merely felt lonelier. Mostly he had sat at home, reading or watching TV and blaming himself for such lethargy. For several years Shaw had wondered whether a move might help. He loved the surrounding landscape; the deep piney swatches of forest that descended into cedar swamps, and the thickets where deer yarded in winter, where bear fed in the fall, the hilly upland hardwood forest of maple, beech, basswood, and slippery elm, and the undergrowth where grouse drummed and cottontails fed at dawn. A hunter from boyhood, familiar with the land as far back as he could remember, he had moved deliberately into wild Kalkaska County after spending the 'sixties with the Detroit police department. It seemed a natural step for him to become a cop after serving as an MP in the Army. He'd hunted and fished to his heart's content, disdaining travel except for a once-a-year hunting trip into Ontario. But the northern landscape was no longer enough. He felt time slipping by and his 50th birthday approached. Watching specials on TV (the National Geographic specials in particular always pulled at his heart and he craved deeply to see just once one of those exotic places, the vast game herds of East Africa, the black water of the Rio Negro where caiman swam and ocelots yowled in the rainforest, the rim of the Himalaya when the clouds opened above Nepal, even the glaciers of the Rockies in his own country), he sometimes wanted to chuck it all, sell the house and car, take his wife and kid and just travel for six months or a year. But it was impractical and Ellen would never agree. Maybe a bigger town, a city, would enliven him again, but he doubted that too. His visits to Chicago and Detroit, his memories of Tokyo and Yokohama, of Los Angeles and El Paso, did not encourage speculation of this sort. He was a country boy and would remain so.

The car skidded out of control, though he pulled hard into the skid and tapped the brakes. It was too late. No amount of experience helped. The patrol car was stuck, nose down, the front buried in a massive drift. Cursing, he got out and began to hoof it down the road, holding a big flashlight, unable to see beyond a few feet, sometimes finding himself wandering into the drifts, only aware of the road and its curves because of the snow laden trees on either side. He hoped no car would strike him. When he found the long drive leading to the Harris cabin, he was relieved. At least in there he could call for help, warm up, and maybe have a cup of java. After he had straightened out the silly fight, maybe...

Shaw heard the noise halfway up the drive. Was it a shot? With the wind and snow and the parka hood up he wasn't sure. He moved quickly, unzipping the parka, and at the door to the cabin he took time to unlimber his automatic, feeling the cold steel. He had never, in all his years, had to use a weapon, but he was always ready. He knocked loudly, shouting against the rising whine of the blizzard, "Hello. It's the police! Open up!"

Nothing. He knocked again, shouting louder. Now he had the hefty automatic in hand and he held it ready while he rattled the doorknob, shouting again. Shaw had seen trouble before and violence, especially in the Detroit riots of '67, when he had seen duty on Twelfth Street. He never forgot the bodies on Brush and John R., or the sense of helplessness as he watched buildings burning, blackening the sky above the Lodge Freeway. The door was not locked and he pushed his way inside.

Warm air hit Shaw's face, and he blinked the snow away. A form loomed before him, in a chair in the kitchen, directly ahead. He realized it was a large man, unmoving, slumped, apparently tied to the chair, head lolling to one side. He saw the blood immediately and looked quickly around. The body was still, no sign of breath or life. A huge quantity of blood, not yet congealed, had flowed onto the floor and he saw blood tracks. In the periphery of his vision he discerned movement and he leveled his weapon, going into the crouch, both hands holding it full front, ready to fire.

"Stop!" he roared.

The figure before him moved again, one hand held high. He held his fire and stepped sideways. The woman held an ax, a small-handled type such as the Scouts used, and she advanced on the body tied in the chair.

"Drop it! Just put it down, Mrs. Harris."

She did not stop, moving as if in a dream, speaking clearly, as if instructing a classroom full of kids, "This one is for Julia, you son-of-a-bitch," and she lurched forward, the ax descending.

Shaw let his weapon go and grabbed her with both hands, holding her with his considerable strength, aware of the surge of adrenalin in her, barely able to twist her wrist until the ax fell to the floor. Her strength almost a match for him, though he outweighed her by at least a hundred pounds, he finally wrestled her to the floor. There she lay sobbing, face turned to the open door where snow gusted in on the rising wind...

Shaw stood for a long time, perhaps a minute or more, taking all of it in. His breath was jagged, hurting in his chest. At first he searched without moving his body, his eyes pulled again and again to the feet of the corpse in the chair. Most of the blood seemed to flow from the right foot, the shoe had been removed, and the stocking too. White bone protruded from the severed toes, and he could see where the ax had done its work. He studied every detail. A 12-gauge shotgun lay on the floor near the stove. He stepped over and around the blood and picked it up, careful not to touch the stock or the finger-guard, marking the spot where it had fallen, checked the breach, and propped it against the table. He leaned forward and felt for a pulse at Harris's neck. Nothing. The eyes were open and dilated.

He examined the body quickly, breathing carefully and deeply, trying to control the rising nausea. He could not remember when he had seen worse. It was obvious and clear. Harris had been shot at close range, with the shotgun. The hole in his torso was enormous. He had probably died immediately.

Shaw looked at the woman, remembering her name, Iris. She was quiet now, her eyes shut as if sleeping. He saw her eyes open. He decided he could leave her for the moment and stepped to the phone, half expecting it to be ripped out. It hummed, working. He dialed quickly.

"Shaw here. I'm at the Harris place. We have a homicide here. You know, that cabin on Valley Road, near that crick? You better call for help. I have a female in custody. Get an ambulance, and you better send a tow-truck ahead with chains. Call Jim's garage. He'll have that big rig ready on a night like this. Right. And make sure he has chains on the thing. Now listen. The dead man is Rodney Harris. Yeah. He's dead. Christ, listen to me will ya. He has a hole in him big as a softball. He's a goner for sure. Yeah, send the ambulance anyhow. My car's in the drift just up the road from the cabin driveway. Can't miss it."

Shaw knew from the dispatcher's voice that he had set the wheels in motion. The phones and police band would be buzzing now for hours. The place would fill up quickly with cops and emergency people, even in the midst of this blizzard.

Then he turned to the woman. She sat now on the floor, eyes open but unfocused. He shut the door and quickly the heat from the stove warmed the little room. He picked up his automatic and holstered it, checking the shotgun to make sure it was empty. She had apparently used only one shell on her husband, but that was enough. And that ax...he felt sick.

"Mrs. Harris. Can you hear me?"

Iris did not respond to him, but he heard a murmur and he moved closer. She was talking almost under her breath, "I loved him. I loved him but he deserved it. He was mean, mean. I loved him though...I really did. No one loved any man more. I tried. God knows, I tried. I gave him so much. I gave him every chance. Oh God. Why did he beat me? What made him hurt me? I had to do it."

Softly Shaw interrupted. This was a confession of sorts, but it would not do.

"Mrs. Harris. I'm Frank Shaw, detective with the Sheriff's Office. Do you hear me?" She nodded. "Good. Now can you tell me what happened? Can you tell me about your husband's death?" Shaw could see the staring eyes of the corpse and strangely the woman's eyes seemed almost as fixed and empty. He had read her no rights, but he figured she was not altogether coherent. He gently asked again, eager to get some sense of what had happened. Clearly, there was no one else around. She had obviously done the deed.

"Dead?" She looked at him as if to see him for the first time, her eyes moving. "He's not dead. I just had to hurt him. Look, he's sitting right there." She began to rise.

It took his considerable strength to subdue her again. This time he used his handcuffs and shackled her hands behind her back. He placed her carefully on her back on the couch, and waited for support. The ensuing minutes, hours, were a jumble. Deputy Mike King was first to arrive, with the tow-truck right behind. King threw up when he saw the sight in the kitchen, his mucus mixing with the drying blood. Eventually calmed, King returned to the patrol car for camera and tape-measure. Then he entered with three more officers, their cars parked out on the road. Then the ambulance personnel arrived, and within an hour or so the body was removed.

Shaw oversaw everything, the pictures taken from every angle, the detailed notes on the location of everything when he entered, the sketches of placements and angles. He conducted a careful search of the entire cabin, both bedrooms, all closets, everything, including drawers and two packed suitcases. He found the boxes of shells and a newly opened box. Photos were taken of the wall where the shot had penetrated after passing through the body. Measurements were made with tape. He tagged and bagged the ax and shotgun, and then noticed the riding crop in the corner, tagging it too. What, he wondered, was that doing here, not a horse within miles?

Iris Harris lay quiet through it all. Then Shaw guided her out into the night, into the storm.

"You guys make sure it's all padlocked, every window secured. We don't want folks poking in. And make sure a team gets out here tomorrow to do it all through again. Now, which one of you is going to help me get my car out, and get her back?"

It took another half hour to free the car, the tow-truck straining at its utmost before the Plymouth was on the road. Iris sat quiet through it all. Then Shaw slid in and drove with care. It was nearly midnight when they arrived at the station, every light blazing from every window.

Iris was aware of blood on her blouse and skirt, blood caked and dried on her hands. Was it her own? Had Rodney hurt her so? She was vaguely aware of unfamiliar walls and voices. Pain throbbed in her skull and she saw through a reddish haze, the people blurred. But words came through, incoherent sounds seemingly not connected to the looming shapes of the men. She gripped her hands and felt the stickiness, and she felt dried tears on her face. Or was that blood too? What had he done?

"You better call the Prosecutor, John Stone, if you haven't already."

The voice boomed, and she looked at the source.

"Yeah. Stone's been notified."

"Well, tell him to get his ass over here. We got a case of open murder here for sure. Jesus, did you see that poor son-of-a-bitch. Jesus, what a mess. This one looks cut and dried."

She moved her head tenderly and looked around. What had she done? She suddenly knew. This was his blood on her, brown and dry now on her skirt but sticky between her fingers.

"How is he?" she said. The men stared and she spoke up, "How is Rodney? I want to talk to him. Please let me talk to him. How is he?"

"She's doing it again. Can you stop her?"

She felt a hand firmly push her into her chair. She tried to rise again, "Please...he can't be dead..." Shuddering, beyond tears, she rubbed her hands.

"Mrs. Harris," it was Shaw's voice, "your husband is dead. It appears you shot him."

"No! No! I loved him. I wouldn't shoot him," Iris screamed. "You killed him, you did it. You bastard, let me see him. I want to see him."

They restrained her and held her down until her struggles ceased. Gasping for breath and sobbing, but with eyes empty of tears, she stared at the men. Then she shook her head slowly at first, then faster. Again they restrained her.

"Where's the matron? Get her over here."

Shaw sat beside her for a long time, ready to help. He felt beyond the struggle now. He sensed tension in his chest and his hands shook. Forcing control, he tried to relax. He knew that adrenalin has sustained him, but now he felt drained. Had he done things right? Done his duty? He waited amid the clamor. The office was full of noise and motion, even at this hour. Heads poked in and out, and people stared. Where in the hell was Stone? He waved them away, angry. Repelled, yet strangely drawn and protective, he sat beside her and thought about the awful scene out there at the lonely cabin in the woods, all socked in by drifts and the howling wind—and the carnage. And this woman sitting right here had done it. She had killed her husband and for some bizarre reason had mutilated him. That he had seen himself. The poor woman. The evidence was concrete, solid, unquestionable.

35

John Stone stopped on the courthouse steps, looking up into the night sky. As quickly as it had come, the storm was gone and a canopy of dazzling stars suffused the heavens from horizon to horizon. The streets of the little town were illuminated by a crystalline nimbus, and he could almost feel the earth wheeling through space.

That poor woman inside...what did she think? Stone knew he would have to prosecute her.

Stone had not come easily to this job. To the casual observer perhaps, his career might seem appropriate and predictable. At thirty-two he was well-spoken, tailored, barbered, and professional in demeanor. Yet doubt had run through every phase of his progress from student to County Prosecutor, from the boozy parties of his undergraduate years at MSU, to the drudgery of law school. He sometimes wondered if others who presented an aura of confidence had such doubts. Maybe all humans did from time to time.

Stone had come from a suburb of Flint, the "G.M. Town" as it was known. He had vivid memories of the village, of open fields and woodlots on one side where a small river flowed to skirt the village, of the "business district" two blocks long, lined with false-fronted stores, a single movie-theater, two drug stores, three barber shops much in use even in that generation of long-haired youths (of which John himself had been briefly part), the town-hall and volunteer firehouse, the Scout meetings in the basement of the Baptist Church. He had dreamed of becoming Perry Mason since eight years of age when Raymond Burr on TV inevitably and relentlessly destroyed poor Hamilton Burge night after night, unraveling what seemed to be air-tight cases against the trapped or framed clients. Stone knew it was not like that in real life, but he had been interested, and without much thought he aimed at becoming a lawyer. Even when he discovered that the law profession required seven years of education after high school, he had persevered. For the most part an indifferent student, he'd been persuaded to major in business at Michigan State. Thoroughly bored by management, marketing, accounting, and computer science, he had gladly turned to pre-law, and in his final year had performed far better in the humanities and social studies classes. Advised that his grades would never get him into a prestigious law school, Stone had settled for the Detroit College of Law. He had no trouble getting in; his scores on the LSAT admissions test had been high. When he put his mind to it he could do damned good work.

His education in dirty, wild Detroit during those vivid and hectic years of civil-rights, anti-war action, and riots had been invaluable. Law school had also taught him how to survive. There was nothing rarified about the Detroit College of Law. An incident in his second year had proved to him that nothing in life was fair. He'd been given an undeserved D by the Dean of the Law School. The Dean's policy was to give credit for class participation as well as for work done on exams. An inadequate answer in class would be remembered and given more import by the Dean than anything else done through the term. Unfortunately, there were one hundred and twenty students in the class and only a handful were ever called upon to recite. John had been called out. Called upon to answer a complicated question for which he was unprepared, he stumbled. When he received the D he'd gone to see the Dean and learned that his grade on the final had been higher than average, but the Dean had stuck to the D on the basis of the incident in class. "I called upon you in class and you were unprepared," declared the Dean, disdainfully looking up from his desk. He had given John a withering stare and dismissed him. Turning impotent anger into determination, John buckled down and graduated without further difficulty, receiving his diploma from the very hand of the man who had nearly flunked him out. This was a singular triumph for a young man who had rarely excelled in obvious ways, but who had built a core of confidence in his capacity to adapt, his ability to bounce back.

The summer after graduation, Stone clerked for a Detroit law firm, attending a bar exam course at the same time. Often going days without adequate sleep, frustrated, overworked, unhappy, he'd triumphed. Passing the bar exam with ease he had the new job in remote Kalkaska, a place he had seen perhaps twice in his life. At first he felt somewhat diminished. Kalkaska, despite its natural attractions, was hardly at the center of action. Indeed the little town and its surrounding and almost empty countryside was a genuine backwater of sorts.

But it was a backwoods town, surrounded by a sportsman's paradise. Responsibility in such a place could teach hard lessons. Stone had gradually come through the stultifying routine of petty cases with a keen sense of how the law functioned. Realistic but not cynical, learning to compromise and adjust in the bureaucratic maze of paperwork and the drudgery of rural legal work, he had become proficient. He knew that real proficiency in anything was not to be taken lightly. He'd tried a range of cases across the scope of legal plains and mountains. In subtle ways, hard to pin-point, but real nevertheless, he had come to respect both the law and himself.

Stone was not a particularly philosophic man. Sometimes when trout fishing on one of the local rivers, a pearl-gray dawn revealing greening foliage and illuminating the riffs of fast water where it turned beneath old logs and roots, waiting for the rush and strike of the rainbow, he might think about himself, about his life and its direction. But he rarely questioned his purpose as he had done when younger. He knew the aphorism that the "unexamined life" is a life not worth living. He had lost his mother to a long illness and had learned through grief that life in itself was precious. Naturally the quality of daily life was vital. Sometimes he pondered deeper questions of the sort that rural living encouraged—for the pace was slower and more natural than in the busy cities—and he had come through a failed and hurried marriage with renewed hope, an even stronger sense of the capacity to give and to share, and with renewed resolve to live even more fully, even with loneliness, even when love came hard. He never doubted greater fulfillment would come one day.

The stars were bright but cold and he shivered. Turning from the steps he ran indoors, fatigue gone. Warm air and light greeted him. He advanced on the tableau...one he would never forget.

Iris Harris sat in the holding cell hunched in a wooden chair, her hands clenched. She had blood on her, visible in several places, and her eyes moved in unblinking otherworldly fear to take him in. He wondered if she saw him at all. There was something almost physically alien in her presence, as if she had been placed here from beyond the stars. This was absurd. He would have to try this woman for murder. The facts as he understood them, even in brief talks on the phone when Shaw and others had informed him of the bare outline of events, pointed to the truth. There was nothing alien about her. She had killed another human being. She had in fact killed her ex-husband. He knew there had to be mitigating circumstances, especially in a case of this sort, but the bare facts seemed to leap at him.

Shaw rose, towering, massive. Stone was glad of the big detective's presence, the unexpected and unnecessary handshake, the strength revealed in the big fingers squeezing his own. But Shaw also expressed a mixture of relief and sorrow in his expression, as if he had something to apologize for.

"I'm sorry, John. This is one hell of a bad deal...sorry to rout you out of bed on a night like this," Shaw's face hung, eyes down.

"It's my job," said Stone glancing again at Mrs. Harris who remained silent, watching. "Besides, the snow has stopped, the storm has passed. The morning will be beautiful."

He realized the incongruity of his words. For Iris Harris, it couldn't be worse. He could see uneven redness on her face, but no apparent bruises. Her face was shadowed by grief, and mystery. As if reading his thoughts, Shaw rumbled his reply, pulling him out into the corridor leading to Stone's office, leaning in close to his ear, "You won't think so, John, not when you hear all the details about what happened out there. I guess we better go into your office. This will take time."

The two men disappeared into Stone's sanctum sanctorum. Approximately an hour later after careful review of the evidence Iris Harris was formally charged on an open charge of murder. She would be arraigned that evening before the magistrate. Since Kalkaska County only had a holding facility and not a jail, Iris would have to be moved. Before dawn, she was taken handcuffed from her cell to a patrol car and then driven to a jail in Traverse City to be held until Tuesday when she would be taken before the District Judge.

The body of Rodney Harris lay cold on an equally cold steel table in the morgue of Munson Medical Center in Traverse City. The cause of death was obvious. The pathologist found few abnormalities in his examination of the corpse. There were several fractures of the ribs which by all appearances had been caused by shotgun pellets fired at close range into the left side of the torso. Multiple foreign bodies were found in the left shoulder region and adjacent to the rib cage, and there were further pellets in the lung, six in all. An examination of the visceral pleura revealed a zone of ecchymoses 6.0 cm in diameter situated along the lateral aspect to overlie the first through fourth ribs. On the anterior surface of the upper lobe of the left lung, there was a 3.0 cm zone of hemorrhage in the center of which was a defect approximately 0.5 cm in diameter. There was extensive hemorrhaging into the paretal pleura in the intralober tissue, and it involved a zone approximately 8.0 cm on the interior aspect of the upper lobe of the left lung and 5.0 cm on the superior aspect of the lower lobe of the left lung. The pathologist also noticed two pellets in the region of the hemorrhage. In his opinion, the cause of death was a gunshot wound of the left chest wall, the left lung, and the left shoulder. He also noticed an enlarged liver and the indication of moderate cirrhosis. The toes of the right foot had been severed, apparently after the time of death, though there was evidence of hemorrhage. Otherwise, the body was robust and in remarkable condition for that of a man in his late fifties at the time of death. The pathologist made a professional guess that the man had probably died almost instantly, barely aware of the cause of his demise, if at all.

No one claimed the body, and when everything was accomplished according to the law, the county buried the remains in a small corner of its cemetery.

Iris woke to bare walls and bars. Oh God, he has done it again, she thought, terrified by the unfamiliar surroundings. "Let me out," she screamed.

"Shut up, bitch," came the guttural reply from the cot next to hers. It was a woman's voice, rough and unfriendly. Then she knew where she was. Swinging her feet to the floor, Iris tried to reconstruct events. Dimly she recalled Rodney talking to the police on the phone and hanging up with a smirk. He had gone into the bedroom and emerged with that riding crop, slapping it against his leg.

She remembered his words, "Now, cunt, you better keep your mouth shut when they get here, or I'll beat the hell out of you when they leave." He had begun to slap her then, not hard enough to bring blood but with stinging force, her eyes tearing at the impact. Taunting her with foul words, he had threatened her again. They sat at the table for awhile. What happened next was muddled. She could not put the images in place. Images of blood, of the weight of the shotgun in her hands, of Rodney reeling back and of the reverberation of the explosion, more blood, tying him to a chair, and of the ax in her hand and the crunch of bone and more blood.

She sobbed heavily, muttering to herself. The woman cursed her again.

Iris studied the derelict woman; the crust of vomit on the painted lips and the yellowed teeth of her cell-mate. No escaping it. She was in jail. Memory flooded back and she sat, holding her face. She had shot Rodney. Carefully she stood and paced a few feet, feeling the pain of his last beating under her skin, against the bones of her face and upper arms and torso. "I shouldn't be here," she thought, "I should be free, even if I did kill him. He deserved it. I had no choice. It was him or me. He was a devil. I should receive a medal." The disjointed phrases seem to flash in and out of her mind. She sat again, aware of the smell of disinfectant and urine, and overcome with grief, fatigue, anger, and fear, she lay back and slipped into restless sleep.

The next morning Stone arrived at his office early. The freshly fallen snow crunched under his boots as he made his way up the courthouse steps. Stone needed coffee. Taking a chance he buzzed Shaw.

"D'you have any coffee brewing?"

"Sure do," replied Shaw, "I'll be right up."

Within minutes Shaw arrived jiggling two Styrofoam cups and the Harris file. Somehow he had managed to maneuver his large frame into the chair across from Stone without dropping the cargo. It appeared Shaw had not slept.

"Y'know John, I think we have a strong case here." He held up a big hand and began ticking off the points on his fingers. "First, she was the only person there, besides the deceased, when I got to the scene. Second, she had to use that gun on him and to use it, she had to go into that bedroom, uncase the weapon, load it, and return to the front room to shoot him. That implies forethought. We also have the evidence that he was the one who called the Sheriff's Department, and we have a quote from him, 'She's going crazy, send a car', or words to that effect. It's all in the report. The dispatcher could overhear screamed threats in the background. It was definitely a woman's voice. So, on each of these points, you can build elements of premeditation and deliberation. Then there's that matter of the ax. I can testify to that."

Stone shrugged. On the surface it did seem open and shut. They had her dead to rights, but this was shaping up as no ordinary case. "There might be difficulty admitting all those statements under the rules of evidence. Harris's statements over the phone before the killing and the things a dispatcher overheard in the background, over the phone mind you; hell, a good lawyer will get that thrown out. Even assuming all that stuff is admissible, the time span between the call and your arrival was what, maybe forty-five minutes at least? Let's assume a fight between them out there...how can we argue persuasively that there was enough time for the cooling needed to argue premeditation and deliberation? We will put the evidence before Manak and let him decide."

Shaw held his silence. He knew Stone would do a competent job, but he could see no reason for any hesitation. He had his own theory about what happened and even sympathized with the poor woman, but he strongly believed the law had been broken, and he was already convinced of certain things.

"Well, boss, we all know who did it, don't we? I mean, aside from all the clear evidence, her behavior amounts to a confession. I wrote what she said out there in the report. She may forget now, but she knew then. Don't tell me we don't have the hard facts to go for it without worrying about motive?"

"Sure," said Stone, "and I do plan to argue premeditation at the preliminary examination. But the Judge might not buy it. Anyway, I'm not sure it will make any difference at the pre-lim level. As I read the law we need only to establish the elements of second degree murder at the preliminary examination in order to get a bind over to Circuit Court. That's how we'll go."

Iris had been held without bond since her arrest because she had no known ties in the community, the proof of guilt was great, and the charge exceedingly serious. Though he knew the District Judge might change it, Stone felt secure for the moment. Iris Harris would not be easily released.

"About the inquiry down in Ionia," Shaw said, "I can't seem to get anyone on duty at this time who knows much. It seems that the Harris's were known there. You want me to keep at this over the phone, or maybe I just drive on down and look around?"

"Yes," Stone said, leaping at the suggestion. "As quick as you can. I wish we'd been able to get her to talk here. I gather you did try, after she was read her rights."

Shaw affirmed this with a nod. Iris had gathered herself enough to ask for a lawyer and to clam up. In the aftermath of the killing, the woman had been withdrawn, disoriented, and for a while apparently half-crazy with confusion and grief. Nothing she had said then made much sense though it was obvious to everyone that she had pulled the trigger on that shotgun, and Shaw himself had wrested the ax from her hands by main force.

"Was she examined by a doctor?"

"No," said Shaw. "We couldn't get one down here before she was transferred into T.C. I gather she'll be examined there today. She complained of pain."

Stone turned once more to his desk. He scanned the warrant again, reading the stark words,

ON OR ABOUT FEBRUARY 17, 1979, AT VALLEY ROAD, CLEARWATER TOWNSHIP, KALKASKA COUNTY, IRIS HARRIS DID MURDER RODNEY HARRIS; CONTRARY TO SEC. 750.31, CL 1970, AS AMENDED; MSA 28.548.

Now the wheels of justice were turning. He looked up at Shaw, "You better get on down to Ionia, Frank."

Shaw was gone immediately. A good detective, he would dig and delve and come up with plenty if there was anything relevant. And John Stone had a hunch there was plenty, though probably not the kind of thing that would help his case. Nevertheless he had a strong case. He remembered his brief glimpse of Iris that morning, just before she had been bundled off to the Traverse City jail. She had stared at him with haunted eyes, obviously in shock. Some of the blood had been hastily sponged from her hands and clothes. She was disheveled, disoriented, dirty, and seemed then to have marginal comprehension of the gravity of her situation. He could see that under normal circumstances she might be pretty in a tidy way, good bones and a good figure, but in her despair and confusion she seemed more like an overgrown child, tear-streaks on her face, hair wild and tangled. For some reason he thought she looked as if she had killed someone. Maybe he was reading his own knowledge into it. He wondered at the mystery of it; the history behind it, the human drama that would inevitably be revealed. He turned to his work, not a thought of fatigue in his head.

The morning cold had crept into John's bedroom. Two sleepless nights and too many shots of Jamesons had caused him to oversleep. He threw a green and white MSU sweatshirt over his t-shirt and stumbled into the kitchen. The tile floor was cold to his bare feet. He started the coffee, and not bothering to slip on a coat or boots, made a dash to the end of the drive to get the morning paper. It wasn't until he'd poured his first cup of coffee that he noticed the article. He spread the paper before him and read:

"'I just want to be free', Accused murderer tells her story."

The article was by Nora Richards, a local reporter for the Traverse City Sun Times. John read what followed with a mixture of fascination and dismay.

"I was his toy, his possession, his plaything. After six months of marriage, I had no life of my own. No matter what I did he would always find a way to bring me back. I divorced him and he still followed me. Finally he brought me back to Kalkaska."

The article encompassed the entire front page and continued on page three. John took the paper into the spare bedroom he used as a home office. Sitting at a battered desk his father had owned, he continued reading. He knew much of it, but some parts, including Iris's first meeting with Rodney at the Michigan Training Unit were new to him. With a yellow marker he highlighted the passages about the several beatings she had suffered at Rodney's hands. He placed question marks next to sections where Iris admitted to returning to the madman on numerous occasions. As he read onward John rocked back in his chair with surprise when he got to the part describing a sexual encounter, when Rodney, using the threat of a shotgun, forced Sally and Iris to engage in a threesome with him. John was amazed that the usually conservative Sun Times would publish this. In disbelief he read further to learn that Julia had killed herself at the State Hospital. As he made notes on a legal pad so that Shaw could follow up on Julia and Sally, John wondered about the woman he was prosecuting and the crazy path the case was about to travel.

He read on:

"That evening, before he called the police on me, setting things up in his favor as usual, he was almost inhuman, like some machine. He dug out this riding crop he used at the farm near Ionia. He had beat me before

with it, and this time I was beyond terror. There was something about him, something worse than before. I always feared for my life when he beat me, but this time he was so mechanical and hurt me so much that I was crazy with fear. I was convinced that he planned to kill me.

So I told him to lay off or I'd kill him. He just laughed and taunted me more in that crazy voice. He made me drink and sat at the table, calling me awful names, cursing me and laughing. The phone rang, and he answered it and told me the police would be there soon. He sat down then, telling me that when the Kalkaska cops were convinced that I was a nutty bitch, then he would have them on his side, repeating that I would never escape him. I don't know how long we sat at the table waiting for the cops, it seemed like hours. Rodney continued to threaten me and taunt me. As he drank I couldn't think. I remembered how one night when he was asleep, I had loaded the shotgun and pointed it at him, but I couldn't use it.

I don't remember this part very well. I walked into the bedroom and uncased the gun. It was another person in me doing it. I had never fired a gun before, at anything. I loaded it and walked back into the kitchen.

He had his back to me looking out at the snow. I called his name and he turned. His face, when he saw me with the gun, was full of hate. But, I could see no fear in him. He muttered something, but I just said, 'Goodbye you son-of-a-bitch' and pulled the trigger. He fell immediately and I threw the gun down."

John lay the paper aside and found the number to ring Shaw in Ionia.

"Hey boss, voice sounds a little raspy. Long night?"

"Just listen," said John, "I can't believe what they've printed here," and he read the article out loud.

"Fuck," cursed Shaw.

36

John Stone wasn't the only one reading the article with interest. The Harris story was the buzz of the coffee shops in the village. Already the patrons were choosing sides. Most assuming Iris Harris must be at fault for staying with such a brute, and, far fewer feeling the bastard had got what he deserved. It had been slightly over a year since the Francine Hughes case. Mrs. Hughes had set fire to her sleeping husband. When accused of murder she and her attorney alleged self-defense and temporary insanity based upon years of violent abuse. The jury found her not guilty by reason of temporary insanity. The trial became famous as "The Burning Bed" case.

Thirty five miles away in her distinctive home on the Old Mission Peninsula—that finger of dales and orchards thrust northward into the blue deeps of Grand Traverse Bay—Robin Blaine threw her newspaper aside. Rising, she stared across the water to the higher hills in the west, on the large Leelanau Peninsula. Clouds reared into the sky over the broad moraines, and she wondered if a storm brewed on Lake Michigan. If so, she would see it come down over those hills and over the bay right up to the beach at her doorstep. She had read the story about Iris with professional interest. A successful lawyer, Robin had moved to the Traverse City region from Detroit in the early 'seventies, seeking the slower pace and relative tranquility of the northland, lured alike by its waters and wooded hills, its excellent entertainments (Interlochen and its concerts were around twenty miles from her home; there was a repertoire theater, summer stock, even a passable orchestra) and its ambiance. She had made a name for herself since the late 'fifties when she represented controversial civil rights figures in the Detroit area, traveling in the early 'sixties into the deep south to take up the cause. She had known Martin Luther King (as a respected acquaintance, she always thought, not a real friend), had marched at Selma in '65, had witnessed harassment, demonstrations and brutality, had fought hard and won cases here, a minor triumph there. She'd been in Memphis when King was assassinated, had been with Bobby Kennedy in Los Angeles, and with Gene McCarthy in Chicago. In Detroit she had slaved at her profession, winning respect but dissatisfied too, until a string of unplanned but marvelous weekends in and near Traverse City, cross country skiing in the National Park out at the Sleeping Bear Dunes, hiking through the autumn colors of the Boardman, sailing down West Bay on a brisk northwest wind, had convinced her to move. Her husband, Edward, had never liked Detroit despite his professional success there, building an architectural business (specializing in small buildings, private homes, schools, annexes), and he had jumped at her suggestion that they try something new. Now Robin considered the bay her own, its changing colors reflecting her moods, and somehow, like the glacial hills that rose all around, comforting her as the years flew by. She was past fifty now, her abundant hair iron gray and somehow not streaked but uniform in sheen, as if the steel in her character had transferred to her hair. She had not entered law school until her early thirties, five years after the birth of their second child, almost on a whim. She had lived the law from the start, even when it seemed to protect those she most despised. Neither a radical by temperament, nor in the least revolutionary in the classic sense— she had only once cracked a book by Marx and that was for an assignment in college—she had nevertheless taken up the cause of the disadvantaged and discriminated-against with genuine passion. That, she had never given up, and was always on call for an important case where her skills might be of help.

Sometimes in contemplative moments, Robin pondered the strange attraction that had kept her married to Edward for more than thirty years. He was dour and conservative to the core. They had met after a football game at Michigan and had been in love ever since. He was a Taft Republican then—she often teased him that he remained one still—nearly eight years her senior, drawn more recently to the Goldwater-Reagan wing of the GOP as a result of the disgusting letdown of the Nixon years. She had never gloated at his discomfort or his dismay in the Watergate years, but had secretly exulted in it, considering it proof of her own views. Together the Blaine's earned a considerable income, kept up a rambling wood and glass house (with one of the best views on a peninsula famous for its vistas), had seen both sons graduate from college, and had presided over the wedding of one. Now they awaited their first grandchild. Of late, Robin had become involved with local conservation and environmentalist groups, lending her legal hand when needed, practicing law out of a successful small firm in Traverse City.

Ed, who had already read the paper, watched Robin with keen eyes, his bald head shining in the late afternoon light. He knew her well. Presently he spoke, aware of her mood.

"I suppose you can't resist it."

"That poor, poor woman. How awful. I've read a bit here and there about abuse of that sort, but, God, it must have been unbearable. I must see her."

"I suppose she deserves the best counsel available, honey. Why don't you call the paper? Maybe you can interview that reporter."

"I think N.O.W. is a better idea. Where's that number?"

Ten minutes later, Robin Blaine drove her Volvo at marginally legal speeds down the peninsula into the city, heading for the dingy frame house where the local chapter of the National Organization for Women had its headquarters. The organization had called an emergency meeting for that very evening. Already the newspaper story by Nora Richards was striking sparks.

Iris couldn't believe the crowd as the patrol car drove into the parking space near the Kalkaska Courthouse. Reporters seemed to be everywhere. The deputies escorted her quickly into the packed courtroom. She recognized the prosecutor John Stone and the big detective. Nora Richards was there and they caught each other's eyes. Iris knew the case was becoming an event and she wondered who the judge would appoint to represent her. She had been informed to expect a court-appointed attorney, but had no knowledge beyond this. That morning she had taken special care to try to look attractive, spending time on her hair, wearing a neat but severe skirt and jacket requested specially through the jail authorities and delivered that very morning.

Judge Manak was stocky, close-cropped hair brushed back from a high furrowed forehead. Square head on a bull neck, he looked more like a football coach than a judge, but he exuded an air of businesslike authority. It was nine o'clock on the dot. Iris wondered. Had a lawyer come to see her before now, would she have consented to the long interviews with Nora Richards? Well, it was too late now. Involuntarily adjusting her hair, aware of the eyes on her, she waited, breathing deeply to maintain control.

"People of the State of Michigan vs. Iris Harris," intoned the judge. Iris realized she must stand and she almost fell back as she rose, slightly dizzy with apprehension. The matron next to her held her elbow for a moment.

"Mrs. Harris," the judge continued, "You are charged, that on February 17, 1979, at Valley Road, Clearwater Township, Kalkaska County, that you did murder Rodney Harris. This Court being a Court of limited jurisdiction, I shall enter a plea of not guilty on your behalf. You should be further advised that you have a statutory right to a preliminary examination within twelve days of today's date. At such examination, the Prosecuting Attorney must prove a crime has been committed and that it is likely that you committed the crime. Do you desire such an examination?"

Iris felt the hush. The only sound was the scratch of pencil on pad, the suppressed cough of a spectator. She spoke again, surprised at her growing calm.

"Your honor, I have not had the opportunity to discuss this matter with an attorney. I am completely without funds to retain a lawyer and would like to ask the Court to appoint counsel for me in this."

The room buzzed for a moment. The many spectators, Robin Blaine included, seemed mildly surprised at Iris's strong statement, her obvious self-possession and awareness. Great speculation abounded about Iris, among the reporters as well as other observers. The most popular theory among those who had read the Sun Times reports was that she was a very screwed-up woman. Most expected an obviously submissive personality, and this articulate lady did not fit the bill. Even her posture, the angle of her jaw, demonstrated pertinacity. The judge raised his gavel in warning and the room grew quiet again.

"Mrs. Harris...if you'll take this form," Judge Manak handed the bailiff a petition that was placed in her hands. "Fill it out and take your time. I'm in no hurry." Again a soft humming filled the room. Iris, forcing her attention to the simple task, blocking out the crowd, completed the task easily enough. Presently she handed the form back across the room.

Manak squared the form and scanned it rapidly, then he spoke again, his eyes fixed firmly on Iris, "Mrs. Harris, having reviewed your petition, I find you presently indigent and in need of court-appointed counsel." Manak snapped his eyes around the room, and Iris could almost sense the wave of impact as the crowd waited. Then she watched the judge's keen gaze stop, resting on the same woman Nora had indicated. Iris knew that there was competition among many lawyers to represent her, but the details remained mysterious to her. She was still not quite sure why this was so since there was clearly no money in it for the lawyer, but the case would be a media event, that much she knew. Her story had attracted more attention than she had expected.

"I appoint Robin Blaine to represent you, Mrs. Harris. Ms. Blaine is seated not far behind you and to your right."

Iris, encouraged, looked again at the woman, who now smiled brightly.

"Ms. Blaine, will you please come forward?" said the judge. "We have several matters to dispose of before we adjourn. These include the preliminary examination and the matter of bond. Ms. Blaine, I'll allow you an opportunity to discuss these with your client. Court will be in recess until you are ready. When you contact me, we will resume." The gavel came down hard.

Reporters rushed from the room, making for the only available pay phone in the lobby. Others ran outside into the brisk air. Iris felt a surge of energy. She shook Robin's hand, aware of the dark brown eyes studying her, keen to the woman's powerful interest, the thrust of the brain behind those deep eyes. She wondered if she would like this obviously competent woman who projected an aura of force and authority. She felt Robin's firm arm guiding her and willingly, excited, she followed her into a conference room.

Alone, the door shut behind them, the two women paused.

"Iris..." Robin began, squeezing her hand with almost painful urgency.

Iris was aware of a glint of tears in those brown eyes. But quickly she sensed the mastery of a strong will and her hand was let go. "Iris, I am going to fight for you every inch. I want you to know you have many people behind you. I'm just lucky enough to be the one to represent you. I think we have a good case."

"Even after what the paper wrote about me, after I talked to Nora and told her everything?" Iris blurted her worst fear. She had talked to Nora by instinct, not really thinking much about it. She had simply wanted to tell the truth, to cry out to the world about her pain and suffering and the events that had led her to this. But after reading the article she had realized how dangerous such an open confession might be. She had admitted everything.

"Well, Iris, I wondered too, at first. But the reaction has been incredible. Nearly everyone I know has voiced support. Even my husband Ed, who is normally very conservative on matters of this sort, urged me to get on this case. There's something about what happened to you. I mean, what you have gone through, that hit people. I think you might have done the right thing."

"But you're not sure are you? Can they actually put me in jail, I mean, for life, or for years and years?" Iris was overwhelmed by emotion but she controlled her tears. Of late, she had regained the capacity to cry and had given way to tears almost too much. But she felt the intensity behind Blaine's apparent control, aware that the woman was also mastering strong emotions, and now she allowed an expression of her own. Impulsively she extended her hand and Robin took it again. Suddenly she was glad her lawyer was a woman, though at first she had wondered, assuming that a man would be better, stronger, more forceful, perhaps more professional. Then they sat at a small table and talked rapidly. An hour passed before they rose to open the door.

When they re-entered the courtroom and informed the bailiff both were calm and prepared. Iris now understood the purpose of the preliminary examination and the issue of bond. As Robin expected, Iris had no funds or resources to post any kind of bond. So, unless the Court lowered the stated bond to personal recognizance, which was not likely, Iris would remain in jail for some time. The first priority of that N.O.W. meeting, which Robin attended, had been to offer Iris the best legal help. The second purpose was to chart out ways of raising funds for bond. None of the women in the meeting wanted Iris to spend one hour longer than necessary in jail. On that the women were unanimous. Robin thought it was one of the most moving experiences in her career. How those women, total strangers to Iris Harris, were determined to help.

Stone entered only a moment ahead of the judge. At once Robin made her intentions clear. A preliminary examination was demanded and Manak set the date for next Tuesday. Then Blaine explained her case for setting personal recognizance.

"As to this matter of bond, Your Honor, I recognize that normally on such a charge the defendant is not entitled to bond, but in this case I can personally guarantee that Mrs. Harris will appear in every hearing set by the Court. She has a place where she can live in the meantime..." There was a buzz in the courtroom, but Robin ignored it. "She is surely no risk to the community. Indeed I believe if the truth were known about this lady, which we shall reveal in her defense, the court would at once conclude she would be an asset to the community. Her teaching record and her experience with young people has been exemplary. She has long helped children, especially handicapped kids. Iris Harris is no more a criminal than I am." Again the crowd murmured. Robin knew the impact of her words. "She is only a woman trapped in an unbelievable set of circumstances. If anyone was criminal in that relationship, it was her husband."

Stone watched all this without expression, suppressing his grudging admiration. Blaine was setting the stage by building up the image of Iris quickly and firmly. He rose to object.

"Your Honor. I respectfully suggest that the defendant has no ties to the community. She is facing a criminal charge with a possible maximum penalty of life in prison upon conviction." He was greeted by a few moans, instantly repressed. Stone knew this was common knowledge, but until now the possible sentence at its worst had not been stated openly.

Pausing for effect, Stone looked at Iris. She glared at him, as if not believing the words. "Any reduction in bond is an affront to the people. The publicity and this circus atmosphere, your Honor, are not relevant. At this moment we are here only to deal with the requirement of bond. Ms. Blaine knows this. We must also consider the possibility that the pressure upon the defendant to run is great. The best of people who come forth to support her can hardly claim they truly know her. We object to any bond being set in this matter."

But he knew he had lost this round. The judge immediately announced bond at $30,000 cash or surety. Stone, watching Blaine's brief smile, suspected that the celebrated defense attorney had already tapped sources of support. Robin was nothing if not resourceful. Up to now he had known her only by reputation. He could not help wondering what she was really like. She seemed personable but the fates had cast the die so that they were in mortal opposition in a case of murder.

To return to her cell seemed a terrible punishment after the high drama of the court, but Iris was at least prepared for it. She had decided to be stoic despite her discovery after but one night in jail (now stretched into the second week) that the place evoked claustrophobia. Small spaces had never much frightened her until she married Rodney. Since then she had felt confined, trapped. It was not so much that she feared anything...at least *he* was dead and gone. It was rather that she could barely move within any realm of space. Her experience with poverty (even the confinement of the smallest apartment did not include doors one could not exit from) was of little use. Jail kept her to a cell (what a perfect word for it) or to a walking and exercise routine. Nothing she did was on her own volition. She resented every moment of it. She felt it as a kind of torture, as if she was still *his* possession. It was not so much because she feared the consequences of the law, but rather that she hated the idea of being held for one more day, one more hour, one moment more behind real bars for what she had done. Couldn't the law see that? It was her reason for telling Nora Richards everything.

Jail had unexpectedly forced on Iris a kind of self-examination, an introspection quite foreign to her nature. Nothing before, neither the worst beatings at Rodney's hands nor the most awful mental anguish and fear, had forced her to think about her fragile mental and emotional state. Now long hours alone forced moments of reflection. Iris found herself wondering too. About herself. Why did I stay with him? Why did I go back? What kind of perverse hold did he have on me? What was wrong with me if I had to stay with him in spite of the brutality? Am I sick like so many people must think? In her cell these thoughts preyed upon her. She managed to put up a face of brave calm and self-possession, a facade she rarely felt inside. That night after a long talk with Robin about legal matters Iris cried long and bitterly, overwhelmed by a kind of self-pity quite different in kind from what she had known before. She could not identify it—only feel it. For Iris this emotional low brought with it a new kind of understanding. She was vaguely aware that it was dangerous territory, but she was determined to tell it all—for in the truth was a stark reality that any human would understand. Even the truth that—terrified of him, hating him, wanting to kill him—Iris had also, could she even think it, had loved him. Loved him.

This thought, springing unbidden, brought a vision of terror; of his body in that chair; of his head lolling back, his chest all blood; that last look in his eyes; then more tears. Would he haunt her forever?

37

The preliminary examination took all morning. Stone called several witnesses: Detective Shaw (whose massive presence seemed to make his testimony more substantial), the pathologist, the crime scene technician, and a fingerprint expert. Stone knew that his objective to prove that Iris was the one who shot Rodney Harris was a foregone conclusion. The case was not going to center on whodunit, but rather on why and whether it was justified in the law. As a consequence of Stone's irrefutable proofs, Iris was bound over to Circuit Court on the charge of open murder. The defense argued that there was no showing of the elements of first degree murder, but Judge Manak relied on a long line of Michigan cases that held that on a charge of open murder the prosecution need only prove the elements of second degree. Robin countered with another motion to reduce bond, but the judge denied this. Arraignment in Circuit Court was set for the first of March.

Robin and Iris, hours into the last preparation for the arraignment, were exhausted. Iris was to stand mute and let Judge Jacob Wilson enter a plea of not guilty on her behalf. They had met seven or eight times since the preliminary examination, and Robin was now certain that she could mount a valid case for self-defense. Her research on the issue of spouse abuse, and her knowledge of law and how the law changed to reflect opinion and attitudes in the larger society, had convinced her. Her law partner, Tom Appleton, was not so sure, but he had always been cautious. Nevertheless, he was behind her. She was forging ahead. She had prepared three motions: Motion for Discovery, Motion for Reduction in Bond, and a Motion to Quash the Information.

Stone, in the meantime, worked hard to prepare his case which was based on the premise that Iris was clearly sane, had ample time and opportunity to deliberate on her actions, and at the very least was guilty of second degree murder. He knew the chances were that Blaine would go for either an insanity defense or for self-defense. Stone still had difficulty in believing that a valid claim of self-defense could be made. He researched them both, beginning with insanity.

The mere fact that one commits an act does not necessarily mean he or she is criminally responsible if the defense of insanity is raised. A jury must determine if a person committed the act charged and then must determine if the person was legally sane at the time the act was committed. The criminal jury instructions define mental illness as a substantial disorder of thought or mood which significantly impairs either the defendant's judgment, behavior, or capacity to recognize reality, or his or her ability to cope with the ordinary demands of life. This was a possibility in Iris's case, although her statement in the paper seemed to indicate she knew what she was doing at the time of the killing. Good Lord, thought Stone, she'd provided graphic description of the act, including the noise the shotgun made. He assumed that if the defense of insanity was going to be raised, Blaine and her partner would probably file notice of insanity at the time of the Arraignment.

John and Robin chatted briefly prior to the Arraignment. He was not surprised when she informed him that she was not filing a notice of insanity. It was the Defendant's position that Iris Harris was acting in self-defense when she killed her husband. The only person who knew exactly what happened in that cabin on Valley Road was Iris Harris. John was reasonably sure that he could make a jury see what seemed obvious on the face of the evidence; namely, that Iris by reason of prior and repeated abuse had decided to kill her ex-husband. It seemed reasonable to assume that she had arrived at a decision, with ample time to premeditate and think about it, and the fact that it was necessary to go into the bedroom, retrieve the shotgun, uncase it, load it, and then shoot Harris while he was off his guard, should support that contention. On that point, Shaw was correct, Stone thought. Sympathy for the victim of abuse, no matter how awful the abuse, should not influence the jury if properly instructed. He felt confident that even if the judge failed to do so it would fall to the prosecution (himself) to argue the law and enable twelve jurors to keep sympathy out of the case.

At his desk Stone outlined the basics of the state law regarding self-defense. Blaine had some advantages. The criminal jury instructions stated that a person may defend himself or herself if at the time of the act he or she honestly believes there is a danger of being killed or of receiving serious bodily harm. Even if later on the appearances turn out to be false, the person is to be judged by the circumstances as they seemed to be at the time of the commission of the act. In fact was it not on record that Rodney Harris had been the one who called the police, not Iris? It was also a matter of record, down in Ionia, that the man had previously called for help on several occasions and there was the testimony of the two deputies that in each of those incidents Iris had been acting strangely.

Robin Blaine's skills before a jury were legendary. Everything about her added up to a formidable challenge. Her very appearance, matronly, trim, iron-gray hair, handsome demeanor, her sense of humor, her obvious compassion, combined into a powerful package. In our system of law, Stone ruminated; the burden was on him, as the State, to prove the defendant guilty beyond a reasonable doubt. What seemed on paper to be a given was turning out quite the opposite. Stone knew that Blaine would work away with relentless skill on that very concept of reasonable doubt, and he knew from her opening moves exactly what her method would be. Blaine would claim first, with ample testimony in support, that Iris Harris was the constant victim of spouse abuse. She would argue that over several years Iris had tried to free herself of this man who kept an iron hold over her, would never let her go, until in the end, in desperation and in fear of her life, she was forced to kill him. Robin would no doubt point out how the police had not been able to help Iris, how she had been abandoned by the law. She would certainly make direct use of Nora Richards' newspaper column which portrayed Rodney Harris as un-redeemably violent. He assumed that Iris would eventually have to take the stand to testify on her own behalf. On such evidence Robin would surely build her case that Iris was in mortal fear of her life because of Rodney's actions and his threats. Stone pondered his situation, reasoning in the rational way that law students learned from day one, that Robin and her crew could hardly fail to make a convincing case. Despite the theory that juries must know nothing of the cases they were chosen to sit, real jurors being human heard what everyone else did, and of course they thought in highly predictable patterns of common knowledge. Despite the hard and clear language of the law Robin's defense would be exceedingly difficult to refute. If she could convince a sympathetic jury that Iris acted in mortal fear of her life, even if the threat was not immediate, she might easily win.

Stone stayed at his desk long after his secretary was gone. When he quit, it was full dark, the air coming in the window was cold now. Michigan in early March still carried winter's chill. Despite a day or two of warm sun, the nights brought hard freeze. It was past midnight when he strode to the Sheriff's Department for coffee, surprised to see Frank's light still on. Both of them were nuts. In Shaw's office, he was greeted by a blue haze, and Frank's large visage.

"Goddamn dedicated public servant." Stone tried to wave the smoke off. "You ought to be home with your wife."

"Don't you mention my wife," Shaw barked. "She's been back only a few days and I never see her. She told me tonight that I should have married Iris Harris, considering the time I spend on the case. Long as you're here, pull up a chair. I have more interesting stuff."

Stone sat.

"The Sandusky Police have come through," Shaw pulled out some papers. "They listed the fire as accidental, although there were serious doubts. I think the newspaper story is validated. The lieutenant I spoke to was the son of the sergeant who investigated the Sandusky fire. He said his dad was first on the scene and talked to the boy. Rodney, of course. The boy's first words were, 'I'm sorry, but they deserved it.' Wait, if you think this is bad news, hold your horses. It seems Harris was married at least three times. There was another woman before Iris and before Julia, by the name of Joan. Two kids by that marriage. Apparently they had to get married. First child came seven months after the wedding and the second kid only eleven months after the first. I gather they were happy for a while, but after the second child things changed. Rodney began to drink and stay out late. Then the beatings started. For no apparent reason. She was hospitalized three times in a two-year period. Finally, one night, after he tied her to a chair and tortured her, sticking pins under her nails, she up and left. Took the kids and lit out."

"Was that the end of it?"

"Nope. Just as you'd expect from what Iris says. For years, off and on, the bastard followed her across the country. Places like Miami, Oakland, Detroit, Los Angeles, and Washington, DC. The way she explained it, I thought of that old TV program, "The Fugitive." She'd take up residence and out of the blue, usually after a year or two, he'd appear and try to take her and the kids back. Once, when the boy, almost grown then, tried to challenge him, Rodney pulled a gun on the kid. When they grew up the kids moved on. Seems they got on with their lives, but kept in touch with their mother. I gather they are close still. This Joan, she told me he last contacted her in Omaha last November, just a day or so before Thanksgiving. She got the cops when he refused to leave, and they moved him on by threatening him on trespassing charges."

Stone whistled. He had read enough to know that Rodney Harris had driven out to gather Iris in Boulder, arriving there on Thanksgiving Day. He shuddered; there was something eerie about all this. That kind of obsession and the energy required. "Maybe," said Stone, "if this lady had allowed him to stay a while, he might not have met Iris, and we wouldn't be staying up late nights on this damned case."

"No, and maybe the cops in Omaha would have a murder case on their hands."

"What?" John forced a wry chuckle, "Are you saying you're agreeing that it was justified to blow him away?"

"Nope. Not at all," Shaw rejoined. He was always the serious type. "But the evidence is piling up. He was no Santa Claus. More of a monster."

Stone thought it was the understatement of the year. "Where is this woman now?"

"She wouldn't say till I swore Rodney Harris was dead. She lives in Marquette. I suppose I have to go up there. Will you want a written statement?" John sensed Shaw's weariness.

"Yes. Get it to me some time in the next two days. And get your hind end up to Marquette."

What Stone had been afraid might happen was now becoming reality. If the defense could shift the emphasis away from Iris and onto Rodney, gaining a guilty verdict would be harder. John knew, because of the discovery motions, he would have to turn this evidence about Joan over to the defense. The character of Rodney Harris was becoming the central issue. Stone knew he had to find ways to focus the jury on the act. He turned to the Michigan Rules of Evidence. The substance was clear. Evidence of a person's character or trait of character, under Rule 404, is not admissible except, and here the language of law appeared to cloud the meaning of its original intent, 'evidence of a pertinent trait of character of the victim of a crime offered by the accused'. John repressed a derisive laugh, since this undermined the prima facie evidence. He shrugged, repressing a yawn. Clearly the pertinent trait in Rodney's case was his aggressive tendency, his habit of beating his wives and never letting them go. Furthermore, under Rule 405, the defense would be able to offer proof of specific instances of his conduct. Certainly Robin had researched this exception, and it would bolster her defense. Not only would she be able to cite specific acts that Iris had knowledge of, but even acts between Rodney and Joan (or any other victims) would be admissible. The pertinent point was that they revealed Rodney's violent nature.

Stone, in effect, was silenced. The substance of the case would be sidelined as the defense focused on the murdered man. It was clear to John that there would be two people on trial. One dead, one alive.

For a time John sat alone. Shaw had gone home two hours before. The empty building loomed about him, as if in reproach. Should I be doing this? Is it right? Of course, it's right. It is my job, my duty. I have no real choice. A trial is mandated. But, God, would I love to be in Blaine's shoes now. What the hell. She killed the man. I present the evidence and let the jury decide.

So his thoughts went, the flow contradicting and challenging and changing. He wanted sleep. He wanted rest.

Sure enough, on the way home, driving through the empty streets of Kalkaska in the wee hours, close to three o'clock, the clear night air changed and flurries began to fall. He stepped through an inch of new snow as he entered his house, alone. So much for the goddamned weather reports.

38

After days of intense give and take, Robin was surprised that she and Iris had become friends. She had been aware of compassion but there was a difference between the willingness to help and a willingness to share emotion and real companionship. But Iris proved worthy, capable of commitment, and this made it all the harder for Robin to comprehend the awful facts of Iris's life with Rodney. She could understand some of it, she knew the power of love—that word with so many connotations—how love could compel what seemed to be irrational actions, and how indeed in some women the capacity to submit and submerge ego to the man's need sometimes took precedent over all else—why else did so many women put up with awful circumstances? Knowing Iris, or feeling that she did, assessing the poor woman's merits and qualities, Robin could not reconcile the character with the actions. Iris simply did not seem to be the right type; if there was such a type.

In this struggle to understand, Robin looked forward to meeting one of the best known experts, a psychiatrist from downstate named Paula Stallman. The National Organization for Women provided the liaison and recommendation. Robin had arranged for a meeting with Dr. Stallman, so as to assess her professional evaluation. If things worked out, Stallman might be a witness in the trial.

In the meantime, Robin had announced at a N.O.W. meeting that the pledges added up to over $30,000, and Iris should be free after the April 7th court date. She played back a statement from Iris to the assembled women in which Iris thanked them and promised to meet each of them in person when she was out of jail.

The next morning, she met Dr. Stallman at the Cherry Capitol Airport.

Stallman was ten years younger by Robin's quick estimate, petite and quick, decisive in action and in speech, strawberry blond hair cut straight across the shoulders, no make-up discernible on rather austere face, a woman of clear force and intelligence whose severe dress and manner belied her fine bone structure.

"I suppose you've read the documents, so I don't need to fill you in on the basics."

"Yes, but I want to hear all your thoughts." Dr. Stallman's voice had an astringent quality to it, and Robin thought she recognized in that slight rasp the force of discipline and will. Without it, perhaps, the voice would be girlish, something quite unacceptable to such a professional. She had always been grateful for her own mellifluous contralto voice, perfect for the courtroom, for the lecture hall, for the cocktail party. It made everything she said seem more important, and she knew it.

"Of course," Stallman continued, "if you imply that Iris Harris is a kind of victim I'm familiar with, you're right. It is all too common, Mrs. Blaine..."

"Robin,"

"Okay, Robin. I wonder if you have any idea of the extent of this syndrome. Of course, it is exceedingly unusual for a woman to strike out in her own defense and take violent action, as Iris did, although in some situations it is the only alternative." This statement pleased Robin, and she made a mental note of it. "Most simply continue in the cycle, some of them in fear of constant beating, or in fear for their lives, for years and years, until the husband dies, or they die, or in some cases they finally escape by divorce. We're only beginning to understand the scope of this. It's pervasive."

"So you're saying what Iris has gone through is common?"

Dr. Stallman glared at Robin and both women were aware of the assessment going on. It was one of Robin's gifts to ask what seemed to be simple things, to draw others out, and to make her own high intelligence unobtrusive and thus appear to enhance the wit of others. She was not one of those bright people whose keenness put others off, but this pro was a mite disconcerting.

"I'm not sure what you mean by common. Perhaps not in gross proportion to the married population, but in sheer numbers, yes, it's common. Estimates are difficult. Few cases get reported. But millions of women—and some men incidentally—suffer repeated abuse of this sort. It seems to be cross-cultural. We're just beginning to look into the phenomena in Europe, and even in traditional societies in the Third World. Don't forget that all the traditional religions, Christianity included, and most legal systems have more or less assumed the right of a husband to beat his wife, or to use physical 'discipline'. For at least five thousand years of civilization, it was at least implicit in the law codes that the men could use force to keep a wife 'in line', and in practice it still is."

Robin wanted to get to the case in point and, growing a bit testy at the lecture, interrupted, showing mild impatience.

"That's fine. But we have this case Iris, you must be aware, did not suffer from an occasional beating or bullying tactic to keep her 'in line.' She was criminally, insanely beaten, tortured, humiliated, raped, sadistically violated, imprisoned. Dr. Stallman (Robin was aware that Stallman did not request the use of her first name), I wonder if you have any idea what this man, Rodney Harris, was like. I've come across many strange ones in two and a half decades of law practice, but this guy takes the cake. He was...well, if you haven't listened to Iris for a few hours, it's hard to explain. He was a man consumed by a need for control...superhuman. I don't believe in the occult, of course, but I'm trying to convey the image of the bastard. He had almost supernatural energy when it came to controlling, torturing, humiliating, and terrorizing the women in his life."

Robin was deliberate in her use of a cliché here and there, falling into the natural idiom of common speech, avoiding the jargon of her own profession. She fervently hoped Dr. Stallman would do so, sooner or later.

"He almost certainly murdered his own mother," Robin continued, "and her lover, and his brothers and sisters, down in Sandusky when he was only ten or so. He never let go of any woman he had anything to do with as an adult. Believe me, he was more than your typical batterer, worse than your typical sociopath. I don't think the typical wife-beater, if there is such a thing, can hold a candle to this son-of-a-bitch. I don't care how common or widespread the phenomenon."

Surprised by her passion and her choice of words, Robin waited, almost ready to apologize. She slowed for traffic.

"I had some idea of that but I'll want to hear it from Iris," said Stallman, nodding, apparently nonplussed, still the pro. "I suppose she's suffering a great deal. Has she had any kind of professional help, that you know of, either before or since the...the killing?"

"Not that I know of, but she is handling it very well. She's strong as hell." Was there an implicit criticism in Stallman's question, Robin wondered?

"That, of course, is a facade. She is in deep turmoil, believe me, and needs help. It would be impossible not to be, given what she's been through."

Robin pulled into the small parking lot behind her office. Crusty mounds of dark snow outlined the pavement around the parking lot, evidence of the lingering winter. Robin directed Stallman to the office behind the kitchen, used as the war room.

"Give me everything you have in writing on Iris," said Stallman with a thin smile, rocking slowly in the chair behind the desk, "and allow me enough time to take it all in." Robin complied.

Hours later, Stallman emerged calling for Robin who was straining at the bit, eager as a new law school grad to hear what this expert had to say.

"Look Robin," Stallman began, "I'm not providing therapy as you imply. I am merely here to give my professional opinion, to help Iris in her defense. The fact that I am a professional psychiatrist is relevant only to the extent that I might ask questions, or go deeper into motives than you or that reporter would feel comfortable with. Iris will open up. I can promise you. I will be able to get at this case. I won't hurt her while doing so. In fact, I intend to recommend that she get immediate therapy, as you say, as soon as she is out of jail."

"Look, I'm sorry if..."

"Forget it. I'll go easy. It's my job you know, but nothing we do with Iris can protect her from the pain she is suffering. I feel as much compassion for her as you."

Stone scanned the pile of notes. He had lost track of the number of legal pads filled. His secretary was inundated by yellow paper, her desk, normally neat, cluttered. Her typewriter never seemed to stop clacking. As anticipated, the defense had filed a motion for discovery requesting copies of all police reports, all officers' notes, the right to have any exhibits examined by their own experts, the complete list of witnesses for the prosecution, the names and whereabouts of all former wives of the deceased, everything. Stone knew that since the early 'sixties, the defendant in such a criminal case had more rights in this respect. If a prosecutor failed to comply with a discovery order from a court, the judge might dismiss the charges altogether. He knew Judge Wilson's reputation, having argued many cases in his presence, and he knew Wilson would almost surely grant the defense broad rights to discovery. John had no objection to allowing the defense to see and have copies of the material building up in his files. It was all part of seeking justice. For this reason, Stone had decided to file his own discovery motion when they met in court on April 7th. He would request a list of all witnesses the defense intended to call. Justice should work equally in both directions. He knew there was no legal authority for such a motion, having researched the matter. Maybe there was a new precedent in this? Sometimes, however weary of the endless work, Stone generally found himself surging with energy as the challenges mounted. It was stimulating to be matching wits with Robin Blaine while the world drew in and watched with ever increasing interest.

Other matters, however, pressed more directly. Already the defense had filed a motion to quash the information, or reduce the charge. Blaine's argument was that Judge Manak had exceeded his discretion when he bound Iris over to Circuit Court on a charge of open murder. She contended that Stone had failed to establish the elements for the charge of first degree murder, and it was improper therefore to bind the defendant over unless the elements of both first and second degree murder had been clearly established. John, however, was ready to reduce the charge to second degree murder if he lost the motion.

As for bond he knew it was lost. Iris would get out of jail for the duration. He knew the rumors about the funds being raised to cover the bond were largely true.

April 7th came cold and with blowing snow. Old Winter blew another surprise in from Canada. From the 1st to the 7th, the sun had blazed from the perfect spring sky, and the nights, though crisp, had been equally clear. With no time to spare John had scarcely noticed the signs of spring. By now he would normally have gone out to seek greening skunk cabbage, to spot the morning ducks dabbling on melting ponds, to hear the mournful flute of Whitman's "shy and hidden bird" warbling its dirge in the swamp, the early thrush, the hermit with its "song of the bleeding throat", its sound,

> "O liquid and free and tender
> O wild and loose to my soul—O wondrous
> singer!"

Now the snow blew into his face as he climbed the courthouse steps, eager for the case but hating this delay of warmth. The rain and sun that ought to be spring. It was too late for snow, damn it. He noted that the crowd was not as large as he expected. Was interest waning? Only a few reporters. There was Nora Richards and that guy she used to go with from Lansing, and the regular from the Grand Rapids paper. He didn't see the Free Press reporter from Detroit. There were several N.O.W. members in the seats, and local spectators, but there were seats to spare.

For two hours after his arrival promptly at nine, Judge Wilson met in chambers with counsel, to discuss the various motions. This was standard procedure in such cases. The action in open court was nevertheless required, necessary, and dramatic.

Stone cast a glance at Iris. He hadn't seen her for days and was surprised that her face was bright and expectant. She had laughed softly at something Blaine said, and John felt oddly at ease. Though he did not relish being her antagonist in court, not in the least, he had his duty. He resolved to keep this trial focused on the law. In theory the law was above persons. It was not as if he felt the need to educate the populace, but the prosecution by its very nature, its origins from a time before the Magna Carta, was not created to be agreeable. Its indispensable mandate was to bring law breakers before the bar regardless, and to bring clarity and order to the law. Such innermost thoughts were best not expressed.

Iris, glancing at him, caught his interest. She wondered if there was compassion in that look. He was the man, however, who was trying to put her in prison. Robin had explained the duties of the county prosecutor and how the "state" had an obligation to prosecute a case if there was evidence enough to convince a judge that a trial must be held. Nevertheless Iris could not find it in her heart to separate the man from the job and she wondered if her eyes revealed the hostility she felt.

She was also aware of the tension in her and in the room. Robin seemed busy, so she looked about her, keen to the nuances, the flow of sentiment. She'd taught school for years and her antennae was still keen. She'd talked with Dr. Stallman over three long days, and suddenly she was scared. Iris truly dreaded the fact that this psychiatrist might use her notes as background to testimony in the trial.

The trial was scheduled to begin in June. These legal moves would soon be past and there would be a jury. She would be on the stand eventually to defend her actions. She was wholeheartedly behind Robin's decision to go for the difficult self-defense argument. It would vindicate her far better than any pretense of temporary insanity. In fact, when she had first heard about the Burning Bed case, she stated clearly that such a defense was not for her. She had told Robin, as she had told Nora, that her action in taking Rodney's life was an act of desperation, done in fear of her own life, a last resort, the final rational act left to her short of suicide. She hated the concept that her act was that of a mad woman. She had repeated this to everyone who asked.

She had another problem too, kept to herself. She fervently hoped that release from jail, planned for this very day, might free her from this awful fear in the night. But she was not sure. A rare night passed without her waking to terror. Usually Rodney would dominate these dreams. She would 'wake' to his face, looming over her cot, right there in the jail, and he would gloat and grin and speak to her, "Iris...yes, it's me. I ain't gone. You might think so, but here I am. You know what, Iris baby? You will never get away. I'll never let you go. Don't you know that?"

Sometimes he would be naked, his penis erect, and he would loom over her ready to enter her. She would awaken to dark reality and the dim walls of her cell. Other times, she would dream that she was making love to a man, enjoying it, exultant in pleasuring her lover and happy, but the man would turn out to be Rodney, and he would lie on her and chuckle and whisper in her ear, and once or twice he would withdraw from her and point to his wounds and the blood would flow from them onto her naked body. "See, Iris, what you did to me. But it didn't help did it? I'm still here, ain't I?"

Haunted by this dream-ghost, Iris was afraid to reveal her night terrors. She had not told Nora, or Robin, and most of all not mentioned it to Dr. Stallman. She hoped they would locate Betty Jean who would listen without judgment. Something had to give. She was not getting half enough sleep. Maybe being released from jail would do it. That awful cell.

Now Iris watched Judge Wilson enter the courtroom. He was courtly, avuncular, his face kindly but his manner stern, his voice rather high and precise, "I'll begin," said the judge, having gaveled proceedings open, "with the motion for discovery filed by defense. Mr. Stone. Do you have objections to any of the material requested by the defense in this motion?"

"No, Your Honor. My only question is when does the Court require those documents to be turned over?"

"If I'm not mistaken, we have set trial for June 15th. Furthermore a final pre-trial conference is scheduled for May 10th. So I expect all material to be turned over no later than May 10th. Of course, I'd suggest, Mr. Stone, since this matter will come to trial in two months that you turn over all relevant material as soon as possible. Now let's deal with this motion for discovery from the prosecutor. Ms. Blaine, what's your position on this?"

"Your Honor, I object to any discovery on the part of prosecution. I know of no legal authority to support Mr. Stone's motion. Maybe granting such a motion might seem just, since the prosecution is required to produce evidence and documents for the defense, but, with no law backing that position, I object."

"Mr. Stone, can you produce any authority to support your motion?"

"No, Your Honor."

"Motion denied," intoned Wilson. "Now we have the defense motion to quash the information or the alternative to reduce the charge. Both sides furnished me with extensive briefs, and we've discussed it in chambers, so I shall listen to argument from counsel."

Both Stone and Blaine restated their positions. Listening to the legal arguments, Iris was aware of a certain malaise. She wanted to get down to cases and, though Robin had explained how important all the maneuvers were, she could feel the impatience of the spectators, perhaps even the attorneys. It was a strange feeling since she was on trial after all. Presently, the judge spoke again, "It is the burden of the prosecutor on an open murder charge to establish the elements of both first and second degree murder. Having reviewed the transcript of the preliminary examination, I agree with Judge Manak that the prosecutor has sustained his burden as to second degree murder. However, it is my opinion that there was insufficient evidence admitted for a charge of first degree murder, and I therefore reduce the charge to second degree murder, or in the alternative, upon a stipulation of the parties, remand the matter to District Court for additional testimony and evidence, if there is any, for a charge of first degree murder. Mr. Stone, do you have a response?"

"Yes, Your Honor," John said, not in the least surprised at the decision, "the People will not desire or request a remand to District Court. We are prepared to file new information on the reduced charge of second degree murder."

Iris noticed Robin's controlled smile. Well, she had been led to hope for this. It was a small victory. Earlier and repeatedly she had complained that a reduced charge made no real difference. She was innocent of murder and wanted complete exoneration, but Robin had advised every avenue, and the reduced charge simply made sense. "If this goes against us, Iris," Robin had opined, "not that I expect it to, the reduced charge could be very important."

Now the judge called Iris and Robin to approach the bench, and Iris was duly arraigned on the new information. Iris stood mute to the charge of second degree murder and the judge entered a plea of not guilty on her behalf.

"Now as to this matter of bond," said the judge. "It's my understanding the defendant has raised sufficient funds to post bond. Upon filing and recording the papers, Mrs. Harris shall be released upon a $30,000 bond. If there is nothing further, Court is adjourned."

Nora Richards was the first reporter at Iris's side as she left the courtroom with Robin. Snow swirled around her, but the weather did not dampen her grin, and strobes flashed. Microphones were thrust forth.

"Do you have a statement, Iris?" Nora asked.

"It feels so good to be free," Iris began and then she burst into tears. Quickly Robin got her into a waiting car, not wanting Iris to make further statements. N.O.W. had located a small house on a wooded hill above Traverse City, overlooking West Bay to the north and east. Iris was to share the home with a couple who had extra space, until the trial was over. Women volunteers selected by N.O.W. would spend at least part of each day with Iris. This, Robin explained, was for companionship, though Robin knew it was also for protection against the severe depression and expected suicidal moments that, according to Dr. Stallman, Iris was bound to experience in the coming weeks. The extra money raised by donors would be used for rent, food and necessities.

Inside, John Stone stood alone with his notes until the room was empty. He had gone up against Robin Blaine on three motions and lost them all. Was this to be the history of the entire case? It had not been a good day for the people. He knew that the trial of Iris Harris had become a cause celebre, that he was inevitably cast as the villain, the hard-nosed county prosecutor who was trying with all his might to put a poor, abused woman away in jail when all that woman had done was to defend herself in extremity against an admitted monster, a man so beastial that no one (not even the prosecution) could come up with a good word to say about him. John also knew that in the minds of many the whole thing smacked of the old 'underdog' syndrome. The woman, weak and abused, versus the man, strong, hateful and domineering. It was to Iris's advantage that in the trial she was defended by a woman, a charming, handsome woman at that; and that she was prosecuted by a man, himself, who was less experienced and less charismatic. It did not look good.

Watching the snow from his office window, John smacked his bulky folder down on the desk and walked down the corridor to Shaw's office. The big detective was back at his desk; though he would soon be off again, downstate continuing his search for more evidence. He had seen Shaw in the back of the courtroom, looking somewhat strained and tired. He entered without knocking.

"Hi, Frank. Big day for Iris. Bad day for us?"

"Shit...a bad day in black rock. I expected it. I didn't expect this snow though. Goddamn it, I was all set to take my boy with me out on the Au Sable, if we got out of here in time this afternoon. We were gonna drift on down in that ol' aluminum duck boat, y'know and trail a few lines in the water and just talk and watch the willows turning green."

"So you called it off?"

"Yeah. I just got through telling him on the phone. The kid won't mind. He's got other plans anyway. But I was counting on it. Why do you ask?"

"I was going to work till dark, but to tell the truth, I haven't got the heart right now." Stone sat on the sharp edge of Shaw's ancient wooden desk, studying the detective's shoulder holster which hung from an equally ancient clothes rack, the dark stubby grip of the automatic just visible, "Well," he continued, "I was wondering what you plan to do the rest of this shitty day. It's miserable outside or I'd go on drifting down the river with you. Got any ideas? I sure as hell don't plan to work till dark. Not today anyway."

"I was gonna work here..."

"Fucking workaholic."

"I know a place," Shaw flashed a weary smile, "over in Traverse, where the beer is reasonable, the clientele don't stare at you like you're from outer space if you look past thirty, and after dinner they bring in this band, mostly youngsters, but they play blues, Detroit style." Shaw accented the first syllable of the word Detroit. "I could call the missus. She's got some meeting anyway, at the school."

"I'm not sure I want blues..."

"I do." Shaw was not joking. His huge face was serious.

"Okay, what the hell. Let's go. I get drunk this time, though, and you drive back."

39

That evening while John and Frank were singing the blues, Iris sat at a table at the Holiday Inn in Traverse with Robin and Ed Blaine and several N.O.W. supporters, men and women she had only met days before. It was a fine night and the wine flowed on her first night out since her release on bond. There were seven in all; besides herself, Ed and Robin, there was Carla Harcourt and her husband Tom, both active in N.O.W, musicians by profession, but known as caring and effective community activists, Monty Calvin, one of the region's most respected environmentalist lawyers, and Dr. Paula Stallman. They were into their second bottle of wine for good reason. Robin had made contact with Joan Harris, now living in the Upper Peninsula. Joan had agreed to testify at the trial. Her story would dovetail with the defense thesis that Rodney was cruel, vicious, and aggressive, and that Iris really had no choice in the end. Joan's tale of constant harassment over decades coincided with Iris's story. Joan had mentioned the possibility of a yet previous marriage when Rodney was a very young man.

Now, despite her attempt to divert the conversation from the details of the case, Robin found herself in conversation with Iris. The subject was Rodney. Robin caught Dr. Stallman's eye wondering if the conversation around a table with other people was okay, but the psychiatrist seemed unconcerned, if not moved. Iris was talking with verve, with real animation.

"Y'know Robin, I still can't believe he kept up contact with Joan all those years. If only I'd known..."

"How could you have?" said Ed, who until now had been listening silently. "I mean, isn't it obvious by now that the man was a cunning pathological liar. The kind who could fool anyone, even the most perceptive cop, even those lie-detectors, I'll bet." Ed spoke with undisguised anger. Robin was somewhat bemused by her husband's open emotion regarding this case. From the first day he had automatically assumed that Iris was a victim, that she ought to go free, be vindicated totally, and the sooner the better. It was an issue that transcended the traditional political divisions in Traverse City. People mostly lined up on Iris's side, or at least so it seemed among her friends, though Robin was aware of strong feelings on the other side as well.

"I agree," said Dr. Stallman quickly, "he was capable of presenting himself publicly, and even privately, most of the time, as quite the opposite of what he was. You couldn't have known his capacity for deception, Iris, or for self-deception either. There are many people who can't really feel emotion or engage in emotional give and take, but who are damn good at pretending to, up to a point. Usually in such a person the lack of capacity to feel becomes evident fairly soon. But there are a few, like Rodney, who have learned somehow to brilliantly act the role, even for weeks at a time, as he did early in your marriage, and every time you reconciled with him. I mean he apparently cried real tears, and the self-deception extended even to the point where he seemed to need you, even when he was beating you."

Robin raised her eyebrows and looked closely at Iris. Was Stallman perhaps pushing this too far, too much, in public? No. Surely it was just helpful talk.

"Yes," cried Iris, "that's right exactly. I really thought he loved me. He was so...so totally convincing. He made me want to believe and he put so much into it, I mean you wouldn't believe..." Iris broke off suddenly as if stricken by something. "But, d'you think maybe it was just me, and maybe other people could see? Was it something in me, maybe, that attracted him?"

Robin knew this was the question on everyone's mind, indeed on her own. Once more Robin was surprised by Iris. She opened her mouth to dissent but Stallman beat her to it. The talk was clearly fueled by the wine.

"No, Iris! I think he could have pulled it off with any of hundreds, literally thousands of women. I mean that literally. I don't mean he didn't find you attractive; obviously he needed a vital woman to fulfill some twisted need, but clearly he fooled nearly everyone. Don't forget that he was able somehow to persuade even Julia to return to him, to remarry him. He could take on two experienced cops and twist things to his own purpose. He could lie convincingly to everyone. I suppose that's one thing that made him such a great salesman. Had he been less preoccupied with mastering and controlling women, he might have made a most effective and dangerous politician."

"We have enough of those already," said Clara, and everyone laughed. Presently the talk drifted to other subjects, but Robin knew, as they all sensed, that this brief exchange touched on something vital. Iris, perceptive about these matters, would no doubt brood further on it. Robin was acutely aware that Iris, though rarely talking about her inner personal feelings in the aftermath of the horror she had experienced, was not by any means out of the woods, no matter how the trial went. Robin, though confident of her abilities, knew that nothing was predictable. Surely Iris must wonder, just as others wondered, whether she had been susceptible in some unknown way to such a man, possessing some masochistic need perhaps, or some unexpressed flaw that caused her to seek submission. Society, after all, taught women to be submissive to their husbands as a general rule. Apparently this had been so for thousands of years, for at least as long as written records had existed, in virtually all societies. Perhaps it went further back. Would Iris be able, Robin thought, to separate her own terrible experience from what she might become, would she be able to accept that what had happened to her—exceptional and unusual as it was—had been part of a pattern that caught hundreds, thousands of women in similar traps, many never to escape? She filed the thought away and turned her attention to the others, quickly resolving to bring up the subject with Dr. Stallman as soon as it was convenient. It might be necessary, as Dr. Stallman had already indicated, to make the jury understand that Iris was the victim of a thoroughly documented pattern of abuse. Try as she might, Robin could not shake the idea until well after the last dish was consumed, the last wine glass emptied. There did seem to be a paradox in it, of sorts. It was vital to Iris's defense that every detail of Rodney's abuse and obsessive and possessive behavior be revealed, but every further detail (even when, and especially when revealed by Iris herself) must in some way reduce Iris as well. It was as if each revelation that might be used to set her free would also add to her already terrific humiliation.

The following morning John drove to his office with a slight hangover. It was a good thing Shaw was the designated driver the night before. The late April weather so perfect it was hard to believe winter had fled only days before. Even before that welcome evening was over John had decided to subpoena the notes of the conversation between Nora Richards and Iris. In the clear light of morning—though he was certain that the newspaper would object on the basis of the First Amendment—he felt increasing confidence in his research. In his firm view there was no privilege protecting such communication. He reaffirmed the importance of the notes when he joined Shaw.

"She's trapped into a story. She as much as confessed to murder in your presence. If she attempts to change her version I will not hesitate to impeach her. Besides, we might find information in Richards' notes that weakens her self-defense claim."

"Goddamn it, John," Shaw put in, "I just can't get used to this. I can't for the life of me figure out the legal justification. But hell, I'm just a simple cop. So he beat the shit out of her. That doesn't justify her killing him. Self-defense hell! She had lots of options short of taking his life. I've really thought about this John."

"I know, Frank," said John supportively.

"I mean, she didn't have to stay. You can bet if I'd got out there and she talked to me, and if she told me all that stuff, hell, I'd have escorted her to safety no matter what. I've done it before."

Iris stood on the great dunes, hand shading her eyes from the glare, gazing across the Manitou Passage to the islands that loomed like mirages. Ed had just explained the islands—revealing something of their history and geology—and now Iris pondered the vista, moved and impressed, trying to catch her breath after the hike. Behind her stood Robin and Monty Calvin, with Ed Blaine just to her right. The four of them had hiked slowly for over an hour through winding forest trails, profuse with wildflowers, up steep pitches through big trees, and across winding dune paths. Monty had identified several species of shrub and flower and now they all stood in awe six hundred feet above the inland sea. The Lake Michigan coast extended north and south as far as eye could see, delineated by the ribbon of yellow sand beach and the steep cut of dune, the cobalt blue of the lake and the darker green of shore caught and seemingly magnified in the vast light that arches these waters when the air is clear and the wind is in the west. Iris, unaccustomed to exercise after weeks in jail, no hiker in any case, felt lightheaded. As she paused to catch her breath, her thoughts went back two days or so when Robin had informed her that Prosecutor Stone had subpoenaed the notes of her jail house interviews with Nora Richards. According to Robin these moves would delay the trial. Iris had responded to this information with bitterness and outrage. She had told Nora the truth. Why was Stone persecuting her? In part she understood the reason behind Robin's insistence that they visit the Sleeping Bear Dunes. Robin was nearby, standing near Monty Calvin and Ed, also seeming to want a brief rest, and silence. Ed plopped down into the sand, cross-legged like an Indian, unlimbering his small pack, his bald head shining in the sun. Presently he broke the silence speaking above the strong breeze.

"Anyone want a drink?" he said, lifting forth a large thermos.

"Is that healthy stuff, or do you mean a real drink?" Monty asked, jocular as always.

"Healthy stuff I guess, just Gatorade. Robin might have her flask. She usually does, if you need real poison."

"I'll have some poison," said Iris, also trying to settle her rump in the sand, squirming for comfort, resting her back against a cut where the dune crested with beach grass streaming in the wind.

"I'm sorry," said Robin, apologetic, "I forgot the flask. No booze."

"Booo..." said Monty.

"All I have is a canteen with water," Robin added, holding it up.

"I'll settle for anything wet," said Monty reaching for the canteen.

"Thus spake the great outdoorsman," quipped Ed, "What would you do, Monty, without duffers like us? You'd die of thirst out here and they would find your bleached bones amid the sand. I see the headlines now: 'BODY OF LOCAL ENVIRONMENTALIST FOUND ON REMOTE DUNES. POLICE INVESTIGATING.'"

"They would suspect foul play. I have enemies, the kind of people who wanted to keep all this for private use," Monty indicated the magnificent sweep of land and freshwater sea. Robin giggled, accepting sandwiches from Ed, who passed the food around.

Watching the banter, Iris felt awful. These people were secure, highly educated, accomplished, seemingly content in their friendships and in their private and public roles. Monty was married, father of five, his wife a part-owner of a local photography shop. They were kind to her, and supportive, but Iris wondered, would they have even met her in their daily routines, or ever invited her to a hike like this? Monty Calvin was, she had read, one of the most knowledgeable people in the state when it came to the wilderness regions, especially the Sleeping Bear through which they now hiked. All the way in to this height above the lake, he had entertained them with a stream of knowledge and humor, and Iris felt drawn to him. He was, she realized, similar to Rodney in some ways, though a decade younger than what Rodney would have been. She studied Monty more closely. Yes, there was a resemblance, the square head and handsome face, though the nose was less aquiline and smaller. The same kind of robust build, though shorter by one or two inches. The same gift of gab. No! He was not the same. He was a fine man who was exactly what he seemed to be. Not, like Rodney, a monster beneath the facade. She listened and looked more closely as Robin persistently questioned Monty about the islands, about pending plans to provide ferry service for tourists to North Manitou Island, and the related problems of increased access to the pristine forests and dunes that lay across those miles of water. Monty spoke in legalese for a while, but then he seemed to notice Iris's concentrated attention, switching effortlessly to what she assumed was his lecture hall mode. Again Iris was stricken by his similarity to Rodney. The same aura of energy, of confidence, of virile force, the same promise of excitement beneath the muscular exterior.

Swept by feeling, moved by something she could not control, swayed suddenly by sheer desire, Iris stared at him. For a long moment that seemed to stretch on and on, she felt his pull on her, like a magnet. It was as if Rodney were present in this man, only disguised beneath another's skin. She cast her eyes on his sinewy legs (Rodney had never worn shorts), wanting to touch him, to feel the dense fair hair, and her mouth fell open and she breathed deep, turning her face into the wind. She wanted Robin and Ed to go, to leave her alone with this man. It was crazy. She barely knew him. He was married. Did he sense this feeling now? It was silly. He caught her eye and winked. He knew! She felt herself caught out...sure of it, with that same burning sense of her own allure she had so often known with Rodney. Lust, sheer lust, melted her sense of place and time, left her panting in the sun and wind. She had thought all such feeling gone forever, destroyed. Now she felt a powerful physical attraction, purely sexual, to this man she barely knew. Surely he felt it too. He moved, stretching out in the sun, his body revealed through t-shirt and shorts, still talking, hands behind his head. She was deeply aware of her own body, of her back against the sand, her breasts arched upwards beneath the denim shirt, the tight Levis on her hips and buttocks. She felt her nipples harden and she squirmed unconsciously, pedaling her legs against the sand.

"Iris..." Monty was talking directly to her now, and she shifted her eyes up his torso to his eyes. "You really ought to go out there for at least a day or two, at least overnight. It's a treat, believe me. Would you be interested, maybe, if you can get some time...?"

"Where...?" She knew her voice seemed strangled. She could not seem to get enough air.

"To the island, the smaller one right there, South Manitou. A bunch of us are going next weekend, and you're welcome...if..."

Did he mean it? He must know...he must see what she felt now. Or did he? He seemed to smile with his eyes, watching her. She felt some control now. Rodney was dead and gone. This man was a casual acquaintance, a friend of Robin's, a supporter, nothing more. Surely this invitation, openly presented, meant nothing.

"I don't think I can. What with the trial and all."

"I think it's unlikely for several weeks, at any rate," Robin put in, kindly.

"Well, I'm taking my two youngest kids and my wife," said Monty. "You're welcome if you can get two days away. We have extra equipment, sleeping bags and so on."

"I see." Iris turned her head from the wind, eyes smarting suddenly. It had all been fantasy then. Was she going nuts? The others were moving about, restless to return. The wind had a bite to it now. Iris shut her eyes and felt the tears. The others had stopped chattering and she turned her back on them. Then she began to sob uncontrollably.

For a time, no one came to her.

The others stood a bit apart, awkward, avoiding speech.

"Shouldn't you go to her?" Ed asked Robin after a time.

"I will, but I think she needs to be alone for a while."

"Was it something I said?" Monty looked embarrassed, shifting his weight from one foot to the other. "I mean, inviting her like that?"

"I'm sure it wasn't, Monty," Robin said, watching Iris who had not moved, though she seemed under control.

"We'd better be heading back," Ed put in, "it's getting cold." They all turned at once. The wail came high, over the small rise on the growing wind. It sounded like a wounded animal, drawn out and full of pain.

"The poor woman."

"Robin, you'd better..."

"Yes. C'mon, Ed. We've got to get her out of here. Dammit I wish I'd brought that flask."

Two days later the oral argument was heard before Judge Wilson to quash the subpoena for Nora Richard's notes. Wilson denied the motion. The newspaper immediately appealed. Feeling the pressure of constant attention, the Michigan appellate court sided with Judge Wilson, and the Supreme Court of Michigan surprised everyone, including an elated John Stone, when it refused to hear the matter. Nora would be turning over her notes. Stone practically floated down the hall, with Shaw alongside, into the courtroom where a buzz greeted them. There at the defense table, next to Robin and Iris, sat Nora Richards and her lawyer Carter. It was eight-thirty and the windows were open to admit the spring breeze. The judge took a long breath to ease the palpable tension. Wilson, who easily kept command of his court, had no real need for his gavel, but he brought it down hard.

"Ms. Richards, would you come forward?" said Wilson, making it sound like an invitation. Nora stood before the bench, Carter beside her.

"Mr. Carter, Ms. Richards, I presume you are prepared to comply with my orders in this matter. You will turn over the papers and notes and any evidence of conversations between Nora Richards and the defendant Iris Harris."

The actual handing over of the notes was anticlimactic, despite several groans of outrage from the press, and the look of horror and surprise on Iris's face. Judge Wilson gaveled silence.

"Thank you Ms. Richards for complying with this court order. These proceedings are dismissed."

Nora looked exhausted as she left the courtroom. A careful reporter, she knew that nothing would be found in her notes that conflicted with her published columns in the newspaper. But that was not the point. She whispered to her attorney, Carter, "Stone's fishing expedition isn't going to find anything to catch." Carter did not reply.

As for Stone he had a brief press release ready and stood on the courthouse steps to read it before the assembled members of the press. He read it equably, without emotion.

"It has been my opinion, supported by the Court, that the First Amendment does not provide a privilege between a reporter and his source when a criminal defendant or a witness in a criminal case—and possibly even a civil case—discusses that case with a member of the press. In such an event, they should both expect to be questioned about their conversations. A frequent question raised by the press during the suit was why I, the prosecutor, needed the notes. Simply put, in the article of February 22nd, written by Nora Richards, there are exculpatory and incriminating statements made by the defendant. I am entitled to those statements. Further, I am under a Court Order as of April to deliver to the defendant and her attorneys evidence of any statements made by the defendant to anyone."

Stone answered scattered questions from the disappointed press corps, knowing his statements would be quoted out of context, but he felt satisfied with it.

The following morning Stone's name was blazoned across the front page of every newspaper in the state, the lead story in every newscast. His name was on the CBS evening news. In other circumstances John would have been pleased, elated even, but not when cast as the villain. Nora, on the other hand, was even more the center, the heroine in the melodrama. Neither could escape nor will it away.

Nora felt the pressure keenly. She did not relish her role in the least, nor the attention. Angry at the assumption of her peers that she should have happily gone to jail over this issue, she had lost sleep and equanimity, and only wanted it over. Though she had originally refused to produce the evidence, primarily to test the case in the higher courts, she had no choice but to obey the court. She'd mentioned as much in her public statement, but the press, her own profession, had overlooked her point. She knew now what it was like to be quoted out of context and misunderstood. True, when the Supreme Court refused to get into it, she was surprised and dismayed. But, regardless of what the papers assumed, she hadn't been willing to go to jail. There was nothing in her notes that had not been summarized in her articles, so Stone's prosecution would not be advanced when she turned over the notes. Those were in the public domain. Furthermore, two courts had stated that no issue of First Amendment rights was involved. She spent Friday night with friends at the Bluebird in Leland.

40

"Hey John," Shaw said, "I agree. It might be a good idea for you to meet with Robin. Isn't that what the judge would want, just between the two of you?" He looked over John's shoulder at the array of documents strewn on the desk, sifted from the banker's boxes of documents that sat at his feet. "Yeah. I guess so," John replied, a bit surprised that Frank backed the idea. "Why don't you call and see if she's in her office. The number is on the bulletin board."

Her office was on Union Street in the Old Town section of Traverse City, where John was met by Robin herself, showing him to a chair in the comfortable waiting room filled with trophies of her past triumphs. Framed newspaper articles about her successful verdicts in personal injury cases shared space with photographs of John and Robert Kennedy, and the Reverend King. In the middle of the wall was one of the famous newspaper photos of the Birmingham police attacking civil rights marchers with dogs and water hoses.

"Let me guess John, you want to talk about whether a plea bargain from the defense might speed things up and satisfy justice."

"I could hardly say it better," John replied, moving up close to one of the pictures. "Robin, at the time this photo was taken, I was a sophomore in high school. We watched the CBS evening news. It was painful."

"I can imagine. I was at least forty. If you look real close you might see me in the far right corner, standing near Martin. I must add, since some people think I post all these clippings to show off, it's good public relations for prospective clients. Besides, these things constantly remind me of what the State will do to the less fortunate."

"Are you speaking," John retorted, in good humor, "of the same State that provided protection for its citizens, the ones marching in that famous demonstration, and the Federal Marshalls, and the cops who provide security while you sleep peacefully in your big house on the bay?"

"Oh. Touche, John. This case has been a grind. I'm going to have a shot of my best vodka. Want one?"

"I better not; I have to drive back to Kalkaska."

"I thought you guys got a pass on that," said Robin, taking any remaining tension out of the air. She left to fix her drink, returning with two.

This John felt, was the real Robin Blaine, casual, funny and friendly. He decided to plunge directly to the point, "Robin, I truly wonder where you draw the line. Do you really think that I, as a prosecutor, can allow a killing because of someone's past behavior?"

"I'm not sure where you draw the line, but Rodney Harris crossed it a long time ago."

John accepted a small glass with the subtle aroma of excellent vodka in it, on ice with a twist of lemon.

"One more thing you're right about," he continued, "and that's the reason I came by. I would be willing to reduce the charge from second degree murder to manslaughter. Further, I would not take any position on sentencing."

Robin smiled, "I would have been shocked if you did not hope to cut a deal. Listen John. When Iris was facing a possible first degree murder charge, and the mandatory maximum of life in prison, that deal might have sounded inviting. But we don't have that pressure now. It will not make any difference if she is convicted of second degree murder or manslaughter. The sentence will be the same. Further, she is not going to be convicted. We expect to win."

John was not surprised at the forcefulness of her statement, but he truly thought the plea made good sense. "Robin, with all due respect, you can't be certain. Present her with a deal. This is Iris's case and not another cause for you and your friends in N.O.W."

Robin stepped back, making a gesture to refill his glass, which he waved away.

"Believe me John, I will pass this deal onto her. Iris is smart. I am not making any final decision, nor are my friends at N.O.W. This is her case and the decision will be hers."

The next morning John was in his office reading a recent book, **Wife Beating: The Silent Crisis** by Roger Langley and Richard Levy when he was interrupted by a call from Robin affirming Iris's refusal to accept a plea. "No deal John. She wants her day in court." Hardly surprised, John returned to the book whose thesis gripped him. It wasn't that he had no sympathy. But the questions on every mind remained. Why did Iris Harris take repeated abuse and why did she return? John knew how easy it was for the layman reading the papers, to jump to conclusions and fall back on the folk wisdom that blamed the victim. Before this case Stone's knowledge of battered women was sketchy, but not empty. His office, like many prosecutors, had instituted a policy of requiring the victim to secure a security bond, plus a cooling-off period before a warrant could be issued, and his experience with this case had already prompted changes in those policies. Further irony lay in the fact that waiting periods rather than helping the victim, tended to make her susceptible to retaliation. He felt it ironic that he, above all people, was allegedly against adding protective measures. He was not one of those in denial about it. Perhaps most absurd was the assumption that there was a particular "type" (male or female) who was susceptible to abuse, a predictable syndrome that fit into personality disorders or worse, tending towards some kind of madness. In his experience as top legal officer for the county, he knew that these things happened to people regardless of creed, color, profession, or education. Something he also knew from his reading was that the batterer often seemed to fit a Jekyll and Hyde pattern of personality; for the most part capable of a modem of loving and caring (at least when sober), but, under the influence of alcohol or job loss or similar stress, often became dangerously violent. Everyone in law enforcement from cop to prosecutor knew all too well what Frank Shaw—in his bluff way—called It's Friday Night Beat up on the Missus Time. That syndrome defied classification by country or region, or even economic status. Stone remembered a passage in **Wife Beating**, he had underlined:

> "There have been a number of attempts to classify wife beater into types, and all of those efforts have been useful to some degree. But the mere act of classifying tends to set the wife beater aside, to remove him from the 'rest of us' to be examined by 'the rest of us'. Spouse abuse needs to be examined as part of the whole fabric of violence. The simple fact is that in America today almost every man is a potential wife beater."

From experience in office and his recent reading Stone knew another problem of equal significance. Abuse within the family was typically not reported. What he'd seen as a prosecutor was the tip of the iceberg. The reasons most people never complained or sought help were many; fear of assault by the abuser, fear of the reaction of police and official personnel, fear of family scorn or rejection, and maybe the most important of all, fear of losing home and security.

It was an odd twist of fate that in knowing this he also knew how stupid the common view was that the abused women love the abuse. Though it was among the most commonly held explanations it was pure rationalization, and anyone who believed it was ignorant at the least, sexist at the worst.

One other thing he knew was the fact that if abuse was not reported and acted upon, it would soon become an accepted form of behavior within the relationship, the family, whatever. Society, since it treated domestic violence as a private or family matter, fell into the trap of thinking it ought to be solved by the family. By then it was usually too late. All this had nothing to do with the reasons for bringing Iris Harris to trial in the first place, or for demanding that the law be applied equitably. Stone sensed that the burden of this trial, thrust upon him by the requirements of justice, was bound to be misunderstood. A deeper irony lay in the fact that he was among those most enlightened on the subject. He realized it was going to be a rough long fight, uphill all the way. It would take time.

It was in this mode that he strode into Shaw's office unannounced.

"Well, Frank. Any doubts about how we're going on this?" Stone knew that a man like Frank Shaw, though stolid in manner, could weigh in with tough and smart advice when the going got rough. As Frank neatly separated a manila file from the untidy pile on his desk, Stone watched in wonder at the nimbleness of those huge fingers, "Have you decided to call Nora Richards as a witness?" Shaw clicked his fingernails on the file, Richards' name inked on the label.

"We just have to wait and see. Some people think we won round one, but I plan to save her for rebuttal if necessary. Iris is locked into the story she told Nora back in February, so if Robin dares call her to the stand, and she can't remember specifics in her original statements, especially the admissions she made to you, and if those don't match the drift of what's in Nora's notes, and her columns, if she says anything to the contrary, I'll simply call Nora to the stand to impeach her testimony."

"Hell John, Robin Blaine is too smart to let her tell a different story, on the stand." Despite his wariness about the case, Frank had no reservations. To him it was not complicated at all. Iris Harris had been abused and had taken her husband's life. "Boss, if you ask me, the simple question is what punishment fits the crime, not whether or not she committed it. Maybe I'm simple, but to me she done the deed—no one doubts that part—under circumstances that overwhelmingly indicate forethought and a considerable degree of rationality and planning. Otherwise we would of had to bring her body back, not his."

"In that case it would have been easier for us," said Stone, getting a laugh from the big man.

"Hey Boss, let me blow off more steam about this. I know how hard you are working, going without sleep for days to cover everything. Me, I have no problem with all the evidence proving Iris was abused all to hell, like the stuff in this file. Maybe Rodney Harris was a shit and did all those things. What it comes down to is that she killed him, in cold blood."

This was just what Stone needed. He was reassured by the big guy's straightforward policeman's logic. Shaw had not budged from his certainty from day one, though Stone had moved from his original conviction that this was an open and shut case. What had seemed an easy case had morphed into one of the most significant and complicated cases of criminal law, and he was in the thick of it. Sure, ten or twenty years back Iris would have been charged, taken swiftly to trial, probably been advised to plead to a reduced charge, convicted, and served a short term in prison. *The Times They Are a-Changin.* But in his public role as prosecutor, Stone did not have the luxury of voicing his feelings. He was under the gun. Practically everything he said might end up in a newspaper column somewhere. Suddenly he remembered the reason he had dropped in on Shaw in the first place.

"Any news on that woman Sally? The one who was Rodney's secretary. It appears she slept with him on and off."

"No luck," Shaw replied, shifting his weight and gazing out the window, its frame bursting with new leaves. "The police in Ionia have nothing since the day Rodney moved up here. I got a list of her friends, and a relative or so, but none of them have any idea where she is. I think she's laying low and they're covering for her. If that story Iris told to Nora Richards is true, then I can see why she'd hide."

"I agree," John said, "Even if we find her it would be disastrous to put a woman like that on the stand. Can you imagine what Robin would do to her in cross-examination?"

Shaw kept his silence. His eyes wandered to the alluring spring scene outside. He had managed almost no time for his spring ritual of fishing, of making contact with the world of trees and the smell of new earth, of water to wade in after the isolation of winter in the North Country, and he was suffering from it. Shaw never complained, but Stone knew better. John felt it himself. Strange, he thought, studying Shaw before he turned on his heel to return to his office, we are so different—emotionally, physically, in age, background, and even in our feelings about this, but in some ways we are so very much alike. Stone felt the pull of the rivers just as much. He wanted nothing more.

41

It would not have reassured Stone had he known what Robin was up to, even as he pined for the trout stream, since she was placing Iris in front of a mock trial designed to prepare her for the real thing in court. The twelve people, all rather flattered that they had been asked to play this role, murmured as they settled into their chairs. When she was brought in Iris was uncomfortable, but Robin patted her arm and Iris saw that most of the volunteers were from the Women's Resource Center. They had answered ads in the Sun Times. Over a hundred people wanted to help so picking a cross sample of thirty-six and then reducing them to twelve had been a pleasure for Robin and her staff.

"Mrs. Harris," Robin began, playing the role of the prosecutor, her deliberately lower voice getting a twitter of laughter. "Why in the name of heaven did you return to Mr. Harris, and then stay on with him, in spite of it all?"

Iris replied, looking straight at the mock jurors, as Robin had instructed, "You must understand, I tried to get away many times. Each time when he connived to get me back he played on the fact that I was alone, and desperate. In two cases when I actually managed to escape, he moved heaven and earth to find me and get me back. Each time, once he found me, he took advantage of the fact that I needed him for support, for protection, even for shelter. I had poorly paying jobs or none at all. When I did allow contact of any kind he was clever enough not to charge right in, but he would insinuate himself. You see, he had the advantage since he knew me so well. He possessed me." Iris said this with emphasis, surprised by the force of her own words. "He played on that need. That last time, when I went to Kalkaska, he set it up in a place where I knew no one."

"But Iris," said Robin, persisting in her role, "couldn't you have just up and left when he was at work, especially after he began abusing you again?"

"That was the worst of all the places, of all the times, since unlike the other times at the farm near Ionia, I didn't even have a job, not a single friend to turn to, no money. Not having any money, that I wonder if any of you can imagine that. It means you can't even go to a grocery store to buy food, or take a cab, or buy a bus ticket."

"I find that not very convincing, Mrs. Harris," Robin continued, pushing the relentless prosecutorial role, watching the mock jury out of the corner of her eye. She saw that they were all totally focused on Iris. "Isn't it a fact that you actually did leave several times, and that you made careful plans to escape him in Kalkaska?"

Iris smiled at this, taking the pretend jury through the list of escape attempts in detail. Though her story was well known to Robin and to those who had carefully read Nora's articles, most of the members of the mock jury shook their heads in sympathy. She saw a tear or two. Well before she finished the litany of violence and intimidations that had grown into sadistic possession, she noticed Robin sliding across in front.

"Thank you Mrs. Harris," Robin said, turning to dismiss the jury with a shrug of approval. Iris studied them all as they left their chairs. One old woman, dabbing at her eyes, gave her the high sign. Two younger people applauded. When they had gone Iris looked at Robin for confirmation. Robin happily replied, "Good job, Iris."

Before they left the spacious basement—with its fireplace and billiard table—owned by one of the mock jury members, Robin explained that she and her staff had given a questionnaire to each faux juror. She and her helpers had prepared it with two goals in mind; first to prepare Iris for the rigors of the real trial, when the prosecutor, and probably most of the jurors would not easily be swayed by appeals to emotion, digging only after facts. Secondly it was to determine which type of person was most sympathetic to Iris, to her seemingly unlikely story, to a woman who apparently had let things go out of control.

Before she retired to her bed, pushing her sleepy husband over to make room, Robin had read through all the replies to the questionnaire. It appeared that Iris would stand up well in court.

"Waa...s up, is that you Robin?"

"Who else would it be Ed?" Robin laughed.

"Are you actually coming to bed? I mean to sleep?"

"I plan to sleep soundly you loving man."

As for her strategy it was already well advanced. Robin's central idea was to divert the jury's attention away from the case against Iris and to focus it onto the culpability of Rodney, the police, and society in general. She had subpoenaed the key witnesses, Harry Pool, Iris's cousin Mable, Joan Harris, Dr. Stallman, a member of the Michigan Domestic Violence Board, various people from Detroit and Colorado, policemen from Ionia, and most important, Betty Jean Benchley. The totality would make a powerful impression on any jury. Yet, Robin knew that in the final analysis the whole case depended upon Iris and how she came across on the stand. One of her law partners had emphatically advised against this move. It was dangerous and so much was unpredictable. Iris, under oath and under cross-examination by John Stone, might be overcome with remorse and blow it all. But Robin had insisted, and Iris wanted to testify. If Iris came through on the stand her own testimony would clinch it.

Up and about early the next morning to a sunrise that filled her east-facing kitchen with glory, Robin remembered how hard they had searched (in vain) for the alleged fourth Mrs. Harris, a woman whose existence no one was sure of. Joan Harris had spoken about "a young ignorant bitch he'd married when just a kid, stupid but good in bed," according to Rodney. When putting Joan down, usually as a prelude to beating her, Rodney sometimes claimed that he wished he had never left the nameless girl. Joan could not recall any evidence of marriage to the woman, but she had allowed that is seemed likely. "Rodney always married his women," she said, "In that way he never changed."

All this speculation about a fourth wife was no longer vital. Robin was certain that she had ammunition enough to convince a jury that Rodney Harris was one mean son-of-a-bitch and that on the night of February 17th Iris had been so in fear of her life that she literally felt she had no alternative except to kill him or be killed.

Dr. Stallman would also become a vital part of the case. Of course she would provide an expert's edge, but people would more likely listen to a cerebral lecture from a professional psychiatrist after the situation had been set up by the previous witnesses. As the puzzlement receded about what really had happened to Iris, as the jury became familiar with the sordid details of abuse, torture, and fear, they would grasp Stallman's clear and logical explanations with a sense of relief and justice. Here, Robin was fairly confident. Stallman's intimate knowledge of the underlying psychic burden of Iris's personal agony, something they had often talked about, could come across with unexpected force. Though the testimony seemed dry and impersonal when read in isolation, Robin knew that Paula Stallman had taken on this task with a growing sense of commitment, and even of passion. This was in some ways equal to her own.

Later that evening, satisfied by another long day's work, several of the mock-juror's questionnaires scattered across a low table, Robin watched the sun disappear over the western hills, over the West Bay waters lit like flame. It was marvelous, the light fading ever so slowly—sails still visible as late as nine-thirty on the darkening waters—almost as if night might be held off infinitely. Low clouds coming in softly were lit from below, reflecting deep orange, as if from earthly fires, and out on the veranda people moved in silhouette. Iris was there, wine glass in hand, talking with Ed and several others. Presently she entered, "Y'know Robin on a night like this it's hard to believe he's dead. I almost miss him."

Iris refilled her glass from one the bottles of Leelanau Chardonnay that Ed had brought up from his better stock. "He was one bastard..." Iris continued, glancing at Robin as if to see if her words could still shock, "but damn him, I did love him and when I'm alone I still miss him."

"I know," said Robin, not knowing what else to say, moved by the simple banality of the words.

"Sure Robin. You try. I agree that you try. But you can't know. Not if you haven't...haven't been in love with a man like that." It came almost as a rebuke, and Robin did not reply, waiting. There was a tale-tell catch in Iris's voice and Robin hardly dared to breathe. She sensed that there was more to come.

"I know you're fighting to find me not guilty, Robin, I want that. I'll fight for it, but..."

"Of course," Robin put in somewhat abruptly, suddenly feeling rather like a mother when confronted with the up now and down tomorrow vagaries of a teenager.

"Sometimes I'm afraid. I'm not sure I want to go on without him."

The two women remained silent. Robin broke her vow to stick to only one glass of wine, and poured a second. At the moment she needed it. A couple approached the panel door and looked in, and sensing something in the posture of the two women inside—poised in front of each other almost like gladiators, necks arched and heads forward—retreated. Ed slid the door shut from outside with a click, gesturing and turning the attention of the guests to the panorama across the water, now black as the night sky. Iris and Robin were alone again.

"Iris. Listen. You have no choice. You must. I'm going to do my best to get you out of this. Then you'll have to fight and keep fighting. I know it won't be over for you."

"No. I don't know if I can face it. Robin?" The words came as a soft cry, not a sob, more a question.

"Yes?"

"What happens if they find me guilty?"

Robin knew this was coming. Of course Iris knew the consequence of a conviction, but was this the right moment?

"We will deal with that only if it comes to that. Listen Iris..."

"No. Tell me, I want to know."

"Okay. If you're found guilty on second degree murder, which I believe is improbable, you face a maximum of life in prison." Robin heard Iris gasp as if this was something they had not been over before. "But I doubt you'd get that much from this judge. My bet, if they find you guilty, is that you'd be convicted of manslaughter at best. In that case, which is also possible, I'd guess the judge would simply place you on probation, give you credit for time served, and impose some fines and costs. But Iris, it's my professional opinion that the jury will altogether acquit you of all charges and you will be free and clear."

"But maybe I am guilty. Robin, honestly, tell me. Do you think so?"

"No. Certainly not." Robin snapped. "Not guilty."

"Never? You never wonder?"

"No. Not from the start. Once I interviewed you and read Nora's article, I knew. You are innocent Iris."

"Only in the law?"

"That's all that counts." Robin tried to control herself, to keep her tone easy, conversational. She was angry now. This was not unexpected, but she was fearful that Iris might not be up to it. Robin continued, speaking gently.

"And even beyond the law, I think you're entirely innocent. Why do you think so many people are helping you?"

"I don't know... I sometimes think about it at night. I guess they feel sorry for me." There was a tone of bitter self-pity in Iris's voice.

"Maybe so Iris, but many people are simply outraged. I am, for one. At what you suffered and how you could not escape. How the law failed you."

"I get it," Iris put in bitterly, "So the cause is more important then?"

Robin withheld her instinctive response. Yes, Iris was on target, in part. Yes. The cause was vital. Yes. Iris's predicament had unleashed energy to alleviate a condition that affected thousands, possibly millions of women and not a few men. That could not be denied. But there was another truth in it too, and Robin felt awkward about it. Her training, her life, had not prepared her for the tides of emotion that this woman roused in her, anger, exasperation, frustration, because she could not really help this woman in her inner struggle. Robin felt genuine pity, yes—which she knew was something Iris did not want—and mixed with real affection, a growing sense that Iris was alienating her, putting her and others off, putting them at a distance. This talk about the cause was not helping. Robin inwardly declined to take up the challenge.

"Have you made plans, for afterwards, I mean?" said Robin, trying to change the subject.

"I think about it. I suppose I'll try to teach. But who would hire me? Even if I'm acquitted, I did kill him."

"You might be surprised, Iris. I've talked with some people, right here in Traverse. I never told you because, with the trial coming up, it seemed premature."

"You've talked with school officials?"

"Yes. Among others."

"But I don't know if I can even teach, again."

"Iris, I know you can. You did so for years before you met him. Now you can start your life over. You're strong and intelligent. This trial is only step one."

"I don't know. Sometimes I am so afraid."

Robin knew the symptoms. Iris's fear was in part a residue of depression; though to what degree it was a consequence of events, or ran deeper, she had no clue. She stepped forward and embraced Iris, awkwardly aware of her own stiffness. Iris held on for a moment and then turned to look westward across the dark sheet of water, the horizon gone. Robin took her elbow and guided Iris to the sliding doors. Ed pulled the panel open and they stepped together onto the veranda into the cool night air and the rumble of voices, the laughter of people.

42

"I've never seen you so spiffy," said Stone as Frank Shaw appeared in his office door. Only minutes before the trial began, Stone was trying to humor Shaw to ease his nervousness, sitting upright in his chair, tapping his fingers on the desk. Shaw wore a new three piece suit, an off-blue shirt and a muted rust-colored tie, looking almost professorial despite his size. Everything was ready, Stone assured himself, or was it? What surprises were in store?

"Like a lawyer? Like you?" Frank quipped. He too was covering up for the hardest part, the count-down to the case for which they had prepared for months. The day was at hand and they could do little but wait.

The two men strode into the Courtroom, aware of the eyes on them. Crammed into some fifteen rows of seats were more than one hundred and fifty prospective jurors, news people and local spectators, some jammed at crowded tables on one side, and many standing where there was no room for chairs. The press had worked out a pool arrangement, drawing straws for privilege. Judging from the crowds both inside and outside the Iris Harris trial was the biggest news event of the North Country in years.

For the moment, the topic of interest was the decision by Judge Wilson announced a few days before the trial that a change of venue was not necessary. The Judge's reasoning, accepted by John's staff and by Robin Blaine and her defense team, was that there was probably no community in all of Northern Michigan where the pre-trial publicity had not alerted most people to the pros and cons. Picking a jury anywhere would be difficult and Kalkaska was as good a place as any.

As for jury selection, Stone and Shaw were old hands, but never had they faced a process of *voir dire* involving so many prospective jurors. Stone assumed that Robin in her long experience had never faced so many, and both prosecution and defense anticipated several days of hard work just to pick the jury.

A murmur in the courtroom alerted Stone and he turned to watch Iris Harris, accompanied by Robin and two of her young law partners, make her way through the crowd to the defense table. Iris was neatly dressed, coiffed hair gleaming, looking pert and attractive, nothing like the disheveled woman he had seen that night when she had taken Rodney Harris's life. Everyone craned to get a good look, though most of the reporters had sat through long drawn out pre-trial hearings, and like the legal staffs, waited eagerly for the real thing to begin.

The noise level rose as Judge Wilson entered, middle aged but quick of step, his eyes sweeping the room. Berobed and contained he somehow conveyed the dignity of his office, moving to his seat behind the bench. When he adjusted the papers placed before him, brushing back his dark hair and not looking up, Stone supposed this was a gesture of self-control. The case had drawn international attention, and everyone was in the spotlight. He felt stage-fright himself.

"Before we begin," said Wilson, his high clear enunciation penetrating easily to the back of the room and hushing the crowd, "I have a few words to the spectators and gentlemen of the press." He had not yet used his gavel, but his assertive words made that gesture unnecessary. Wilson introduced himself and the prosecutor, but when he introduced Robin and her defense team the quiet audience was broken by a few cheer leader cries, down came the gavel. Wilson intoned the proceedings to begin, explaining the process by which the one hundred and fifty members of the jury panel would be utilized in selection. It was a vital step in the trial, perhaps the most important of all.

"Ladies and gentlemen," Wilson added, "I shall have the clerk draw fifty names from among the one hundred and fifty persons already pre-selected for possible jury duty in this trial. Those fifty people are to remain in this courtroom today." The judge paused to look carefully across the mass of people, his eyes kindly but unblinking, as if everyone in the room saw him looking directly at them. "When this is done, the clerk will draw an additional fifty names. Those persons shall return tomorrow morning at nine o'clock. The remaining fifty shall come on Wednesday morning at nine. Is this clear to everyone?" he paused, and John noticed Robin also taking in this judicial display with admiration. "If for any reason it is unnecessary for any of you on these lists to return, the clerk of this Court will so notify you. Now, I would ask that all of you remain in this courtroom until I excuse you. Ladies and gentlemen, I cannot impress upon you enough the importance of retaining an open mind throughout these proceedings. I am ordering you not to discuss this case with your family or friends, hard though that is, nor to read any newspaper or listen to any media reports concerning this matter. It is important to our system of justice that you, once you are chosen as jurors, try this case based upon the evidence presented at trial and not upon information from some other source. This case will not be tried in the media."

Stone noticed how Wilson emphasized the last sentence, taking time to gaze up from his notes to look around the room. He knew of course, as did Judge Wilson, that the case was being tried in the media, emphatically so. He watched the judge, catching the trick of appearing to catch everyone in his quick gaze around the room. It was a skill practiced by many judges, college teachers, coaches and politicians.

"If the first fourteen names selected," the judge continued, "will have a seat in the jury box, and the remaining thirty-six will be escorted to the jury room by the court officer as their names are called, we may proceed. Madam Clerk, will you please begin by calling the first name?"

Iris sat unmoving through the name drawing. She did not find it dull or tedious, and she listened attentively through the hour and a half it took to merely draw the names. After all the selection would be the people who would convict her or acquit her. When Judge Wilson excused the remainder who were to return the following days, she noticed that most of them avoided looking at her, as did some members of the press. Wilson was not finished when Iris noticed Robin's increased attention.

"Now, Mr. Stone," said Wilson, "would you please introduce any witnesses in court. If not, if you have witnesses not present, please produce their names and occupations."

The judge then asked Robin to introduce her client, the defendant. Iris, though warned of this, was suddenly shaky, having not moved a muscle for nearly two hours her knees felt weak. Robin touched her arm reassuringly "You have to stand up with me," she whispered. There was something in Robin's manner that was almost charismatic, but also maternal, as she stepped away from the table, smoothing her skirt and patting her hair. For a moment, nodding to the judge, Robin paused, and in that pause was a certain power, an awareness of her impression, of competence and grace, of rightness and assurance. Turning, Robin glanced around the room, her level gaze traveling without a flicker across the rapt faces, back to the judge.

"Thank you, Your Honor," Robin suddenly smiled, her teeth flashing and her eyes twinkling, her iron-gray hair catching the light. She seemed incredibly aware of everything. Then Robin's resonant contralto echoed like a bell in the chamber.

"Ladies and gentlemen, I am honored to be here to represent Mrs. Iris Harris. Iris...?"

At this cue Iris rose and nodded to the judge and turned slightly to nod at the crowd. Silence reigned. She had begun to sit again when Robin held her elbow for a moment.

"I think we'll all have the opportunity in the days to come to get to know Iris, to observe her in this unique forum where the only thing we seek is the truth." At this came a perceptible hum, then silence returned. "And, ladies and gentlemen, I am confident that when you do get to see Iris and know her, as I do, that you will be convinced as I am, that by all rights she ought not to be here."

Stone instantly wanted to rise and make the obvious objection to this display of irrelevance, but he held back, feeling it would look bad to the jury. As Shaw nudged him, wanting the objection, Stone knew that this woman was going to be more than formidable.

"And," Robin continued, "We shall do that." Iris felt her elbow released and took her seat.

The first day of jury selection was tiresome as defense and prosecution questioned prospective jurors. Literally every one of them admitted some knowledge of the case, though some were clearly better informed than others, or at least admitted such. By ten that evening, with some thirty-four challenged for cause, everyone was exhausted. Stone calculated at least another four days if the rate continued, and this was only the first step.

It was late Thursday before fifty-five of the one hundred and fifty prospective jurors had successfully passed challenge for cause, making it possible for the attorneys to exercise their peremptory challenges. The defense had twenty such challenges, the prosecutor fifteen. The four days of interviewing—done in the judge's chambers—had also eroded the reports by about one-third.

The peremptory challenges were held in open court, and only one juror at a time could be called and questioned, respectively, by the attorneys on both sides. Sometimes there was a minor drama in this, but all through Friday and Monday the process went on with little interest to all but the most dedicated courtroom buff.

Alone in her room Iris read the note again, anger rising. Someone in the courtroom had passed her the note during jury selection. It was crudely written, but conveyed what Iris felt many thought.

"No matter what happened to you, you still killed the man. You are guilty of murder, and I hope the jury convicts you."

There was more but Iris balled the offending paper and threw it against the wall. Was it true? No! How could she doubt it? Rodney had left her no choice. Containing her anger and fear, she dialed Robin's home number. Robin answered at once.

"Robin? What about the note?"

"It's nothing to worry about, Iris."

"But what if...what if most of the members of the jury believe the same thing?"

"Don't worry about it. You leave that to me."

"I must prove to them that I had no choice. Robin...we must find a way to make them know that I did the only thing I could do."

"I'm sorry," Iris knew her voice sounded abject, confused, but she could not do otherwise. "It's just so hard to wait. And letters like this one... they make me feel so isolated."

"Well," Robin said, "such opinions are in the minority in this town, I assure you." Though this was stretching the truth she continued, "Remember, Iris, that, to convict you, all the members of the jury must agree that you are guilty of the charge beyond a reasonable doubt. If only one member of the jury has reasonable doubt you cannot be found guilty."

"I know. But doesn't it work the other way around too, Robin? I mean, if only one juror thinks I'm guilty beyond a reasonable doubt, doesn't that mean I won't be acquitted? I want the world to know I am not guilty. I don't want a hung jury."

Iris felt she needed the formal stamp of legal vindication. No inner sense of righteous justification could otherwise solace her. Rodney had taken so much. He had left her no option. And no leeway. He had pared away so much self-confidence and esteem that the core was thin and brittle. Iris somehow understood this, and Robin's reply, firm and reasoned, seemed strangely distant.

"Iris...you know that I feel this as strongly as you. I never aimed for anything less than acquittal. Try to think on the positive side. Think about what you'll say when you go on the stand. Think about how you will prove that you had no choice. And remember, we have the truth on our side."

But, Iris thought, Robin can't know this fear. She can't know how he affects me. It was as if Rodney stood behind her. She could feel his knowing grin, and, with flesh crawling, she turned. But she was alone. Controlling her voice, Iris thanked Robin and said goodbye. For a moment she held the receiver to her ear, the click and hum a reminder of her desolation. Replacing the receiver in its cradle, she felt his presence again. She looked around the small room, as if to inventory the meager possessions that marked her presence. A small bed, not her own, not even the sheets and blankets. A bedside table with two novels on it. These at least were hers to choose, one by Mary Renault and the other by John Irving. The portable TV was not hers. Clock-radio and portable cassette-player radio, hers. A small bookcase about three by three, not hers, but with her own magazines and books. Her old electric typewriter, unused now for months, a reminder of happier days. A small dresser, not hers, with the lower part of the mirror mostly obscured by scents, creams, powders and other toilette items. All of it would fit into two suitcases and perhaps a fair-sized box. In the closet, not quite filling it half way, her clothing. As if to reassure her senses, she opened it and stared at the familiar garments. She was alone. Yes. He was gone. He was dead and gone. And I am alone. Alone. I am nothing. I have nothing. The words seemed to echo in her head and she turned around the room, finally falling to the bed, her hands pressed against her temples, her head moving slowly from side to side, as if to obliterate fear and feeling.

Presently she fell into a half sleep and he was there. Leaning over her, he smiled, his strong teeth revealed until the grin became a snarl of feral hate. He reached to touch her and she saw red blood, and she screamed aloud, "Leave me alone!" Then she was awake and aware once more.

Wondering if the Snells heard, she curled herself into a fetal position and lay with open eyes staring into the darkness beyond the window.

43

The courtroom was packed. It was already close to 90 outside, one of those hot days when most people headed for the water. It was pleasant enough inside, the air-conditioning units in several windows humming.

A few hours more and the jury selection was over. Having used his challenges up, John could do nothing when the defense used their last challenges to dismiss four of the jurors on his plus list. But, since three of the four replacements were negatives on his list, the final make-up was hardly to his liking; fourteen jurors (two of them alternates) of whom eight were women and six men. At noon the judge called a recess and advised both sides to be ready for opening statements at one-thirty. Then he called counsel to meet in his chambers.

"I've given this considerable thought, and the crowd in there is only more evidence," said Judge Wilson. "So, I will sequester the jury from here on." Wilson gestured to a stack of clippings on his desk, taken from major newspapers throughout the nation. "These piles of mindless nonsense and media driven poppycock speak for themselves. I see no other option. The members of the jury can hardly avoid being exposed to this publicity if they go home every day. Furthermore, since this is such a small town and their names have already been printed in the papers and broadcast over the media, it would be a temptation for friends and neighbors to call them and seek gossip or genuine information concerning the case." Wilson paused to let this sink in. Both Stone and Robin remained silent.

"I'll inform the jury after lunch," Wilson concluded, "It will be my decision entirely. I will make that clear so none of the jurors can hold it against either side."

Quickly Stone and Blaine agreed. Both had expected this.

Back in the courtroom, John shuffled his notes. He had elected to use a small podium to set his notes on; this would give him more freedom to move around, especially to pace across to confront the jury. Being up close worked better for most people. Every seat was filled, the press table packed and several reporters stood along the wall. He began, speaking carefully, with no dramatics, building his case step by step, outlining the legal justifications for bringing Iris Harris to trial, explaining what the law required, and, he knew, fully engaging the jury's attention. Then, having listed all the witnesses and giving a synopsis of the testimony expected from each of these, Stone raised his voice several decibels, pleased to see the surprise on several faces.

"Ladies and gentlemen, during the selection of the jury, the defense asked each and every one of you questions concerning your views about domestic violence and spouse abuse, and we all clearly understand by this time that a strategy of self-defense based on years of abuse would be used at this trial. I think anyone who has not been living in a cave for the last few months knows this."

There was knowing laughter at this.

"I do not intend," Stone continued, "to submit evidence to rebut the fact that Iris Harris was an abused spouse. At this juncture it would be futile to argue that the defendant did not suffer abuse at the hands of the deceased. I recognize the fact that you will be hearing abundant testimony that may make you sympathetic to Mrs. Harris. You may remember that during *voir dire* I asked you if you could decide this case based upon the evidence and not allow sympathy or prejudice to influence your decision. All of you replied affirmatively to that question. I ask you to remember that promise as you listen to the testimony." John took time to look directly at each juror until their eyes met his.

"Even though you will hear plenty of testimony that will elicit feelings of sympathy for the defendant, I am prepared to prove to you beyond a reasonable doubt," and here John spoke each word with added emphasis, even daring to point a finger upward with each word, a mild rhetorical flourish, "that the defendant was not acting in self-defense on the evening of February 17th. The evidence will show that she had other means to free herself from Mr. Harris short of killing the man. The only thing I ask of you, ladies and gentlemen, is to listen to the evidence and base your decision on that evidence. Thank you."

Returning to his seat, Stone was pleased. The silence in the courtroom was proof of the force of his words. He felt confident and optimistic, and glancing at Robin, he caught her eye. She nodded almost imperceptibly, as if to acknowledge the quality of his statement. The crowd hummed and then fell silent again as Robin rose to her feet. Robin's style, as Stone already knew, was one of studied casualness. She deigned notes and ignored the podium, preferring to pace the entire space between the Judge's bench and the various tables, often approaching the jury to within two or three feet. This created an impression of careless and natural ease. It was, thought John, the product of iron discipline and years of training. Like an accomplished actress, Robin knew when to move towards the jury and when away, when to stand under the gaze of the Judge, when to lean easily against the defense table, and Stone watched with total fascination. He would learn from this no matter what.

Now, Robin's voice, rich with emotion, grew more dramatic, "Ladies and gentlemen, we do not deny that the action of Iris Harris on the evening of February 17th resulted in the death of Rodney Harris. We have never disputed certain facts in this case, and we do not dispute her action that night. But, we do deny and defy the prosecution to prove to you beyond a reasonable doubt that Iris Harris is a killer, a murderer." Robin emphasized the last word. "In a criminal case, the burden is on the prosecutor to prove each and every element of the crime beyond a reasonable doubt. The defense needs to do nothing of the sort. But Iris Harris has a story to tell, and she does not want to sit here and be silent. For too long she has been silent. It is time for her to tell her story, here, where our only object is to get to truth."

Robin now stood before the jury, slightly angled towards the audience as well, her bearing authoritative and yet friendly at the same time, her face stern but her eyes kindly. She seemed almost like a proverbial schoolmarm, full of wisdom and rectitude, yet able to give a lesson and impart a moral message to her charges. She leaned in yet closer, her mellow voice reduced somewhat, but heard clearly by everyone in the courtroom, "It is not a pretty story. Iris Harris's story is a chronicle of years of physical, mental, emotional, and sexual abuse at the hands of a man who seemed to possess two distinct personalities. But I need not tell you the details here. Iris will do that herself. She will tell you about her life with this man, of her early months of hope and happiness, of the first awful beatings, of her attempts to leave him, of his successful efforts to persuade her to stay while he promised to seek help, of repeated and even worse beatings, of various forms of imprisonment and captivity, of her flight and divorce, all to no avail."

Robin moved back to the defense table and now stood near Iris, who sat unmoving, watching her counsel with complete absorption. So was everyone else in the room. She had them all.

"Iris will tell you," Robin continued after her dramatic pause, "of her last attempt to find freedom and how it led to a fight, if that is the word, during which Mr. Harris told her that she would never be free of him. He threatened further beatings after the police had gone, and worse. Iris will tell you why she had no other choice but to take his life before he might take hers."

"Ladies and gentlemen, Iris Harris is not proud of her act that night; but, as Mr. Stone says, she only wants you to listen to the evidence and to keep an open mind while listening to the prosecutor's case and to wait until all the evidence is produced."

This, Stone knew, was a clever and effective tactic, to speak as if through Iris to the jury.

"And she believes you will do that. All of us believe that. That is why our system relies on juries, like you, to ascertain facts and make judgments. So, ladies and gentlemen, we, Iris, and the rest of us who are here in her behalf, further believe that when you hear all the evidence and testimony there will be only one verdict you can return. A verdict of not guilty. A verdict that will finally allow Iris Harris to be free. Thank you."

The silence lasted for some time, then the buzz grew gradually. Stone wondered if he had ever heard a more effective opening statement. It was not so much Robin's words, which were predictable, he would have written almost exactly the same words himself, but rather the way she presented them. He had no doubt that, despite his own effective presentation, Robin had won this round. But the thought did not bring dismay. Rather it prodded him more.

Together the two statements had taken the rest of the afternoon. Wilson, glancing at his watch, adjourned for the day, dismissing the jury until the next morning. Then he called counsel to meet him in chambers. Stone was familiar with the judge's chambers, which in the Kalkaska courthouse consisted of a single room; hardly deserving of the name, it had barely room for a desk and two easy chairs, which looked as antique as did the banker's style desk with old fashioned cubby holes, and a small rack of nicely bound legal volumes across the back. Judge Wilson and others had made it comfy. Behind his desk Wilson put the four lawyers who crowded in at ease, Stone and Blaine taking the easy chairs. He lit a pipe and reached around to open the only window, allowing the smoke to escape. Robin thanked him for that, and got a chuckle from the judge.

"Let's agree to meet every morning at eight-thirty to discuss any evidentiary or other problems that any of us can foresee might occur that day," said Wilson. "I think I can promise to provide a decent cup of coffee to aid us each morning, till we face the mob. But please pay attention to this. I need not repeat what I said in court, that I will not allow this trial to become a sideshow or circus." Stone nodded, knowing that Judge Wilson had repeated exactly what he said he would not repeat. "We all know," the judge added, "that this is an important case with many complex issues that go beyond any of us here. Let's work together to make it go smoothly."

"In the meantime do any of you have questions about the trial that you are burning to ask? Don't forget I was an attorney myself, not all that long ago."

Stone could hardly believe himself as he blurted out a major concern, "Your Honor, we both know this community well. It's inevitable that gossip, especially about the more sordid elements of this case, will grow rather than subside until the trial is over. Is there anything you or any of us can do to suppress the taunts and awful hateful language that are thrown at those of us involved, including you, Ms. Blaine, and of course the defendant?" Stone felt Robin's approving hand on his arm. He was not alone in this.

"Well John," said the judge, "I am not the Lord God himself. I aim only to control the case itself, in the courtroom, and I hope to command enough respect on the part of the jurors to expect them to rise above that nonsense. I shall do my best, and fully expect both of you to help."

For the next two days Stone presented his witnesses, the essence of his case in chief.

Some of it was routine and there was nothing to be done about that. All the measurements and photos and prints and proofs had to be presented. But there was a collective gasp from the jury during the first morning when Shaw testified to what he had seen when he first entered the cabin out in the woods. There was the corpse of Rodney Harris tied to a chair, Iris virtually in the act of cutting off his toes with a hatchet. Shaw's testimony was harsh and powerful, as Stone had anticipated, and even Robin's objections, aimed to keep such testimony out of the record, claiming that since it occurred after the shooting, it wasn't relevant, seemed to be misplaced since the judge overruled the objection immediately.

When questioning Shaw, Stone tried to make full use of the big man's certitude, and his commanding presence. What Shaw had found in that cabin, the blood and carnage and the evidence of some planning or forethought had to be impressed on the mind of each juror. Stone's questions to this point were effective.

"Detective Shaw, where did you find the gun case?"

"In the back bedroom."

"And the box of shells?"

"The same place."

"Now, where did you find blood?"

"There was a trail from the back door to where he was tied to the chair."

"As if he was shot while looking out the window and then was dragged across the floor to the chair?"

"Objection," Robin said, "at the minimum Mr. Stone is leading the witness, but it sounds to me like he is testifying. If Mr. Stone wants to testify, let him be placed under oath and take the stand."

"I would be happy to testify," replied a smiling Stone.

"Counsel, please address all statements to the bench," Judge Wilson intoned with a slight disapproving smile. "Mr. Stone, please refrain from leading the witness. Let him testify what he saw and heard."

"Detective Shaw, would you describe Mr. Harris physically."

"He was a big man, much larger than the defendant," Shaw knew he had an opportunity to bolster his testimony. "It is my opinion he didn't even know she had the gun. Otherwise, he could have taken it away from her."

"Objection," interrupted Blaine.

"Sustained," said Judge Wilson. "Please just answer the questions, Detective Shaw." A small smile came across the faces of both Stone and Shaw, since they both knew that despite the objection nothing could obscure the point, and the jurors would not easily separate the suppressed idea from the evidential facts.

"Detective Shaw, did you notice any injuries on Mrs. Harris?"

"No. I couldn't even determine if there had been any slaps or choking as it appeared she was unmarked."

"Thank you," said Stone. "Your witness."

"Detective," Robin circled behind Stone as she spoke, standing next to the jury, "Did you seize a riding crop from the residence?"

"Yes," replied Shaw. Robin took the instrument from Detective Shaw and had it marked as an exhibit.

"Were there any horses at the cabin?"

"I don't know for sure. It was winter." Stone loved the way Frank looked directly into Robin's eyes, without a blink.

"Detective," said Blaine sternly, "you have been there numerous times. Now answer me, did the Harrises have any horses?"

"Not that I know of," replied Shaw.

"Thank you. Now, did you find any other evidence of a struggle in the cabin, besides what was in the kitchen?"

"I noticed a broken lamp in the living room and a clock-radio on the bedroom floor."

"Thank you, Detective. Nothing further."

Stone was impressed. Robin had managed in a few short questions to place in front of the jury the possibility of a fight in another room and also get the dreaded riding crop admitted as evidence. As with all good cross-examination, Robin did not have the Detective repeat the damaging testimony.

Stone quickly called the remainder of his witnesses. By late afternoon, he was done. He was surprised by how quickly and easily it had gone.

That same evening Robin Blaine remembered that book by F. Lee Bailey, **The Defense Never Rests**. A truism, she reflected, as she reviewed the testimony of the witnesses she planned to call. Stone had used two days for his case in chief.

As she reviewed her notes, quickly jotting thoughts on the margins of her already well-scribbled legal pads, Robin noticed that Ed had entered her study, a smallish elegant room at half a level above the broad expanse of the family room below. A small window filled with beveled glass (taken from an old Victorian manse in the Upper Peninsula but purchased in Sutton's Bay) let the light in and allowed a lovely but distorted view of the bay. Robin loved the room for its brightness and cozy separateness, yet it was but a dozen steps from the kitchen and the utility room. She had neglected Ed for too long and she knew it. Watching him set a pot of herbal tea at the corner of her desk; she stood and leaned into him, accepting his tentative but comfortable embrace. She nuzzled his seamed and leathery neck and ran her hand over his tanned bald head.

Long since he had accepted a cancellation of their planned—and twice postponed—trip to the Yucatan and Guatemala. Ed was something of an amateur archaeologist, with a sizable library on Pre-Colombian cultures including the Mayan Civilization. He had been down to the Yucatan thirty years before, on a brief dig while in college, before deciding on a career as an architect over that of a globe-hopping weather-defying digger-into-ruins. This trip was special and Robin had asked him to go on alone, but he had refused, preferring to wait until both could go.

"It should be over in another two weeks, at the most."

"Maybe we can try for a late September visit. It isn't the dry season then, but we could do it. If you don't mind getting wet from time to time."

"October is out then?" she asked, knowing it, only wanting to talk more with him. She missed him, though they were together almost every day. Her routines on this case required late work and she almost always went to bed much later, finding him asleep, unwilling to wake him. It was not that she felt a need to make love, so much as a need to communicate as before. This had happened before, a work load that cut into their personal time, but rarely quite so deeply. Since their young days with children and endless chores and career concerns were behind them, Robin felt some guilt. Still, Ed had not complained. Only now, she detected a note of mild sarcasm.

"You know October is impossible, sweetheart. I have three projects to start, and a heavy schedule till Christmas. Hell, next spring sounds like the best bet, if we can't make it in September. You sure that trial will be over in time?"

"If I have anything to say about it, it will."

She let her weight shift onto him, forcing him to hold her, her breath on his neck, her hands moving in the practiced touch of decades on his broad back. When his body gave signs of response, she pulled her head back, neck arched and let him kiss her at the joint of her neck and shoulder, until their lips met. In a while he pulled back, holding both her hands, moving as if to take her to their room. But she shook her head.

"We're alone, for once. Everyone's gone. We have the whole place, remember?"

"So...?"

"So follow me." She led him, unfastening the buckle of her comfortable old robe and throwing it aside before she was halfway down to the spacious family room. She preceded him, barely, to the couch that normally faced the fire but now, in summer, was turned to the vast glass doors. She watched as he disrobed, characteristically placing his clothes in a neat pile on an easy chair, nodding in approval as he came to her, looming over her in muted light from a new moon reflected glowing from the waters of the bay.

They were arm in arm, sharing expensive Cognac, luxuriating in the night and each other, when the phone rang. Only moments before she had teased him, happy at his willingness, evidenced unmistakably, to make love again, and now he cursed, a lifetime of civilized restraint betrayed by Alexander Graham Bell's pernicious instrument. "Dammit. Your goddamned case again." This, from Ed was considerable.

Robin lifted the receiver, her voice forced. "Yes. Who is it?"

"Mrs. Blaine?" came the voice, "My name is Sally Tuttle." Robin whirled to make signs to Ed to bring her a note pad and pen and struggled into her robe, "Go ahead Sally,"

"I need to talk to you," Sally continued, "about the Harris trial. I know it's late, but I must tell you. I just got here. Could you please meet me, somewhere, soon?"

"Sally, we've been trying to locate you for weeks. Can you find the Holiday Inn, here in Traverse City? I gather you're in town." Robin gave directions and hung up. Quickly she was dressed and on her way to the car. Ed watched, his frown speaking volumes. Perhaps as a reminder, he had not donned a stitch, and he was still stark naked when she ran from the house, promising to be back as soon as possible. It was already well past midnight.

At the still busy bar, she had no trouble finding Sally, who stuck out like a harlot of Babylon even in this somewhat overdressed night crowd. Iris had described her perfectly. From the frumpy but striking "big-hair" piled to her shoulders, to the skin-tight red slacks and beaded scarlet slippers, Sally was unmistakable. The band was on a break and Robin guided Sally from the bar, where two slightly inebriated night denizens were trying to stake their claim, to a table in the far corner.

"Where you takin' her, lawyer lady?" said the largest of the two men with a studied leer. "Just so's you don't drag her away. I'll wait, darlin', right over here."

Sally laughed, but once seated she grew earnest, conspiratorial.

"I know Iris never liked me. I suppose she hates me. But that's the way it is with most women. Y'know, the way I dress. I guess I dress sexy for some screwed up reason. But Mrs. Blaine, I ain't no slut. You see, I really liked him, Rodney I mean. He always ignored the way others looked at me and put me down, and he treated me like royalty."

Trying to ease the tension, Robin tried a joke, "I hope you don't plan to testify to that."

Sally's peal of laughter caused Robin to look around the ballroom though the volume of noise was so high that no one paid attention. "Nope.

I'm not gonna testify to that. That ain't why I come all the way up here. I come to help, if I can. I never really understood what Rodney saw in Iris. I was more his type, it seemed to me. But he took off after her and, God, he just never let her go."

"You know about all the beatings too? Is that why you came?"

"Well, no. I heard all them rumors and saw her with sunglasses an' all to cover up the black eyes, so I guess I had some idea. But he never beat on me. He always explained the situation between him and Iris and made it out to be her fault that he had to keep her in line once in a while. He used those words a lot, y'know, to keep her in line."

"But, you did have an affair with him, while he was still married to Iris." Robin stated this casually, as if asking the time of day.

Sally quickly turned defensive, alert, "I admit I slept with him some, but when I did it is my business. He was a hell of a lover most of the time. Anyhow, it was then that I wondered about Rodney. I'm only just now startin' to understand that he might'a been at fault for her problems, Julia's I mean. It was after he put her in that hospital, though, that he really started dating me, if you wanta know. Rodney was always considerate and took care of me."

"Then why did you come here?"

"Haven't you heard about that one night?" Sally went on, "I mean... when the three of us...when we were in bed?"

Robin nodded. Half the country knew it from Nora's articles.

"Well, when Rodney brought it up, I thought he was joking at first. He never did anything like that before. I'd had too much to drink and we was smoking dope." It occurred to Robin that Sally enjoyed an audience, no matter what the subject.

"Then he pulled that shotgun. Jesus, I was scared. There was no way, lady, I was gonna object. When he fired the weapon and blew a hole through that wall, I wanted to run and hide."

"Would you be willing to testify about this?" Robin blurted the question, unable to contain her eagerness. This was vital stuff.

"You're damned right I will. That's why I come up here. Well, when I saw that gun and he shot it off, I had to go along. Believe me, when I tell you I didn't want to have sex...with Iris, and with all three of us into it. I'm not inclined that way. But I was too afraid of him to object."

"So, you were forced to comply with the act, against your will?"

"Yes. I guess you could put it that way."

"You'll testify to this? In court?"

"I got to. I got to clear my name, y'know. I hear rumors. Besides, now I know what he did to her. I read some of the stuff that's been printed in the papers, and I seen it on TV." Suddenly Sally broke into tears, and the image of the sexy, brash blond, cool and cocky and full of piss and vinegar, simply evaporated. Before her Robin saw a childish woman, unsure of herself, revealed for what she was, confused, insecure, craving of approval and in need of love.

Robin could scarcely control her sense of elation despite her fatigue. This would support that part of Iris's story that seemed incredible. Furthermore, Sally's testimony would help answer that question everyone worried about. Why didn't Iris leave Rodney, and why couldn't she stay away. The fact that Sally, after only a brief "affair", also felt trapped, was powerful evidence. With Sally on the stand, in support of Dr. Stallman, Robin could show the jury that no matter what Iris wanted to do, no matter how strong her will to free herself, her fate remained in Rodney's hands. Any efforts to leave him, including divorce, would be futile in the end, for he would always find some way, through terror, to bring her back. This was the part of Iris's tale that needed hard fact in support and here it was. This had to be the clincher.

Before leaving, Robin got Sally's motel address. Then still high on the unexpected break, she drove home. What strange lives some people led, like the most melodramatic soap opera, but entirely without the glitter. That was the sad and sordid truth; the violence and fear and pain and the unexpected shifts of routine, all that was real enough to many people. But, in these cases, almost never was there the converse, the glory and triumph, so beloved of the soap opera and novel of romance. These were simply lacking. Ask Iris, she thought. Ask Sally.

Driving home, Robin gazed up at the brilliant moon, marveling at her good fortune. She tried to imagine Iris's response when tomorrow she would call and tell her the news.

44

Watching from the defense table Iris thought her defense was going well. The witnesses came one after the other, each seemed to deepen the impact of the previous testimony. Pool said his piece with icy detachment, a contrast to Mable's tearful effusions. Then came Betty Jean, taking up nearly an afternoon, explaining and supporting the details of Iris's stormy marriage to Rodney.

"Then, Betty Jean," Robin asked, "even after Iris rented that flat in Ionia, even then, you half expected that she'd go back to him?"

"Yes."

"Would you say he had control over her of some kind, even after divorce proceedings had begun?"

"Definitely. He did. Believe me. I could see it clearly and I tried to warn her. I could see clearly what was happening. Iris was being manipulated and made to feel guilty, as if she was to blame."

"Please be specific, Betty Jean."

"Turning the blame onto yourself. She would try to find out what she was doing wrong and how to make him happy, and the more she tried, the more he played on that and the more guilty she felt."

There was more, but that was plenty. By the time Betty Jean stepped down and Joan came to the stand for her testimony, the jury was primed. Joan testified simply, without elaboration, to the effect that she had desperately feared Rodney all her life. Wisely, Robin let the words sink in and dismissed Joan quickly, calling on the Ionia Sheriff's Deputies, Barnett and Fitzgerald, in turn, effectively making the point that the officials in Ionia had—in truth—done little to protect Iris.

To Iris, as to everyone, it was clear that Barnett was a willing witness, and his frustration at the procedures and laws that had impaired his ability to help had bothered him in the case from the start.

Fitzgerald was abrupt, almost dour. Briefly he confirmed Barnett's testimony. Stone watched, knowing what Shaw had collected from Fitzgerald. Stone approached the podium, in one hand incident reports of the Ionia County Sheriff's Department, in the other his outline of cross-examination questions of the Deputy. If he and Shaw were correct, Fitzgerald would be a wealth of information.

"Good afternoon Deputy Fitzgerald," said Stone. "I want to direct your attention to the afternoon of November 10th, 1977. Were you on duty that day?"

"Yes," began Fitzgerald. "Deputy Barnett and I were working the afternoon shift. We received a call that there was a disturbance at Mr. Harris's office on Main Street. Although technically it would be a City Police matter since it was inside the city, we were on Main Street and responded."

"What happened when you arrived?"

Fitzgerald seemed almost too eager to tell the story, as he began. "We were ushered into Mr. Harris's office by his receptionist Sally. Mr. Harris was behind the desk. It was clear there had been some sort of argument. Folders were scattered on the floor, pictures overturned. In the corner, I saw fragments of a statuette or figurine."

Guiding Fitzgerald, Stone inquired what happened next. "Mrs. Harris was standing by the corner of the desk. She was screaming, 'I have a Restraining Order, I have a Restraining Order. Do something.' Deputy Barnett moved toward her and she picked up a brass paperweight in the shape of an eagle from Mr. Harris's desk. She eventually put it back on the desk. The best we could make out was that she and Mr. Harris were in the process of a divorce. She complained that he was following her around town in violation of a Restraining Order that her attorney Harry Pool had filed."

"What did you do?" asked Stone glancing across the courtroom to check the jury's response to this story.

"We advised Mrs. Harris that we would be filing a police report on this matter. She could check with the Prosecutor in five days to see if he had cause to sign a warrant. She should also call Mr. Pool immediately and report any violations of the Restraining Order, in order that he could take appropriate steps in Civil Court."

Stone, feeling the tension in the Courtroom, continued, "Deputy Fitzgerald, I gather you were involved in responding to numerous complaints at the Harris residence. Would you please describe the behavior of the parties."

Fitzgerald responded with visible zest. "It was Mr. Harris who was generally cooperative and cool. In all of those instances it was Mrs. Harris who was agitated, yelling and screaming. It is not that I always believed Mr. Harris, but of the two of them he usually was easier to deal with. Deputy Barnett and I talked about it, and we agreed on that. She was often enraged and out of control."

"Objection," Robin called out, "This is hearsay, and opinion Your Honor."

"Objection overruled," said Judge Wilson.

"Were you involved in the arrest of Mr. Harris at one point?" Stone continued.

"Yes. Mrs. Harris had filed a complaint and the Prosecutor issued a warrant for Mr. Harris's arrest. Deputy Barnett and I picked him up. He eventually pled guilty. It was my understanding that prior to sentencing Mrs. Harris dropped the charges."

"As a law enforcement officer, how did that make you feel?"

"Objection," Robin intoned again. "This man has not been qualified as an expert. His feelings are irrelevant."

"Overruled," said Judge Wilson. There he paused, knowing that none of the attorneys knew what to expect. "Ms. Blaine, since you have raised the fact that law enforcement did nothing to prevent the abuse of Ms. Harris, I'm allowing this Deputy's response."

Fitzgerald, a good looking officer, sat erect in the witness chair. "It's hard Mr. Stone. We responded to her complaints. We advised her of the policies of the Prosecutor's office. We arrested him. The Prosecutor prosecuted him. The system had him, and then she let him off. What more could we do?"

"No further questions," said Stone. Robin knew from years of experience that there are times in a trial that you take the blows. This was one such time. Fitzgerald probably would relish a confrontation with her over these issues. Robin would use Iris and Stallman to explain Iris's actions.

Deeply aware of her mistake, Robin knew she should have checked Fitzgerald more closely beforehand. She had subpoenaed both deputies to increase the impact of the officers' testimony, reasoning that even reluctant testimony about the system that failed Iris would be more convincing to the jury. Now, as the Courtroom emptied, she spoke to Iris who sat still, eyes downcast.

"That wasn't expected, Iris, but I don't think it'll hurt us very much in the long run."

"He made me look like a liar." Iris did not look up. She held both hands clutched on the table.

"No. I don't think so. We'll put it all in perspective later when you take the stand. Dr. Stallman will have things to say about that. I promise." Robin sensed how hurt and disturbed Iris was by this unexpected testimony. It wouldn't help at this point for Iris to express the slightest doubt about her act. She tentatively placed a hand on Iris's shoulder, encouraging her to leave the defense table, and together they made their way to the door.

45

The next day Robin called Dr. Paula Stallman to the stand. Almost at once, following introductory comments on her qualifications, research, and a general introduction about technical terminology—a blackboard was brought in for this purpose—Dr. Stallman moved to the point. Robin's questions were perfunctory, Stallman's answers elaborate and effective.

"So certain generalizations can be made, then, about this cycle of abuse?"

"Exactly. Most people seem to think things like this are individualized. To an extent, of course, any abuse is...but we have lots of research on this. Typically, a battering like that experienced by Iris Harris has a distinct three-stage cycle. It's amazingly predictable in virtually all the documented cases."

"Can you explain, in laymen's terms?"

"Yes," said the psychiatrist, using her best classroom style, "first is a tension-building stage. This may vary in length, often it lasts for a long period, weeks, months, occasionally longer than that. During this period the woman is increasingly provoked to constant attempts to placate the man, to accommodate to his wishes and desires. She is aware that things are changing, perhaps he insults her, throws tantrums, and she wonders what she is doing wrong. Stage two is the acute battering cycle. Usually this episode begins as a result of some minor, insignificant incident. This lasts anywhere from an hour to over twenty-four hours."

"This second stage," Robin asked, "you're not sure what triggers it? That is, it is not necessarily brought on by some provocation?"

"We still have much to learn about the trigger...if in fact that's the right word. We simply know the battering itself is a stage in itself. I hardly need say that the emotional, not to mention the physical, repercussions are enormous. Most of us have little comprehension of it. We are not talking here about a little slap on the face. The beating is usually protracted and violent. Through it the man seems to lose all control. Often he is potentially suicidal as well. Then comes the period of anger. While the man is...well, remorseful or at least apologetic since remorse in these cases seems to be a fleeting emotion, the couple, trying to communicate perhaps, begin to piece things back together. In this third stage they often seem to agree on everything, even conspiring, for example, to lie to the authorities about what happened in the event that someone has called for help."

"Does the battered woman, then, tend to believe things will go back to normal as they were before?"

"In this third stage, yes. The battered person invariably thinks that with extra effort on her part, she can patch things up, love the man more, keep the relationship going. Of course, it is all on the surface. Beneath outward loving behavior the tensions and problems remain."

"Is this what you call a form of denial?"

"Yes, but of course nothing is really changed."

"Tell us, Dr. Stallman, what will change it? What will break the cycle?"

"I'm afraid the evidence on this is rather bleak. So far as I know only three things will break the cycle. First, the abuser consents to the woman leaving him. Second, society steps in and protects the woman. Suicide is the third."

"Once the pattern is begun, then, the couple cannot break it, change it, solve it?"

"No." Stallman paused as a low growl of disbelief came from the audience. The judge gaveled silence without uttering a word. Stallman was aware of the general doubt of most people when confronted with this. She looked keenly at the citizens in the jury box, some frowning in concentration. One or two shook their heads; it was hard to tell whether they were simply shocked or in disagreement.

Robin picked up on the vibes immediately. "You seem so certain Dr. Stallman. I'm sure many of us would disagree. We are creatures of free will."

Stallman responded in hard flat tones, "I am merely testifying to fact. Scientific, objective fact. The fact is that we have no evidence of people in a battering relationship solving it...period. I suppose, with professional help, it is possible or might be someday. I have yet to see a single example. I'm sure my colleagues will concur."

"You're not talking about the kind of fight all married people have from time to time, even with threats, and so on..." Robin got a murmur from this and waited for it to subside.

"No. Of course not. But people know the difference, don't they? The degree of that 'so on' is the important thing."

Robin threw back her head and laughed. Iris pealed forth too and everyone joined, relieved for the moment. This, Robin thought, was a mite unexpected, this droll aspect of Dr. Stallman's persona. But it was perfect.

"Shall we proceed?" Robin said presently.

"Yes. I was about to add," said Stallman, "that society has little input in the first, and unfortunately the last, of these three means of breaking out of the cycle. The second, that is, when society intervenes to protect the abused person, that is vital. A restraining order, enforced by the courts, is one avenue, often difficult however...as we've seen in previous testimony. The police can take action immediately upon receiving the complaint. This too is not as easy as it seems. Usually there is no action taken and even if a prosecutor, apprised of the complaint, might refuse to dismiss complaints and proceed to prosecute them to the fullest, this is rare. My point is that, if society takes strong action to protect the battered person the batterer will begin to get the message. He will realize that his behavior is not acceptable and not tolerated by society."

"Then the hope is there, in that process?" As usual Robin was quick to see the point.

"I suppose so. A couple might, just possibly, with outside help, with firm and loving family support, if the problem has been brought out into the open so that people know, be able to struggle through it."

"Now, Dr. Stallman, don't all of us know, deep down, despite all this psychological stuff, that when a woman is beaten she deserves it. Isn't it true that it happens because she asked for it?" Robin's contralto rang like a gong on these five words. Stallman seemed mildly startled for a moment. From the crowd came a muted "Yeah, yeah", and the judge glanced at the offender until silence returned.

"Absolutely not," Stallman came back firmly, almost with anger. "That is pure myth. Let me explain. There are several myths to this effect, that the woman provokes the beating, that she enjoys it, that in some perverse way she 'asks for it' as you said."

"All our folk wisdom on this is wrong?"

"I'm sorry to say most folk wisdom is wrong. On this in particular. Society supports the man, of course, when inklings of the abuse get out, as many do. After the beating, the abuser will experience guilt feelings, self-hatred, and may promise to make changes. He will vow not to do it again. I'm sure in most cases the batterer wants to stop, but he cannot. More importantly, his every justification for his act is reinforced by society, by ancient conventions about how a woman must be submissive, especially in the face of a challenge by her husband. The man will come to believe that the woman is at fault and the woman concurs in this belief."

Robin waited, letting the words sink in, then she asked, "Can you play that by us again, Dr. Stallman? Are you saying that even when she is not at fault the battered woman will take the blame?" Robin was surprised that an objection from Stone did not come regarding this comment, which seems to stretch belief.

"Yes. The same conventions that reinforce the man's view that she is to blame also pull the woman in that direction. If she goes to a friend, a mother, anyone, the typical response is that she must be doing something wrong, not doing enough to placate the abuser, and is somehow provoking him. Furthermore, a male batterer is rarely physically afraid of the woman and doesn't think she can hurt him in turn. Even if, in the anger of reaction, the woman makes threats—as many do—he is certain that she cannot carry them out."

"So, she *is* trapped?" Robin looked directly at Iris, and then turned back to Stallman, a glance everyone noticed, as she intended.

"Exactly. It isn't at all unusual for the man to call the police after he has beaten the woman. He tells them he is afraid of her, that she assaulted him first, or things to that effect. He does this to humiliate her and to make any future complaints ineffective."

"Isn't it possible, in some cases, that the man is telling the truth, and that in fact he has been threatened, provoked, even beaten himself? Couldn't the woman be the liar?" Asking this, Robin was aware of an increased tension. She had debated whether or not to take this tack, deciding it was worth the risk of confusion.

"Certainly, and in such cases the man is usually the battered spouse. It does happen. Cases are known."

"So, this isn't all some feminist plot, concocted by N.O.W. or some other organization?"

Laughter broke out again, a welcome relief as before.

"Hardly," said Stallman, flashing an unexpected smile. "Sooner or later, no matter how careful the abuser is, the battered person will show obvious signs of the abuse. These are eventually unmistakable. There are only so many doors you can walk into or steps to fall down."

Again, a titter of incongruous laughter. Judge Wilson merely raised his gavel and the spectators were mute. He had firm control of his courtroom.

Stone, leaning back behind his table, taking rapid notes, knew the sinking feeling of impending loss. Dr. Stallman's testimony was made to order for Iris Harris. The theories and beliefs seemed to fit the facts of the case like a key to a lock. He would do what he could in cross-examination, but he knew he could do little to shake this powerful evidence and the way it was presented. It was unlikely he could counter her expertise. He had been unable to find a single reputable expert in the same field, with knowledge of such cases, who was willing to take the stand on the people's behalf.

Now Stallman began speaking again, the entire Court her classroom so it seemed, "Often, in fact commonly, the battered woman feels safer if she stays with the man than if she leaves him. Or, if she does leave, she soon returns. We have devoted some research to this...what seems to be irrational behavior. What seems to happen is that the woman feels that if she is with the beater she can monitor his actions the better. She feels he has power of life and death over her. In some ways she is like the prisoner of war, or the victim of a terrorist kidnapping, who comes to depend on her captor. Not unlike the famous Stockholm syndrome, where the victims of hijacked planes allied themselves with the criminals."

"Can you tell us, Doctor, aren't there certain personality traits common among abused women?" asked Robin, avoiding a glance at Iris.

"Yes. I have a list of several common traits. Let's see, ten or so of these may be found in victims of spouse abuse: an aura of loving the abuser, sense of his supernatural power, dependency on him, taking responsibility for his assaults, dread of defying his wishes, fear of leaving, detachment from feelings, hope for his reform or his acceptance of the situation, acute awareness of his feelings, and inhibitions against killing him."

Stallman's litany was related in a monotone, and only on the last part did some of the spectators indicate profound interest, with a palpable breath. Now Robin took a deep breath herself, entering a new phase of questions that were absolutely essential to her case.

"That last one you mentioned, inhibitions...against killing her tormen-tor? Tell us, Doctor, are there things, ways, circumstances, that might over-come that inhibition? Assuming it is natural for us not to kill. Going even beyond the restraints of morality, religion, and society?"

"I think so. All of us possess an animal instinct for survival, that is very basic. There are some cases where the battered woman kills the batterer." A silence fell over the room, uncomfortably long it seemed. The allusion was universal and unspoken.

"In such cases," Robin said eventually, "what happens?"

"Well, speaking in general, in the documented instances, the situation changes for the woman. She feels, senses, perceives, that the abuser's behavior is becoming a direct threat to her life."

"She believes he is going to kill her?"

"Yes. Her perception is based on the situation, her immediate sense of her inability to keep going, to get help, to escape. In such a situation, she is acting on instinct. In such a state she cannot form an intent to kill. She simply acts."

So there it was, Stone thought, shaking his head, scribbling furiously on his pad. The foundation block of the edifice of defense that Robin was building was firmly in place. Given the previous testimony, already shocking enough, that the authorities had not been able to help, this was strong indeed. From this basis Robin would argue that Iris Harris had no choice but to take Rodney Harris's life, not with the intent to kill—which it was his job to prove—but in simple instinctive self-defense.

On the edge of his pad he wrote the words clearly, sliding it to where Shaw could see, HOW DO WE REBUT THAT?

Reading it, Shaw merely shrugged his big shoulders. There seemed to be no way.

When he rose to cross-examination, Stone gave it his all. When, finally, he fell back into his chair, arms extended across the table, it was as if a collective sigh rose in the air, and everyone held it in suspense for a moment, until the Judge, knowingly, adjourned for the day.

For a long time Stone sat, accepting Shaw's heavy pat on his back, surprised when he looked up in exhaustion to see Robin leaning forward over the table. Smiling, she murmured kind words, "Good work, John. You had me worried for a moment. Too bad you couldn't get an expert like her."

"Well," John replied with asperity, "I guess you coached your witnesses well." This slipped out before he could stop it, the bitter tone undisguised.

"Stallman doesn't take well to coaching of any kind."

"Yes. I can see that. Thanks anyway."

46

Walking together from the Courtroom into the hall, the two lawyers paused a moment at the water fountain. Reporters were clustered around Dr. Stallman, firing questions. Stone noticed Iris, standing nearby with Betty Jean. Catching her eye, he held her gaze for a moment, aware of some primal communication; was it a plea or something else? He turned away, mildly puzzled, walking to his office, bidding Robin goodbye, both of them happy to have an extra day free from the trial. Judge Wilson had adjourned proceedings until next Tuesday to catch up with other court business. The break was needed, in any case, to recuperate.

Robin and Iris talked late into the long summer night. Next week, for perhaps all of two days or so, Iris was scheduled to testify in her own behalf.

Both knew the risk well, knew how Stone could come in to cross-examine, how the emotions evoked might prove volatile, dangerous. Robin seemed far more confident as they planned and reviewed every contingency. Iris seemed plunged in gloom.

On Robin's spacious deck, light spilled across the slanted planks, leaking in the protracted twilight of the northland, a sunburst from beneath bunched mackerel clouds, illuminating the broad bay and turning its blue to purple and gold. Even at ten in the evening, this light topped a tall sail beyond the sandy shore, and in the stilling breath of night air, all wind ceased, came voices from the myriad boats, the clink of an ice bucket, and the strum of a guitar. Out there on the shimmering water people celebrated their private triumphs or drowned their inner woes, and laughter came in muted echoes. Robin had tried to cheer Iris up, but now they simply sat on reclining deck-loungers, drinks in hand, just looking and listening.

"It is beautiful up here," said Iris when Robin returned with a refilled glass of semi-sweet white wine, which Iris preferred, nicely chilled.

"D'you plan to stay on?" asked Robin, willing to help her client, her friend, hoping for an opening again. It had been some time since they had discussed the future, Iris's hopes and dreams. She couldn't help but wonder if—like others who had suffered less—Iris really had dreams in that sense.

"I don't know. I like it, of course, but everyone here knows me now. My whole past...all those details. I think it would be kind of hard."

"You will be starting over no matter where you go. You might find it harder in some ways if people know...but you'd have nothing to hide." Robin sensed the defensive barrier in Iris to this kind of communication. She wanted to push it aside, somehow. Directness, her forte, seemed the best way to try. Robin had tried before and failed. It wouldn't hurt to try again. It could be touchy. She didn't want anything to impair Iris on the stand, beginning next Tuesday.

"I might feel better if people where I find work, if they didn't know, or if they only know part of it..." Iris let her voice trail off. Clearly she was not at ease on this subject.

"A big city? Even there the people closest to you would know. They'd have to wouldn't they?" Robin was blunt, less guarded now.

"Maybe. Like Detroit. Lots of people hate it. I was happy there once. Maybe there. If I can find work."

"You have new friends here, of course. Support people. That has to be important, Iris."

Iris turned towards Robin, eyes wide. Casually dressed in the summer twilight, the breath off the water tepid, arms and shoulders bare and lightly tanned, evidence of some time on the local beaches, Iris seemed young in the almost horizontal rays of the westering sun, the shadows deep on her skin, accentuating but not sharpening, somehow, her angularity, the revelations of time and life. Robin wondered if Iris had any idea how attractive she might be, could be, if—through some inner rebuilding of confidence and hope—she might emerge from this, struggle through it, triumph somehow by it. She wanted to voice this thought, but held it in, thinking it too intimate to speak. Instead she prevaricated a little, filling the silence when Iris failed to respond to her promptings.

"I don't think you know your strengths, Iris. I mean, after all this, you'll be free of the fear. You can put it behind you. You need to find a new life." Aware of the triteness of her words, Robin could think of no others.

"Everyone says that."

"Because it's true, Iris. Think of what you know. How you might use it to help other people. You were a good teacher, good with all kinds of kids, and every time you tried to get free...and long before Rodney, you succeeded. You heard Mr. Hayward's testimony on the stand."

"Yeah..." Iris drawled with a weariness in her voice that caused Robin to glance closely at her. "But don't expect Mr. Hayward to offer me a job now. Can you imagine that? No. That's the truth of it, isn't it, Robin? I can't go back there even if I wanted to. If I get off, I mean. Up here, I just can't believe...I could teach..."

Robin was slow to answer, knowing the truth in it. Further investigation by members of her staff had revealed exactly this point. Any school system in the state was unlikely to hire Iris Harris under any circumstances. The hullabaloo of hiring a woman, acquitted or not, who had taken a person's life, would outweigh all other factors. Robin understood the dilemma. Parents would raise hell.

"You might have to start over altogether." Several times before, she had tried to raise this point with Iris; now she decided to push it in spite of her concern about the coming testimony.

"I don't know," said Iris bleakly, "how to start over."

"You'll have to, Iris. When you're free..."

"Right," Iris interrupted, her anger spilling over. She sat up straight and took a deep sip of wine. "Like you say...when...if...I go free, when all this is over one way or the other?" Iris seemed to stammer over the next words. "What...what you mean...is when this damned case is over, when you win your cause, and when I'm gone...after all of you have proved your point...you mean, I'll be on my own."

The two women looked at each other in fading light. Finally the sun had sunk far enough below the western hills to bring that gloaming that preceded genuine darkness. All was shadow now. A shout came across the water, the voices of youths, piping and unrestrained; a barking dog on some boat out in the night.

"I guess so," Robin replied. "You'll have help, but you'll have to want it, to ask for it. You can't just retreat."

Lights were appearing now on some of the craft. The bay seemed to deepen, as if the bottom had dropped out of it. So calm was it on this midsummer night, as the last remnants of light leaked from the sky, that the appearing stars were reflected below, and the lights from boats seemed strangely detached.

"Why...why shouldn't I?" said Iris. She was fascinated by this phenomenon, the moving lights and reflected stars. She had seen it, or something like it, before, from her room in the Snell house over there across the bay somewhere, but this was stranger yet. Robin's house was right on the water, not distant and high above it. She rose and leaned across the rail of the deck, looking to see the water, almost invisible now. She barely heard Robin's reply.

"You can't let him win, Iris. That's why."

"I don't know..." Iris turned and finished the wine, her head back. She felt Robin next to her at the rail, and now could see lights from the boats and distant cottages reflected on water. The stars hung on high where they belonged. The void was there still, mere water now. "Did you see that?"

"See what?" asked Robin.

"Oh...out there, a minute ago. A strange thing."

"The light is tricky, this time of year. Over the water especially." Robin grasped Iris, reaching out with an arm impulsively, wanting to accentuate her concern. "Iris, you can't just let him win. You must keep on."

"I know...I know," said Iris, accepting the words, the embrace, "but he knows better than that."

47

The next afternoon in the mall outside Traverse City, where Iris had gone shopping with Mrs. Snell, Iris was ordering an ice cream cone from one of the stalls in the middle of the busy passage, aware here and there of a curious stare as the occasional alert shopper recognized her face from the frequent pictures in the papers. Mrs. Snell was chatting nearby with a friend when a harried-looking young woman came by, pulling a little boy by one arm. The child, obstreperous, whined and resisted, "No...ooo. Mommy, I don't wanna. Let me go. I don't wanna."

"You shut up...you shut up," the woman cried, her voice rising. The child, a boy about four by Iris's guess, pulled away harder, struggling now. "No...ooo oo. I don't wanna..." Then the woman hit him with an open hand, trying for his rump, but missing and hitting him hard on the back. The boy struggled, crying now, screaming, twisting. It was not an uncommon sight and passers-by turned to watch and turned away, embarrassed. Some shook their heads in disapproval. The mother and child were just opposite Iris when the boy, kicking and fighting, managed to tear the bulging shopping bag held by the mother. At this she hit him a hard smack across the head and he yowled. "Shut up! You behave...you shut up!" cried the woman, hitting him again, a glancing blow to the head.

Iris, frantic with outrage, grasped the bewildered mother by one arm, her ice cream cone fallen upside down to the floor. "Stop it! Just stop it...stop it, stop it!" She only let go when Mrs. Snell stepped between them.

"It's okay, Iris...It's okay. Let's go now."

"Do you really think she's ready?" Betty Jean asked Robin, hands on hips, insistent and concerned. They stood at the entrance to the courtroom, "I mean, can't you find some way of postponing it for a day or so? Say she's sick or something?"

"I don't think so, Betty Jean. An extra day or so won't make any difference. We have to risk it." It was true, thought Robin. Iris had returned to her seemingly normal behavior at once, immediately after the incident at the mall. She had been apologetic and willing to acknowledge that her behavior was unusual, but she also rationalized excessively, explaining it away. Robin recalled her words.

"I knew what I was doing, I really did," Iris explained when Robin confronted her two days before, "that kind of thing...people just turn away and do nothing. Why do people allow it? She was beating on that kid. That's wrong. Don't you agree? Can you understand that?"

"Yes, I think I can," Robin replied, avoiding the obvious questions, not sure how far she should push it now. The rumors were all over town. A reporter from the Sun Times had called wondering if Robin could confirm the incident, and Robin had refused comment. Perhaps among active and involved people, secure in themselves, a brief word in public indicating disgust or disapproval might be considered acceptable, but what Iris had done went far beyond the norm. Maybe she had a point. Maybe people should intervene if the situation clearly indicated abuse, but it was also possible that the particular young mother was not acting characteristically, perhaps harried beyond patience, perhaps she had—as all parents are wont to do—in a rare occurrence, only lost her temper. The woman might be a good mother, though probably Iris was correct in her judgment. But it was not for her to judge. Paula Stallman, who had also briefly spoken with Iris, was certain the outburst was further evidence of deep trouble. But even she had concurred. It would not do now to postpone the trial; an unlikely possibility in any case. Judge Wilson was fair and open minded, but such an excuse would probably backfire, nor would it be wise at this point to change the strategy. Iris was bound to take the stand. Stallman had even gone so far as to explain that not to allow her this testimony might do great damage. It was necessary to push on and hope.

Moments later, Iris emerged from the women's room, freshened, smiling. She looks good, thought Robin, as Betty Jean tried to put forth a smiling upbeat attitude, wishing Iris luck. For a moment they stood in a tense cluster outside the door, the murmur of the press inside humming like some vast machine, full of potential danger, full of expectation, capable of great change. Over the same busy weekend, Paula Stallman had surprisingly suggested that Iris get herself a still newer outfit and now she was dressed in almost elegant fashion, far less severely, more appropriate to the heat of mid-summer; a light tan skirt, pleated enough to show some leg, full and fluffy yellow blouse, a pastel green silk scarf, even a small yellow bow in her dark bobbed hair. Maybe this was better...this image of the mature woman who had lived a bit, who knew the ups and downs of life. Stallman's idea was that the jury would respond more readily to this than to the more obvious schoolmarmish, subdued style that Robin had preferred. Watching Iris, Robin felt far better. She would make it.

They walked into the Courtroom, finding their seats just as Judge Wilson entered briskly from chambers. It was now or never.

"Iris," asked Robin, getting to the point as soon as Iris was seated and sworn. "I simply want you to start from the beginning. Tell us how and where you met Rodney Harris. Tell it all."

For three grueling days, Iris was on the stand. Much of her testimony was routine, filling in details of her earlier life and career, building the basis of her personality and character, but parts of it were difficult and emotional. There were tears. Iris herself cried twice, especially when relating, at Robin's almost relentless questioning and probing, how Rodney had managed to convince her of his love, exploiting her regard for him, her need of him, and tricking her again and again into making another try. Telling the story of the awful time in the cellar, however, had revealed in Iris a toughness that few expected. Her narrative came pouring forth in short clipped sentences, detailed, full of suppressed anger, the edge to her voice as hard as the oak table where John Stone scribbled on his pad. Stone, sensing the response of the jury, a reflection of the larger and fascinated audience, guessed that Iris was especially effective when her anger showed. Her tears, evoking tears in many, even once—so it seemed—moving Judge Wilson to an unexpected recess, were also effective, but more expected, even predictable. But this calm and almost detached, almost emotionless litany of fear and violence and terror, clearly this impacted on the listeners like steel bullets on wax.

As Stone expected, Robin built the case firmly on Iris's words. Never was there any attempt to deny that Iris had shot Rodney Harris. She even admitted that he had been standing in the kitchen when she had finally gone into the bedroom to get the weapon and load it. This had been elicited by Robin, a minor surprise, but clearly in anticipation of Stone's cross-examination, where questions of this sort would dominate. At the end of Robin's questioning, when after three days Iris had brought her harrowing story up to the act itself, Stone thought there was probably not a soul in the room who didn't feel deep sympathy.

When it came time to cross-examine, Stone was patient, controlled, and for most of the time, kind. Much of what he asked was routine. Yes, Iris agreed, she had made the choice herself, on those occasions noted by Stone, to return. No. Rodney had not used physical force to get her back on all of those occasions, at least not initially. Yes, she had given up jobs, twice, to return to him. No. he had not kept her tied up all the time. Yes, she had been free on many occasions (each duly recorded by Stone from his detailed notes on her own testimony) to leave him, to leave the farmhouse near Ionia, to refuse his calls, to leave letters unanswered. Yes, she had ignored the advice of Attorney Pool and of others and failed to follow through with complaints.

Stone was pleased by the nature and tone of the cross-examination. He had to walk a thin line between being aggressive and compassionate. He sensed the jury liked Iris but he felt they had unanswered questions concerning her behavior. He made notes on his legal pad to emphasize the fact that she returned to Rodney on numerous occasions, apparently of her own choice. Was Rodney's control over her so strong that even when she had a job and the assistance of friends, she could not resist him? Stallman's testimony explained much of Iris's behavior but did the psychiatrist's elaborate thesis explain these return trips? The case may very well hinge on what the jury believed on this issue.

Forcing her to simple affirmative or negative answers, Stone did his best to remind the jury of the pattern of actions, seen outside of the heavy emotional context, and he hoped this record would make them wonder again—as surely they had all wondered at first—about Iris's behavior both before and at the time of her final act of violence. What he wanted was to establish in their minds a linkage between her earlier behavior, including those incidents when—according to the testimony of Deputy Fitzgerald, Superintendent Hayward, and even Harry Pool and Betty Jean—Iris had exhibited a potential for violence especially when inebriated, or at least aberrant and erratic behavior, throwing things, screaming, accusing, losing control and so on. The idea was to at least lay the seed of doubt—that the violence done to Iris by Rodney Harris had in some degree been reciprocated, that she had also acted abusively, in public no less; that it was a question at least worthy of consideration that Iris might be prone to violence herself, and that her final act fit that pattern. Stone did not state these things openly, of course, but the implication was there throughout. He thought when that part of his questioning was completed that he had done well.

Then on the final day he came to the core of his cross-examination. He sensed Iris was tense, on edge, her eyes usually following his movements, often glancing with some confidence around the room, now shifted rapidly to Robin and back to him, her eyelashes fluttering. He had been closely questioning her about the events leading up to that final act.

John sipped slowly from a glass of water as proof that he was in control of the proceedings. "Mrs. Harris," he said walking back to the podium, "I want to focus my next line of questions on the events following Mr. Harris calling the police the evening of the 17th. Are you there?"

Iris nodded. The jury as a collective body became more alert. The courtroom was silent.

"After Mr. Harris called the police he took a seat at the kitchen table?" asked Stone.

"Yes," said Iris, her voice flat.

"You then sat at the table?"

"Yes," replied Iris, casting a glance at Robin.

"How long did you sit there?" inquired Stone, first looking at Iris, then turning to the jury.

"I'm not sure, Mr. Stone."

"It was more than a couple of minutes," emphasized Stone.

"Probably," replied Iris, looking down.

"After this period of time, sitting at the table, you then went to the back bedroom to locate the shotgun?"

"Yes" Iris replied sullenly.

"You uncased the shotgun?" John could have been reading from Nora Richards' story.

"Yes" Iris said, looking querulously at Robin, avoiding Stone's eyes, and continued, "Mr. Stone, I don't remember...like, I'm not sure what I did then."

"Mrs. Harris, by your own admission in the accounts published in the newspapers, according the story you told to Nora Richards, you went to the dresser and found the box of shotgun shells?"

"Yes."

"How long did this take, Mrs. Harris?"

"Probably a couple of minutes," guessed Iris. Robin was beginning to fidget ever so slightly in her chair. She did not want to give the jury the impression that the testimony was bothering her but this was the Achilles Heel in her defense. If Iris had time to locate and load a shotgun, it followed that she was not under immediate attack. In fact, her own recorded testimony, allowed as evidence in the case, was clear on this. Robin withheld an objection, sensing that Judge Wilson would overrule it.

"Did Mr. Harris follow you into the bedroom?" John knew the answer, probably anyone who had read an account of the murder knew the answer.

"No. I mean I'm not sure. Maybe he did."

"I must ask you for a direct answer, yes or no. Remember, you are under oath and your own published testimony is clear on this." John saw that Robin was not rising to object. On this one Iris, however carefully coached, was on her own.

"No. As far as I know he was in the kitchen."

"Was he threatening you during this time?"

"As far as I know he was still in the kitchen." Iris repeated stubbornly.

"So the answer is no," asked John.

"That is correct, Mr. Stone."

"Then you took the loaded shotgun back into the kitchen area. Is that correct?"

"Yes."

"Did Mr. Harris come rushing at you when he saw you enter the kitchen with the shotgun?" John knew the answer as did the jury, and as did anyone who had read a portion of Iris's public confession to a newspaper reporter.

"Do I need to repeat the question, Mrs. Harris?

"No. Mr. Stone, I don't even think he was aware I was in the room until I called his name."

"Did he have his back to you?" Stone asked, as if amazed by this revelation.

"Yes, I think so. But I am not sure."

"You then called his name, he turned towards you and you shot him. Is that correct?"

Iris did not reply immediately. "Yes, I guess so," came as a whisper. John felt no need for her to repeat it.

"Mrs. Harris, wasn't your sole goal that evening to get a ride into Kalkaska, so you could catch a bus to the airport in Traverse City?"

"Yes." Iris lifted her bowed head to glance at Stone, her hostility self-evident.

"According to the record you had a plane ticket waiting for you, a job in Boulder and a place to live in Boulder? Isn't that correct?"

All Iris could say was, "Yes," in a sullen whisper.

"Mrs. Harris, based upon your past experience you must have known that the police would arrive?"

"Objection," Robin said, on her feet. "Mr. Stone cannot read the defendant's thoughts, then or at any time."

"Overruled, Mrs. Blaine." Wilson moved his gaze to the jury and then across the courtroom, "The question is relevant. But Mr. Stone, you must re-phrase the question."

"No problem, You Honor," he turned back to Iris, who was mutely shaking her head, obviously overcome, if not openly sobbing.

"Iris, did you expect the police to send a cruiser?"

Iris did not answer, though she nodded her head mutely. The judge instructed her softly but firmly, "You must orally reply, Mrs. Harris."

"Yes," Iris said.

"Mrs. Harris, why did you have to shoot him if he was not attacking you and you knew the police were on their way?"

One of the first lessons a trial attorney learns is never ask a question that you do not know the answer to, but there are exceptions. If all possible answers have been analyzed and mapped out in advance then there may be no harm in asking the question. In this instance John had determined that the worst answer he would obtain was that she was afraid of future attacks. This was the core of the defense. Furthermore Paula Stallman had said as much about Iris's state of mind, as to the reason Iris took violent action.

It was as if Iris had been given a shot of adrenalin. She sat up in the chair, glaring directly at Stone, and replied, "Mr. Stone. The son-of-a-bitch deserved to die. No one was willing to protect me or help me, so I took the matter into my own hands."

Stone held back. The court, the counsels, the spectators, the press, all silenced by this surprising, strongly stated affirmation. He let the jury soak up her statement of intent to kill.

"And that allowed you to become Judge, Jury and Executioner."

"Objection."

"Sustained. Mr. Stone, be careful," Judge Wilson intoned.

"So you feel no remorse?"

"No. It's tough to feel sorry for the bastard." A murmur rose in the courtroom.

"I have no further questions," John ended it. It was out there. How far would society and this jury go in excusing or justifying an act of murder?

The noise gradually subsided as Judge Wilson used the gavel. Aware of the change in the room, John looked at Robin. She sat unmoving, expressionless, her pencil tapping, eraser down, on the table. Stone felt modestly confident. He thought Iris had seemed heartless and cold. Would enough members of the jury feel the same way? He was hardly objective on this, but surely the jury would be disturbed by this revelation. Iris's final outburst was as damaging as her public confession via Nora's interview several months ago.

John was surprised to notice that Robin, leading Iris back to her seat behind the defense table, was beaming at her, actually patting her back.

"Will attorneys meet me in chambers?" said the Judge, after Iris had taken her seat. Then he adjourned for the day. Robin entered directly behind Wilson and Stone followed. He took a glance through the window, vaguely aware that a brilliant summer day had turned, in typical Michigan style, wet and cold.

"Well?" said the Judge, a thin smile veiling his weariness, also glancing out the single window in his small office. "How much longer do you two think we have to go? Do I sense an end in sight?" John knew Wilson and understood that his joshing tone concealed an unspoken direction to get on with it.

"Are you two just about through?"

"As for me, Your Honor," said Robin, "I'm ready to complete tomorrow. I have two more witnesses."

Stone wondered who they might be. It was typical of Robin to be ready for another surprise, even at this final phase.

"And you, John?"

"I'm ready to wrap up as soon as Robin's last witness is finished."

"Okay. I'll hold you both to it. Let's expect one more full day."

Shaw was seated behind Stone's office desk. His pipe was lit and he puffed away with a relaxed demeanor for the first time in weeks. He pulled a cigar from his suit pocket and slid it across to Stone.

"A little early for a victory cigar, Frank." Stone didn't ask the big detective to move, not sure of what he would do if Shaw refused.

"I know but it is just like I told you from the start. She as much admitted that she didn't have to shoot him. After the Judge instructs the jury on self-defense there is nothing they can do but return a guilty verdict to second degree murder or manslaughter." Shaw's joy faded as he watched Stone's face. "What's the matter? You did a fine job on cross."

"Frank, have you ever wondered why sometimes we lose cases that we should win?"

Shaw's eyes brightened, "I just thought you did a lousy job."

John allowed himself a weary smile. The case was in its fourth week and he was bone tired. He wondered if he should spend the time discussing with Frank the notorious Jury Nullification case made in 1735 by a famous Philadelphia lawyer named Andrew Hamilton, who came to New York that year to defend an immigrant German pamphleteer named Zenger, who had been arrested on charges of sedition and slander. Hamilton had swayed the jury and got Zenger acquitted of all charges. Stone keenly remembered one of his law professors summing up the concept, "As cynical as it seems, the jury has the final say. Many a judge knowing the law has faced this fact to his disgust. Many a prosecutor has lost because of it. The jury decides the case no matter how conclusive the evidence of guilt. Frankly," the professor continued , "it hardly matters what the law says. This process, when emotion among jurors overrides reason, well, it is the ultimate defense."

John decided not to mention it and simply said, "Jury nullification."

Frank stopped puffing on his pipe. Of course he had heard of jury nullification. "What you're saying, John, is that the jury could agree with Iris, that Rodney Harris was one mean son-of-a-bitch and deserved to die. Regardless of the jury instructions, regardless of the facts. They could acquit."

"That's right," said Stone. Shaw reached across the desk and with his big hands retrieved the cigar.

48

In her room Iris sat, slouched, hands limp at her sides, feet placed flat on the floor. She wanted to move but couldn't find the will. The radio was playing a soulful and vaguely familiar bit of jazz from long ago, from sometime in her past. It was Charlie "Bird" Parker, and the wrenching wail of the notes held her for a long time. When she finally rose, she turned off the radio, unwilling to listen. It seemed silent at first, but then came the ever-present sounds of life, a car on the highway not far off, the throb of a powerboat on the bay, crickets in the yard. For them life goes on. What about me? That bastard Stone did it. He revealed me. I said exactly what I felt. It was all the truth. Now they'll find me guilty, but it doesn't really make any difference. I am not important. I never was. They've all had their big event. They've put on their show. I'll be left aside and forgotten.

She could not stop the vicious chain of self pity and yet tears would not come. She finished a glass of wine and started another. When the phone rang, she was mildly high, letting the forgetfulness come, as she knew it would, sooner or later. She held the receiver limply, her voice listless and neutral.

"Yes. Who is it?"

"Iris, are you all right?" It was Betty Jean. "I waited, but you didn't call." Iris remembered that she had promised to call Betty Jean to arrange to be picked up for a late meal in town. Robin and Ed were supposed to join them.

"Yeah. I'm a bit tired. I'll be ready." Reluctantly she agreed, forcing herself to shower and make ready. She still had something of a buzz on when Betty Jean honked out front. I'll go through with it, she thought, for them. But not for me. Not for me.

Ten minutes later, as they met at the entrance to a new elegant restaurant on the top floor of the Park Place, Robin paused and said, "Be prepared for a surprise, Iris, there's someone here I want you to meet." And forthwith, with a gentle prod, she directed Iris to a large corner table where the crescent lights of the city could be seen curling round the western arm of the bay. Ed was already there and Iris forced a smile. And standing next to Ed, a total stranger.

Sally's much anticipated testimony proved to be the stuff of soap opera. Reporters seemed especially fascinated. Not only did Sally dress the part, gaudy, flashy, plenty of leg and cleavage showing, abundant hair in studied disarray, tossing her head at every opportunity, flashing sexy looks at the Judge, at Stone, at Shaw, at nearly every man present it seemed, but she played the role to the hilt, and Robin expertly milked every nuance. One exchange was typical.

"Sally," asked Robin in her kindest tone, "How would you characterize your ah...relationship with Rodney Harris?"

Not in the least offended, apparently relishing the part, Sally beamed.

"Well...it was fun. I mean, Rodney was...he knew how to make a woman happy." Laughter echoed in the crowded courthouse. Sally seemed mildly offended, "I mean...at first."

"He was kind then, considerate?"

"Oh...yes. Absolutely. He was...ardent. Yeah, that's the word."

More laughter. Judge Wilson gaveled quiet and the titters subsided.

"Did you think he cared for you?"

"Absolutely. He was incredible. He had a terrific line."

"You mean it was all an act?"

"Well, not all of it," subdued laughs, dying quickly. Again the intensity of interest was palpable. Sally's artless use of superlatives and her flamboyant personality brought a welcome element of comic relief; but Robin knew this would only turn things more to Iris's favor.

"Like he had two sides? One good, the other bad?"

"Yeah...like Jack Palance in that old movie..."

"Do you mean Jekyll-Hyde?" Robin asked, guessing that Sally had no awareness of the famous Stevenson story.

"Yeah, that guy. Rodney was a hell of a lover sometimes, but he lied like hell too. And he changed...he turned bad, just like that." Sally snapped her fingers dramatically.

"Now Ms. Tuttle," said Robin in a soothing voice, "Can you tell us about the evening when Rodney forced you and Iris into a sexual threesome? In your own words?"

And Sally did, in expressive, vivid, and unabashed language. When she stepped down, Stone had stopped writing on his pad. This was very damaging since it showed that Rodney had fired a gun at Iris in the past, apparently trying to kill her. And it bolstered the concept that he was capable of almost anything. Stone decided it would be dangerous to cross-examine Sally. Anything he asked her in open court would probably reinforce the damaging information now lodged in the minds of each member of the jury.

Then Robin called her final witness. It came as a surprise to everyone connected to the case.

"I call Mary Harris Tome."

Everyone stared at a heavy sixty-ish woman who now took the stand, swearing to tell the truth, the whole truth, and nothing but the truth.

Iris had met her the evening before at the Park Place restaurant. Mary Tome was the missing first Mrs. Harris, materialized out of Rodney's hazy youth. Her story was almost unbelievable. She had been in virtual hiding for thirty-five years, constantly fearful that at some time, somewhere, Rodney would reappear and claim her as his. She had married him, while three months along with his child, at the age of fifteen. Rodney was then in his late teens. Now her testimony stunned the audience.

"Even when my parents found out that I was expecting, they told me not to marry him. They didn't trust him. But I was just a kid and I wanted to get away from them so bad, and Rodney, he had that gift of gab, and he sure was one hell of a handsome boy, so I guess I persuaded myself I loved him. So we got married and moved to Boston where we found a small apartment on the south side. He started drinking right away, and kept at it most every day after work, from then on. It didn't seem to affect his job selling insurance door to door. You see, Rodney never seemed to need sleep, and sometimes I'd wake up and find him pacing the floor at three or four in the morning with a drink in his hand. Then one night he started beating me. I never knew why.

I thought maybe he didn't want to be married, so I tried to make him happy. I wondered if he didn't want the baby. I even offered to leave. Soon enough I just wanted out, though I had no place to go…I wasn't barely sixteen. But he wouldn't let me go. Sometimes he'd be very considerate, after beating on me. He had two personalities."

"But you did try to escape?" Robin asked, making a point to glance from Mary over to Iris, and then to Joan who sat in the front row. No one missed the point.

"Well, in my fifth month I had enough. I packed and told him I was leaving. I didn't expect it, but he didn't make a scene. He just opened the door to that dumpy little flat and let me out. I was at the landing, just ready to go down the steps when I heard his voice. It was like a voice from hell, kind of high and strange, 'You will leave only when I say, bitch.' I remember his big hands pushing against my back. There were twenty-five steps on those stairs. I counted them after I got out of the hospital. I lost the baby. I remember the first face I saw when I came to was Rodney's. He was leaning over me in the hospital, with tears in his eyes. He told the nurses I tripped. Of course they all believed him."

"And even after that you stayed on?"

"Yeah. I know it's hard to believe. We was married for four and a half years. Then one day he just up and left, without a word. I had started to work and I put on some weight, and he just disappeared. I moved back to my folks near Toledo. I was with them two years when he showed up suddenly one day. My parents wasn't home and he just came in and grabbed me and forced himself on me, and he took me with him. He kidnapped me actually. We traveled all over for about two years. I don't think we stayed in one town more than three months in all that time. Rodney worked at carnivals, he sold stuff, used cars, encyclopedias, everything. He was good at it, but he'd cheat on his share and we'd have to move on. He'd take good care of me for weeks and weeks, and then he'd turn on me and beat me something awful. I never did figure out why. For a while he starved me, made me lose weight and he used me as bait, sort of, to attract these guys from that army base—at that time we was living near Fort Benning down in Georgia—to set up card games. Then he'd cheat at poker and take their money. I was pretty back then. But I kept eating and put weight on again. Then one night he just up and left again. He left a note this time. I remember every word because I kept that damned note for almost twenty years. It said, 'Mary, you are free now, but someday, sometime, I might want you back, so remember, you are mine forever.' I was barely twenty-four years old. I never saw the man again, and never heard of him again, until I read about this case."

"What made you come forward then, after all this time?"

"I guess it took me some time to get used to the idea that he was dead. I was in hiding from him you see."

"For thirty-five years?" Robin asked with a tone of obvious skepticism.

"Yeah. I never married again. I was always afraid he'd come back. Then, I was living down in...well, you don't mind if I don't say where do you?"

"Of course not."

"I was reading all about Mrs. Harris here...Iris." Here the first Mrs. Harris paused, looking at Iris with eyes suddenly luminous, flooded with emotion. A muffled sob came from one of the spectators.

"Anyhow, I started thinking about her. She's young. I mean, compared to me. I'm gettin' on towards sixty. I got hypertension, I'm diabetic, I smoke too much and I got emphysema. I have no children. I guess you might say it's too late for me. But he's dead and I wanted to make sure she...if it's the last thing I do...I want Iris to be free. In a way, she's allowed me to be."

Robin and all the others remained silent, in token of respect. Stone, controlling his own emotions with effort, knew it was over. This was the final nail in the coffin. There wasn't a jury in the land that would convict Iris after this testimony. He didn't know how Robin had managed to find this final witness. Whatever, it was masterful. So, to everyone in the room it seemed obvious that Iris had told the truth from the start. She had found it impossible to free herself, his entire possession until, obviously she had done the only thing left to do; and in doing so she had freed not only herself, but two others as well.

Of course Stone knew that his genuine case, also based on the chain of events leading to Iris using the shotgun, was not refuted in the least. It was simply ignored.

When Robin spoke again, it was in simple words, "Your Honor, the defense rests."

In his office Stone and Shaw stood next to the tall window, feeling the breeze against their skin, a day comfortable enough to keep the windows open and shut off the noisy air conditioner. It would be a good day to be outdoors.

"What next, John?" asked Shaw, flinging a great arm around John's shoulder with unrestrained affection.

Stone looked back with a gleam of comprehension. Words seemed unnecessary, but presently he spoke, his voice a little thick, "After the acquittal you mean?"

Shaw nodded. It was a foregone conclusion.

A deputy was at the door, announcing that the jury was returning. The jury had deliberated since nine in the morning and people were clustered on the lawns and sidewalks enjoying the bright, dazzling summer day. The speculation, rampant throughout the trial, had turned overwhelmingly in favor of acquittal. As news of the jury's return reached them, the clusters broke and the expectant crowd filed into the courtroom.

"Boss?" Shaw filled the doorway, blocking it for a moment. Footsteps rang in the hall as the last of the people pushed into the courtroom. "You did a good job."

At the announcement of the verdict, the room erupted in cheers. Iris was on her feet, embraced by Betty Jean, by Robin, by many others. Stone stood alone at the prosecutor's table, a faint smile on his face. For a long time the crowd eddied around Iris, and then people began to leave. Most of the reporters were gone, the well of their stories dry. There was some collective relief in victory. John did not exactly share it. Some spectators gathered around Iris and Robin and the defense team, jabbering happily. Robin detached herself and walked over to Stone. He extended his hand and she grasping it firmly in a brief shake, then she nudged him towards Iris.

"I don't think..." he mumbled.

"No, John. I think she'd want to."

Iris, standing now, a fragrant bouquet of roses in one hand, surrounded by friends and well-wishers, smiling and looking a bit confused, glanced up and saw Stone. For an instant she frowned, her eyes lit by a flash of challenge, but quickly she smiled.

John took her extended hand in both of his, releasing it after a quick squeeze.

"I wish you luck, Mrs. Harris...Iris."

Iris thanked him, nodding politely, then her eyes shifted away, gazing into the distance. Stone glanced around but all he could see was the bright window and the blue sky beyond.

EPILOGUE

Far off to the west lay the blasted peak now mantled in snow, the leveled forest now greening in its vast arc and filled once more with life. Deer teemed in the bushy secondary growth and grouse fed on abundant berries. Many of the smaller streams ran clear again, minnows flashing in rivulets once choked with ash, and trout rising in the deeper pools. On the slopes of Mt. Adams lay a campsite; two tents, with several sleeping bags thrown across a rope slung between two trees. A navy-blue backpack was propped against a massive Douglas Fir and the remains of a campfire darkened the place where they had eaten. Within the visible perimeter of the camp no one moved, nor was anyone in sight on the higher slopes where the trees fell away. From her vantage point up above the tree-line, she could see the perfect dazzling cone of Mt. Adams, rising still above her, close, and beyond, around its flank, the scooped and hollowed mass of Mt. St. Helens. There had been fire in that mountain, magna and steam and heat, and even now, five years after the eruption, it lay stoked with power. From her perch she could clearly see places where the forest had been laid low by that blast, and yet the damaged regions seemed to glow brighter than the surrounding undisturbed forests of great trees, like those just below under the shadow of Mt. Adams.

For a long time she studied Mt. St. Helens. The mountain and the land—had recovered. She framed the words one by one in her mind. Her headache gone, as fleeting as the thin clouds that had covered the peak when she began to climb from the camp. Resting, despite the thin air of some 10,000 feet, her head had cleared. The air too had cleared so that the view was unimpeded for endless miles, maybe a hundred or so. Mt. Hood was visible far to the south, and lesser peaks.

She looked at Mt. St. Helens again. It sits there with that strange feminine name, as if waiting. When, I wonder, will it go off again? What year was that? Yes...it was not even a year after I came out...to a job in Portland; and it has taken all of those five years, or so, to really absorb this...to get an acquaintance with this vastly different landscape. I'd never have come up here this far, never alone, in those days, before...

The teaching job in Portland had lasted three semesters, then trouble, and near oblivion and recovery in the hospital and that intrusive and—at first—hated therapy they had forced on her. Then the job in the school near Tacoma. And a few friends.

Remembering the climb, so hard and steep in places that she had nearly turned back, limbs shaking, head throbbing, she felt a mild triumph. Breath came short as she rested, still, but she had come high enough to feel—at midsummer—the icy breath of snow. Where she sat on rock, amid moss and sparse alpine grass, the snow thickened perceptibly. She would not venture there. Already there came a cold breeze downslope, and she pulled a sweater forth and put it on over her flannel shirt.

Remembering...so much. Times and times she could not escape memory and the harrowing pain of that past. The struggle and the pills and the allure of the void. Of that dark pool. Wind on her, blowing her hair so that she pulled her hat tighter, reminded her of time and of hunger. She unwrapped her lunch and ate, slowly, aware of a mild nausea at first, the swallowing difficult until appetite grew with need for repletion. She must return, after all, down that hard slope, into trees, along craggy paths, to the camp where the others would meet her.

Two years ago, even last year, I wonder...would they have let me do this? Alone? So much had changed. So much was the same. I can handle this solitude. Now. Knowing it, welcoming it. They tell me not to seek escape, but there are things I need. I did not know this feeling, quite. Not before...

No. I remember mountains from before. I was still his then. Am I my own? On this mountain? Whose am I?

Laura down there, and Patsy, with her plump little guy, slow but solid Will, who would be wondering by now why she had not returned. She could see movement now in the camp, but it was too far to see who was there. Probably Patsy, worried about supper. Fussy, but prepared, she would have everything ready long before necessary.

Now the sun was low enough to cast a deep shadow on the eastern slope of the great white peak. She was still in the sun and warmed by it, though the wind carried cold from above. Her back cold, front warmer, she turned and sat facing north, and watched Rainier emerge from cloud. Higher, yet it seemed far smaller from this distance. So white. Pure white. Whiter than cloud, it rose dazzling above deep green forests, so deep now as to look almost black in shadows. Scattered high clouds came in from the west, from the Ocean, and stippled the sunlit valleys, moving.

It was hard to rise, turn, and lift the small pack, hunching to take it on her back. Night was closer than it seemed. Cold prompted motion, so she moved down, easily at first, then more careless of step as she entered the tree line. Within the scent of fir and pine, climbing down now on rock and needles and through laden thickets, and along the sudden plunge of canyon where the stream, tiny above, dropped over a ledge into a cleft so deep she could barely see the bottom. Down there it roared, the sound rising up to her through craggy rock, an animal sound, she thought.

Pulled by hunger and thirst, she looked to where the trail rose again, and then to the winding descent (not in sight) where it skirted the cliff and dropped sharply to cross the stream, and to the wide shoulder where it rose in fading light, across to the camp. Patsy would have supper on by now. All of them, all middle-aged, would wait for her and she could almost feel the relief, so obvious in their eyes so often, when she came into the trampled perimeter of their camp, where they had slept two nights, and would one night more.

So this is it? Light like fire drenched the top of the mountain now, the white transformed to a glowing orange, and the trees and rocks gave back an emanation of their own. Her upturned face caught this light, but she turned to look down into the darkness of the cleft. One step, two, and she might soar, like that hawk off to the south. Soar forever. The void beckoned. And she remembered.

The tree at her back felt warmer, though shivers ran through her limbs. Propped from behind, her legs crooked and both feet flat, toes but inches from the precipice, she waited. Night sounds, evening song of high nesting birds, of the roar of water below in dark depths, came and faded and came on wind. When it grew so dark that she could not see to the white-froth of water, she rose, standing right at the edge, a seeming emptiness below. Was there light enough...she did not care.

On the back of the letter, she had written spare words, in pencil. Why had the letter caused such pain? Only memory? She could practically recite the words, commonplace words. She pulled it from her shirt pocket and held it high, just able to read, knowing the words:

"Iris, this might dredge up old wounds, I know."

Robin continued in her slanted scrawl:

"As incredible as it may sound, Rodney had a fifth wife, at least that is what she is claiming. She says she was married to him for a couple of years. It appears it was before he married Julia. A couple of the local television stations have been interviewing her. I don't know what her intentions are but she stubbornly claims Rodney never beat her and she can't believe he would beat any woman. I wanted to make you aware of this before a local reporter tried to contact you. I'm sorry, Iris. I wish this was over."

She could not read more. In deep shadow of tall trees, it was night. On the back she had written words in pencil. Hard pressed into the papers, she had scratched them on the back of the letter that very morning. Her farewell. He haunted her still. Now there was a woman claiming he couldn't have been a beater. The obvious questions of where was she during the trial and why she was coming forth now escaped Iris. All she could think of was here was a woman, claiming Rodney never beat her. The inference was clear. If Iris was beaten, it must have been her fault.

The dreams had receded. Less frequent over the years. Now only rarely did he visit her dreams, virile and alluring so often before his visage turned to hate and before that powerful torso bled red blood. But there had been no other man to drive him out, all the way out, into the past where he belonged. She was prepared for life without one by now, forever if need be. She thought there had to be one big thing, and that was her freedom, or her space, or something. And now this woman. Why? This news from Robin came like a breath from hell. In the morning chill, before the night rain had gone, inside her tent and alone, reading it over again and again, she had scribbled the painful words.

A strange cry rent the air, far down the trail. She did not know it. Not Will, or Laura, or Patsy, surely. Not human. It came again, a cry without echo, almost triumphant. What was it? She felt goose bumps, and not from cold, though it was cold now, and her hair tingled at its roots. A chill came up her back to the nape of her neck. She shuddered, aware of the keenness of sensation. To step that step...so easy. Into the void. Blackness below.

She balled the single page in her fist and threw it now, without plan or thought. It was gone. Only words.

Whose am I? I am not his. Not his, nor anyone's. The words she had scrawled in pencil were...were only half true. Yes, he haunted her. But she was no longer his. Maybe she was the mountain's. The trail back was rough and treacherous at night. It would not be easy. If she belonged here, and this mountain claimed her...so be it. But she knew, turning now from the chasm, her first step moving her away and down the trail, that the fire would be warm and blazing. And her friends were waiting.

CPSIA information can be obtained at www.ICGtesting.com
Printed in the USA
BVOW02s1524181213

339184BV00001B/20/P